Praise for Lyn Ho

Darlin' Irish
Texas Devlins, Jessie's story
(formerly Darlin' Druid)

"It blends a compelling romantic story line . . . with a coming-of-age story line for the heroine, Jessie . . . Fans of historical romance and possibly even those who are into westerns, sans romance, should find much to like in *Darlin' Druid*.   —*BigAl's Books and Pals*

"I'll admit I was completely thrown by the title of this book. If for some reason you are as well, "fuhgeddaboudit"! This is an engaging, page turning, can't put it down, don't know where the time went, read."   —*Todd Fonseca, Reviewer*

"A touch of the Irish in the Old West is the best description of this story. . . . I would definitely recommend this book to everyone."
—*Laura Wallace, Paranormal Romance Guild*

DARLIN' DRUID by Lyn Horner should be made into a movie! It has all the right ingredients: wild west setting, lots of fast-pace action, a feisty heroine, a truly nasty villain and a hero-to-die-for. It's a real page-turning tale, historically accurate, beautifully written and lots of romance to make your heart race
—*Tori Phillips, Harlequin Historical Author*

Dashing Irish
Texas Devlins, Tye's Story
(formerly Dashing Druid)

"The author gives a very realistic view of life on a cattle drive. The perils involved with moving thousands of head of cattle cross

country, bad weather alone can get these animals stampeding. Anyone who enjoys western books will love this one. "
—*Linda Tonis, Paranormal Romance Guild*

"I enjoyed Darlin' [Irish], the first book of this series. It's combination of a solid western romance storyline with . . . a significant amount of the supernatural was a fun read that was very different. Dashing [Irish] continues the story, this time focusing on Tye Devlin, the brother of the heroine in the first book . . . In the final analysis, I enjoyed this book even more than the first."
—*BigAl's Books and Pals*

"Lyn Horner does a wonderful job of bringing the old west to life in a way that makes the reader sigh with contentment when the last paragraph has been read. I can't wait for the next book in this series to be published." —*mesadallas, Amazon reviewer*

Dearest Irish
Texas Devlins, Rose's Story
(formerly Dearest Druid)

"Lyn Horner has done an outstanding job . . . This story has it all. The fact that she has brought Irish immigrants, with a Druid history into the melting pot just makes it that much more interesting. The plot is realistic and the characters were wonderfully portrayed."
—*Big Al's Books and Pals*

Can two people with troubled pasts find the one thing they have been without, love? . . . This was a beautiful romance and it was a book filled with amazing characters. I loved this book and although there is no need to read the series in order you would be missing out on two other wonderful love stories.
—*Linda Tonis, Paranormal Romance Guild*

White Witch
Texas Devlins Origins, A Prequel

"I really enjoyed reading this prequel . . . I had never really heard of the Chicago Fire and to read of the suffering and loss was just tragic. This is where Jesse's gift makes an appearance leading into Darlin' Druid. Also Tye's gift which leads to his story, Dashin' Druid. These books are wonderful and I would highly recommend them to anyone." —*Bev Harro, Australian reviewer on Amazon*

Titles by Lyn Horner

White Witch
Texas Devlins Origins, a Prequel

Darlin' Irish
Texas Devlins, Jessie's Story

Dashing Irish
Texas Devlins, Tye's Story

Dearest Druid
Texas Devlins, Rose's Story

Texas Devlins Duo
White Whitch & Darlin' Druid

****

Six Cats In My Kitchen
Photo Illustrated Memoire

Dearest Irish

Lyn Horner

This is a work of fiction. All of the characters, organizations, and events portrayed in this novel are either products of the author's imagination or are used fictitiously.

Dearest Irish

Copyright © 2013 by Lyn Horner

All rights reserved.

ISBN:1490384839
ISBN-13:9781490384832

Dedicated to Native Americans past and present.
I am lucky enough to have a little Choctaw blood, or Cherokee
depending on which family story I choose to believe.

CHAPTER ONE

Bosque County, Texas; February 1876

Rose Devlin stood outside the corral fence, tensely watching her brother Tye struggle to stay on the brown stallion he was attempting to subdue. Horse breaking, he called it, but man breaking seemed a better description. With head down, the infuriated animal kicked out both hind legs, raising his rump high in the air. Somehow, Tye hung on, but when the stallion performed a wild twisting movement, he succeeded in throwing his rider. Rose cried out in alarm, but to her amazement, her brother hit the ground rolling to avoid the horse's hooves and rose nimbly to his feet.

Brushing himself off, he cornered the horse with help from a ranch hand named Micah Johnson, an older cowboy who mainly worked around the homestead. Mr. Johnson had lost the use of his left arm in the War Between the States, but he deftly threw his lasso over the horse's head with his good right arm. While he controlled the animal, Tye climbed back into the saddle.

Rose clutched the small gold cross suspended on a delicate chain at her throat and whispered a prayer as the battle between man and beast resumed. She gave a start when a man walked up beside her. Going rigid, she stared at him as he folded his arms along the top rail of the fence. She'd never laid eyes on him before. If she had, there'd be no forgetting him. Almost a head taller than her, with copper colored skin and long black hair, he wore a wide-brimmed black hat with a black-tipped white feather jutting from the leather hatband.

"Howdy, Miss Devlin," he said, casually glancing at her.

"Ye . . . ye know who I am, sir?" she asked, wondering who *he* was and where he'd come from. She thought she'd met all the Double C hands over the past three months.

He turned his head and studied her with eyes as dark as night. "Everybody on the place knows you're Tye Devlin's little sister."

Embarrassed by his close inspection, she looked away, but her curiosity got the better of her. "Who are ye?" she blurted. Then, instantly regretting her bluntness, she stammered, "I-I mean I've never seen ye before. Are ye new here?" Darting a sidelong glance at him, she was relieved to see him watching Tye and the bucking, snorting horse instead of her.

"Depends how you look at it," he replied. "I just rode in yesterday. That's why we haven't crossed paths before. I return about this time every year to help out with the roundup and the drive north."

"Oh, I see." Rose knew he referred to the yearly cattle drive to Kansas. She'd listened to Tye and his in-laws discuss plans for this year's drive several times. Herding thousands of cattle over such a long distance sounded like a daunting task to her.

"I heard you fixed your brother's eyes," the stranger remarked. "How'd you do it?"

Rose licked her lips and clasped her cross again, seeking an answer that wouldn't require mentioning her unusual ability. Before she could find words, the horse Tye was on emitted an enraged shriek and ran straight at the fence where Rose and her companion were standing.

"Look out!" Tye shouted.

Frozen in terror, Rose stared at the charging animal. She gasped when two arms closed around her from behind and whirled her aside just as the crazed horse reared and slammed his front hooves down on the top rail of the fence. The wood split with a loud crack, accompanied by a pain-filled neigh from the horse. A hiss of pain also sounded from the man pressed to Rose's back, his broad shoulders hunched around her. Had the horse struck him while he shielded her from harm? Or perhaps a piece of the broken fence rail?

With the danger past, he released her and stepped back. Turning to face him, she gazed wordlessly into his dark, fathomless eyes. They showed no emotion and not a hint of pain, yet they unsettled her. Quickly looking away, she saw Tye dismount and watched the troublesome stallion stagger along the fence, limping on his right foreleg.

"Stupid beast!" Tye shouted, shaking a fist at the horse. Leaving him for Micah Johnson to catch, he spun around, concern on his face. "Rosie, are ye all right?" he questioned, rushing toward her.

"Aye, I'm fine," she replied a bit unsteadily. "But Mr. . . . ." She looked askance at her protector, who'd moved a step closer.

"Call me Jack, Miss," he said with a barely noticeable crook of his lips.

"J-Jack, I'm thinking you're hurt. When the rail split I heard ye . . . ." She stepped behind him and blurted, "Oh, dear!" There was a tear in his shirt several inches long, and blood plastered the fabric to his back.

"It's nothin', just a scratch," he said.

"A scratch! 'Tis far more than that."

"Let's have a look," Tye said gruffly, stepping over the damaged fence. He joined Rose, scowling as he took in the other man's injury. "She's right. Ye need tending. Go on up to the house with Rosie. She's got the healing touch."

Jack pivoted to face them. Eyeing Rose, he nodded. "What they say is true, then. You have magic."

"Nay, nay! There's no magic. 'Tis merely a skill I've picked up." It was a lie, but she dared not admit the truth.

* * *

In the kitchen of the main house, Rose gathered a pan of water and a rag while Jack swung a chair around at the table and straddled it. Uncomfortably aware of him, she waited for him to unbutton his shirt and push it down, allowing her to see the cut running across his left shoulder blade. Hesitantly, she stepped close and began to gently wipe blood from around the wound with the dampened rag. Her tall sister-in-law, Lil, stood watching nearby. Tye had stayed out at the corral, wanting to examine the stallion's injured leg if the horse would allow him close enough to do so.

"It doesn't look too bad," Lil commented. Her protruding stomach brushed Rose's arm as she bent close to study the wound. She was due to give birth to her and Tye's first child in late March or early April.

"Nay, the cut isn't very deep," Rose agreed.

"Do you need me to fetch a needle and thread?"

Rose shook her head. "I think not. A bit of healing salve would help, but I haven't any with me."

"That's all right. Ma keeps a jar of the stuff, something her ma's people use. I'll get it."

Left alone with Jack, Rose nervously cleared her throat. "I need to wash out the cut. 'Twill hurt a bit."

"Go ahead," he said, the first words he'd spoken to her since entering the house.

Biting her lip, Rose wiped bits of wood and dirt from his wound as gently as she could. He didn't so much as twitch, causing her to admire his fortitude. While working over him, she contemplated his copper skin. She'd thought his face to be dark from working outside in the sun, but he was the same copper color beneath his shirt. It dawned on her that he must be an Indian. Her heart skipped a beat and a tremor of fear raced through her. She'd heard terrible stories of atrocities committed by Indians upon white settlers.

Rose reminded herself that Lil and her mother were part Cherokee, and she'd never been afraid of them. Yes, but Jack was a man. White or red, that was reason enough to fear him. Yet, she couldn't forget he'd saved her from injury, possibly even death, with no thought for his own safety.

Warily stepping around him to rinse out her rag in the pan of water, Rose surreptitiously studied her silent companion. His features were square-cut, with a high brow, hawkish nose and sharply chiseled mouth, bringing to mind the term *noble savage*. He turned his head and caught her staring at him. Face heating, she lowered her eyes and hastily returned to cleaning his wound. To her dismay, she encountered a small, jagged edge of wood embedded near the top of the gash. "Begorra! You've a sliver buried under your skin. I'll have to remove it."

"Do it," Jack said curtly.

By now, Lil had returned with a small jar, which she deposited on the table. Looking up, Rose asked, "D'ye perchance have some nippers I could use to pull out the sliver?"

"Nippers?" Lil looked mystified.

"Uh, tweezers, I mean."

"Oh. Yeah, I think Ma has a pair. I'll see if I can find them."

Again, Rose found herself alone with her stoic patient. She couldn't think of a thing to say. Hoping Lil would hurry back, she wiped more blood from Jack's seeping wound then rinsed out the rag once again.

"You come from Chicago?" Jack asked, drawing her surprised glance.

"Aye, I did."

"Mm, I figured."

"Ye did? How d'ye . . .? Oh, ye knew Tye and my sister came from there, I suppose."

He nodded. "You got more kin up there?"

"Only Da. Um, my father that is," she explained, wringing out the washrag.

He didn't say anything more. Stepping behind him to dab at the troublesome cut, Rose dared to inquire, "And yourself? Where d'ye come from?"

After a moment's silence, he said, "I grew up in Texas, up near the Red River, but I've moved around since then."

"I see." She wanted to ask where he'd moved around to, but Lil returned at that moment.

"Here you go." She handed Rose a pair of tweezers that had seen better days. "They're kind of bent."

"They'll do," Rose said, squeezing the small instrument. Finding it operable, she stepped close to Jack. "Are ye ready?"

"Do it," he repeated.

"Very well." Rose gingerly probed with the tweezers, trying to get hold of the end of the embedded sliver. When she finally succeeded, she took a deep breath and pulled.

Jack sat stone still through the probing process, but Rose felt him stiffen as she carefully drew out the long, ugly sliver. He made no sound, however, and Rose wondered how he could be so brave. When it was over, she breathed a sigh of relief and staunched a fresh flow of blood from the wound. Pressing gently along the length of the wound, she felt no other bits of wood.

"I think that's all of it," she said, hoping she was right. She was tempted to use her hands to close the gash, but resisted the urge. Instead, she reached for the jar Lil had brought, uncapped it and took a sniff, detecting the scent of yarrow and other herbs she might use in her own healing ointments. Reassured, she dipped her fingers into the aromatic concoction and scooped out a generous dollop. It had to sting as she spread it over Jack's wound, but once again, he showed no sign of pain.

"There, that should be enough." She glanced at Lil. "Will ye help me wrap a bandage around him to protect the wound?"

"Sure. Just have to work around Junior here." Grinning, she patted her rounded middle.

* * *

Rose lay tossing and turning in her bed. The house was silent. No doubt everyone else had long since fallen asleep. Not her. Her mind kept dwelling on Jack, wondering if she'd been wrong not to use her healing power on his wound. Truly, it ought to heal well enough on its own if he didn't get it dirty. If he did, infection might set in, leading to far worse trouble.

She could have saved herself the worry, and him a good deal of discomfort, by laying her hands on his torn flesh, but she hadn't wanted to confirm his suspicion that she possessed some sort of magic. What if he went around telling everyone? She couldn't chance that. They'd likely believe her a witch, as some had when she was a girl in Chicago, and in the convent after . . . . No! She refused to relive the dreadful events leading to her expulsion by Mother Superior – and the horror that followed.

Forcing her restless mind onto a different path, she wondered how the injured horse was faring. Tye had stabled the animal in the barn but couldn't get close enough to thoroughly examine his leg for fear of being trampled. He hoped the fractious stallion would calm down by morning. Was his leg broken? Rose hated to think of the poor creature suffering.

Slipping out of bed, she shivered as her bare feet touched the floor. The night had turned chilly. Hugging herself, she padded over to the window. It overlooked the ranch yard, affording her a view of the barn and the bunkhouse where the ranch hands were quartered. No light shown from either building. Coming to a decision, she donned the dress she'd removed earlier, stepped into her scuffed high-tops and laced them up. She grabbed her shawl and, realizing she would need light to examine the horse's leg, crossed to her dresser and picked up a squat oil lamp and a lucifer to light it.

As quietly as possible, she crept from her room and down the stairs, ears tuned to any sound from the sleeping household. Once outside, she paused to look at the bunkhouse again. Still seeing no light or sign of movement, she set off toward the barn, stepping carefully in the dark.

The barn doors were closed. Lifting the heavy wooden bar that held them shut was no easy task, but she managed it without making too much noise. A glance around assured her she went unobserved. Retrieving her lamp from the ground where she'd set it, she drew one door slightly ajar and edged into the humid, animal scented interior. It was pitch dark without even the meager light of stars and moon.

Fishing the lucifer from her pocket, she fumbled a bit but finally succeeded in striking the match and lighting her lamp. With the darkness held at bay, she walked past a stall occupied by a sleepy mare and her foal, another that stood empty, then paused outside a third. Within it stood the angry stallion. Only the animal didn't appear angry now; he looked forlorn with his head down, facing a far corner.

* * *

Jack eased past the open barn door and glided noiselessly into a dark corner where Miss Devlin wasn't likely to see him if she happened to glance his way. Unable to sleep thanks to the aching gash in his back and his unwanted thoughts of Tye Devlin's pretty sister, he'd gone for a walk. Moments ago, he'd been on his way back to the bunkhouse, determined to sleep, when he spotted the young woman leaving the main house. Curious, he'd followed her to the barn, careful to remain in deep shadows in case she turned to look behind her.

Now, he watched her walk quietly to the last stall on the left, where Tye had placed the troublesome stallion. She paused outside the enclosure, raised her lamp to see the horse, and began to speak in a soft tone. Jack crept closer, straining to hear what she said.

"Hello, darlin'. Come here to me. Ye needn't be afraid. If you'll let me, I'll try to take the pain away." She continued to croon reassuring words until, to Jack's amazement, the horse limped over to her and extended his head over the stall gate. As docile as a pet pony, he allowed her to scratch his forehead and rub his muzzle. All the while, she kept talking to him in that soft, sweet tone.

Jack was fascinated by the sight, but when she lifted the latch, preparing to enter the stall, he tensed in alarm. He opened his mouth, ready to order her not to go in there with the dangerous stallion, but something stopped him, perhaps the horse's calm behavior. Or maybe he was just curious to see what the fool white woman would do next. Edging closer still, he watched her enter the stall. She didn't bother closing the gate, and Jack expected the mustang to make a break for freedom, but surprisingly, the horse didn't move.

Setting her lamp down near the gate, Miss Devlin slowly approached him, offering her hand. He snuffled at it and allowed her to step close. She gently stroked his neck, causing a visible tremor to pass over the glossy brown surface. The stallion butted her with his head, obviously liking her touch. She giggled and scratched around his ears. Jack shook his head, hardly believing his own eyes. The woman sure did have a way with horses.

She went on talking to the big brute as she slowly stroked downward along his injured right foreleg. He gave no sign of fear or rebellion, although he did shift sideways when she touched the sore area. She said something Jack couldn't understand, in Irish? – and the horse immediately settled. Then she squatted, rubbed her hands together briskly, and wrapped them around the swollen part of his leg. She bent her head and her lips moved, praying, Jack guessed.

All at once the stallion whinnied and danced away from her. Jack prepared to dash into the stall and drag her to safety, but she calmly rose and resumed speaking to the wary horse.

"There now, don't be afraid. I'm sorry it hurt for a moment. 'Tis feeling better now, aye? By morning you'll not know 'twas ever sprained." She moved close again, patted the mustang's neck and gave him another good scratch around his ears. He nickered softly in response.

"There's a good lad," she murmured. "Now, I'd best be getting back to my bed. Good night to ye." With a final pat, she bent to pick up her lamp and exited the stall.

While she paused to latch the gate, Jack slipped out of the

barn, not wanting to get locked in there. He hid himself in deep shadows again and waited while the young woman struggled to replace the heavy board that barred the doors. He would have helped but didn't want her to know he'd been spying on her. He also didn't want to frighten her.

Once she was safely inside the main house, he headed for his bunk. Sleep eluded him as before, this time because he was anxious for daylight so he could see the results of Miss Devlin's midnight visit. As soon as dawn broke, he rolled out of bed, pulled on his boots and strode back to the barn. The brown stallion greeted him with a fierce neigh and charged the stall gate. However, he didn't try to knock it down, evidently having learned his lesson yesterday. He stopped short, stuck his head out and bared his teeth. Smiling at the threatening display, Jack stayed well out of reach.

What interested him was the horse's right foreleg. Crouching to look it over between the slats in the gate, he clearly saw the swelling had disappeared and the horse wasn't favoring the leg at all. It appeared completely healed. Jack straightened and slowly retraced his steps to the barn's open doorway. Crossing his arms, he stared at the house.

"So, Rose Devlin, you do have magic. You're a medicine woman." He chuckled. "You're also a little liar."

CHAPTER TWO

"I can't believe it," Tye said in amazement, seating himself at the breakfast table. He'd just returned from the barn. "The stallion's leg appears completely healed. The swelling is gone and he's his usual ornery self." He glanced at Rose as she placed a platter of fried eggs and ham on the table.

"Sis, if I didn't know the horse would never let ye get close, I'd swear ye worked your magic on him during the night."

"Oh, aye? But as ye say, he'd doubtless not allow me to touch him." She avoided meeting his eyes for fear he'd see she wasn't being honest.

He shrugged. "The injury must not have been as bad as I first thought," he said, running a hand through his dark hair.

"Will you try to work the fight out of him again?" Lil asked, carefully lowering her bulky form onto a chair across from him. Her parents, Del and Rebecca Crawford, sat at opposite ends of the table. Her Uncle Jeb was away on a trip to Waco.

Rose looked at Tye as she took a seat next to Lil. Frowning, he hesitated a moment before answering his wife's question.

"Aye, I suppose I'll try one more time, but if the devil behaves as he did yesterday, we may have no choice but to put him down."

"You'll kill him?" Rose blurted in shock, a forkful of egg halfway to her mouth.

"If need be, aye. He's no good to us if he can't be ridden or safely handled. Del and I hoped to keep the great brute for stud purposes, which is why he wasn't gelded as soon as we captured him. But mean as he is, even that's too risky."

"Could ye not set him free?"

"Can't do that, missy," Del said. "He knows his mares are here. Like as not, he'd try to steal 'em back. Could cause us a peck of trouble."

Rose gazed at the older, gray-haired man, then at her brother again. "But he's a grand horse. It seems such a . . . a waste to throw his life away."

"I know how you feel," Lil said, patting her hand sympathetically, "but Pa's right. Setting a wild stallion loose on our range might end up with us losing our own mounts along with the wild ones. He'd get them all stirred up and lead them off, and we'd be left afoot."

"I see," Rose replied in a small voice. Letting the subject drop, she toyed with her food, having no appetite left. She kept seeing the stallion she'd made friends with last night, imagining him lying lifeless on the ground. Praying it wouldn't come to that, she hoped the horse would settle down and allow Tye to ride him.

A while later, after helping Lil and Rebecca clean up the breakfast dishes, Rose excused herself, letting the other women think she was on her way to the outhouse. Instead, she made a beeline for the corral, needing to know the stallion's fate.

Tye was just stepping into the saddle. Two men, Jack and Micah, held the skittish brown horse in place, each with a rope around his neck. Neighing in protest, the animal fought against the restraints.

"All right, turn him loose," Tye ordered, gripping the reins.

The two cowboys pulled off their ropes and ran for the fence. Climbing over it, Jack locked gazes with Rose and nodded. She smiled shyly then turned her attention to the scene in the corral. Her heart jumped in her chest when the stallion reared, trying to unseat Tye. He didn't succeed. Fingering her cross, Rose prayed fervently for both man and beast as the stallion bucked and twisted, determined to rid himself of the weight on his back. Equally determined, Tye hung on until the horse performed the same seemingly impossible gyration as yesterday. Seeing her brother go flying, Rose gasped when he landed hard on his back.

Not content with unseating him, the stallion reared again, ready to strike him with iron hard hooves. Thank the saints, Tye rolled out of the way just in time. Cursing a blue streak, he scrambled to his feet and made a dash for the fence, with the stallion at his heels. He hurled himself under the bottom rail, leaving the animal to neigh and dance from side to side in angry frustration.

"Ye loco fiend!" Tye shouted. Regaining his feet, he jabbed a finger after his nemesis, who'd begun to trot victoriously around the corral. "Ye just signed your own death warrant."

"Nay!" Rose cried. Rushing over to him, she clutched his arm. "Can't ye give him another chance? Please, Tye."

"Are ye daft? Give him another chance to kill me?" he retorted, trying to shake her off.

"Nay, nay, but I don't wish him to be put to death if there's any other way."

Controlling his temper, he pried her fingers from his arm and spoke slowly, as if to a child. "Sis, the horse tried to stomp me into the ground. Ye saw that for yourself. He's vicious."

"Nay, he's not, he's only fearful and –"

"Boss, you might want to have a look," Jack interrupted, pointing into the corral.

Tye turned to look. "What the devil?"

Rose craned her neck to see past him and caught her breath when she saw the stallion ambling peacefully toward her. Stepping up to the fence, she extended her arm over the top rail, offering her hand to him. "Hello, boy," she said softly. "How are ye this fine morning?"

"Rosie, get away from there!" Tye cried. He grabbed her shoulders, ready to drag her back, but stopped when the stallion nickered and nosed Rose's outstretched hand.

"There now, you're a sweet lad, aren't ye," she murmured, stroking his muzzle.

"Begorrah!" Tye muttered in a tone of disbelief, hands sliding from her shoulders.

"Seems like the stallion's decided who he'll let ride him," Jack drawled.

"Are ye mad?" Tye shouted, rounding on him. "Petting him is one thing, but allowing her on his back is another. The mean tempered beast would toss her off in a heartbeat."

"Maybe, maybe not. Only one way to find out."

"Nay! Absolutely not!"

"Tye's right," Rose quietly agreed, scratching around the stallion's ears the way he'd enjoyed last night. "I don't even know how to ride."

"That's easy enough to fix. I'd start you out on a quiet mare. Once you get the hang of it, you can try riding him." Jack nodded toward the stallion.

"You're daft, man. *I'll* teach my sister to ride if she wishes, but she'll not be climbing onto that monster's back," Tye declared.

Rose met Jack's stare, reading challenge in his dark eyes. "I would like to try riding him," she said timidly, wondering where the words came from.

Tye glared at her. "Have ye lost your mind? That fiend would likely kill ye."

She regarded the stallion, who was now rubbing his neck on the fence rail separating him from herself. His warm brown coat gleamed in the sunlight. Raising his head, he nibbled at her open palm with his lips. It tickled, making her giggle.

"We're friends. He wouldn't hurt me, would ye, Brownie?"

"Brownie? You've named him? Woman, you're as daft as Choctaw Jack," Tye said crossly. Bending close, he whispered, "And ye plied your healing arts on the beastie last night, didn't ye?"

Rose gave him a tiny smile, not denying his accusation.

Her riding lessons began the next morning. For the first few days, her brother attempted to teach her, but she had trouble getting used to the lady's saddle, was afraid of falling off and found it impossible to obey his directions. He became impatient and snappish, driving her to tears at one point, until he finally turned her over to Choctaw Jack for instruction. Tye was not happy about the Indian cowboy being her teacher, why she didn't know, but Lil convinced him his sister would learn more easily from a stranger, for which Rose was very grateful.

Jack insisted she learn to ride on a man's saddle, saying it was more natural and safer. Tye grumbled but couldn't say no since his wife pointed out she'd always ridden astride before growing heavy with child. Rose expressed no opinion in the matter until Lil casually mentioned she would need to wear a pair of men's trousers for riding. Horrified at the thought, Rose stared at her wide-eyed from her chair at the kitchen table, where she sat peeling apples for a pie.

"What? No! I can't," she protested.

"Why not? I did," Lil said, frowning from across the table as she shucked corn for dinner. Her mother stood between them, preparing dough for the pie.

"Ye did? But how could ye display yourself so . . .?" Rose bit back the word she'd been about to utter, not wishing to insult her sister-in-law, but it was too late.

Lil narrowed her eyes. "So brazenly? Is that what you were going to say?"

"I-I meant no offense," Rose stammered, clutching a paring knife in one hand and a half peeled apple in the other. "But I'm not as b-brave as yourself. I simply can't wear trousers."

"Even if it means never riding your Brownie and knowing he'll be shot?"

"Oh, please don't say that!" Rose cried. Her eyes filled with tears. Dropping the knife, she clapped a hand over her trembling lips, fighting to hold back a flood of regret.

"There is another way," Rebecca said. Wiping her hands on the long white apron draped over her dress, she glanced at Rose. "I could make a riding skirt for you."

"You mean one of those split skirts like Jessie wears?" Lil asked dubiously. "I don't know how she climbs aboard a horse with all that skirt dragging on her."

"She manages." Motioning Rose to her feet, Rebecca looked her up and down carefully. "You are about the same size as your sister. Perhaps she will let me use one of her skirts as a pattern."

"I'm sure she would," Rose said, a surge of hope helping to dry her eyes. Recalling the riding skirt she'd once seen on Jessie, she thought she could stand to wear such a garment. Certainly it was better than figure-hugging trousers. If it allowed her to ride Brownie, thereby saving his life, she would do it.

Word was sent to Jessie and she immediately supplied not only a skirt, but the paper pattern she'd used to make it. At Rebecca's request, Tye escorted Rose and her into Clifton, the nearest town, where Lil's mother chose a durable corded fabric suitable for their purposes. While there, Tye also outfitted Rose with a plaid work shirt, a pair of thick-heeled western boots, and a Stetson hat much like the one he wore.

Once back at the ranch, Rebecca wasted no time in cutting out the pieces for Rose's skirt. With Lil pitching in to help, the three of them finished sewing it within two days.

On the morning her lessons were to commence with Jack, Rose hesitantly stepped out of the house wearing her blue plaid shirt and grayish blue riding skirt. She'd pinned her long hair into a tight knot at her nape beneath the brim of her brown hat. Walking cautiously in the unfamiliar boots, she tugged on a pair of leather gloves borrowed from her sister-in-law.

Lil had assured her she looked fine; Tye had merely raised an eyebrow and shrugged at her appearance. Still, when Rose spotted Jack standing by the corral, watching her approach, she blushed hotly, feeling self-conscious in her strange new clothes.

"Morning. You ready to learn?" he asked as she drew near.

"Aye, I'm ready." Painfully aware of his gaze upon her and his imposing size, she studied the ground. Much to her relief, he made no comment about her changed attire.

"Good. Come on. I saddled Betsy for you," he said without any inflection in his voice. Ushering her into the corral, he led her over to the quiet mare Tye had previously chosen for her. She was a muddy brown color, not the lovely warm hue of Brownie's coat, but she was sweet-natured and patient, qualities Rose had come to value during her inept attempts to ride.

"Hello, Betsy," she murmured, patting the mare's neck. The animal turned her head and eyed her, perfectly calm.

"The first thing you need to learn is how to mount and dismount," Jack said. With that, he demonstrated the proper way to do both. Then it was her turn.

Dearest Irish

She felt horribly exposed with her backside partially outlined by the riding skirt and practically in his face as she clumsily lifted herself into the saddle, but he seemed not to notice. All he did was adjust her feet in the stirrups and order her to sit straighter. Once he was satisfied with her posture, he had her climb down and repeat the process. This went on for close to an hour, with Jack patiently, if somewhat coolly, correcting her mistakes. Finally, he seemed satisfied with her efforts.

"That's enough for today. I'll meet you here tomorrow morning," he said, touching his hat to her.

"All right," Rose replied as he pivoted and led Betsy toward the watering trough. His dry, impersonal manner left her wondering if he resented having to instruct her. But he'd volunteered to teach her how to ride. Hadn't he?

Choctaw Jack's standoffish behavior lingered in her thoughts as she assisted Rebecca with cooking and household chores. Following Tye's stern order, Lil spent most of the day on the sofa with her swollen feet propped on a pillow, complaining about her bossy husband – and smiling over his concern for her.

* * *

With the spring roundup now underway, Jack spent the rest of the day rounding up cattle and helping to brand calves, all the while struggling with his unruly thoughts of Rose Devlin. She was as skittish as the stallion she wanted so badly to save. At least with him, she was. Maybe she wouldn't be if he were white. The thought galled him even though he wanted nothing to do with the woman outside of teaching her to ride.

Despite his resolve to hold himself aloof from her, he kept seeing Rose's lovely, pale face in his mind's eye, not to mention her womanly curves. Recognizing her embarrassment that morning, he'd pretended no interest in her new duds, but the sight of her nicely rounded bottom as she stepped into the saddle time and again was imprinted on his brain.

The scent of roses that clung to her, so fitting with her name, also tormented him. He remembered that scent from his youth, when his father had planted rose bushes around their house, a surprise for Jack's mother. She'd been awestruck, never having seen roses before. Like her, Jack had loved their bright color and sweet scent.

He spent the night in camp with the roundup crew that included Del Crawford and Tye Devlin. Tye questioned him tersely about his sister's riding lesson. Jack answered in the same tone, well aware the Irishman didn't trust him around his baby sister. He guessed the reason had to do with Lil, Tye's wife. Last year on the trail drive to Kansas, when he'd occasionally made Lil grin with a flirting comment, Jack had caught Tye's angry scowls. He'd been jealous, plain as day. Now, he was suspicious of Jack's intentions toward Rose.

Lying under the stars with her shy smile haunting his thoughts, Jack admitted Tye Devlin had cause for concern. Then he angrily reminded himself not to get any foolish ideas. The woman was not for him. They came from different worlds. He was more red man than white. With her blue eyes, light hair and creamy skin, she was his exact opposite. Not that he'd never had a white woman, but the ones he'd been with were the kind a man paid for. They weren't ladies like Rose. If he was stupid enough to go mixing with her, her brother would come after him with a gun.

* * *

Rose met Jack outside the corral after breakfast the following morning. He must have risen before dawn to arrive so early, she realized. Recalling how indifferent he'd been to her attire yesterday, she didn't blush as hotly as she had then, but she was still uncomfortable in his presence.

"Good morning," she said nervously. "'Tis a might chilly today." She rubbed her arms to make her point.

Jack's lips twitched as if he wanted to smile. "A might," he agreed. Then he barked, "Let's get started," and turned to open the corral gate.

Rose frowned at his broad back while following him toward the waiting mare. He hadn't even returned her greeting. The man needed to learn some manners. She wanted to tell him so . . . if only she possessed the courage.

Today, he showed her how to hold the reins and use them along with pressure from her legs to start, stop and turn the horse. Now and then he touched her arm or knee, demonstrating how she was to position them. At his touch, sparks shot through her like small bolts of lightning, and she could hardly resist jumping in the saddle. She told herself this unnerving reaction was fear of being touched by a man, any man.

Like yesterday, Jack made her practice every move over and over until she could do them without having to think about it. He curtly announced when her time was up and said he'd see her tomorrow. With a cursory touch of his hat, he led the mare away. Stung by his blunt dismissal, Rose opened her mouth to call out an angry retort but snapped it shut, too afraid to speak. Once again, she swallowed her annoyance.

The following day was much the same. After reviewing what he'd already taught her, Jack allowed her to walk Betsy around the corral. Now and then he ordered her to correct something she was doing wrong, or not doing, but he never lost his temper with her. Grateful for that, and realizing he'd gotten her over her fear of falling off the horse, she tried to make allowances for his unsociable manner. Perhaps he was like that with everyone. He was an Indian, and she knew nothing of their ways.

Over the next three days, Jack taught her to increase Betsy's pace to a jog and then a lope. Calling a halt to her lesson on the third day, he declared, "Tomorrow you will ride the stallion."

Rose's jaw dropped. "Ye think I'm ready for him?" she asked uncertainly.

"As ready as you'll ever be. I will tell your brother. He'll wish to be here." With a wry crook of his lips, he pivoted and led Betsy away once again.

She watched him go then raced for the house. Bursting in the front door, she found Lil and Rebecca in the parlor. Lil sat with her feet up, darning one of Tye's shirts, while her mother swept the floor. Both women paused to look up at her.

"Jack says I'm ready to ride Brownie!" she exclaimed, pulse pounding wildly.

"Now?" Lil asked, half rising from the sofa in alarm.

"Nay, tomorrow morning."

Lil relaxed. "Oh, well, that's fine. I'll send word to Tye."

"There's no need. Jack said he'd tell him."

"That oughta make for an interesting *discussion,*" Lil said dryly, focusing on her sewing repairs again.

Rose considered for a moment before replying, "Aye, I suspect so. Tye doesn't appear to like Jack. Can ye tell me why?"

Her sister-in-law gave an amused laugh. "It has to do with me. I've known Jack for years, ever since war's end when he first rode in to let us know my brother, Toby, had been killed in a skirmish somewhere up in Tennessee." Lil darted a glance at her mother, who now stood with her hands wrapped around the broom handle, silently staring out the front window, obviously thinking of her lost son. Clearing her throat, Lil added, "They were in the same outfit, you see, and Jack was with Toby when he died."

Rose quietly seated herself in a chair near the hearth as Lil explained how Jack had returned every year at roundup time and how they'd become friends. Jack had gotten into the habit of teasing her, playfully suggesting they get together. "We both knew it was only a game, but last year on the cattle drive, Tye got the wrong idea. I was a might put out with your brother back then, and I kind of enjoyed making him jealous." Lil grinned at the memory. "Not very kind of me, I reckon. Of course I've told Tye he never really had anything to be jealous about, but he still doesn't quite trust Jack. That's why he didn't like the idea of him teaching you to ride."

"He needn't have worried. Jack's never shown the least bit of interest in me. In fact, I'm sure he'll be glad to be done with my lessons," Rose said with a twinge of hurt she instantly smothered.

Lil smiled at her. "I wouldn't be so sure of that. Jack's close-mouthed most times, but there's a lot going on behind that blank stare of his. And he's a man like any other, with an eye for a pretty woman like you."

"Oh!" Rose gasped, flustered by the compliment and by the suggestion that Jack might be attracted to her. Not that she cared. She certainly wasn't attracted to him – or any other man. They were all brutes. Well, not all of them. Not Tye or her brother-in-law David.

* * *

Rose paid a brief visit to Brownie after supper as she'd done each evening, just to let him know she hadn't forgotten about him. She always made sure to bring him a treat, an apple in this case, that he eagerly took from her hand. Stroking him as he devoured the fruit, she said, "I'm to ride ye tomorrow, me beauty, and ye must allow it. For if ye don't . . . ." Her voice caught and she gave up trying to speak.

The stallion merely snuffled at her hands, searching for another tasty tidbit. With a final scratch around his ears, she bade him goodnight and trod the well beaten path back to the house.

Tye had arrived home earlier, just in time for supper, and was now intent on talking Rose out of risking her life for the sake of a horse. She adamantly refused to give in to his urging, which resulted in them both going to bed angry. In the morning, wearing a stern scowl, he accompanied her to the corral, where Jack and Micah waited, holding the stallion in check with lead ropes. Brownie neighed in protest and fought to break free. He'd already been saddled and no doubt disliked the weight on his back.

How would he react when she climbed into that saddle? Swallowing hard, Rose fought a threatening tide of fear. Perhaps sensing her wavering courage, Tye laid a hand on her shoulder, stopping her just outside the corral gate.

"Rosie, are ye sure ye want to do this? No one will think less of ye if you've had second thoughts." Worry wrinkled his brow.

She hesitated a second, then shook her head. "Nay, no second thoughts. Jack says I'm ready, and I believe him." With effort, she called up a convincing smile.

Her brother's lips thinned. She expected him to argue, but he only sighed and said, "All right, but promise me one thing. If the horse tosses ye off and you're still alive, you'll not try to get back on him."

"But that's not fair! What if –"

"Nay! No what ifs. Give me your word on this or I'll not let ye near that devil."

Rose wanted to protest further but recognized it would do no good. "Very well, ye have my word I won't try again if Brownie throws me. But he won't," she asserted with more confidence than she actually felt.

"I hope you're right." Opening the gate, Tye walked her over to the agitated horse and his handlers. "Morning," he said to Micah, then nodded stiffly to Jack. The two men replied in kind.

"You ready to mount up?" Jack asked Rose.

"Aye, in a moment." Stepping close to Brownie's head, she greeted him and stroked his soft muzzle. He quieted at her touch. Reaching up on tiptoes, she whispered to him, "This is our only chance, my dear. Please don't be angry with me. 'Tis the only way I can save your life."

His ears twitched and he peered at her with an eye the same rich brown hue as his coat. He seemed to consider her request. Then he nickered and bobbed his head up and down as if giving his permission. A silly notion, Rose thought.

Patting his neck, she took a deep breath, collected the reins and prepared to mount. She failed the first time. The stallion was quite a bit taller than Betsy, her trusty mare, and with the heavy riding skirt dragging at her leg, she couldn't quite reach the stirrup. Gnawing her lip, she was about to try again when Jack wordlessly handed his lead rope to Tye and came to her aid. Bending over, he cupped his hands and quirked an eyebrow at her expectantly. She hesitated for a second, then gripped the saddle horn and placed her left foot in Jack's hands. He lifted her as easily as she might lift a small child.

"Swing your leg over like I taught you," he told her.

She did as he said. Settling herself in the saddle, she smiled gratefully at Jack. Then, suddenly, the stallion sidled away from him and bucked, drawing a startled gasp from Rose. She clutched a handful of brown mane while Tye and Micah fought to control the fractious animal.

"Talk to him. Let him know it's you up there," Jack ordered sharply.

Nodding, Rose bent low and said, "Be calm, lad. 'Tis only me, your Rosie. Ye needn't be afraid." As she spoke, she gently caressed his sleek neck.

The stallion's ears swiveled toward her and he stilled.

"Good. Keep it up," Jack directed. "Give him time to get used to you on his back."

Rose continued to pet and croon to the horse. After several moments with no further trouble from him, she looked at her brother and said in the same soft tone, "Let him go. He'll not hurt me."

Tye scowled. She feared he would argue with her and cause Brownie to start bucking again, but he must have had the same thought. Removing his rope, he signaled Micah to do the same. The two of them slowly backed away. Now it was only her and the horse, Rose thought.

"What should I do?" she asked, looking to Jack.

"Tell him to walk," he said. "You know how."

Gathering her courage again, Rose signaled Brownie to move forward. Much to her delight, the great beast instantly obeyed.

"I'll be damned!" Tye exclaimed. "I can't believe my own eyes."

Grinning at him, she directed the big horse to circle the corral, employing the lessons Jack had drilled into her. All three men retreated to the fence, where they stood watching. She waved at Tye as she rode past him and caught his annoyed scowl. However, the next time around, she was pleased to see him wink and tip his hat. He was proud of her, she happily realized.

"Should I ask him to trot?" she called out to Jack.

"No. Stop and turn him in the opposite direction."

She followed his orders, and again Brownie responded easily to her signals.

"Good. Walk him around a couple more times, then we'll quit for now."

Rose did as she was told, feeling Brownie's powerful stride and basking in the knowledge that she was the only one he would allow on his back. She also experienced a rush of gratitude toward Jack for making this possible. Flushed with success, she drew Brownie to a halt after their final circuit of the enclosure and dismounted without assistance. Scratching his ears and brushing a hank of forelock away from his left eye, she murmured, "Thank ye, love, for allowing me on your back. 'Twas a grand ride ye gave me."

"You did good," Jack said, gathering up Brownie's trailing reins. "Meet you here tomorrow morning. We'll see how he trots for you." Surprising Rose, he gave her a brief smile before turning to lead the stallion back to his stall. Skittish again, Brownie resisted for a moment before settling down and following Jack's lead.

Rose stared after them, pleased by her reticent teacher's approval and thinking how very handsome he was when he smiled. She jumped when Tye walked up and wrapped his arm around her shoulders.

"Well, ye proved me wrong, and glad I am to admit it," he said with a gleam in his blue eyes. "You've become quite a horsewoman, little sis."

She gave a deprecating laugh. "If I have, 'tis all Jack's doing. He's a good teacher."

Her brother's mouth turned down, making her realize she'd just implied *he* wasn't a good teacher. She opened her mouth to say that wasn't her intention, but he spoke first.

"Aye, I suppose I should be thanking him. If he hadn't taken over your lessons, I'm thinking ye might have run off to Jessie and David with word of how wicked I was to ye. And certain sure, I'd have been in for a tongue lashing from our dear sister." He grinned at the prospect.

Rose laughed in relief, glad he wasn't truly offended by her remark. "That ye would. Jessie still thinks of me as a child in need of her protection."

"Oh, and you're not an innocent babe anymore, I suppose?" he teased.

Her smile wobbled. "Nay, not anymore." Ignoring his raised eyebrows, she gently shrugged off his arm. "I'd best go see what I can do to help Lil and Rebecca."

CHAPTER THREE

Several more days passed while Jack put Rose and Brownie through their paces. The stallion trotted smoothly, loped as if he had wings on his feet, and never failed to obey Rose's command to stop, turn or even back up. Yet, Jack continued to call for more practice, watching for any trouble from the horse.

Rose longed to give Brownie and herself a taste of freedom. Timidly, she asked if they might go for a ride on the open range. Jack said no, not yet. Disappointed but fearing to argue, she abided by his decree until, on a warm mid-March day, he was finally satisfied that the stallion wouldn't rebel and throw her.

"I'll take you out tomorrow," he announced. "Best tell Lil you'll be gone for a while." Pivoting, he led Brownie away as usual, leaving Rose's heart thumping with excitement.

She hardly slept that night and was up and dressed shortly after sunrise. Thank goodness her brother was out on the range helping Del Crawford supervise the roundup, or she suspected he would have refused to let her go anywhere beyond the corral with Jack. Fidgeting through breakfast, hardly knowing what she put in her mouth, she helped clean up afterward and bade Lil and Rebecca a hasty farewell, to which they both laughed and advised her to be careful.

In her rush to get going, Rose arrived at the corral earlier than usual. Jack wasn't yet there. Hearing a clang of metal striking metal, she thought it came from behind the barn. Curious, she strolled in that direction and found a large, open shed, from whence came the metallic hammering. It was a blacksmith's workshop, she realized. Acrid heat struck her as she approached the open portal.

Wearing no shirt, the smith stood working at an anvil with his back to her. Even so, she recognized Choctaw Jack by his long, midnight black hair, tied back with a leather thong at his nape, and by the healed red scar across his left shoulder blade. But what was he doing here, working in the smithy? No one had ever mentioned he was a blacksmith.

Coated with sweat in the heat from the forge, his muscular arms and torso gleamed like molten copper. Rose stared in awe as he skillfully wielded his hammer and tongs. A strange excitement curled through her insides at the sight. She must have made some sound, for he stopped in mid swing and pivoted to face her. A startled look crossed his face; then he pinned her with his black stare.

"Miss Rose," he said with a nod. "Didn't think it was time to meet you yet."

"Uh, nay, 'tisn't. I'm early. I-I heard the hammering." She gestured toward the heavy tool in his hand. "I didn't know ye were a blacksmith as well as a cowboy."

He shrugged one shoulder and mopped his face with the bandana draped loosely around his neck. "Pays to know more than one way to earn my keep."

Nodding, she cleared her throat nervously. "No doubt my brother and the Crawfords set great store by your skills."

"Saves them a trip to the blacksmith in town," he replied with another one-shouldered shrug. "While I'm here."

"Mmm. And what are ye working on?" Rose asked, hoping her questions didn't annoy him.

"I'm making up extra horseshoes. We'll need them on the drive to Kansas."

"Ah, I see." Feeling awkward, she stammered, "Well, I-I'm sorry for disturbing ye." She ought to turn and leave, but her feet seemed rooted in place. Her gaze skittered across his broad, glistening chest then darted uncertainly to his chiseled features.

He cocked a raven eyebrow and laid aside his tools. Setting hands to his hips, he sauntered forward until he stood no more than three feet away from her. His mouth curled into a smile. "I don't mind being disturbed by a pretty lady."

"Y-ye flatter me, sir." Flustered by his compliment, so unusual coming from him, she fiddled with the open collar of her shirt, touched her cross and stared at the ground.

"No. Just speaking true."

Intimidated by his male scent and sheer size, she backed away a couple steps. She peeked at him from beneath her lashes, seeing his smile give way to his usual expressionless mask.

"You afraid of me?" he asked, tone hardening.

"Nay, I-I . . . ." Hunting for an excuse for her nervous behavior, she blurted, "I need air is all. 'Tis hot in here."

He crossed his arms, muscles bulging. "A smithy has to be hot."

"I know." Rose cleared her throat again and licked her dry lips. "But I'm not accustomed to the heat." Which was true. Extracting a handkerchief from the cuff of her sleeve, she dabbed at her damp forehead.

"If you can't take heat, Texas isn't for you," he said in a challenging tone.

Miffed, Rose met his onyx stare and snapped, "I'll get used to it. Excuse me. I'll go wait by the corral." She started to turn away, but his voice stopped her.

"You sure you still want to ride out with me?"

"Of course." Her pulse pounded in her ears. In truth, she was a wee bit afraid to be alone with him, away from the safety of the house – perhaps more than a wee bit – but she couldn't bring herself to admit it. Besides, she dearly wished to take Brownie for a real ride. "I've looked forward to this day," she added, lifting her chin.

He stared at her for a moment and said, "It'll take me a few minutes to finish up here. Then I'll clean up and fetch the horses."

"Fine." Nodding, Rose swung on her heel and hurried away.

Jack watched her hasty retreat. She might deny it, but she *was* afraid of him. Once again, he wondered if it was his being an Indian that spooked her. Scowling at the thought, he reheated the horseshoe he'd been forming and hammered it into shape, reminding himself that he wanted nothing to do with the red-blonde girl with shy blue eyes. Eyes that reminded him of beautiful blue agates he'd once seen mounted on an ornate cross.

Why did you call her pretty? Fool! Are you looking for trouble? Then and there he decided today would be her last lesson. She'd have to find someone else to take her riding.

He would be gone from here before long anyway. The roundup was almost finished. Soon they would start driving the longhorns north. He'd already agreed to scout for David Taylor, who was to boss the drive this year. Del Crawford would not be going along. Like his brother Jeb, he'd declared himself too old for another trip up the Big Trail. Jack agreed. Pushing longhorns over rough country, sleeping five or six hours a night on hard ground, and risking death in stampedes, flooded rivers, and a passel of other ways, was not for the old.

Tye Devlin wouldn't start out with them either. He refused to leave Lil when she was so close to her time. After the birth of their child, he planned to catch up with the herd. Jack couldn't fault his decision. He might not be on cordial terms with the Irishman, but he was glad Lil's husband loved her well.

Done shaping the horseshoe, he thrust it into a bucket of water to cool. The fiery metal hissed and sent up a cloud of steam. Depositing his hammer and tongs on a workbench, Jack banked the forge fire to keep the coals hot for later and prevent any accidents. He didn't want to return from his ride with Rose to find the shed and barn burned to the ground.

Plucking the cooled horseshoe from the bucket, he used the warmed water to scrub himself free of sweat and grime, as much as possible without a dunk in the creek. In no hurry to spend an hour or more in Rose's company – she tempted him too damn much for his good and hers – he donned his shirt, strapped on his gun belt and retrieved his hat. He slicked the ruffled feather with his thumb and forefinger and, stepping from the shed, settled the hat in place over his long, damp hair.

* * *

Rose waited by the corral, leaning against the rails as she poked at a pebble with the toe of her boot. Acutely disturbed by her encounter with Jack in the smithy, she battled an urge to run for the house and the safety of Lil and Rebecca's company. The only thing holding her back was her keen desire to ride Brownie beyond the confines of the corral. That's what she told herself, but she knew there was another reason. Deep inside lurked a dangerous yearning to be with Jack, to watch him and perhaps see him smile again. It was this yearning that frightened her so, even more than her ingrained fear of men.

Hearing a muffled clip-clop, she swung around in time to see Jack lead Brownie and a handsome bay gelding from the barn. Both animals were saddled, and Brownie pranced along, head high, looking eager for some exercise as he was led toward her.

"Let's get mounted," Jack said in his usual curt tone.

Nodding, Rose let him boost her into the saddle, tensing at his nearness. He mounted his own horse with a fluid grace she both envied and admired.

"We'll ride west, away from the branding ground."

Wondering why that was important, Rose said, "I'd rather like to see how the branding is done."

Jack shot her a skeptical glance. "No you wouldn't. It ain't pretty. Besides, I don't want that stallion anywhere near the cattle. If he was to get ornery, he could start a stampede."

"Oh! I hadn't thought of that. You're right, of course."

He didn't bother to reply as he led her away from the homestead. They rode at a gentle lope across the prairie, toward a low, hazy line of hills. After a long silence, Jack asked, "You want to give him his head and see how fast he really is?"

"Aye! I'd love to!" Rose blurted in excitement. Then doubt set in. "But d'ye think I'll be able to keep my seat? I'd not wish to tumble off and crack my noggin."

Jack's lips quirked and for a brief moment his eyes danced with amusement, but he quickly reverted to the wooden expression she'd grown used to. "If you do like I taught you, you won't have any trouble."

"All right," she said, still a trifle anxious.

Tugging his hat down low, he kicked his horse and gave a yell that sent the startled bay into a gallop. Without any signal, Brownie lunged after the other horse, wringing a gasp from Rose. She grabbed a handful of his mane, bent forward and forced herself to move with the stallion as Jack had repeatedly instructed. To her amazement, Brownie caught up with Jack's gelding in a matter of seconds, his long legs eating up huge chunks of ground.

Rose waved at her teacher as she shot past him. His startled look made her laugh joyously. She felt as free as a bird soaring across the earth below. She wanted never to stop, but after a few glorious minutes Jack shouted from far behind for her to pull up. Reluctantly, she drew on the reins and leaned back in the saddle. For a moment, Brownie resisted stopping. He was obviously enjoying his run as much as she was, but he finally slowed and came to a halt. Jack caught up moments later.

"Damn, that stallion's fast! In a race, I bet he'd beat every horse in the county."

Astounded by his gush of enthusiasm, she said, "D'ye really think so?"

"Yeah, I reckon," he said more calmly, looking faintly embarrassed by his outburst. "Let's walk for a while. The horses need a rest after that run."

"Aye, I see that." Jack's gelding was blowing hard, his sides heaving. Brownie looked a bit winded, too.

Dismounting, they ambled along side by side, leading the horses. Shades of spring green surrounded them, brightened by many-hued wild flowers. Rose appreciated the beautiful scene, but she grew uncomfortable with the lengthening silence between them. Clearing her throat, she glanced at Jack and vented her curiosity.

"How did ye learn the blacksmith's trade, if ye don't mind me asking?"

He met her gaze briefly. "I don't mind. My pa taught me when I was a boy. He worked as a smith over in Louisiana before we moved to Texas."

"But I thought . . . I mean, how did he happen to –"

"You mean how did an *Injun* become a smith?" he interrupted in a caustic tone.

"No! 'Tisn't what I was going to say."

"Maybe not, but you were thinking it, weren't you?"

A fiery blush swept up Rose's throat, burning her cheeks. "Aye, I suppose I was," she admitted, turning her face away in shame. "I'm sorry. I wasn't meaning to offend ye."

Jack sighed. "Forget it. Truth is if you didn't wonder about it, you'd be the first paleface who didn't. And the answer's simple. Pa was a half-breed. He learned blacksmithing from his French Creole pa. His ma was Choctaw."

"Ah, I see. And your mother?"

"She's pure redskin." Not giving her time to ask more questions, he said, "It's time to head back. Come on, I'll give you a hand up."

They rode back at a slower pace, and although neither said much, Rose felt more relaxed in Jack's company than ever before. Thus, it came as a blow while they were dismounting near the corral, to hear him say she needn't meet him there the next day. Her lessons were over.

"I've taught you all I can. Keep practicing. You have a great horse here." He patted Brownie's sweaty neck. "And you've got what it takes to be a fine rider."

Rose searched for words to convince him she still needed his instruction, but the only thing that came out was a choked, "Thank ye for everything, Jack. I . . . I wish ye good fortune."

"Same to you, Miss Rose." Touching his hat, he led the horses back to the barn.

An odd sense of loss swept over Rose as she watched him disappear into the shadowy interior. She hated to admit it, but she would miss seeing him each day. She'd never expected to feel that way about any man. Walking toward the house with lagging steps, she wondered who would take her riding. Then she told herself not to be foolish. Riding Brownie was a delight, but what she needed was a job, a way to earn her keep as Jack had put it. She couldn't continue to live off her relatives forever.

Once she'd had a purpose for her life, but she'd lost it – and so much more – when Mother Superior ordered her from the convent. Shying away from painful memories as fresh as yesterday, she thought of Jack again and how he'd made a life for himself in the white world. That couldn't have been easy. Aye, but at least he was a man and he had skills that were in demand. She was a woman with no particular skills – unless she counted her healing ability. Ha! She could hardly support herself doing *that*. She'd either be laughed at or driven away by those who saw evil in anything they didn't understand.

She ought to ask Jessie's advice. Her sister had once worked as a maid and later as a serving girl in a restaurant. If she could perform those tasks, Rose thought perhaps she could too. She'd spent nearly a month with Tye, Lil and the Crawfords. It was time to visit Jessie and David again, but she didn't know the way to their ranch well enough to chance making the ride alone. Tye planned to be here tonight, to make sure his wife was taking care of herself, he'd said. Rose decided she would ask him to escort her back to the River T.

Of course she would return here in time to be with Lil when the baby came, but that looked to be another two or three weeks away. There was nothing to hold her here just now. Her riding lessons were over, Jack had made clear. Again, that feeling of loss struck her, but she pushed it away, telling herself he meant nothing to her.

Rose put her request to Tye after dinner. Del had ridden in with him and Jeb Crawford had returned from Waco with the extra cattle drovers he'd set out to hire. The brothers sat on a pair of ladderback chairs near the parlor hearth, smoking their pipes. Rebecca had claimed a cowhide upholstered easy chair, where she'd resumed sewing a new shirt for her husband. Lil reclined on the sofa – also leather-bound – with her feet propped on Tye's lap. Rose perched on the edge of her own chair, anxious for her brother's reply.

"Aye, I'll be glad to escort ye to Jessie and David's place, sis, but you'll have to wait a bit. Del, Jeb and I are to meet with David at the River T in a few days to finalize plans for the trail drive. Ye can go with us, but I'm too busy to make a special trip over there with ye right now."

Impatient to talk over her employment possibilities with Jessie, Rose suggested, "Jack could take me there. He knows the way, does he not?"

"No! I won't hear of it," Tye declared. "You're not to go anywhere with him."

"But I already went riding with him today," she said, thinking to assure him of Jack's trustworthiness. The result was quite the opposite.

"What!" Setting Lil's bare, swollen feet aside, he sprang upright. "Ye rode off with him without asking my permission? Are ye daft, woman?" he shouted. "D'ye know what he might have done to ye? Some men have no qualms about forcing themselves on a woman if they get her alone. Ye mustn't be so trusting."

Gulping down words she couldn't speak, Rose was immensely grateful when Lil spoke up. Pushing up from the sofa with difficulty, she faced Tye, chin jutting forward.

"Rose told me she was going riding with Jack. I thought it was a real good idea."

Tye stared at his wife in shock. Then he scowled. "Ye did, did ye?"

"So did I," Rebecca said without looking up. "Jack is a good man. He would not hurt your sister."

"Rebecca's right, son," Del agreed. "Jack's not the kind to force a woman."

Going red in the face, Tye exploded. *"Begorrah!* The lot of ye plotted behind my back, is what ye did. I'll have no more of it!" he roared, strongly reminding Rose of their hot-tempered father and sister. Pointing at her, he decreed, "You're not to go near the man again!" With that, he stomped out of the house, slamming the door behind him.

Rose wondered if he intended to confront Choctaw Jack and order him to stay away from her. She found that laughable, considering Jack had already put an end to her riding lessons.

"Durn man!" Lil grumbled, easing down to her spot on the sofa. "I've never known him to be so ornery before."

"He is a true brother. He feels it his duty to protect his sister," Rebecca said, sending Rose a heartening smile.

Del chuckled. "He's a might techy right now, too," he said around his pipe. Removing it from his mouth, he pointed the stem at Lil. "All he can think about is you and that young'un you're carrying."

"Humph! If he's so worried about me, he oughta calm down and come back and rub my feet. They look like balloons. Feel like balloons too."

"Stop complaining," Rebecca said. "Soon you will have a little one to hold." Setting aside her sewing, she took Tye's place and began to gently massage her daughter's swollen feet.

Listening to their exchange, Rose missed her own mother desperately. Feeling glum over Tye's angry reaction, she swallowed past the lump in her throat, bid Lil and the others good night, and hurried up to her room. If she shed a few tears, it was no one's business but her own.

* * *

Since he had more blacksmithing to do in the morning, Jack slept in the bunk house that night. Or he tried to. Filled with thoughts of Rose Devlin, his mind refused to let him sleep. He was about to give up and go for a midnight walk when the door squeaked open. Immediately alert, he saw a shadow move across the doorway, a deeper shade of black than the night beyond. It couldn't be Tye

Devlin again. The man had said his piece, and he wasn't the kind to murder a man in his sleep.

Grasping the knife he'd tucked under his pillow, Jack rolled quietly from his bed and crouched beside it as the intruder padded toward him between rows of mostly empty bunks. Micah Johnson, the only other ranch hand who wasn't out with the roundup crew, sawed wood loudly toward the far end of the room. Their visitor sounded as if he wore moccasins. An Indian here?

"Ah-p'ah-be? Brother, are you there?" the man called out softly in his native tongue. His voice was instantly familiar.

"I am here, *Tsoia*," Jack whispered in the same language as he pushed to his feet. "Be silent," he added, motioning toward the door. The other man nodded and noiselessly followed him out of the bunkhouse and around back, where they could speak without waking Micah.

"What are you doing here, my brother?" Jack asked. "How did you find me?"

"Your mother gave me the map you once drew for her. She is ill and wishes you to come to her."

"Is it the spotted sickness?" Alarmed, Jack remembered too well how smallpox, the white man's scourge, had decimated his mother's people in years past.

"No, thank the Great Spirit. It is her belly. She cannot eat and is in great pain."

Alarm turned to anger. "Did she eat rotten meat from the agency?"

"No, Ah-P'ah-Be, it is not that. Her pain is like a fist in the belly, she says." Tsoia made a squeezing motion to demonstrate. "She says she is dying."

Jack found no words. His mother dying? Despair clutched at his own vitals. In a daze, he aimlessly retraced his steps, halting at the corner of the bunkhouse. He leaned against the log structure, gaze drifting to the main house, and a memory surfaced abruptly. It was an image of Rose Devlin crouched beside the injured stallion with her hands wrapped around his swollen leg. He straightened. Swinging around, he found Tsoia standing nearby, waiting.

"Brother, there is a thing I must do to save my mother," Jack said. "I need your help, but there is great danger. If we are caught, we will die. Are you willing?"

Tsoia gave a low laugh. "Why do you ask such a foolish question? Danger makes my blood sing. What would you have me do?"

* * *

Rose had fallen asleep with Tye's dire warning about men preying on her mind. Now a threatening male form peopled her dreams. A leering face closed in and hands reached out to grab her. She tried to shake them off, to escape, but they held her fast. Even when she opened her eyes, a shadowy form hovered above her. Her sleep befuddled brain awoke to the fact that she was no longer dreaming. The hands gripping her arms and the man bending over her were real.

Terror flooded her. Heartbeat soaring, she opened her mouth to scream, but one of those steely hands clamped across her lips, smothering her cries. She pushed at his encroaching chest and fought to twist free.

"Shhh! It's me, Jack," her captor whispered.

Rose stilled instantly. Jack? Jack was doing this to her?

"I won't hurt you, but you must stay quiet. Will you do that?"

Still fearful, she made an agreeing sound and he slowly lifted his hand from her mouth.

"W-what d'ye want?" she squeaked.

"Your help," he said simply. To her great relief, he released his hold on her arm and straightened away from her, sitting on the edge of the bed.

She hastily scooted up, pressing her back to the headboard. Realizing her top half was now covered only by her thin nightdress, she snatched the bed covers higher. "Help? What kind of help?"

"I just got word that my mother is very sick. She may be dying."

"Oh, Jack, I'm so sorry," Rose whispered, heart going out to him. "But . . . but what does that have to do with me?" Even as she voiced the question, she guessed the answer. He'd somehow learned about her gift.

"You are a healer. You have magic in your hands." When she shook her head, he added, "Don't deny it. I saw you that night, when you healed the stallion."

"Och! Ye spied on me!" she accused, horrified to know he'd watched her with Brownie.

He shrugged. "I couldn't sleep. I'd gone for a walk and was on my way back when I saw you heading for the barn. I got curious and followed you."

"Well, ye should have let me know ye were there."

"If I had, would you have helped the horse?"

"I . . . I can't say," she mumbled, twisting the blanket at her throat.

"Uh-huh. I figure you would have run like a scared rabbit back to the house."

His words stung. "I'm no scared rabbit!" she hotly denied.

"Aren't you?"

"Nay!"

"Then come with me and heal my mother."

Rose realized she'd stepped into his well-laid trap. If she refused, he'd think her cruel and unfeeling, but she couldn't go with him. Stalling, she asked, "And where is your mother? Ye haven't said."

"She's with her people up in the Indian Territory. Near Fort Sill."

"B-but that must be hundreds of miles from here. Ye can't mean for me to go all that way with ye, surely."

"Surely I do," he said in a determined tone.

"Nay, I'm sorry, but that's impossible. Tye would never agree to it."

"I'm not planning to ask his permission."

Rose swallowed hard as his meaning sank in. "Ye think I'll pick up and leave without even telling him? Ye must be mad."

"Maybe, but that's the way it has to be. You've got the power to save my mother, and you're going to do it."

"Nay!" Rose gasped, frightened anew. She tossed back the covers, ready to run, but he stopped her, throwing an arm around her waste. She had time enough to issue a strangled cry, then his fist caught her on the chin. The world spun and dwindled to black.

"Sorry, *Toppah,* I hoped you wouldn't make me do that," Jack whispered, gathering her into his arms.

CHAPTER FOUR

Rose regained her senses slowly. Feeling herself rock to and fro, she groggily recognized the loping gait of a horse beneath her. But how could that be?

She forced her eyes open, taking in the starlit sky and the dark landscape passing by. Blinking at the sight, she realized she was seated crosswise on the horse – in a man's lap. Just like that, the scene in her bedroom with Jack came back to her, and she knew whose chest she leaned upon and whose arm was locked around her.

Panicking, she cried out in fright. Pain lanced through her jaw, reminding her of the blow her teacher-turned-abductor had delivered just before she'd sunk into oblivion.

"Easy now," the brute murmured. "You're all right. Nobody's gonna hurt you."

She threw her head back to see his shadowed features. "I'm not all right, ye . . . ye kidnapper!" Cupping her painful jaw, she demanded, "Take me back this instant!"

"Can't do that, Toppah."

"But ye must! Tye and Lil will be looking for me." Catching the odd word he'd spoken, she repeated it. "Toppah? What's that?"

"It's you. It means yellow-hair."

"Oh. Well, don't be calling me that again. Now turn this horse around and take me back," she again demanded.

"Nope. We're heading for the Nations. You might as well relax and enjoy the ride."

"Enjoy the ride, is it? You're daft!" She pushed at his steely arm and attempted to twist free, but, although his hold caused no pain, it was unbreakable. Feeling smothered and panicky, she shoved at his chest, managing to create a small space between them.

"Be still," he ordered sharply. "Do you want to fall off and break your neck?"

Before she could reply, another man's voice sounded nearby, speaking in an unfamiliar tongue. Unaware of his presence until that moment, Rose uttered a frightened cry and instinctively shrank against Jack. His arm tightened around her for a moment. He said something to the other man then spoke softly to her.

"Don't be afraid, *Poe-lah-yee*. That's only Tsoia. He is my friend, my blood brother. He won't touch you as long as he thinks you're mine."

"Yours! I'm not yours!" she shrilled, once more stiffening against him.

"You might not want to let him know that."

Twisting her upper body and craning her neck, Rose caught a glimpse of the other Indian's shadowy form. He rode near them and, unless she was mistaken, he led another horse.

"What did he say?" she warily asked.

"He said you screech like an owl," Jack replied, a grin in his voice.

Rose huffed in annoyance, not liking the comparison. After a moment's silence, she asked in a softer voice, "And what did ye call me a minute ago?"

"Poe-lah-yee. It means rabbit."

"Rabbit! I told ye before I'm no scared rabbit." Although she did feel like one just now, she privately admitted. "Oh, and my hair's not yellow, 'tis strawberry-blonde. That's what they're calling the color back in Chicago these days."

"That right? Well, I guess I could call you *Poe-aye-gaw*. That means strawberries."

"For goodness sake, can't ye call me by my proper name?"

"I dunno," he drawled. "Poe-aye-gaw is kinda nice, or maybe *P'ayn-nah*. That means sugar. Yeah, I like that one."

Sugar? Did he think her sweet? And what if he did? It made no nevermind to her. Snorting in disdain, Rose squirmed uncomfortably in his lap. She remained silent for several minutes, racking her brain for a way to escape, unable to think of anything. When she squirmed again, Jack gave her a sharp squeeze.

"Be still," he ordered again. "What's wrong, you hurting someplace?"

She felt a blush warm her face and was grateful for the darkness. "I . . . I need to relieve myself if ye must know."

"Oh. Why didn't you say so?" He called out to the other Indian and both men drew their horses to a halt. Easing Rose to the ground along with the blanket she was encased in, Jack said, "You'd best put your boots on. You don't want to step on a cactus with bare feet." Reaching into a bag tied to his saddle, he produced the boots and handed them down to her.

"Go on behind those bushes. See them over there?" He pointed off to the left as she struggled into her boots, fighting to hold the blanket close at the same time.

"Aye." She barely made out the shadowy foliage.

"Be quick about it, and don't try to run."

Not bothering to reply, she picked her way cautiously toward the small clump of bushes. As she took care of her urgent need, Jack's warning echoed through her head. It was very dark, with the moon hidden behind a bank of clouds. If she stayed low, perhaps she could make it to some hiding place before Jack and his friend noticed she was missing. She didn't give herself time to reconsider the idea. Bunching up her blanket and nightdress – her only garment – she crept stealthily away, praying for a hidey hole she could duck into.

She hadn't gone far when a hand clamped around her arm, wringing a terrified shriek from her lips. Dragged upright by that iron grip, she lost her hold on the blanket but hardly noticed as her captor shook her.

"I told you not to run," he growled. "Little fool! Did you really think you could escape me so easily?"

"I had to try!" she cried.

He gave her another, harder shake. "What if you fell and broke a leg or cracked your head open on a rock? What then? And where did you think to go when you don't even know where you are?"

"I . . . I don't know." Trembling with fear and cold, she couldn't hold back a despairing sob.

He sighed impatiently and raised his hand as if to strike her. Cringing in terror, Rose threw up her free arm to ward off the blow, but it never came.

"What the . . . ? I'm not gonna hit you, woman. I told you I wouldn't hurt you, didn't I?

Lowering her arm a little, Rose peeked at him. She couldn't see his expression in the dark, but he sounded more disgusted now than angry.

"Course, if you try running again, I just might have to beat some sense into you."

"No, please!" she begged, voice quaking like the rest of her. "I-I won't, I promise."

* * *

Jack felt her tremble and knew he could never carry out his threat. Retrieving the blanket she'd dropped, he wrapped it around her shoulders. As he led her back to the horses, more gently than he'd first intended, he puzzled over her terror-stricken behavior. True, he'd wanted to frighten her so she wouldn't do something stupid again and maybe get herself hurt, but he hadn't expected her to cower before him as if waiting for him to strike her. She'd made him feel ashamed when all he'd meant to do was brush a lock of starlit hair from her face.

Once they remounted and set off again, he continued to mull over Rose's reaction. The fear and timidity she'd shown him on other occasions had angered him because he'd thought it due to him being an Indian. Now, he was beginning to suspect some man, somewhere, had treated her cruelly, causing her to fear all men. The thought spread fire through his veins, making him long to get his hands on the lowdown coyote and give him a strong dose of his own medicine.

For a while, his captive sat stiff as a statue, not making a sound, never looking at him, but exhaustion caught up with her. Her head drooped and she relaxed against him. He carefully adjusted her position so that her head rested upon his shoulder. Dawn was breaking, allowing him to see the red swelling along her jaw where he'd struck her. His stomach turned over at the sight. He regretted having to knock her out. He'd never struck a woman before, but she'd left him no choice.

His gaze wandered over the delicate curve of her cheek, her dainty nose and the fine, slanted arch of her brows. They were rich, reddish brown the same as her lashes, like a pretty chestnut pony he'd once owned. He found the dark color startling in comparison to her light hair, but not unpleasant to look upon. No, not unpleasant at all.

She sighed, lips parting in sleep, and Jack was caught by the tempting sight. He wondered dangerously if she tasted of sugar, as he'd called her earlier. Unhindered, his gaze slid downward to the swell of her breasts and his pecker began to rise. Shit! He quickly aimed his gaze straight ahead and shifted beneath her, trying to alleviate his sudden discomfort. He'd better keep his eyes off the woman, and his thoughts too, or he'd end up proving she was right to fear him.

Still, he couldn't stop himself from glancing down at her now and then. As the sun rose higher, her red-blonde hair glowed like pale fire, captivating him. He longed to comb his fingers through the shimmering strands.

Damn! Jack frowned and reminded himself he preferred women with black hair like his own and skin the warm color of autumn leaves. A honey and cream complexion would turn an ugly red under the prairie sun. With that in mind, he dragged off his hat and gently settled it on Rose's head. That ought to protect her for now, he thought, experiencing an odd flood of tenderness. He wished he hadn't needed to drag her from her bed and the safety of her brother's home, but she was the only one who might save his mother's life. Once she worked her magic, he would return her to her family, he vowed.

* * *

"Damn that no-good Choctaw! He's made off with my sister!" Tye Devlin shouted, pounding his fist on the kitchen table, causing his wife to jump in her chair.

"Tye, you don't know that for sure," she protested.

"Oh, I'm as sure of it as of my own name. He's had his eye on her from the day they met, and he's nowhere to be found. Moreover, her brown stallion is gone. Who else but Choctaw Jack would think to take her and the beast, I ask ye?"

"Rose isn't a child. I'm betting she took the bit between her teeth and asked Jack to guide her over to Jessie and David's place."

"Aye? I ordered him to stay away from her. If he disobeyed

Dearest Irish

that order, I'll fire him. That's if he hasn't laid his hands on Rosie." The thought of the bastard raping her sickened him. "If he harms her, he's a dead man!"

Lil started to reply, but stopped at the sound of pounding hooves. Tye spun toward the sound. Hoping it might be Rose returning, he strode to the door. He threw it open in time to see his sister Jessie scramble off her horse.

"Tye! Thank the saints you're here!" she cried, running toward him.

He met her halfway, catching her by the shoulders as she barreled into him. "Jess, I was about to ride over to the River T. Is Rosie there?"

"What? Nay, of course not. Isn't she here with you?" Breathing hard, she stared at him, wide-eyed.

Tye's stomach knotted. Closing his eyes briefly, he shook his head. "Nay, she's gone. Either run off or taken against her will."

"Oh God! I'm too late." Swaying on her feet, Jessie went white as a sheet.

Moving fast, Tye slipped an arm around her waste. "Here now, don't be going into a swoon." Helping her stumble up the steps, he found Lil standing in the open doorway, a hand pressed to her throat, the other splayed over her rounded belly. Her face was drawn in distress. Alarmed, he motioned her inside. "Sit ye down," he told her, "before ye have our babe on the doorstep."

Once he had them both safely seated, Tye bent over Lil. "Are ye all right, mavourneen?" he asked worriedly, hands framing her face.

"I'm fine, just . . . afraid for Rose," she said, giving him a wobbly smile. "See to Jessie."

He studied her for a moment, kissed her brow and moved to squat beside Jessie's chair. She sat unmoving, staring blankly ahead. When he gripped her cold fingers, she turned her sorrowful gaze upon him. "I'm too late," she repeated dully. "Why? Why couldn't the vision come sooner?"

Sudden dread engulfed Tye. His sister's visions had often preceded terrible events, including the Chicago Fire back in '71. Before he could ask what she'd *seen* concerning their missing sister, Rebecca approached, carrying a cup of hot coffee. Tye scented the whiskey she'd added to it as she pressed the cup into Jessie's shaking hand.

"Drink," she ordered, and Jessie silently obeyed.

Keeping one eye on Lil to make sure she really was all right, Tye waited impatiently until color began to seep back into Jessie's cheeks. Then he questioned, "Sis, can ye tell me what ye saw?"

She wrapped both hands around her cup and gazed into the dregs of her coffee. "I saw Rosie," she said, barely above a whisper. "There was a man with her. His back was to me. I couldn't see his face, but he was big, with long black hair." She choked on a sob and forced out in a rush, "He had hold of her and was forcing himself on her. She was f-fighting him." Her voice broke and she bent over, weeping.

Tye took the cup from her hands, set it aside and gathered her close. Clenching his jaw, he struggled with his own feelings as well as hers. She was one of the few people who could break through the mental barriers he'd built up over the years to fend off the emotions that bombarded him from all sides. With Jessie's sorrow pounding at his brain, he had all he could do to keep from breaking down and weeping along with her. What saved him was white-hot rage, directed at the man who'd taken Rose.

A hand touched his shoulder. Lifting his head, he saw Lil standing beside him. Her wounded gaze revealed the sympathy she felt for him and Jessie, but mixed with that, and with her fear for Rosie, Tye detected denial. Her words confirmed it.

"I can't believe Jack would do such a thing," she said with a catch in her voice. "I've known him for more than ten years. In all that time he's never shown a mean streak." She shook her head. "It just doesn't seem possible that he'd hurt Rose." Silent tears slipped down her cheeks.

Releasing Jessie, whose sobs had begun to let up, Tye rose and pulled Lil into his arms. "I know ye don't wish to believe it of him, but Jessie's visions are seldom wrong." Burying his face in her unbound hair, he muttered, "God knows I hope this one is."

Their child kicked, letting him know he or she didn't like being squeezed so tight. Loosening his hold, he took a half-step back and stared into Lil's eyes, wondering what in God's name he ought to do.

As if reading his mind, Rebecca Crawford asked, "What will you do?" She stood in the middle of the room, between the kitchen side and the parlor, hands folded over her long white apron, calmly waiting for an answer.

Turning away from Lil, Tye paced to the open door and stared out. "I don't know," he admitted, grinding his teeth in frustration.

"You'll go after them," Lil said quietly.

Pivoting to face her, he shook his head. "No, I can't, I won't leave ye. Not now, when 'tis almost time for the babe to come."

She walked over to him. Laying one hand on his chest, she stroked his bristly cheek with the other, making him aware that he hadn't shaved this morning, so riled was he over Rose's disappearance. "You have to go, Tye. Rose is your sister."

"Aye, and you're my wife, *mavourneen,*" he replied, holding her loosely so as not to aggravate the babe again. "I can't go off and leave ye at a time like this."

Lil shook her head. "You don't need to worry about me. Ma's here. She'll be with me for the birthing."

"So will I," Jessie said, on her feet now. "And Maria Medina as well. She's helped me bring three wee ones into the world. Lil will be in good hands."

"There is nothing you can do for your wife at such a time, anyway," Rebecca chimed in. "It is your duty to find your sister."

Tye stared at her uncertainly then turned his eyes back to Lil. He wanted more than anything to be with her when she gave birth to their child, but how could he abandon Rosie to captivity in Choctaw Jack's hands? Especially after what Jessie had foreseen.

"You have to go," Lil said again. "Rose gave you back your sight. Now it's up to you to save her, to bring her home."

He sighed heavily, accepting what he'd known all along. "Very well, but where am I to look? Where would that devil carry her off to?"

"I expect he'll ride north into the Nations." Lil looked to her mother. "Don't you think so, Ma?"

Rebecca nodded. "It is possible. Jack is Choctaw. He might go to his people."

Tye was far from convinced by her vague answer, but he had no idea where else to search for Rose. "And where exactly would I be finding these people?"

"The Choctaw Nation is over on the eastern side of the

Territory," Lil said with a shrug. "That's all I know, but Uncle Jeb ought to be able to give you directions. He lived up in those parts when he was a young man." She glanced at her mother again. "Fact is, that's where my folks met, too. Isn't that right, Ma?"

With a sound that could have been either a yes or a no, Rebecca stepped to the kitchen table and began to scrape the breakfast plates. None of them had had an appetite after discovering Rose was gone. The largely untouched food went into a scrap bucket, destined for a pair of hogs being fattened for slaughter in the autumn.

A few minutes later, Tye hoisted his saddlebags – packed with an extra shirt, pants and whatever else Lil could cram into them – over one shoulder. Bidding Jessie goodbye with a vow to bring their sister back, he drew Lil toward the door, wanting a moment alone with her outside. His mother-in-law's voice halted him.

"I would ask one thing of you, Tye Devlin. Do not kill my dead son's friend if you do not need to."

He met her dark gaze. Did she realize what she was asking? "I wish I could promise ye that, Rebecca, but I can't." Biting out the words, he added, "If I find Jessie's vision has come to pass, the *bligeard* will wish for death before I'm done with him."

Not giving her a chance to plead for mercy for the man he intended to kill, he grasped Lil's elbow and led her outside.

* * *

It was mid morning when Tye reached the roundup campground, and he had to wait another agonizing hour or more before Del and Jeb Crawford rode in, shagging along several longhorn calves in need of branding. Refusing to waste anymore time, Tye didn't wait for his brother-in-law, David Taylor, to show up. In as few words as possible, he informed Del and Jeb about his sister's disappearance. By the time he finished, the two men looked as grim as he was feeling.

"Damnation! Are you certain it was Jack who took her?" Del queried.

"I'm certain." Tye didn't bother going into all the reasons. Turning to Jeb, he said, "Lil told me ye know your way around Choctaw territory. Can ye be giving me a few directions?"

Dearest Irish

Tall and lanky like his brother and niece, Jeb scrubbed at several days' growth of gray beard and studied the ground for a long moment, making Tye long to shake an answer out of him. Looking up at last, he shook his head. "Don't reckon I'll do that."

"What! But ye must. Without your help, I don't stand a chance of catching up with that bastard in time to save Rose from –"

"Hold on, boy. I didn't say I wasn't gonna help you. All I said is I'm not giving you directions. Like as not you'd get yourself lost along the way and waste all kinds of time. It'll be best if I go with you."

"You'd do that?"

"Course I will. You're family, aren't you? And that makes young Rose family too."

Speechless with gratitude, Tye could only nod.

Luckily, Jeb had stashed spare duds in his saddlebags – in case he was to get bloodied by an ornery steer, he said, adding that it paid to be prepared. Following the older man's example, Tye chose a fresh horse from his string, more for stamina than speed. Endurance would likely be the key to hunting down their quarry.

Packing enough rations to keep them going for several days, and grabbing a plate of bacon and beans from the chuck wagon, they wolfed down the food and mounted up.

"You boys watch yourselves up there in the Territory," Del advised. "Those Choctaw are supposed to be peaceful, but some of 'em have no more love for white folks than do the Comanche and Kiowa."

"I know that. As you durn well oughta remember," Jeb barked, more testy than Tye had ever heard him.

Del scowled and rubbed his neck. "Yeah, I reckon so. Just don't go losing your scalp, little brother. And bring Tye and Miss Rose home safe."

Jeb nodded. "I'll do that." Saluting Del, he told Tye, "Come on, we're burning daylight." With a rebel yell, he sent his startled horse into a gallop.

"Tell David I'll catch up with him on the trail to Kansas after I bring Rosie home," Tye called out to his father-in-law. "And take care of Lil." Spurring his mount, he raced after Jeb.

CHAPTER FIVE

Rose stretched and yawned. Something hard supported her head, and another something lay half across her face. This object felt like cloth and gave off a vaguely familiar scent. Swatting whatever it was away, she opened her eyes and had to squint at the bright sun glaring down at her from on high. In the time it took to blink and shield her eyes with her hand, everything that had befallen her during the night burst upon her like a waking nightmare.

Realizing she lay on the hard ground – she had the aches and pains to prove it – she turned her head to the right and saw Choctaw Jack lying a hand's breadth away. He lay on his back, head pillowed on his saddle and one arm thrown over his eyes. Where was his hat, she wondered absurdly. Recalling the object she'd pushed off her face, she rose on one elbow and twisted to look behind her. First, she saw that she'd also been sleeping with a saddle under her head; then she spotted the hat she'd knocked into the high grass surrounding them. Jack must have placed it over her face to protect her from the sun's burning rays. In view of his threat to beat her if she tried to run away again, she was surprised by this small kindness.

A throaty snore sounded from her left. Looking in that direction, she saw Jack's Indian friend sprawled on his stomach, with his face turned away from her. He was naked from the waist up, his lower half covered by hide leggings and what she guessed was a breechcloth, never having seen one before. His long black hair lay in disarray over his dark copper shoulders.

He snored again, louder this time. Rose's lips twitched; then she scolded herself for finding anything remotely amusing in her situation. Glancing around, she wondered how far they were from the Double C. Jack had been right to chide her last night. She'd had no idea where they were or in which direction to run for help. Even more true now, she conceded with a disheartened sigh.

She heard a horse snuffle. Sitting upright, she craned her neck to see over the grass and spotted three horses tethered among a stand of nearby trees. She caught her breath. Was one of them Brownie? Aye, she was certain of it. Excited and anxious to greet him, she folded aside the blanket cocooning her and started to rise, but a sharp tug on her ankle made her fall back with an astonished gasp. Only then did she notice the rope tied loosely around her ankle. To her dismay, the other end of the rope was wrapped around Jack's hand.

"Going somewhere?" he asked, startling her.

"You're awake!" she blurted, meeting his frowning, half-lidded gaze.

"Thanks to you, I am. You didn't answer my question. Where were you going?"

"I saw Brownie over there." She pointed to the trees. "I was only wishing to let him know I'm here, nothing more." She swallowed hard, fearing he would think she'd meant to climb on the stallion and make a run for freedom – though without a saddle on his back and no one to boost her up, 'twould be well nigh impossible.

Staring at her a moment longer, Jack evidently came to the same conclusion. "I reckon he'll be glad to see you," he said, sitting up and freeing her ankle. "Go ahead. Say howdy to him."

She again started to rise, but he forestalled her, saying, "Hold on. You'd best put your boots back on." Reaching behind his saddle, he retrieved her footgear.

"Aye, I suppose there could be cactuses about," she said tartly, recalling what he'd said last night. She forced a tight smile.

"Yeah, or snakes."

Rose shivered at the thought of encountering a snake and gladly jammed her feet into the boots. As she did, Jack dug into his saddlebags, drew out a pile of clothes and extended them to her. "You might as well get dressed while you're back there in the trees. I hope I got everything you need. It was dark in your room and I wasn't sure what all you'd want."

He'd brought her riding skirt, plaid shirt, a pair of knitted cotton stockings, and a set of unmentionables. "Thank you," she muttered, mortified to know he'd handled her personal things.

Pushing to her feet, she clutched the blanket and her garments close as she trudged through the tall grass, over to the grove of scrubby trees where Brownie and the other two horses stood grazing on shoots of green.

"Hello, boy," Rose murmured, patting her friend's silky neck. He raised his head, nickered a greeting, and nudged her affectionately.

Laughing, she scratched around his ears the way he loved. She petted and crooned to him for several moments, then quickly donned her clothes and finger combed her hair as best she could. Thankful to be fully dressed, though God knew a few pieces of clothing wouldn't save her if Jack or his friend chose to attack her, she walked out to face them.

The two men sat cross-legged on the ground, speaking quietly in their native tongue between mouthfuls of some sort of food. Hearing her approach through the swaying grass, both of them twisted around to watch her. The bare-chested Indian looked her up and down, grinned and commented in a suggestive tone, causing Rose to halt and glance at Jack in apprehension. He frowned at his companion and waved him to silence.

"Come and eat," he said, motioning Rose forward.

She hesitantly knelt beside him, keeping a wary eye on his companion, who now ignored her as he bit off a sizable chunk of strange looking stuff and wolfed it down. Hoping for coffee, Rose was disappointed to see they hadn't started a fire. Jack handed her a strip of the same stuff he and his friend were eating. It appeared to be a mixture of meat, fat and some sort of berries. She stared at it dubiously.

"It's pemmican," he explained, lips quirking at her reaction. "It will give you strength. Eat it," he ordered.

Rose warily bit off a small piece of the greasy mixture and chewed thoroughly before swallowing. She couldn't say she liked the taste, but it wasn't terrible. Jack passed her his canteen and she downed a sip of tepid water before taking a larger bite of pemmican.

"Finish it all," Jack said. "You'll need it."

Finding his comment ominous, she ate her *breakfast* while he turned his attention back to his friend, whose strange name Rose couldn't remember. The two carried on a brief conversation, then stood and set about preparing the horses for travel. Jack saddled his gelding while his half-clothed companion slapped the saddle Rose had used as a pillow onto Brownie. Did he intend to ride her horse? Ha! She'd like to see him try. He'd be tossed off in the blink of an eye.

It came as a surprise when Jack led Brownie over to her. "Before we move out, you need to visit the bushes?" he asked.

Wondering if *he* meant to ride the stallion, she parroted, "Visit the bushes?" Then it dawned on her what he meant. "Oh! No, I, uh, saw to that before," she replied in embarrassment, gesturing toward the trees.

"Then let's get you mounted."

She caught her breath. "You'll let me ride Brownie? By myself?"

He lifted one dark brow. "Ain't that what I just said? Come on. We're wasting time."

Relieved to know she wouldn't need to sit perched in his lap again, with his arms enclosing her, Rose hastened to obey. However, once he'd helped her mount, instead of handing her the reins, Jack gathered them up and swung onto his bay gelding.

"Catch hold of the stallion's mane and hold on," he directed.

"Ye . . . ye don't trust me to guide him myself?"

He glanced at her over his shoulder as he started off, leading her. "I trust you to guide him right enough, but not where I want you to go."

"Ye think I'll try to run away again after I promised I wouldn't?"

"You promised, but that doesn't mean you'll keep your word," he replied without bothering to look back at her.

"Oh! Are ye calling me a liar, sir?" she snapped.

"Take it any way you want. I've seen that horse run, lady, and I'm not going to chance you getting away."

Rose opened her mouth to voice an angry protest but closed it. Her jaw still ached where he'd punched her last night, and she vividly recalled his threat to beat her. She didn't wish to provoke him into doing so.

"Hang on tight," he called, picking up the pace.

Grumbling under her breath, Rose wound her fingers tightly through Brownie's mane as Jack urged both their mounts into a gallop. His Indian friend rode beside him, moving with his brown and white paint horse as if he and the animal were one, with only a dark, curly-haired blanket – a buffalo robe, perhaps – over the horse's back.

The afternoon and evening passed in stretches of hard riding, relieved by periods of walking the horses to save them from breaking down. Twice, they stopped to drink and rest the animals, and on one occasion eat more pemmican, but these brief stops didn't help Rose's growing discomfort. She wasn't used to such long hours in a saddle. As the day wore on, the inside of her thighs and her bottom became so sore that she had to clamp her jaws together to keep from crying out. Her legs grew wobbly, threatening to collapse when she touched ground. The last time Jack called for them to mount up, he had to lift her into the saddle.

"We'll ride a short distance more before stopping to sleep," he declared.

She made an indistinct sound, refusing to speak. In truth, she was too tired and in too much pain to say or do anything. She was aware of Jack standing there studying her in the dim evening light, but didn't look at him. After a moment, he muttered something cross in his throaty Indian tongue and stepped over to his horse. As he led off once more, Rose heard him exchange a few unintelligible words with his friend. Outside of that, they rode in silence.

By the time they halted for the night, the stars and moon were well up. Not that Rose took much notice. She was more exhausted than she'd ever been in her life, and she hurt so badly that she couldn't choke off a whimper as she slid – fell was more like it – from her horse.

Jack was there to catch her. She found no strength to protest when he slipped an arm around her and led her, stumbling, to a spot beside the bole of a large tree. She groaned when he lowered her to the ground. "I'll make you a bed," he said gruffly. Moments later, Rose barely registered being lifted and placed on a blanket. She was asleep almost instantly.

* * *

Jack wrapped her blanket snuggly around her to ward off the night chill. Her face was only a pale blur in the darkness, for which he was glad. He didn't want to see signs of the suffering he'd caused her.

"Toppah did well," Tsoia remarked as they cared for the horses. "I thought she would complain about the pace you set, but she did not."

"No, she did not, but today cost her much. I fear she will be unable to ride tomorrow."

"But she must. You will make her ride, will you not?"

"Yes, I will make her ride," Jack gritted, hating the fact that he'd have to put her through more agony.

* * *

Come morning, Rose was so stiff and sore that she could hardly move. Her nether parts were on fire with pain and her legs ached abominably. She wanted to cry when Jack announced it was time to move on. Wondering how she would survive another day in the saddle, she limped to Brownie's side, where Jack stood waiting. He'd folded her blanket into a pad and laid it over her saddle, she noticed.

"That oughta help some," he said, gesturing at the blanket.

"Thank you," she choked out, unable to meet his gaze. It embarrassed her to realize he knew what part of her hurt the worst. She jumped and looked up when he brushed a finger across her tender jaw.

"There's a bruise. I'm sorry for that. If there'd been any other way . . . ." His husky voice trailed off.

Disturbed by his touch and unexpected regret, she turned her head aside.

After a brief silence, he said in his usual curt tone, "We'll take it easier today." Without further conversation, he gave her a hand up and mounted his own horse while she gingerly adjusted her sore posterior on Brownie.

The blanket did help, she discovered, and Jack was true to his word, setting a slower pace and calling for more frequent rest stops. Still, by the time they halted long after sundown, she was done in again. She stiffly dismounted, bottom and thighs aching, though not quite as badly as the night before thanks to the blanket pad.

Excusing herself for a few moments – her captors now trusted her that much, at least – Rose returned to find the horses staked out for the night and the two men preparing to eat. Along with the ever-present pemmican, she was pleasantly surprised to find a tin of beans on the menu. Although they had to be eaten cold due to the lack of a fire, she gratefully consumed every bite of her helping. Moments later, in a replete, exhausted daze, she watched Jack lay out her usual bed of blanket and saddle.

"Lie down," he ordered. When she wordlessly obeyed, he pulled a flap of the blanket over her and said simply, "Sleep."

Rose made an agreeing sound. That was the last thing she remembered before sinking into fretful slumber peopled by a ghostly being who chased her down dark tunnels, a dream she often suffered. This time, though, it took a different turn. Out of nowhere, Jack appeared, opening his arms to her and driving off the evil one. Smiling in her sleep, she sighed, secure in the safety of his imaginary embrace.

Watching her from his sleeping place, Jack saw her smile and wondered what she was dreaming about. Could it be a man? Had he guessed wrong the other night? Maybe he was the only one who terrified her, and there'd been no cruel man in her past. Instead, maybe she'd once loved a man, a *white* man. Even though he'd told himself she was not for him, the thought of her in the arms of another made him scowl and roll over, turning his back to her.

Tsoia's snores irritated him further. Then came the call of a lonely coyote. That sound was like a lullaby to him most nights, but not tonight.

* * *

Rose's dreams faded away when Jack woke her at first light. He seemed even more taciturn than usual, remaining silent while they ate and prepared to ride on. She dreaded climbing back on Brownie. Her legs and backside had stiffened over night, but surprisingly, once they got underway, her muscles loosened up.

With her aches and pains receding to a tolerable level, Rose began to notice the changing country. Gone were the lush fields of spring wild flowers and groves of trees. They now rode across a dry, windswept landscape, dotted with scrub brush, tufts of tall, wiry grass and tumbleweeds. Once, they happened upon a narrow stream, low and easily crossed.

Dearest Irish

It was only late March, and the farther north they traveled, the cooler temperatures became. Rolled in her trusty blanket that night, Rose curled up close to the small campfire Jack had built, the cause of an argument between her two captors. Tsoia, whose name she'd finally committed to memory, was against starting a fire, obvious from his sharp words and gestures. She'd gathered he feared discovery by enemies, white men no doubt. However, Jack had prevailed, laying a fire made up of dried cattle droppings – cow chips, he called them – and sage brush that gave off a pungent, strangely soothing aroma.

Had Jack insisted on lighting a fire for her sake, going against Tsoia's and his own better judgment? The possibility warmed Rose's heart briefly, until she recalled his threat to beat her and the fact that he continued to retain hold of Brownie's reins each day.

* * *

"Time to move on," Jack said, walking to his horse. Their noon stop was over. The gelding turned his head and gave him a white-rimmed glare as Jack tightened the cinch he'd loosened only a short while ago.

Adjusting the canvas bag filled with food supplies that hung from his saddle, Jack glanced over at Rose. They'd stopped beside a narrow creek, and she was down on her knees beside it, washing the tin plates and forks he'd brought along with her comfort in mind. Surprised by her effort to help, he was also mindful of her quiet acceptance of the cold food he'd served up. Since their first day on the trail, when she'd looked suspiciously at the pemmican, she hadn't once complained about their tiresome fare.

"Toppah is not so useless as I thought," Tsoia remarked. "She will make you a good wife."

"She is white. I will never take her to wife," Jack muttered, staring at Rose's profile. He eyed the curve of her breast, outlined by her plaid shirt, and her rounded bottom, molded by the divided riding skirt. The woman was tempting, too damn much so.

"Then let me have her. I do not mind her white blood, and I will teach her to be a good *Ka'igwu* woman."

Jack turned on his friend. "No! She is not here for your

pleasure. I told you she has magic. I bring her to heal my mother. Nothing more." He slashed the air for emphasis. "Anyway, Juana would slice off your balls if you took a second wife."

Tsoia chuckled. "That is so. But you protest too loudly, my brother. I see how you look at this woman. You want her for yourself. Do not deny it."

"I said I will not take her to wife," Jack ground out.

"But why should that stop you from having her? If she means nothing to you, you need not care what she wants."

Glancing at Rose as she got to her feet, clutching the eating utensils, Jack experienced a fresh surge of temptation. He had wanted her for weeks. She'd driven him half mad, invading his dreams with visions of her lying beneath him, moaning as he pleasured her. But Tsoia was wrong. If he were to take her against her will, she would likely refuse to work her healing magic on his mother. Besides, never had he forced himself on any woman and he wasn't . . . .

She looked up, encountered his gaze and halted in her tracks. Returning his stare, she licked her lips provocatively.

Tsoia elbowed him in the ribs. "Go ahead, brother, Toppah wants you," he prodded with a sly laugh.

"Don't call her that. She doesn't like it," Jack muttered distractedly. He forgot his reasons for not touching her. Powerless to resist his desire, he walked slowly toward Rose. Her blue agate eyes widened as he neared, and she licked her lips again as if in invitation. It occurred to him that she just wanted to find out how an Indian kissed, and he stiffened in anger.

He grasped her arms and hauled her close, drawing a gasp from her lips. Plates and forks clattered to the ground as he crushed her breasts against his chest. She cried out, but he silenced her with a hard kiss. Drawing in her woman's scent, he plunged his tongue into her mouth and tasted her honeyed warmth. Then he noticed her violent trembling, heard her muted whimpers, felt her twist in his grasp and pound frantically at him with her fists. He remembered what he'd been thinking moments ago, that he'd never forced a woman and wasn't about to start with her.

Kneading her slim shoulders, Jack gentled his kiss in an attempt to sooth her. Her breath hitched, she went still, and for one searing moment he forgot everything but her. He simply wanted to go on kissing her, wanted to discover her mysteries and coax a response from her. Yanking off his hat when it got in the way, he tossed it aside and slid his mouth across Rose's velvety cheek then nibbled her earlobe, drawing a gasp from her lips. On the verge of sliding his arms around her, he caught himself.

What was he doing? Why had he let Tsoia's goading and his own mindless desire drive him to kiss her? She was meant to heal his mother, not serve his needs.

Anger returning, he lifted his head and glared at her. "Does that satisfy the white lady's curiosity? Or should I show you what a redskin can do on a blanket?" Not trusting himself to touch her a moment longer, he shoved her away.

"Nay!" she gasped, stumbling backward. Her wide blue eyes were pools of fear. "Stay away from me!" she cried, raising her arms in a defensive gesture.

Abruptly, Jack remembered her terrified behavior the other night when he'd caught her trying to run away. Whether caused by memories of a man who'd hurt her in the past or by his own threatening actions, he hadn't liked watching her cower before him. He didn't like it any better now. Disgusted with himself, he raked his long hair back and forced himself to meet her panicky gaze.

"I'm sorry," he said gruffly. "I got the wrong idea. I shouldn't have touched you."

She cautiously lowered her arms. "Wr-wrong idea?" she stammered in a high-pitched, trembling voice.

He snatched up his hat, slapped it back on and cleared his throat. "Yeah, when you stared at me a minute ago and licked your lips, I, uh, thought you were inviting me to . . . ."

"To kiss me? Nay, *attack* me! Because you're an Indian and I wanted to how you . . . ?"

"Yeah, that's what I thought," he barked, uncomfortable beneath her accusing gaze. "It won't happen again. I give you my word."

She studied him for a long moment, clutching the small gold cross at her throat. Then dark lashes shielded her eyes and she nodded. "I accept your word, sir, and I hope you'll believe me when I say I'd never lead ye on out of mere curiosity. I couldn't be so brazen and cruel."

He felt guilty for thinking her capable of such behavior, even for a minute. If he'd learned one thing about Rose Devlin over the past few weeks, it was her sweet nature. He should have known she wouldn't play the kind of game other white women had played with him in the past. If he was honest, he *had* known, but he'd let his own wild urges convince him otherwise.

"It's time to move on," he said gruffly. Crouching, he hastily gathered up the utensils Rose had dropped and stowed them in his saddlebags. When he glanced at Rose, he found her watching him, arms crossed, hugging herself. "Get mounted," he ordered.

"I-I can't. Get mounted, I mean."

Jack cursed under his breath and went to perform the service she'd come to expect. He wished the stallion was smaller so she could mount by herself, because after kissing her, he needed to keep his distance. He didn't want to break his word to her.

* * *

As they rode on, Rose relived Jack's angry kiss. He'd terrified her with his imprisoning hands, his big, threatening body and predatory mouth. Then he'd suddenly changed, becoming gentle. She didn't know why and didn't understand the disturbing effect upon her. All she knew was the taste of his mouth and the way he'd used it had sent sparks shooting through her body, frightening her in new, unexpected ways. She prayed he would keep his word and not do that again.

Except for an occasional brief halt, during which Jack ignored her, the afternoon passed to the thud of their horses' hooves and the howl of the wind. The sound was enough to drive a person mad, Rose thought. Would it never let up? Instead of weakening, the wind strengthened and the sky turned ominously dark over to the west.

She watched Jack study the rapidly approaching storm clouds and heard him exchange a few words with Tsoia. Glancing at her over his shoulder, he said, "I don't like the look of those clouds. We need to find shelter fast. Here." He tossed Brownie's reins to her. "Ride hard and stick close."

Astonished by his sudden trust in her, she nodded mutely. When he and Tsoia kicked their mounts into a gallop, she did likewise. Before long, rain began to pelt them, growing heavier by the minute, forcing Rose to blink fast to see where she was going. Mixed with the rain were small, stinging pellets of hail that made her hiss in pain and bend low over Brownie's neck as she struggled to guide him after Jack.

The wind screeched like a banshee, blowing sheets of rain sideways, slashing at her like knives. The hail stones grew larger, the pain they inflicted more intense. Brownie let out a piercing neigh when an especially big one smashed into his shoulder, and Rose had all she could do to control him. He was in a near panic, as were the other horses.

Where was the shelter Jack sought? Was there any to be found out here in the middle . . . ?

Pain exploded through her head, radiating from above her left ear. Seeing bursts of bright colors, she swayed precariously in her saddle. Instinctively, she grabbed her saddle horn to keep from tumbling off the galloping horse. Somewhere in her stunned brain, she realized she'd been struck by a large hail stone.

She had no memory of screaming, but she must have because Jack was suddenly there, scooping her from Brownie's back with an arm around her waist and swinging her onto his lap. "It's all right, I've got you," he shouted above the raging storm.

Huddled against him, she felt the beating of his heart beneath her ear and, despite the terrible pounding in her head, she took comfort from his rock-solid strength. The rain and hail continued to beat at them, but in her groggy state, Rose trusted Jack to bring them safely through. She was not surprised when, moments later, he drew up outside a broken down cabin. Jumping off his horse, he lifted her down into his arms and carried her to the cabin. He kicked open the sagging door and stepped into the dark, musky smelling interior. After a brief hesitation, he set her down near the cold hearth. As he did, Tsoia shouted something from outside, accompanied by the terrified shriek of a horse.

"Stay put," Jack ordered. "I need to help with the horses."

Rose caught his hand. She'd regained her senses enough to ask, "Brownie, is he –?"

"He's here. He stayed with us all the way."

"Buíochas le Dia," she breathed in relief, thanking God in Irish.

The two men herded the horses inside with a good deal of

tugging, pushing and a few cuss words from Jack. At last, he slammed the door shut, closing out the storm. Rain and hail continued to hammer the roof as he and Tsoia settled the animals on one side of the one-room shack. Next, they broke up a rough hewn, lopsided table and used the wood to start a fire. Shivering in her cold, wet clothes, Rose scooted close to the flames and stretched her hands toward the blessed warmth.

"How's your head feel?" Jack asked, squatting to wrap her blanket about her shoulders.

"It hurts a bit," she replied, darting a quick glance at him. He was just as wet as she was, but the cold didn't seem to affect him.

He pointed at the spot above her ear where the hail stone had struck her. "You bled some. Best wash it before your hair dries and sticks to the cut."

Surprised to learn she'd been cut, Rose touched the side of her head. Her hand came away stained with red.

"I'll do it for you, if you'll let me," Jack offered.

Her first instinct was to say no, she could do it herself, but something stopped her. She tilted her head in acceptance. "Thank you. I would appreciate that."

He used his bandana, doused in water from his canteen, to gently wash the blood from her hair. "Sorry," he muttered whenever he touched an especially tender spot, causing her to flinch despite her determination not to show pain.

"I got most of it," he said after several minutes. Then he pulled a bottle of whiskey from his saddlebags and removed the cap. Rose stiffened, knowing what he intended. He cocked a raven eyebrow at her. "You could always heal yourself."

"Nay, I can't. It doesn't work that way," she said, staring in dread at the whisky. When he dribbled the fiery liquid over the gash in her scalp, she hissed and bit down hard on her bottom lip, but she sat still, knowing this was necessary. She didn't want the small wound to become infected.

"Too bad we don't have some of Miz Crawford's ointment. It wouldn't burn so much," Jack commented. "But it's done now, and the cut's mostly stopped bleeding. It oughta close up good in a couple days. Then you can wash the rest of the blood outta your hair."

"Thank you," Rose repeated, giving him a wobbly smile.

He nodded and turned away. "Since we've got a fire again tonight, we might as well heat up some vittles."

Working together, he and Tsoia soon had supper ready. It consisted of more beans, bacon and flatbread heated in a small skillet over the fire. Jack called it frybread. It was quite good. The hot food and the fire's heat warmed Rose, driving away her shivers.

She cleaned up after their meal again, needing something to occupy her hands. While she scraped and rinsed their tin plates clean with more water from Jack's canteen – he would need to refill it tomorrow – her companions sat cross-legged, talking in their own language. Tsoia brought out a long-stemmed pipe, different from any Rose had ever seen. Adding tobacco to the bowl from a small leather pouch, he fished a brand from the fire, lit the tobacco and drew on the pipe. Then he handed it to Jack, who took a long draw before passing it back to his friend.

A sense of nostalgia swept over Rose. "My da always used to enjoy smoking his pipe," she remarked softly.

"Used to? You told me he's in Chicago. Now you're saying he's dead?" Jack asked, frowning.

"Nay, nay, he's alive." She fastened her gaze on the plate she was drying. "'Tis only that I was thinking of days long ago, before I left home. The first time that is."

"You left home once before?"

"Aye, after Mam, uh, I mean my mother died."

"Oh. Sorry." After a moment's silence, he asked, "Where'd you go?"

"To a convent. D'ye know what that is?"

"Course I do. My pa was Catholic." He stared hard at her. "You were a nun?"

"Nay. I never took my final vows." Rose didn't like his probing questions. Setting aside the dried plates, she tried to distract him. "I enjoyed that frybread. Perhaps I could try making it next time."

"Mmm. But you meant to become a nun," he persisted. "How long were you locked away in the convent?"

She glanced at him sharply. "I wasn't locked away. I could've left any time I wished."

"Fine. But how long you were there?"

"Nigh unto seven years."

"That's a long time," he said slowly. "You must have been a child when you left home."

"I was thirteen, old enough."

At that point, Tsoia said something, distracting Jack as Rose hadn't managed to do. She hoped he would forget about questioning her.

CHAPTER SIX

Morning dawned clear and cold. Huddled in her blanket, Rose watched with envy as Jack shook out a fringed buckskin jacket he'd kept tied behind his saddle. She was surprised when he walked over and handed her the garment.

"Put this on. It's big for you but it'll have to do for now," he said, lifting away her blanket. "I didn't think to grab your wrap back at the ranch."

"But what of yourself?" Rose asked, donning the heavy leather jacket. It smelled of horse and Jack, and it was huge on her, hanging almost to her knees.

He shrugged as he helped her turn up the sleeves. "I'll get by with a blanket 'til we reach Fort Sill. Should be able to pick up a coat for you there."

"Fort Sill. I recall ye saying 'tis near where your mother lives."

He nodded. "It's an army post on the reservation. The soldiers make sure the *good* Indians behave themselves and they chase down the bad ones."

"Oh." From his derisive tone, she concluded this was a topic best avoided. She held her tongue while he wrapped himself in his blanket, helped her mount up, and stepped into his saddle. Tsoia waited on his paint, cloaked in his furry horse blanket. Jack led out once again trusting Rose to guide her own horse, making her feel as though she'd won a small battle.

They rode until midday, when Jack called a halt to eat and let the horses graze. Rose dutifully chewed her cold rations, dreaming of hot fry bread and coffee to warm her insides.

"We're not far from the Red River," Jack informed her

between bites of food. "If we're lucky, that storm we rode through didn't hit this far north and we'll cross with no trouble."

"Aye? But what if the storm did pass this way?"

Swallowing another mouthful, he replied, "The river will likely be running high and fast. I won't risk crossing it, not with you along. We'll have to wait for it to go down."

"How long might that take?"

"Could be days, depending on how much it rained up here."

"Auch, no! We need to get to your mother as soon as possible, do we not?"

He stared at her, wearing a dubious expression. "Yeah, we do, but why do you care? She's nothing to you."

Insulted, Rose glared at him. "I care because she's suffering, and perhaps I can help her. That's why ye abducted me, after all."

A slow grin spread across his lips. "Yes ma'am, it sure is and I'm glad I won't have to convince you to work your magic on her."

"There's no magic! 'Tis a gift from God, and of course ye needn't convince me. I'm a healer. I'd never let a person suffer if I can take away their pain." She paused then admitted, "Although, without knowing more about her illness, I can't say if I'll be able to heal her."

"Tsoia said she has a pain in her belly." Jack squeezed his fist and pounded his midsection. "And she can't keep food down."

Rose frowned, thinking his mother's ailment sounded serious, perhaps too serious for her to cure. "How much farther do we have to go after we cross the river?" she asked.

"Another day, day and a half, and we'll have to stop at the fort. I need to ask permission to take you to her."

"What? But why?"

He cocked his head and gave her a mocking look. "Because an Indian riding with a white woman on the Kiowa reservation will stick out like fish in a dry creek. It's asking for trouble, but a letter from Colonel Mackenzie, the post commander, ought to satisfy any troops we meet."

Rose frowned and shook her head in confusion. "I don't understand. Why would your mother be living on the Kiowa reservation?"

Finished eating, Jack said something to Tsoia and received a one-word reply. Then he pushed to his feet, saying, "Because she's

Kiowa." Holding his blanket together with one hand, he extended the other to Rose and she accepted it without thinking.

"But I thought ye were Choctaw," she blurted, letting him pull her upright.

"Pa was half French and half Choctaw, like I told you, but not *Khaw*. Mother, I mean. She's fullblood Kiowa."

"Then why are ye called Choctaw Jack?" Withdrawing her hand from his, she overlapped his huge coat snuggly around herself and followed him to the horses.

He gave a bark of laughter. "The first time I met the Crawfords, Miz Rebecca asked what tribe I belonged to. I figured it best to let her and everyone else think I was a *civilized* Indian like her. So, I said I was half Choctaw." He hung the bag of dwindling foodstuffs back on his saddle and motioned Rose over to Brownie. "They started calling me Choctaw Jack and the name stuck. My pa would have gotten a good laugh from that," he added dryly.

"Why d'ye say that?" she asked as he boosted her into the saddle.

"Because when I was a boy, I didn't hold much respect for the Choctaw. Seemed to me they shamed themselves, Pa included, by trying so hard to fit into the white man's world. I wanted to run off and roam free with my mother's people. Tried to once, but Pa tracked me down and hauled me back home. Then he blistered my backside 'til I had to eat standing up for two days." Chuckling at the memory, Jack stared into the distance, one hand resting on Rose's knee.

Acutely aware of that hand and wanting him to remove it, yet oddly warmed by it, she cleared her throat. "Ye keep referring to your father as if . . . as if he's no longer alive."

Recalled to the present, he immediately lifted his hand from her leg, "He's not. He was killed in the war," he said curtly, striding back to his own horse.

"'Tis sorry I am to hear that." Watching him swing onto his horse, she asked, "D'ye have any brothers or sisters?"

"Enough! You ask too many questions, Toppah. Let's go." With that, he headed his bay gelding north, kicking it into a gallop.

"Don't call me that!" she shouted, miffed by his sharp rebuff. Encountering Tsoia's amused grin, she narrowed her eyes at him and kneed Brownie after the devil up ahead, gritting her teeth when she heard laughter from the one behind her.

If I were bigger I'd pop both of them on the nose, she thought in annoyance.

They arrived at the Red River perhaps two hours later. Rose had feared being the cause of a delay if the river turned out be in flood, but halted between the two men on the high bank overlooking the water course, she sighed in relief. The river was low, so low that it ran in several narrow streams with sandbars dividing them.

"Look up there," Jack said, directing her attention to the opposite bank. "That's how high she gets after a long, hard rain."

Rose caught her breath. High up the red clay bank, driftwood was jammed among the trees that grew there, showing the power of the water when it came rushing through here. Jack was right not to want to cross the river at such a time, especially burdened with the likes of her. She offered up a silent prayer to the Blessed Virgin for sending the rain storm farther south.

"This was a buffalo crossing for more years than my mother's people can remember," Jack informed her, leaning on his saddle horn. "They and their Comanche brothers often followed the same trail on their raids into Texas. But the great herds are gone, slaughtered by buffalo hunters, and the tribes no longer ride south. Now cowboys are starting to cross their cattle here instead, on their way to Dodge City up in Kansas." His words held bitter resignation, for which Rose found no response.

"I'll take the lead," he said, straightening. "You come next and follow exactly where I go. There's quicksand in some spots that could swallow you and your horse."

Rose nodded, gulping down a knot of fear. While Jack spoke briefly with Tsoia, she unconsciously twisted Brownie's reins, causing him to dance nervously. She relaxed her hands and patted the stallion's neck.

"Easy, boy, you're all right," she murmured.

"Are you?" Jack asked, snaring her gaze.

"Aye, I'll do."

He eyed her for a moment, then turned his mount and headed down the bank. Rose urged Brownie after him and Tsoia fell in behind her again. In case she got into trouble, she realized, for the first time grateful for his presence.

She stuck so close to Jack that Brownie's nose was

practically buried in the bay's tail. At one point the horses had to swim across a narrow channel, but they took it in stride and within moments all were climbing up the far bank. Glancing over her shoulder, Rose was glad to see the last of the Red River.

* * *

Tye Devlin cursed the storm for delaying Jeb and him by nearly a full day. The hail had driven them to beg shelter late yesterday at a small homestead along their route. Meeting them with a shotgun, the widow woman who owned the place had questioned them closely before allowing them to spend the night in her barn, the roof of which leaked in several places. Not that Tye blamed her for being cautious when strangers showed up at her door. Besides herself, she had two young sons to protect and no man to help her.

It was that fact that led Jeb to insist on taking time to repair the barn roof for her this morning. Anxious to track down Rose's kidnapper and free her from his heartless clutches, Tye had begrudged the further delay, but needing Jeb's knowledge of the Indian lands in order to find Choctaw Jack, he'd been forced to pitch in and help patch the roof. Then the good widow, whose name was Abigail Fuller, had shown her gratitude by convincing Jeb – his arm hadn't needed much twisting – to sit down for a hearty dinner at her table. Wanting to butt his head against a wall in frustration, Tye again hadn't had any choice but to stay.

They were finally underway now, but the day was more than half gone and a long ride still lay ahead of them before they reached the Red River. Tye gave up hope of making it tonight.

Having angled northeast from the Double C over the past few days, they were aiming for Colbert's Ferry, which, according to Jeb, would carry them across the Red and land them near the Choctaw Nation's western boundary. From there he recommended they head for Durant, a nearby settlement, and begin their search. "I know you're put out with me for sticking around Widow Fuller's place so long," Jeb said. "But I just couldn't ride off without repaying her for taking us in."

Tye resettled his hat against the sun. "I felt the same way," he conceded. "'Tis only that I'm in fear for Rose and wanting to find her as quickly as we can."

Nodding, Jeb squinted into the distance. "I know that, son." After a moment's silence, he cleared his throat. "There's somethin' you'd best keep in mind. The Choctaws aren't gonna be anxious to tell us where Jack's taken your sister. He's one of them; we're not."

"But he kidnapped her. Surely they won't wish to protect him."

"Taking women captives isn't looked at as a crime by a lot of tribes, even now, even among some of the *civilized* ones."

It took Tye a moment to realize what Jeb was trying to tell him. Feeling a heavy weight settle in the middle of his chest, he said, "You're saying we may never find Rosie."

Jeb sighed heavily. "With luck, we might run into somebody who's willing to talk. If not, our chances aren't too good."

* * *

That night, Rose sat wrapped in Jack's coat and her blanket, with her arms locked around her knees as she stared into the campfire. Also watching the flames dance, Jack reclined nearby, back propped against his saddle. Tsoia had ridden on ahead with word for Jack's mother that he was on his way.

Oddly enough, Rose wasn't afraid to be alone with her kidnapper. He'd kept his word, making no further advances since that one disturbing kiss. He was nothing like the evil creature who haunted her dreams. Besides, Jack needed her to help his mother. For that reason, if no other, she realized he wouldn't harm her.

Feeling lonely, she thought of her own mother, recalling a day from her childhood when Mam had held her and kissed away her tears after neighborhood children had taunted her, calling her a freak. She'd brought it on herself, of course, trying to impress them by healing one boy's scraped knee. What a little fool she'd been! Hadn't Mam warned her many times that other people wouldn't understand her strange ability? It was a gift from God, only to be used when someone was seriously ill or injured. After that day, she'd never again ignored her mother's warning.

However, even when she used her gift out of true necessity, there was always a price to pay. She wondered what that price would be this time. How would Jack's mother and their people react when she laid her hands upon the woman and healed her? *If* she was able to, that is.

"I had a brother and a sister," Jack said suddenly, startling Rose out of her reflections. "My sister was twelve when she died, my brother ten."

"So young," she murmured, wondering why he chose to tell her now, when he'd refused to do so earlier.

He nodded, frowning grimly. "Too young to die."

"How old were you then?" she asked, testing his readiness to talk.

"Fifteen. I was off fighting in the war. Hadn't been home in two years."

"D'ye mean to say ye were only thirteen when ye joined the army?" Rose couldn't believe a thirteen-year-old had been expected to bear arms.

"I was."

"But ye were only a boy."

"Yeah, but I was big for my age, and stubborn. Pa gave up trying to make me stay home after the third time I caught up with him."

Seeing him smile at the memory, Rose envied him the obvious love he'd felt for his father, and visa versa. "I never knew Indians took part in the war," she said.

Jack shrugged. "It was mostly the Five Civilized Tribes. The Choctaw and Chickasaw Nations lie in the southeastern part of Indian Territory, near Texas, so most sided with the Confederacy. The Cherokees, Creeks and Seminoles split, some fighting for the North, some for the South. Pa and me joined Cooper's Choctaw-Chickasaw Mounted Rifles. Every man had to supply his own pony and gun. We didn't have uniforms and most of us wore our hair long. Some even painted their faces for war."

Sitting up, he glanced at her as if expecting her to make some disparaging remark. When she calmly returned his gaze, he tugged his blanket more firmly around himself and continued, "We did some hard fighting here in the Territory. Then, in the summer of '62, Colonel Cooper led us into Arkansas along with Colonel Stand Watie's Confederate Cherokees and some Texas cavalry. General Hindman needed our help over at Fort Smith. From there we moved into Missouri and hooked up with Jo Shelby's Rebs near the town of Newtonia. Those boys were fighters. Got to be called Shelby's Iron

Brigade later on."

Jack paused in thought, and Rose studied him, admiring his chiseled copper profile. After a moment, he said, "The Union troops were gathering north of Newtonia, and early in the morning on September 30th one bunch attacked us. Guess they didn't know how outnumbered they were. Still, they gave us a good battle for a while, until Tandy Walker, one of our Choctaw chiefs, led us and the Chickasaws on a charge straight through town. Those Yankees didn't much like our war cries. They scattered like flushed prairie hens." He grinned, but his humor quickly faded.

"Four days later, Federals drove us from the town. Pa was killed in our retreat."

"Oh no," Rose uttered softly, filled with sympathy for the young Jack.

He ignored her, never taking his gaze off the fire. "I didn't want to leave him, but Toby made me. Toby Crawford, I mean, Lil's brother. He dragged me off and we made our way across the border into Indian Territory with the others, went into camp at old Fort Wayne. Toby was a few years older than me and he kind of took me under his wing after Pa died. We served together for another year, until he was killed."

"Aye, Lil told me ye were with him when he died."

"Mmm. And not long after that, my mother found me."

Rose stared at him blankly. "Your mother?"

"Yeah. It took her weeks to locate my unit." Stretching forward, he poked a stick at the fire, causing orange sparks to shoot upward, brilliant against the blue-black sky. "She came to tell me border raiders had struck our plantation. They looted and burned the house, even torched the cotton crop – after they raped my sister and murdered her and my brother."

"Sweet Mother of God!" Horrified, Rose pressed a hand to her lips, holding back grief for those poor children and her own remembered terror.

"Khaw had gone to a neighbor's to help birth a baby, or she'd be dead too."

"W-was it she . . . who found them?"

Jack pulled off his hat and smoothed the feather over and over. "Yeah. She buried her children and mourned in the Kiowa way. Then she went looking for me."

Rose moved her lips, but no sound came out. Before she could find words that wouldn't sound trite, Jack replaced his hat, leaned back on his saddle and turned to her.

"That's enough about me and my family. Why don't you tell me more about yours?"

Caught off guard by his request, she tensed. "There's little to tell."

"You said your mother died. I reckon you miss her. Tell me about her."

She met his dark eyes warily, wondering if he'd sensed her loneliness a while ago. Was that why he'd begun to speak about himself, to distract her from her glum thoughts? Or was he merely trying to make amends for his earlier harshness? Either way, she decided there was no harm in telling him about her mother, at least to a point.

"Mam was kind and beautiful. She had a sweet, soft voice and hands as gentle as an angel's, it seemed to me. She's been gone over seven years now, but I do miss her still. Very much." Hearing her voice quiver, she pressed her lips together.

"How'd she die?" Jack asked quietly.

"'Twas typhoid," she said once she could speak. "An epidemic swept through our part of the city. She caught it, and I tried to save her but I-I couldn't." Rose broke off, afraid to say another word. Tears welled in her eyes. Swallowing hard, she dabbed at them with a corner of her blanket. She'd barely regained her composure when an eerie, barking howl rang out.

She sat up straight. "That wolf sounds close," she said fearfully, straining to see into the darkness.

"No wolf, just a coyote yipping at the moon," Jack replied casually, rising to add more fuel to the fire. "He won't bother us."

"Oh." Reassured by his lack of concern, she relaxed, until he spoiled it.

"Not that some red wolves, maybe even a big lobo or two aren't out there somewhere," he said, returning to his resting place. "A lot of wild critters are gone, wiped out by hunters, but not all of 'em. And night's when they go hunting for a meal."

Rose shivered, wishing he hadn't said that. She wanted to be brave, but it wasn't easy. Scanning the darkness again, she prayed the critters he'd spoken of weren't out there watching them, eager to make a meal of *them*.

"Don't worry, I'll keep you safe," Jack said, drawing her gaze back to him.

Not knowing what to say, she nervously licked her lips. Instantly, his gaze dropped to her mouth, and her pulse kicked up. His eyes lifted to meet hers and something flared in their depths. He made a jerky movement as if he was about to reach for her. She stiffened, fearing he would try to kiss her again – and half wanting him to. He didn't do it. Instead, a curtain seemed to descend over his face, and Rose experienced a foolish rush of disappointment as he settled in his blanket.

"Get some sleep," he said tersely.

"Aye." She lay back, turned onto her side away from him and tried to relax, difficult to do since she could swear she felt him watching her.

The next morning, Rose wondered if she'd imagined that charged moment between them. Jack acted as if nothing had occurred, which it really hadn't. Yet, every time she glanced at him, his dark good looks and manly physique caused an odd quickening within her. When she happened to meet his gaze, her breath caught and her heart raced.

Why did he affect her so? Was it because he was so very different from *him*, the slavering beast she hated? She hadn't wanted any man ever to touch her after what he'd done to her. *And I still don't*, she sternly told herself.

* * *

As they rode on, Jack was preoccupied with troubled thoughts of his captive. Although he pretended to feel nothing, his desire for her ate away at him. She'd felt it last night the same as him, he knew, and he'd come mighty close to acting upon it. Thank God he hadn't. She likely would have panicked if he'd broken his word not to touch her again, and she might have tried to escape. That was still a possibility.

Riding into Fort Sill later that morning, he studied Rose, wondering if she would scream for help from the bluecoats. At the moment, she was gaping at the stone buildings surrounding the parade ground and the hills beyond. She seemed not to notice the stares they drew from the soldiers and civilians they passed. None made a move to stop them, but their sour glares told Jack they weren't happy to see a white woman riding beside him. He'd expected as much.

"This is your chance to escape," he said, deciding he might as well find out where she stood. "All you need to do is say I forced you to come here, and they'll throw me in the guardhouse. You'll be free."

She turned her head and stared at him with wide blue eyes. "But your mother needs my help. I can't turn away, and I . . . I've no wish to see ye behind bars."

Her words lifted a weight from Jack's mind. "I'm glad to hear that," he said, leading her toward the commander's headquarters. Dismounting out front, he pulled off his blanket and tossed it over his saddle.

She did the same with his jacket, then smoothed her riding skirt and tucked a stray blonde lock behind her ear. "I'm ready," she said, smiling.

"Don't expect a real warm welcome inside."

Her smile fell. "All right."

With that, he escorted her up the steps and into the building, being careful not to touch her. It wouldn't help his cause if Mackenzie and his aid got the wrong idea about them. As it was, the aid looked up from his desk and scowled when they walked in. It was a moment before the thickset officer remembered his manners enough to stand and greet Rose.

"Ma'am, can I be of help?" he asked, ignoring Jack.

"Aye, we need to speak with . . . with . . . ." She darted a glance at Jack, blue eyes pleading for help.

"Colonel Mackenzie," he finished for her.

The aid was forced to look at him. "Is that right? And who might you . . .?" Pausing, the man narrowed his eyes. "You're Lafarge, the breed who blacksmiths here on the post every winter, aren't you?"

Catching Rose's surprised glance, Jack realized she'd never before heard his last name. "That's me," he replied laconically.

"Thought you'd already left for wherever you go come spring," the bluecoat said.

"I did. Now I'm back."

"Yeah? What for?"

"Like the lady said, we have business with Colonel Mackenzie."

"What kind of business?"

"It's personal, between us and him."

The man's beefy face turned an angry red. "Listen, if you're not going to tell me what this is all about, I'm not –"

"Please, sir!" Rose interrupted, stepping forward. "We truly need to speak with your colonel. 'Tis a matter of life and death."

The officer stared at her uncertainly. Then his expression softened. "All right, ma'am, for *your* sake, I'll let him know you're here." Shooting Jack a hostile glare, he turned and rapped on the door to Mackenzie's office. Opening it, he stuck his head in and said, "Colonel, there's a young woman who needs to see you. She says it's urgent. That breed, Lafarge, is with her."

Jack caught Mackenzie's curt order to show them in. A moment later, they stood facing him as he stepped out from behind his desk. Slim and middling tall, the youngish looking man was far from imposing, but Jack knew him to be a ruthless Indian fighter. He'd defeated the Comanche, Kiowa and Southern Cheyenne in what whites called the Battle of Palo Duro Canyon, burning lodges and winter food supplies and ordering more than a thousand Indian ponies shot. Left afoot and starving, the tribes had been forced onto reservations.

The commander nodded at Jack and gave Rose a smile. "Col. Ranald Mackenzie, ma'am. May I ask your name?"

"Aye. 'Tis Rose, Rose Devlin, sir," she said, fingering the cross at her throat, a habit Jack had noticed before, whenever she was nervous.

"I'm pleased to meet you, Miss Devlin. I understand you need my assistance."

"Aye, sir, we must go to Jack's mother. She's very ill and perhaps I can help her, but I won't know until we get there, and –"

"Whoa, slow down," Mackenzie said, holding up his good hand, keeping the other with its two missing fingers – the reason Indians called him "Bad Hand" – behind his back. He aimed a piercing look at Jack. "What's this about your mother, Lafarge?"

"I got word a few days ago that she's near death."

"Sorry to hear that, but I suspect I'd rather not know how you found out." When Jack didn't respond – he wasn't about to admit Tsoia had jumped the reservation to bring him the bad news – Mackenzie turned to Rose again. "May I ask why you think you can save the woman, Miss Devlin?"

"I-I'm not a'tall sure I can, but I'm a healer, ye see. So when Jack, uh, Mr. Lafarge asked if I might help his mother, I . . . agreed to try."

Jack hid his amazement behind a blank stare. His captive had just told an outright lie for his sake. No, for his mother's sake, he corrected himself.

"You mean you're a physician?" the Colonel asked, sandy brows knitting.

"No, but I've knowledge of herbs and such. 'Tis a skill passed down through my family."

"Ah, I see." Mackenzie turned to Jack. "I take it you want my permission to escort Miss Devlin to your mother's lodge, is that right?"

Jack nodded once. "I figure a paper from you ought to prevent trouble."

"Mmm." Crossing his arms, Mackenzie paced slowly back and forth in front of his desk, thinking. After a moment, he stopped to face Rose. "Ma'am, are you sure you wish to do this? You could be putting your life at risk."

Briefly meeting Jack's gaze, she lifted her chin. "I'm sure, Colonel. Mr. Lafarge has protected me from danger several times. I trust him to keep me safe on the reservation as well."

She trusted him to protect her. Pleased as he was to know that, Jack knew she did not, in fact, trust him completely. Along with the flash of longing in her eyes last night, he'd read fear. What lay behind it, he didn't know, but he vowed to find out.

Accepting her decision, Mackenzie scrawled the authorization they requested and wished them good luck. Back outside a moment later, Jack stopped Rose with a tap on her shoulder. "I'm grateful for what you did in there."

She smiled shyly. "I merely bent the truth a bit. 'Twas necessary, aye?"

"Yeah." Clearing his throat, he said, "There's a hotel over past the parade ground." He pointed north to where the commander's quarters and the hotel stood. "It's not fancy, but if you want to stay the night and get some rest before we head for my mother's lodge . . . ?" He wanted to ride on immediately, but he owed his beautiful captive, who was no longer a captive, this much at least after what she'd just done for him.

"A real bed would be nice, and a bath," she said wistfully, gazing in the direction he pointed. Then she shook her head. "But from what ye said about your mother's illness, there's no time to lose. We'd best be going now, don't ye think?" She looked up, worry creasing her brow.

"Yeah, I do," he said, hoarse with gratitude. Wanting to kiss her, he settled for smiling into her blue agate eyes. Her strawberry-pink lips curved upward in reply, making his mouth go dry and testing his self-restraint. Desperate to put some distance between them, he gently nudged her toward their waiting horses.

They made a quick stop at the trader's store, where Jack purchased a woolen coat for Rose, though the days would soon be too warm for it. Then they headed out.

* * *

Riding away from Fort Sill, Rose gazed at the jumble of mountains extending northwest from the fort. "What are those mountains called?" she inquired, lagging a bit behind Jack.

"The Wichitas. Stick close now," he ordered, glancing at her over his shoulder. When she obediently caught up, he kneed his horse into a lope, and she followed suit.

She'd never seen mountains before and couldn't keep from staring at them. They weren't terribly high, surely not as tall as the majestic Rockies to the far west, which she'd seen pictured on postcards and travelers' Guides. Cloaked in shades of green and brown, these peaks reminded her of dignified old women basking in the sun. She giggled at the thought and wished she could explore them.

"Toppah!" Jack shouted, giving her a start.

"Aye?" Responding without thinking to the Indian name, she jerked her gaze away from the rocky heights. To her surprise, Jack had stopped and turned his horse to face her, a short distance ahead.

There was no sign of the gentle smile he'd given her back at the fort. With a fist planted on his thigh, he scowled fiercely. "I said stick close, didn't I?"

She kneed Brownie, hurriedly closing the gap between them. "Aye, and I'm sorry. 'Tis simply that –"

"You're not out for a pleasure ride, woman. This is rough country."

Pulling abreast of him, she watched him warily, half expecting him to cuff her for being so thoughtless. "I know, but –"

"And I'm not talking just hills and gullies. I mean bears and panthers that sometimes come down out of those mountains. I mean the wolves I already warned you about, and poisonous snakes that can kill you with one bite. Cross paths with any of 'em, and that stallion's liable to shy and dump you on your backside if you don't stay alert. You want that to happen?"

His mention of snakes made her quake. "No," she muttered, eyes downcast.

After a brief silence, he added more calmly, "There's something else you'd best keep in mind. We're on the Comanche-Kiowa-Apache Reservation. You don't want to be trailing behind if we meet some braves who've had too much firewater. From now on, keep up. All right?"

Feeling like a fool, she nodded meekly.

"Good." Jack pivoted his gelding and once more kneed the animal into a smooth lope, with Rose right beside him, determined not to give him a reason to chastise her again.

CHAPTER SEVEN

Skirting the foothills of the Wichitas some while later, they topped a windswept rise and Jack hauled back on his reins. Approaching from the north, a cavalry patrol was no more than two hundred yards away. He saw no way to avoid them.

"Damn!" he muttered. This was what he'd dreaded. He pointed to the advancing column as Rose drew up alongside him. "I hope your hide's tougher than it looks."

She stared at the troopers, saying innocently, "We have Colonel Mackenzie's letter. They must abide by his order, nay?"

"Yeah, but they're still not gonna like you riding with me."

"But they've nothing to say in the matter."

Jack shook his head, not knowing whether to laugh or curse. The woman didn't know what she was in for, but she would soon find out. The bluecoats were almost upon them.

He recognized the young lieutenant leading the patrol. His name was Proctor. Not long out of West Point, he enjoyed pushing around the reservation Indians he'd been sent out here to guard. He'd just as soon see them dead, Jack figured, but then, most whites felt the same way.

The gawky shavetail raised his arm, signaling a halt. His gaze traveled from Rose to Jack and back again. "Good afternoon, ma'am," he said, touching his hat to her briefly. His tone was on the cool side.

"Good afternoon," she replied, sounding uncertain.

Proctor eyed Jack arrogantly. "I heard you rode out, Lafarge. So what are you doing here now, with a white woman?" He aimed a sharp glance at Rose.

Jack held his temper, barely. "I'm taking the lady to my

Dearest Irish

mother's lodge. We have permission from Mackenzie."

"Indeed?" Proctor's one word carried a load of contempt. "Do you have proof of that?"

Withdrawing the Colonel's note from his pocket, Jack held it out to the scornful upstart, who reluctantly accepted it. He read its contents, frowned and looked at Rose. "Lieutenant Abel Proctor at your service, ma'am. Might I ask what prompts you to –?"

"Hey, Yellow Jack, how come you not dead yet?" a voice rumbled in broken English.

Jack stiffened, recognizing that voice and the slur on his name. As the lead troopers turned in their saddles, he followed their gazes and spotted the speaker three rows back in their ranks. His weathered copper face twisted in a mocking grin, but Jack noted with satisfaction that his hands were bound to his saddle horn.

"Guess I'm just smarter than you, Nahotabi," he retorted. "Leastways I'm not headed for the hoosegow."

The backwoods Choctaw snorted. "I plenty smart. Sneak whiskey in from Kansas, sell to Comanche, make money 'til get caught. White partners put up fight, get killed. They dumb." He leered at Rose. "You tell pretty white gal about war, Jack? I bet no. She no like you then. Maybe I tell."

"What I tell her is my business," Jack snarled. "Take your dirty eyes off her!"

"Enough!" Lieutenant Proctor barked. "Keep that whiskey runner quiet back there. As for you, Lafarge, I want to know why you're escorting a white woman to your mother's lodge, as you say."

"That's my business, too, Proctor," Jack bit out, knowing he was asking for trouble. He couldn't help it.

The officer's pale eyes glittered maliciously. "We'll see about that, breed." He turned to his sergeant, a veteran with deep frown lines around his mouth, probably caused by fools like Proctor. "Sergeant, take this man into –"

"No! Please don't do this," Rose cried. "Ye needn't be concerned, Lieutenant. I'm a . . . a doctor, and Mr. Lafarge's mother is very ill. He's asked me to see if I might help her."

Proctor peered at her suspiciously. "You're a doctor? I've heard of a few women docs back east, but not out here. Where'd you come from?"

"I-I recently moved from Chicago to Texas. I've relatives

there."

"Is that right? And how did you come to hook up this uppity half-breed?"

Clenching his jaw to contain a furious curse, Jack heard Rose draw a sharp breath.

"*Mr. Lafarge* works for my brother," she snapped, "and I wish ye wouldn't speak of him that way. I'm sure he doesn't like it."

Jack stared at her in astonishment. Several troopers choked back laughter and the sergeant coughed. Proctor flushed bright as Red River clay. His voice quivered with outrage. "I suggest you worry less about what he likes and more about yourself. It's a mistake to trust an Indian."

"Sir, I thank ye for your advice, but I believe I can trust him." Rose smiled at Jack, giving him pleasure, but making him uneasy when the troopers' laughter turned into scowls.

"Madam, you're obviously new to the frontier," Proctor said sharply. "Thus, your error in judgment is excusable. But I tell you you're putting yourself in jeopardy by traveling with this man. Moreover, it's improper. White women – decent ones – do not keep company with Indian bucks."

Rose gasped. This was what Jack had warned her about. She'd ignored the hard looks they'd drawn at Fort Sill, but Proctor's insult was impossible to ignore. Out of the corner of her eye, she saw Jack tense and feared he might lunge at the insufferable lieutenant. Knowing she had to stop him, she drew herself up and unleashed her long-buried temper on Proctor.

"Sir, I don't care what ye consider proper or improper. I shall *keep company* with whomever I please. And I much prefer Mr. Lafarge's company to yours."

Disapproving mutters sounded from the column of soldiers. They obviously concurred with their leader's opinion. Glad she couldn't hear their remarks clearly, Rose watched Proctor's thin mouth curl in anger.

"So be it, madam. I leave you to your fate." He flung Colonel Mackenzie's letter at Jack, gave Rose a loathing look, and chopped the air with his arm. "Move on!"

Rose met the same scathing look from his men as they rode past. Their prisoner eyed her and laughed. "Jack no man for you, pretty gal," he called. "He old woman. You ask about war."

Dearest Irish

Hearing Jack growl a curse, she pivoted her horse to face him. "What is he talking about? What happened in the war to be causing such ill will between ye?"

He remained silent, watching the patrol ride away. Finally, he said, "We were in the same outfit during the war. He thinks I'm a coward for deserting."

Rose stared at him, open-mouthed with shock. "Y-ye deserted? But why?" She couldn't picture him running away from anything.

"Because I refused to fight for those who destroyed everything I cared about." Jerking his hat lower, he sent his horse into a trot.

"D'ye mean the raid on your family's place?" Rose called, hurrying to catch up.

"Yeah." Gazing ahead at the dry, rolling landscape, he said, "The plantation was in Texas, east of here and a little south of the Red River. Pa named it Belle Rouge. That's French for beautiful red. We grew mostly cotton, but it wasn't a real big spread, and we didn't own any slaves. Pa didn't hold with that. When he needed help, he hired men from up in the Nations." Jack paused to glance at Rose.

"The night of the raid, my mother was on her way home from a neighbors' place when she spotted the glow from the fire. Like I told you, she found my brother and sister. She saw what the bastards had done to her children, all because they were Indians."

Hearing the hatred in his voice, Rose fully understood it. She moaned in pity for his poor mother and watched his hand clench against his thigh, the knuckles standing out white as he continued the grim tale.

"But they weren't the only ones killed. It was cotton pickin' time, and Ma had three hired hands, Choctaws, staying on the place. The raiders shot and killed two and wounded the third man. He played dead and watched . . . and listened. Afterward, he told Ma how the raiders bragged about taking what oughta be theirs from the stinkin' Injuns, and how some of 'em wore gray uniforms. They were Confederate renegades who decided Indians oughtn't to live better than whites. It didn't matter that my folks worked and scraped to build a home from nothing, or that we were loyal to the South."

Jack went silent, and Rose didn't push him to say more, knowing full well how past horrors could hold one in their grip.

After several moments, he went on.

"When Ma found me and told me about the raid, I wanted to kill all white men, North and South. The Confederacy made all kinds of promises to win over Choctaws and the other tribes, but they'd already broken most of 'em, and now southerners had destroyed my family. They were no better than the bluecoats. I could not go on fighting for such as those!"

Jack pounded his thigh and Rose flinched at the savagery of his tone. His gelding whinnied and pranced skittishly.

Gentling his voice, he calmed the animal then tersely finished his account. "Nahotabi and others called me coward for walking away. They accused me of bringing shame to my father's name, but I knew he would not want me to fight for his children's murderers."

Rose swallowed hard, searching for words. Hesitantly, she said, "I realize sympathy doesn't help much, but --"

"No, it doesn't." Jack's dark gaze stabbed her. "It won't bring back my family or undo any of the wrongs done to my people by whites."

"I know," she whispered, flinching at his bitterness.

"You know nothing of the red man's suffering, white girl," he said, spurring his mount ahead, leaving her sick at heart as she hurried to catch up.

A few minutes later, he said gruffly, "I'm sorry. I had no call to lay into you. What happened to my family is not your fault."

"Apology accepted," she replied quietly, spirits lifting a bit. Still, they both remained wrapped in their private pain, barely speaking until they neared their destination.

By then they'd left the mountains behind and the sun hung low in the west, bathing the scene in the golden glow of late afternoon. Rose was surprised to see barely a half dozen tipis situated beside a meandering, tree-lined creek. A short way off, a large, rounded hill jutted from the surrounding plains. "I thought 'twould be bigger. The village, I mean."

"The Army frowns on large camps. They're afraid the warriors, what's left of 'em, might plot trouble." Jack pointed into the distance. "You can't see 'em from here, but there are more camps farther along Rainy Mountain Creek." He crooked his thumb toward the lone hill. "That's Rainy Mountain. For the Kiowa, it's kind of a signpost or a guardian, you might say."

Dearest Irish

Rose thought the mountain and the peaceful setting quite lovely. Viewed up close, though, the village lost much of its charm. The hide tipis were patched and shabby looking, their painted designs faded. Several women, wearing a variety of animal skin and cloth costumes, worked at campfires, evidently preparing supper, while the men sat cross-legged outside their shelters, talking or simply staring at nothing. A few small children, both boys and girls, ran back and forth, kicking around a beat up cloth ball. Two older boys stood watching the game, while here and there an adolescent girl worked beside the women. All of them, except the youngest, had a dispirited air about them, Rose noted.

As she and Jack rode in, several mangy, underfed dogs set up a racket, barking and circling their horses. Everyone in the camp turned to stare. Jack raised his hand in greeting, drawing stilted nods from some of the men. One of the little boys who'd been playing ball shrieked, "Jack!" and came running as they dismounted. The child hurled himself at Jack's legs, shrilling something in Kiowa.

"Whoa there," Jack said. Chuckling, he scooped up the boy and returned his fervent hug. He rattled off what sounded like a question, and the boy gave a high-pitched reply, pointing toward the creek. Turning to Rose, Jack explained, "This is Tsoia's son, Tsahlee. He says his pa is hunting for supper."

Rose smiled brightly at the little boy. "Hello." She didn't try to pronounce his name, fearing she'd mangle it. He gave her a shy grin, revealing two missing baby teeth, and hid his face against Jack's shoulder.

By now, the adults had gathered around. They began speaking and gesturing at Rose, no doubt asking who she was and what she was doing here, making her uncomfortable and causing her to clutch her cross. Jack answered casually at first but grew visibly irritated, wanting to go to his mother, Rose assumed. He scowled when one young woman pushed forward, gazing at him hungrily and tugging at his sleeve. She was lovely, with flawless copper features and coal black hair plaited into glossy braids. Surprisingly, she spoke in broken, heavily accented English.

"You come back, White Eagle. For Star-girl, yes?" Batting her eyelashes coyly, she pressed up against his side, ignoring the child he held.

He nudged her away. "No. I come for my mother. No other."

The girl's flirtatious smile dropped into an angry pout. She opened her mouth as if to protest, but Jack gave her no chance. Grasping Rose's arm, he ordered, "Come with me." Still holding Tsoia's young son in his other arm, he hurried her toward one of the tipis. It was set off a short distance from the others, as if to give the occupant more privacy.

"That girl, she called ye White Eagle. Is that your Kiowa name?" Rose asked.

"Yes. She thinks to impress me with her English."

"And did she? Impress you?"

"No," he said curtly.

Before they reached the isolated tipi, a woman pushed aside the hide flap covering the low entrance and ducked out. Seeing them, she smiled. She was a few years older than the lovely Star-girl, and her complexion was a shade or two lighter. Her black hair hung in soft waves about her shoulders instead of in braids, and she wore a patterned skirt and a long red blouse cinched in at her waist. She wasn't as pretty as Star-girl, but her face lit up when she smiled.

"Ah, *bueno,* I am happy you are here, *Señor* Jack," she said, revealing her Mexican origins. "Your *madre,* she has been asking for you." She eyed Rose curiously as they walked up to her.

"*Buenos días,* Juana," Jack replied. "I came as fast as I could. Tsoia told her I was on my way?"

"*Sí,* and she is anxious to see you." Reaching out for the child hanging onto Jack's neck, she said, "Come here, *mijo.*" As the boy went into her arms, she turned her attention to Rose. "I am Juana, wife of Tsoia. You are the medicine woman my husband spoke of, *Señorita?*"

Rose nodded. "Aye, my name is Rose. I'm a healer."

"That is good, Rose. Ghost Woman needs you."

"Ghost Woman?"

"My mother," Jack explained. "Our people gave her that name when she returned to the tribe. They'd believed her dead for many years."

"Oh, I . . . I see." Rose wanted to ask how his mother had come to leave the tribe in the first place and how she'd met his father, but Jack was impatient, and rightly so.

"How is she?" he asked Juana, slanting his head toward his mother's tipi.

Juana shook her head sadly. "Not good. Go to her and you will see."

Without another word, Jack led Rose to the tipi entrance and held the flap aside, allowing her to enter ahead of him. The dim interior smelled faintly of smoke from a small fire pit in the middle of the circular space. Pausing near the entrance, Rose hung back as Jack walked to the bed of piled furs where his mother lay. Even from a distance, it was easy to see how thin and frail the gray-haired woman was, causing Rose to seriously doubt she could save her.

Jack knelt on one knee and gently clasped his mother's hand. " Khaw?" he said quietly. "Can you hear me?

The old lady's eyes opened and she gave a strangled cry. "You are here," she said in a dry, cracked voice. Lifting a boney, trembling hand, she cupped her son's cheek.

"Yeah, I'm sorry I didn't come sooner," he replied thickly.

Ghost Woman pressed her fingers to his lips. "No. You came. That is enough." She switched to Kiowa, and the two of them spoke in emotional tones.

Not wishing to intrude, Rose averted her eyes and glanced around the dusky interior. She saw cooking pots, gourds of various size, odd looking utensils and objects she couldn't put a name to. More furs were piled on the opposite side of the tipi from Ghost Woman's bed, suggesting someone stayed with the sick woman at night. Could it be Juana, Tsoia's wife?

Still wearing the coat Jack had bought for her, Rose found the tipi too warm. She patted dew from her brow and upper lip with her sleeve then slipped off the heavy wool garment. Jack must have caught her movement because he looked her way and motioned her over to his mother's bedside. After a brief hesitation, she crossed the small space and knelt beside him. Ghost Woman stared at her warily with eyes as dark as her son's.

"Who is this you bring into my lodge?" she questioned. "Has she come to watch me die?"

"Haun-nay! No. This is Toppah. Rose. She has come to take away your pain."

Ghost Woman gave a disdainful snort. "Only *hêmà* can do that."

"No! Death won't take you. Rose will heal you. I have seen her power," Jack declared, causing Rose to nervously swallow and wish he wouldn't make such promises.

His mother lay silent for a moment, studying her through narrowed eyes. Then she trained her doubting gaze on her son. "What is this power you saw?"

Jack shot Rose a quick glance and said, "I watched her lay her hands on a horse's lame leg. The next day the leg was healed."

Frowning, Ghost Woman asked Rose, "You did this thing?"

"Aye, 'tis a-a gift I have, ma'am," she answered timidly, feeling as if she were facing her own private inquisition.

"Come closer," the woman ordered, voice stern despite being little more than a whisper.

Bending over until her face was only inches from the old lady's, Rose jerked when two papery hands grasped her head, their claw-like fingers digging into her scalp. Startled and a bit fearful, she tried to pull away.

"Be still," her inquisitor snapped. "Look at me and do not try to hide the truth. I will know if you do."

Hardly daring to breathe, Rose stared into the black, bottomless orbs that seemed to peer into her very soul. Wondering if the woman could read her thoughts, or perhaps absorb her feelings the way her brother Tye was able to do, she trembled at the thought of what the woman might discover. Her heart galloped in her chest; her mouth felt dry as ashes. Finally, after what seemed like forever, but may have been only seconds, Ghost Woman released her.

"You speak true, but I do not believe you can kill the thing that grows in me." She tapped her blanket-covered belly, rounded as if she were in the middle months of pregnancy. A grimace of pain swept across her wrinkled features, the first she had allowed Rose and Jack to see.

"Ye may be right," Rose conceded, sitting back on her haunches. "Until now, I've used my gift only to mend wounds, knit broken bones and cure illness. I've never tried to destroy something inside a person." She shrugged. "Whether 'tis possible, I can't say until I try. If nothing else, perhaps I can lessen the pain a wee bit."

"Let her try, Khaw," Jack pleaded, adding something more in Kiowa. He'd been so quiet that Rose had almost forgotten he was there beside her.

His mother smiled wearily. "As you wish, my son."

With a nod from Jack, Rose folded back the blanket to just

above his mother's hips. However, when she started to pull up the woman's baggy dress, made of some sort of animal skin, Ghost Woman stayed her hand.

"Jack, you must leave," she said.

Jack's black brows dipped into a vee over his nose, but he didn't argue. Giving Rose a forceful look that willed her to succeed, he pushed to his feet and stepped outside. The weight of his expectations settled heavily upon her. Managing a weak smile for her patient, she carefully worked her dress up out of the way. She inhaled sharply at the sight of the old woman's swollen, blue-veined belly.

"It is not a good thing to look upon," Ghost Woman said. "I did not want Jack to see me this way."

"I understand." Feeling panicky all of a sudden, Rose grasped her cross, wondering how to even begin.

"You fear doing this."

"I . . . I'm afraid I might do ye more harm than good."

"Mmm, but as you say, we will not know until you try."

Rose fought down her fear. "Very well, but first, there's a prayer I must say. 'Tis in the language of my ancestors."

At Ghost Woman's nod of assent, she bent her head and whispered the Gaelic prayer of healing her mother had taught her long ago. Then she rubbed her hands together briskly, gathering the fiery impulses that streamed outward from her mind. The fire burned through her, making her palms and fingertips smart. Ignoring the familiar discomfort, she said, "Twill likely hurt, I'm sorry to say."

"I am used to pain. Go ahead."

Rose took a deep breath, laid her hands gently upon the woman's mounded belly and, closing her eyes, searched out the size and shape of the invader that was eating Ghost Woman alive. She directed sizzling energy from her fingertips into the demon and felt it writhe and shrink away from her touch. Faintly aware of her patient's strangled groan, she gritted her teeth and struggled with all her might to dislodge the monster, but it clung tenaciously to its host.

She tried to gather more power, but it was no use; she was too tired. The waves of energy died back, leaving her spent. Letting her hands fall to her lap, she swayed on her knees. She might have toppled over if Ghost Woman hadn't clutched her arm, steadying her.

"This thing you do . . . it steals your strength," the old lady said, breathless from what she had endured.

"Aye, but I'll be better in a short while," Rose said, voice quaking. "Forgive me. I couldn't free ye from the demon."

The old lady squeezed her arm and released it. "No, but you did much. The pain is not so bad now."

"I'm glad of that." With trembling hands, Rose tugged the woman's dress back down and pulled up her blanket. "Perhaps we can try again tomorrow."

"We will see. Now send my son in to me."

"Aye." Rising on shaky legs, Rose crossed unsteadily to the exit.

"Toppah, I thank you," Ghost Woman said, halting her.

It flashed across Rose's mind to protest being called Toppah, but it was unimportant now. "You're welcome," she replied and hurried out. Emerging from near darkness into the late afternoon light, she blinked against the brightness and staggered straight into Jack. She gasped as his arms encircle her. Lifting her head, she met his searching gaze.

"You all right?" he asked.

"I'm fine. The light blinded me is all." For some reason, pride perhaps, she didn't want him to know how exhausted she was. Captured by his intense dark eyes and musky male scent, she grew aware of how his muscular arms held her pressed to the hard wall of his chest. Then it struck her that she was clinging to him. Alarmed, she stiffened her spine and pushed at his shoulders. "Let me go."

His nostrils flared and his mouth hardened. "Yes, ma'am. Whatever the white lady says." Releasing her, he backed off.

Trying to ignore his sarcasm, she wet her lips and blurted, "I wasn't able to heal your mother. I'm sorry."

"Did you really try?" he barked.

"What?" Rose stared at him, not believing he could ask such a thing. "Of course I did! I'd never let the poor woman suffer needlessly. I've told ye that before, have I not?"

"Yeah, but she's just a dirty redskin, after all."

"Oh! How dare ye imply that I'd not do my best for her just because she's an Indian? If I was that kind of person, d'ye think I would have stood up for ye before Colonel Mackenzie and that obnoxious Lieutenant Proctor?"

He blew out a ragged sigh. Yanking off his hat, allowing his long hair to fall forward, he bent his head and toyed with the eagle feather. "That's the second time today I've insulted you. Sorry," he muttered rather grudgingly.

Rose considered telling him what he could do with his apology, but she was far too exhausted. She also feared what he might do. Even so, she wasn't about to forgive him as she'd done earlier. "Your mother asked for ye," she said tersely.

Nodding, he met her unbending gaze. "Find Juana. She'll get you something to eat." With that, he stepped around her, bent and disappeared into the tipi.

Rose grumbled under her breath and glanced around, finding herself the subject of several pairs of curious eyes. One pair, belonging to Star-girl, glared at her furiously. Taken aback, she realized the girl must have seen Jack holding her for that brief moment, and she was enraged with jealousy. Could it be she and Jack were promised to each other? But if so, why hadn't he seemed glad to see her? Not that it mattered in the least, she told herself.

Juana walked up just then. "*Señorita*, I can see you are very tired. Come, I will get you some food. Then you must rest. I have prepared a bed for you."

"My thanks to ye, Juana. 'Twould be nice to lie down for a while." Glancing at the spot where Star-girl had stood, Rose found her gone. Relieved, she turned and followed Tsoia's wife.

CHAPTER EIGHT

Rose awoke long before dawn. Her pallet of furs was in Tsoia and Juana's lodge, near their son's small bed. She vaguely recalled Juana leading her in here early last evening and coaxing her to lie down. Everything after that was a blank. She didn't even remember any dreams. Too often, she came awake haunted by the specter of a man chasing her down dark, endless passageways. Not this time, thanks be to God!

Her thoughts turned to Ghost Woman. How was she? Had her pain lessened enough for her to sleep? Was Jack keeping watch over her? Had *he* slept at all? Not that she should care after the harsh words he'd cast at her, Rose told herself. Yet, she did care. Worry for him and his mother gnawed at her, preventing her from going back to sleep.

Quietly, she turned back her blanket and sat up. Embers glowed in the fire pit, giving off just enough light for her to see Tsoia, Juana and little Tsahle-ee bundled in their fur robes, asleep. Rising, she tiptoed from the tipi. Outside, the night was clear and cold. Shivering, she rubbed her arms, wishing for the warm coat Jack had gifted her with. She recalled leaving it in Ghost Woman's lodge and decided to fetch it, since she wanted to check on her elderly patient anyway. Guided by the dim light of a fading moon, she walked cautiously toward the isolated tipi.

She paused outside the entrance, suddenly thinking this a bad idea. If Jack was in there as she assumed, he'd probably snarl at her for intruding in the middle of the night. But she was here and she really needed to know how Ghost Woman was faring. Before she could talk herself out of it, she pushed aside the flap and entered. Her uncertainty abated when she saw Jack sitting cross-legged on the dirt floor beside his mother's bed. His coat, hat and gun lay forgotten nearby. Hunched over with hands slack in his lap and raven hair trailing from his bobbing head, he was obviously fighting sleep and losing the battle.

Rose's lingering resentment toward him faded away. How could she stay angry at a man who cared enough about his mother to sit up with her all night when he was plainly as tired as she had been last evening? Treading softly over to him, she glanced at Ghost Woman, seeing that she was asleep, and touched Jack's shoulder. He jerked and his head shot up. At the same instant, he whipped out the knife he carried in his boot, ready to strike. Gasping in fright, Rose stumbled backward.

"Dammit! I could have killed you," Jack whispered furiously. Lowering the knife, he slipped it back into his boot. "What are you doing here?"

Pressing a hand over her hammering heart, she said breathlessly, "I-I was worried." Unable to force more words out, she waved her hand toward the sleeping woman.

He glanced at his mother and sighed tiredly, pinching his eyes. "She's asleep. Don't wake her."

"Nay, nay, I only wished to know she's all right." Nervously fingering her cross, she added, "I . . . I'll sit with her if ye want to lie down for a bit."

He eyed her in silence for a moment then nodded. "I could use some sleep. Thanks."

Rose watched him rise and cross to the empty pallet, hardly making a sound. As he wrapped himself in a buffalo robe and lay on his side facing her, she retrieved her coat, slipped it on and took her place beside his mother. Glad to see Ghost Woman still slept, she glanced over at Jack and found him watching her. She caught her breath, unable to look away. His mouth twitched, almost smiling at her. Then he closed his eyes.

Freed from his compelling gaze, she released her breath. With his half-smile lingering in her mind's eye, she pulled her coat snug and settled at her post, waiting for dawn. In the still silence, her eyelids soon grew heavy and she caught herself dozing off again and again. Each time, she looked anxiously at her patient but saw no change. Giving up finally, she laid down on the dirt floor, thinking to rest for only a short while.

A groan woke her. She scrambled onto her knees to find Ghost Woman's eyes squeezed shut, her teeth clenched in a rictus of agony, and her hands clawing at her blanket covered belly.

"Oh, ma'am, I'm so sorry," Rose murmured, laying a hand on the woman's frail shoulder.

The old lady's eyes cracked open. "You knew . . . the pain . . . would return," she struggled to say.

"Aye, but I hoped 'twould leave ye in peace for a few days, at least."

"It is bad. More than . . . before. Can you . . . stop it?"

Rose hesitated, fearful of what the results might be. "I can try, but are ye sure ye want me to? I could make it worse still."

"Nothing worse . . . than this. Try again!" she cried, writhing in pain.

"Khaw?" Jack called out from his sleeping place. Almost instantly, he was kneeling beside Rose. "What happened?" he demanded accusingly, clutching his mother's hand with his much larger one.

"H-her pain is back, worse than before I laid hands on her, she says."

"What? How can that be?" He glowered at her. "Has this happened with others afterward, and you didn't tell me?"

"Nay, never, I swear!" She shook her head adamantly. Biting her lip, she added, "She wants me to try again."

"No!" he exploded. "I won't let you touch her. You might do more harm."

Agreeing with him, yet hurt by his cutting words, Rose started to rise, meaning to dash from the lodge. Ghost Woman grabbed her arm, stopping her.

"Stay," she gasped. Pinning Jack with her pain-filled gaze, she said weakly, "Toppah will do this thing. It is my body . . . not yours."

"But *Khaw* –"

"No more words. Go! You cannot . . . be here."

"Ma'am, I really don't think –" Rose began.

"No more!" Ghost Woman declared more forcefully. "Jack, go. Toppah, stay."

Rose cast a helpless glance at Jack. He scowled darkly but gave in to his mother. Rising, he stalked from the tipi. Once he was gone, his mother let out an agonized moan.

"Help me!" she begged piteously.

Choking up, Rose could only nod. She gently worked the old lady's blanket and dress out of the way and, positioning herself, chafed her hands together to bring forth the necessary heat. Laying them upon her patient's swollen belly, she murmured the traditional prayer, adding in Gaelic, "Please let this work, Lord."

Pulsations surged through her hands, into the flesh she touched. She aimed them at the stubborn growth buried beneath the surface. Like the first time, it writhed and shrank from her touch. Ghost Woman's cry of agony reached her but didn't break her concentration. Pressing down, she blasted the invader with her power and felt its tentacles loosen. That wasn't enough. Ruthlessly, she renewed her attack.

This time, the demon's deadly grip broke loose in part, drawing another shriek from Rose's patient. Knowing the thing wasn't dead yet, she tried to blast it again, but the lethal energy refused to come forth. Swamped by a terrible pounding in her head and a sudden, enveloping weakness, she sank onto her side in the dirt. How long she lay there, she didn't know.

When she at last gathered enough strength to sit up, Ghost Woman was sleeping peacefully. For now, she was free of pain, but it would return. Not so soon this time, Rose prayed, but she hadn't killed the monster. It would rebuild itself and launch a fresh attack.

* * *

When Jack heard his mother shriek the second time, he started to charge into the lodge and drag Rose away from her, but he stopped himself. *Khaw* had made clear that he was to stay out of this. Gritting his teeth, he backed off, determined to abide by her wishes. He just hoped Rose knew what she was doing. She had a gift for healing, there was no denying, but could she always control it? Had he been wrong to bring her here?

He paced back and forth, ignoring the curious glances he got from others as they began to emerge from their shelters in the light of dawn. Now and then, he paused to listen for any sound from his mother or Rose, but none came. Increasingly impatient, he was almost ready to ignore his mother's order and enter the lodge when

Rose emerged, stumbling and nearly falling. She straightened, swaying from side to side, her face bone-white.

Alarmed, Jack stepped close and slipped an arm around her. She leaned heavily against him, allowing him to feel the fine tremors that shook her. Tilting her head back, she lifted tear-wet eyes to his, shooting an arrow of fear into his gut.

"What's wrong? Is she . . . ?"

"I-I wounded it, the thing that eats at her," she whimpered, "but I couldn't kill it."

"But she's . . . all right?" He couldn't bring himself to ask if his mother was alive.

Rose nodded. "She's sleeping."

He breathed easier. "You must have stopped the pain."

"For now, but d'ye not understand? I wasn't able to k-kill the d-demon." Her voice cracked and she sobbed brokenly, burying her face against his chest.

"Easy. You did help her," Jack said softly, wrapping his arms around her quaking body. He was sorry for ever doubting her. Not knowing what else to say, he rested his chin atop her head, feeling things he didn't want to feel for this beautiful, tender-hearted white girl. His gaze wandered toward the main camp and caught Star-girl watching them. Stabbing at them with her eyes was a better description. Wishing the girl would forget her foolish notions about him, he turned Rose and led her toward the screen of trees that grew beside the creek, in search of a private place.

He spotted the downed tree he recalled from prior visits. Torn from the clay soil during a storm, it lay with roots exposed and branches half in the trickling stream that fed its neighbors. Urging Rose over to it, Jack seated them both on the upended trunk, keeping his arm around her. She'd managed to stop her flood of tears by now, but her face was red from weeping and she sniffled loudly. Not having anything else to offer, Jack unknotted his bandana and offered it to her.

"Here. It's not clean but it'll do the job."

She accepted the rag, using it to mop her face and blow her nose. "I'll wash it for ye later," she said hoarsely. "I need to wash my clothes, anyway. Not to mention myself." Making a disgusted face, she stuffed the bandana into a pocket of her travel-stained riding skirt.

Jack looked down at his own filthy duds. "Reckon I could do with a wash too."

"Aye, that ye could," she agreed with a critical glance and a twitch of her dainty, upturned nose.

"You want to help?" he teased straight-faced.

Her jaw dropped. *"Begorrah!* What d'ye take me for?" she cried, jumping to her feet.

He grinned, snatched her hand and gave it a shake. "I was only joshing. Don't run off. I want to know how it went with my mother."

She scowled at him for a moment then sat down, keeping several inches between them. "Ye shouldn't say such things," she chided.

"You're right." He smiled ruefully. "Sorry. Now, tell me why you're so sure you didn't cure Khaw."

Shoulders slumping, Rose turned troubled blue eyes toward him. "The thing inside her fought me hard. I summoned every bit of power I could and part of the vile demon let loose of her." She drew a breath and looked away, staring into the green woods. "But it still lives. I had no strength left to attack it again. 'Twill feed upon her and grow. I fear I can't save her, Jack." Her voice wavered. "I couldn't save my mother either, and my father blames me still."

He wondered why her father blamed her, but at the moment he was more interested in preventing more tears. Gripping her arms, he turned her toward him. "If you're thinking I'll blame you if . . . if Khaw doesn't make it, don't. I was a fool for not trusting you a while ago, and yesterday. I know you did everything you could."

"H-how d'ye know?"

He shrugged and scraped a hand through his hair, flicking it back out of the way. "I know because when you stepped from my mother's lodge just now, you were so white, I feared for you as much as for her."

"Ye did?" She stared at him, wide-eyed.

"Yeah. I thought I was gonna lose you. I'm glad to see you've got some color back." He stroked her cheek, needing to touch her. "Your skin is as soft and smooth as a rose petal," he whispered.

Her lips parted invitingly, drawing his gaze. Damning himself for giving in to his yearning, he bent close and kissed her gently. When she shyly responded, he stroked his tongue between her lips. She parted them more fully, allowing him in. With growing fervor, he probed her mouth, savoring the taste of her. He drew her close and wrapped her in his arms, delighted to feel her breasts press against his chest as her hands crept upward to hold him.

Eager to explore every inch of her, he kissed his way across her cheek, over her brow and delicate eyelids, and back down to her trembling lips. Lifting his head for a moment, he took in her enraptured expression and knew a burst of satisfaction because he had put it there. He wanted desperately to reclaim her mouth but burning for much more, he feared he wouldn't be able to stop with kisses.

Her eyes popped open. She returned his gaze for a few seconds. Then an appalled look swept over her face. "No! Let me go!" she shrilled, pounding his back with her small fists.

Caught completely off guard, Jack released her. "Have you gone loco?" he barked, scowling at her furiously as she shot up and stumbled backward.

"Ye mustn't do that again!" she cried. "I-I can't let ye. Not you or anyone else!" Wild-eyed, she looked as if she expected him to rape and scalp her.

Jack had wondered before if something had caused Rose to fear men. All men. Now he was certain of it. Rising, he approached her slowly. She turned, ready to run, but halted when he called out to her.

"Rose, don't run from me. I won't hurt you." He watched her head turn partly toward him, listening. "I never will, I swear," he added quietly, close behind her. As he spoke the vow, he knew it was true. He couldn't use her as he'd used other women, both white and red. She was too defenseless and, although he hated to admit it, he cared for her too much to hurt her.

"You don't need to be afraid of me," he murmured, laying his hands lightly on her shoulders. She trembled but didn't jerk away.

Slowly turning to face him, she locked eyes with him, searching for the truth. At last she said, "I believe ye, Jack, and *you* must believe me when I say I . . . I can't give ye what ye want. There are reasons I'll not speak of, reasons that prevent me from . . . ." She looked down, wringing her hands.

"From being with a man," he finished for her.

"Aye," she choked out.

Jack sighed. "All right, P'Ayn-Nah – Sugar – we'll leave it at that for now. But one day you'll tell me what keeps you from me."

She shook her head adamantly. "Nay, I said I'll not speak of it. And don't call me that. I'm not . . . ." She broke off when her stomach growled loudly. "Oh!" Slapping a hand over her middle, she turned bright red.

Jack laughed. "Sounds like you need to eat, Toppah."

She screwed her face into angry lines and planted her hands on her hips. "Don't be laughin' at me, ye blitherin' idjit! And don't be callin' me Toppah either. I may answer to it for your mam and Juana, but not for you."

Grinning, Jack winked at her. "How 'bout that. The meek white lady has a temper."

Her anger turned to surprise, followed by a shame-faced expression. Dropping her hands to her sides, she mumbled, "I'm sorry. I've a bit o' my da's Irish temper, I suppose."

"Nothin' wrong with that." He took hold of her elbow and turned her toward the village. "Come on, Irish, I smell coffee. Sure could use a cup."

"Coffee? I didn't think Indians drank coffee."

"They drink it when they can. Depends if there's some included in their rations. I think Juana was fixing tortillas, too. They're kind of like that frybread you liked so much, only she makes 'em with cornmeal."

Rose's tone brightened. "I've had tortillas before. Jessie and David's cook, Maria, fixes them. I'm rather fond of them."

Jack couldn't resist another grin. Maybe the way into the lady's good graces, and her secrets, was through her stomach.

* * *

Near the outskirts of the small village, Rose stood gazing at the Wichita Mountains. Rain had fallen during the night, diminishing to a fine mist this morning. It lent the distant peaks a ghostly appearance. How she'd love to explore them, she thought wistfully, stuffing her chilly hands into her coat pockets. But she'd need a guide for that, and Jack was unlikely to volunteer.

Over the past week, Ghost Woman had been able to eat and

keep her food down. She'd gained enough strength to be back on her feet. Rose was glad for her, although she knew this was only a temporary recovery. So did Jack. She felt certain he wouldn't wish to be away from his mother, and Rose could hardly fault him for that. Besides, she doubted he'd want to escort her anywhere after the way she'd rebuffed him that morning by the creek.

For at least the hundredth time, she revisited the scene between them. She'd been right to stop him, right not to let him carry matters too far. Her brain knew this, but her heart . . . her foolish heart yearned for him to kiss her and hold her close again. For those few moments in his arms she'd forgotten the past – until he stopped kissing her, allowing the torrent of ugly memories to flood back.

Jack wanted to know why she couldn't accept his attentions, but if she told him the truth about herself, she was certain he'd think her lower than the red dirt beneath his feet. Better to avoid his probing questions and anymore dangerous kisses, she'd decided. Thus, she'd done her best to keep busy and out of his way.

She'd rapidly become friends with Juana, who'd kindly lent her a long skirt and blouse to wear while she washed her own soiled garments. Whenever the two of them weren't caring for Ghost Woman, Rose had insisted on helping with food preparation, mending clothes, gathering wood, whatever needed doing. With her new friend acting as interpreter, she'd enjoyed getting to know the villagers, especially the women. They'd been wary of her at first but had gradually opened up, asking questions about her and her family and telling about themselves. All had lost loved ones in the Kiowas' long war against white settlers and the Army. Hearing them speak of their former nomadic life, it was clear they missed the old ways. Rose commiserated with them, but she'd heard enough horror stories about Indian raids from her Texas kin to be glad such depredations were at an end for the most part.

One person she felt no sympathy for was Star-girl. The little witch never missed a chance to express her hatred, sending Rose black looks, pinching her when no one was looking, and once deliberately tripping her, nearly causing her to fall into a campfire. Thank goodness one of the older women had witnessed the girl's cruel act and had castigated her, sending her off in a huff. Later, after learning about the incident, Star-girl's mother, whose name translated to Walks Softly, had come to Rose and through Juana, had apologized for her "foolish child."

Star-girl was indeed foolish. She ought to see from Rose's avoidance of Jack that there was nothing between them. There never would be.

As if she'd conjured him with her thoughts, Jack walked up to stand beside her, giving her a start. "Morning," he said.

"M-morning."

"I forgot to get you a hat at the fort. Your hair's getting wet." Removing his hat, he set it on her head, exposing his own long hair to the mist. He wore his fringed buckskin jacket for the first time in several days, the weather having warmed up until last night, when cooler temperatures had swept in along with the rain.

"Oh. I hadn't noticed," she said with a tentative smile. "I . . . I was just admiring the mountains. They look so hazy and mysterious."

He trained his gaze to the rounded peaks. After a moment, he said, "They speak to you, don't they."

"I hadn't thought of it that way but, aye, I suppose they do."

"You want to ride up there with me and take a look around?"

She gaped at him, not believing her ears. "You'd do that? Take me there?"

He shrugged. "*Khaw* is doing much better. If we're gone for a couple days, Juana and Tsoia can watch out for her."

Rose hesitated, recalling her reasons for not being alone with him. But she did want to see the mountains up close, very much so, and Jack had vowed never to hurt her. She'd said she believed him, and she did. Trusting her instincts, she made up her mind.

"When can we leave?" she asked, thrumming with excitement.

Jack flashed a grin, bright against his copper skin. "As soon as we pack some vittles and saddle up."

* * *

Riding out a short while later, Jack adjusted his gun belt, reassured by the familiar weight of his Colt 44. As usual, he'd stopped carrying the gun after their arrival in the village, knowing it bothered his mother and the others. They associated such weapons with soldiers and the hated Texas Rangers, *Los Diablos Tejanos* as the Mexicans called them. But he'd strapped his rig back on for this trip into the mountains, where outlaws of all races sometimes hid out.

He glanced over at Rose, noting the smile that played across her lips, and was glad he'd decided to indulge her curiosity about the Wichitas. By his reckoning, this was small payment for all he owed his lovely Toppah. He'd kidnapped her and dragged her across rough country, putting her in danger more than once. Yet she'd done her best to heal his mother, putting up with his contrary moods in the bargain. She deserved some reward.

The trouble was he knew he was really indulging himself. He'd allowed her to keep her distance for the past few days, but he wanted this chance to have her to himself again for a short while, although he'd have to hold his desire for her in check. That was going to be torture, but he refused to break his promise not to hurt her.

He set an easy pace, hoping to learn more about her as they rode. "You told me your mother died of typhoid," he said casually. "Did you lose anyone else to it? In your family, I mean."

"Nay, thanks be to God, though I easily might have."

"But your father blames you for your mother's death?"

Rose shot him a wary glance. "Aye, he does."

"You tried to save her, so why does he blame you?"

She frowned and looked away. After a moment's silence, she said, "When the epidemic broke out, I volunteered to help nurse the sick at a charity hospital, without telling my parents. That's where I caught typhoid."

Jack turned his head to stare at her. "You recovered, though."

"Aye, but Mam nursed me through it, ye see, and she soon came down with it herself. She'd been sickly that winter and still had a cough. The typhoid was too much for her. I tried to heal her, but I was still weak myself." Her voice grew hoarse. "I hadn't the strength to save her."

"So your father blamed you for catching the disease and giving it to her."

She nodded. "He's never forgiven me."

"Is that why you went off to the convent?"

"Aye, I had to get away from Da, from everything. And if I devoted my life to helping others, I thought perhaps God would forgive me for causing Mam's death."

"But you changed your mind and left the convent. After seven years. Why?"

Rose shifted in her saddle and clasped her little gold cross. Jack wondered if he'd pushed her too far, but after another long silence, she replied, "When the sisters took me in, I made up my mind never to use my gift again and never to tell any of them about it for fear they'd think me a witch. Mam had warned us, Jessie and Tye and me, not to reveal our powers to others unless we had no choice. She told us about gifted ones such as ourselves – Druids, we're called according to some musty book – who were beaten and driven from their villages back in Ireland. Some were even burned because they were thought to be in league with Satan."

Jack knew Rose's sister and brother were rumored to possess some kind of secret ability that allowed them to *see* things other people couldn't. She had just confirmed the fact.

She paused to sip from the water skin Jack had hung from her saddle. Closing it, she continued, "I abided by my decision until I was close to taking my final vows. Then, one day last August, a young novice fell down a flight of stairs. Her neck was broken. She couldn't move and could barely breathe. There was nothing to be done for her, Mother Superior said, but I thought perhaps I could save her. So I set aside my fears and laid hands on the poor girl, and it worked. Her injury healed and she rose from her bed like Lazarus rising from the dead. I was proud of myself, I can tell ye."

The memory brought a smile to Rose's lips, but it swiftly faded. "However, when the nuns discovered what I'd done, 'twas as I feared. They shunned me as though I'd suddenly grown horns and a tail." She sighed and shook her head. "But that wasn't the worst of it. Mother Superior informed me I was no longer welcome in the convent. She ordered me to leave at once."

"What did you do?" Jack asked, trying to imagine what it must have been like for a sheltered young woman to be suddenly thrust into the big, bad world.

She sent him a sidelong glance and nervously fingered her cross again. "Why, I went home, of course. I had no other choice."

"Your pa took you in?"

Avoiding his eyes, she admitted, "He wasn't best pleased about it, but I stayed with him for several weeks. Then Jessie's letter arrived, asking me to come to Texas and help Tye to see again." She shrugged. "That's all. There's nothing more to tell."

Jack didn't believe her. There was more to the story, something having to do with her fear of men perhaps? Sensing he wasn't going to get anymore out of her right now, he let the subject drop but promised himself he would learn the last of her secrets sooner or later.

They reached the foothills of the mountains by mid-afternoon. Shortly before dusk, Jack called a halt near the mouth of a tree-lined canyon.

"That's Timber Canyon," he told Rose as he helped her unsaddle Brownie. "It runs through the mountains. Buffalo herds used to pass that way on their way south to fresh pastures, with Kiowa hunters trailing them. Come morning, we'll head in there and do some exploring."

"That sounds grand. Can we have a fire tonight? And possibly some frybread? Juana showed me how to make it, ye know."

Jack chuckled. "I reckon we can have both. You can do the cooking."

* * *

Kneeling by the campfire a short while later with Jack beside her, making sure she got the proportions right, Rose combined flour, water and a pinch of salt in a small wooden bowl. She mixed the ingredients thoroughly then kneaded the dough until it was a smooth consistency.

"It's good with sugar, too, but I don't have any," Jack commented. "Some folks add saleratus to make it puff up."

"Saler . . . oh, ye mean baking soda."

"Yeah. Now let's see you fry some up."

Wishing he would stop watching her every move, Rose spooned a dollop of lard into the small skillet he'd produced from his saddlebags. Once the lard melted, she broke off a chunk of dough, flattened it between her palms and dropped it carefully into the hot, sizzling fat.

"Let it fry a couple minutes, then flip it over," Jack instructed.

"I know," she said testily, arching her brows and glaring at him.

He grinned and raised his hands in mock surrender. "Don't get mad, Irish. I was only trying to help."

Rose was unnerved by the firelight dancing in his eyes. "I-I'm sorry. I shouldn't have snapped at ye." She dropped her gaze to the open collar of his shirt and the patch of smooth copper skin showing there. The site further disturbed her. *He* disturbed her. Their heated embrace by Rainy Mountain Creek flashed across her mind and, despite her determination to the contrary, she yearned for it to happen again.

Fighting her treacherous senses, she quickly looked away, calling herself a fool.

"Rose?" he murmured after a moment's silence. When she hesitantly turned her head to meet his gaze, he framed her face with his hands. "You're not afraid of me again, are you?"

"N-no." She was afraid of herself, but she was too mesmerized by the warm glow in his eyes and the nearness of him to break away.

"Good." He gently tilted her head back, and she opened her mouth the slightest bit, knowing she was inviting his kiss. His head lowered slowly, making her heart race and her breath catch as she waited for the first touch of his lips.

A sizzling pop sounded and hot grease splattered from the skillet, just missing Rose's arm. A scorched smell reached her at the same time.

"The frybread!" she cried, scooting away from the fire and Jack. "'Tis burning."

"Ah hell!" he muttered. Yanking off his bandana, he wrapped it around his hand and snatched the smoking skillet from the campfire.

CHAPTER NINE

"Magnificent!" Rose cried over the howl of the wind. "'Tis as if we're standing atop the world." She stretched out her arms and laughed ecstatically.

Watching her hair stream out like bright feathers on the wind, Jack thought he'd never seen a more beautiful sight. They stood on the summit of Mount Scott – Big Mountain to his mother's people. The hike up here from down below, where they'd left the horses, had not been easy for Rose, but he didn't think she minded it now. Clamping his hat down to keep it from flying off, he enjoyed the look of pure joy on her face as she gazed at the scene laid out before them.

It was magnificent, he agreed, with smaller peaks stretching away into the blue-gray distance. He'd seen it many times before, but it still moved him.

"Oh, look! There's a deer down there." Rose pointed at the animal running along the base of the mountain. Her childlike excitement made Jack grin. She'd gotten just as excited around every bend, over every odd shaped pile of boulders along the mountain pass. And all the while, he'd wanted to take her in his arms and kiss her until she forgot everything but him. Like he wanted to do right now.

Ha! He wanted to do a lot more than kiss her. The afternoon had grown warm, and they'd removed their coats before hiking up here. Now, with the wind plastering Rose's shirt to her chest, Jack couldn't keep from staring at her high, firm breasts. Dammit! Maybe this trip was a mistake. The woman was driving him loco, just as he'd known she would.

Forcing his thoughts in a less dangerous direction, he said,

"Too bad you'll never get to see the buffalo thunder through down there the way they used to."

She turned to him, catching her hair back with one hand when the wind whipped it across her face. "Perhaps I'll return here one day and see them."

He shook his head. "They'll never come again. Used to be millions roaming the plains, but they're gone now, shot by white hunters, skinned and left to rot by hide men. You'd be lucky to see a few lonesome strays still alive."

Her mouth dropped open in shock, her russet brows dipping into a delicate vee. "But that's horrible! I'm not surprised ye hate all white people."

"I don't hate all whites," he said, gazing into her eyes. "I don't hate you."

Those blue agate eyes grew huge, and her lips formed an "Oh!" that flew away on the wind. In that one word, Jack heard surprise, doubt and maybe a trace of gladness. Or was he imagining it?

"Come on," he said, tearing his gaze away. "It's getting late and there's one more thing I want to show you before we head back."

"Very well," she replied, sounding regretful.

For a brief moment, Jack wondered if Rose had wanted him to show her he didn't hate her, but seeing her gaze one last time at the mountaintop view, he knew she was only sad to leave the summit. Deflated by the realization, he led the way down. She stayed close, accepting his hand at treacherous points along the path. Winded by the time they reached the bottom, they took time to drink from their canteens before Jack boosted her onto Brownie.

"Is it another mountain ye wish me to see?" she asked as he mounted up.

"Nope. It's a surprise. I think you'll like it." He winked, drawing an uncertain smile from her strawberry lips.

* * *

Rose hadn't long to wait for Jack's surprise. They left the rocky heights behind, riding onto a level plain covered by a variety of grasses swaying in the wind. This soon gave way to an open field that appeared to stretch for miles. The field was dotted with short cropped grass and sandy mounds from which tiny furred animals popped in and out, chattering and scampering about. Seeing one pair stand up on their hind legs and touch their mouths together as if kissing, Rose laughed in delight.

One nearby creature heard her and came to attention. Catching sight of her and Jack, the little fiend set up a racket, barking in a high-pitched voice, warning of intruders. Within moments dozens of others were standing on their mounds, watching intently for signs of danger.

"Welcome to Prairie Dog Town," Jack said with a chuckle.

"Oh my! They're adorable!"

"I figured you'd think so, but they're dangerous as all get out."

"Dangerous!" She stared at him in disbelief. "How can such small creatures possibly be dangerous?"

"It's their burrows," he replied, pointing toward the field. "Every one is a trap set to break a horse's or a steer's leg."

Gazing at the prairie dog town, she realized he was right and felt sick at the thought of such a terrible thing ever happening to Brownie.

"In a stampede," Jack continued, "if a horse steps in one of those holes and goes down, the rider doesn't stand a chance. Del Crawford lost his lead rider that way on last year's trail drive. He was a good man. I counted him as a friend."

"I'm sorry," Rose said, impulsively reaching out to touch his arm.

He looked down at her hand, moved his arm out from under her touch, and said hastily, "There's a creek not far from here. I need to refill our canteens before we start back."

She jerked her hand back, stung by his rejection of her touch.

"If you want you can wait here and watch 'em." He nodded toward the prairie dogs.

"Aye, I'll do that," she snapped, handing over her canteen without looking at him.

He hesitated a moment, perhaps wondering why she was suddenly testy. As if he didn't know! Then he said, "Don't try walking out there. You could break an ankle if you step wrong."

"I realize that." Again, she refused to glance at him.

Dearest Irish

"I won't be gone long."

She trained her eyes straight ahead until he headed his horse toward the creek. Then she glared holes in his broad back as he rode away. "Insufferable man!" she grumbled. "One moment you're making me think ye want me, then the next ye can't stand for me to touch ye. Idjit! And I'm tired of ye ordering me about as if I were a child."

Fuming in silence, she watched the prairie dogs' antics. Despite everything Jack had said, she still found the small animals endearing. Determined not to take his orders any longer, she dismounted and, leaving Brownie to graze, marched out among the prairie dogs, being careful where she put her feet. She wasn't stupid, after all. She knew better than to step in one of the burrows. Except, she couldn't always tell where they were because of the short grass disguising some of them.

That explained why she didn't see the burrow in front of her until she was practically on top of it. Thank heaven, a small brown head popped up just in time, causing her to stop short. Startled, she laughed softly, thinking him – she just knew it was a boy – like a furry jack-in-the-box.

"Hello there," she murmured. "Aren't ye the sweetest little fellow."

The animal stared at her with black button eyes, seeming as fascinated by her as she was by him. Curious to see what would happen, Rose moved a step closer. That's all it took to break the creature's trance. She expected him to dive underground and hide, but instead, he darted from his burrow, reared up and began barking frantically, putting himself at risk for the sake of his friends. Rose admired his bravery. Bending over, she held out her hand, offering him her scent as she would to a true dog.

"There now, I won't hurt ye, little one," she crooned. She was blithely unaware of approaching danger until a rattling noise made her turn her head toward the source. She screamed just as the snake struck.

* * *

Jack was on his way back when Rose's scream rent the air. It shot through him like an arrow to his gut. Shouting her name, he kicked his bay into a run. He found Brownie grazing peacefully where he'd left Rose. Glancing around, he spotted her huddled on the ground out among the prairie dogs. His heart pounded in his ears as he ran toward her, barely watching out for burrows.

"What happened?" he demanded, crouching beside her and slipping an arm around her. She shook from head to toe, clutching her right arm to her chest. When she raised her head, she looked pale as death.

"A snake! It bit me," she cried.

"Ah hell!" Icy fear ripped through him. "Did it have diamond shapes on its back? Did it rattle?"

She gave a jerky nod. "Aye."

Jack glanced around and saw the snake's zigzag trail, but the rattler itself was nowhere in sight. Knowing there wasn't a minute to waste, he drew his knife. "Give me your arm," he ordered.

She stared wide-eyed at the knife. "What d'ye think to do?"

"I'm gonna slit open your sleeve so I can see where the snake got you."

"But this is my only shirt," she protested.

"I'll buy you a new one." Not giving her a chance to argue, he gripped her wrist and drew her arm forward, noting the thin streaks of blood staining her sleeve. Carefully, he slipped the point of his knife under the cuff and sliced open the cotton material high enough to let him see two punctures about an inch below her elbow. Blood pearled from the small wounds. Judging by how far apart they were spaced, he guessed the snake was only a two-to-three-footer, but small ones could deliver plenty of venom.

"I told you not to come out here. Why didn't you listen to me?" Jack growled, furious with her and even more furious with himself for leaving her alone. Pulling off his bandana, he twisted it around itself several times.

"I-I was angry. 'Twas foolish of me, I know."

"Damn right it was." Wrapping the bandana around her arm above the elbow, he tied it tight, but not too tight, recalling a Chickasaw trooper he'd known during the war. The man had been shot in the leg. An overworked surgeon had applied a tourniquet to stop the bleeding until he had time to work on the Indian, many hours later. By then the injured leg had turned black. Jack could still hear the Chickasaw's screams as his leg was being amputated. That wasn't going to happen to Rose. Not if he could help it.

"Did you see where the snake went?" he asked unnecessarily, trying to distract her from what he was about to do.

"It slithered off that way," she said, turning her head and gesturing toward the trail he'd already spotted. While she was looking away, Jack made two swift cuts across the bite. Rose shrieked and tried to pull away, but he hung on to her arm.

"Hold still," he ordered, tossing his hat on the ground. "I've got to suck out the venom." With that, he bent, circled the bloody wound with his lips and sucked as hard as he could. Ignoring her gasp of pain, he spat and repeated the process. When he figured he'd drawn out as much venom as he could, he loosened his bandana and retied it directly over the wound.

"W-won't the poison sicken you?" she asked.

"No. It doesn't work like that. Come on. Let's get you back to the horses." Slapping his hat back on, he helped her up and carefully guided her out of the prairie dog colony. Once on safe ground, he had her sit on a small hillock near their mounts. She was still shaking despite the warmth of the day. Retrieving her coat from Brownie's saddle, he draped it around her shoulders, hoping it would stop her trembling.

"I want to find something to treat the bite. Stay right here. Understand?" he said sternly.

"Aye. I won't move."

"Good." Striding away, he headed back up their trail, toward where he'd seen the bush he was looking for. It didn't take long to find. Hurriedly, he gathered what he needed, turned and ran back to Rose. She sat hunched over where he'd left her with her injured arm cradled close and her cross clasped in her other hand. The arm was beginning to swell, Jack noticed when she straightened and looked up at his approach. He read fear in her blue eyes.

"How do you feel?" he asked, crouching beside her.

"My arm hurts."

"I expect it does. I'm gonna make a poultice and spread it over the bite. Then we'll start back."

"To the village?"

"Yeah. My mother's a medicine woman, remember? She'll take care of you." For a brief instant, he wondered if he'd do better taking her to Fort Sill for doctoring, but he dismissed the idea. He trusted his mother's medicine more than the Army sawbones.

"Oh. That's nice," she said distantly.

He frowned, realizing the venom was starting to affect her. "This is buffalo currant. It's good for snakebite," he explained, using his knife to quickly strip away the outer bark from the branches he'd gathered. They gave off a spicy scent. Next, he peeled off pieces of tender inner bark, wadded them into his mouth and began to chew. They tasted bitter as gall. He'd seen his mother boil the bark into a poultice but had never known her to chew it. Was it poisonous? He didn't know and didn't care. As he chewed, he untied the bandana from Rose's arm. Once the bark had softened into a pulp, he removed it from his mouth and spread it over the oozing wound.

Rose jumped. "Ayeee! That hurts worse," she complained.

"I know, but it'll help," he told her, securing his bandana in place over the poultice. His mother, like her people, believed snakes were afraid of the buffalo currant bush and that it was a cure for snakebite. He prayed to the Kiowa gods that it was true.

"Up you get," he said, helping Rose to her feet again. She leaned heavily upon him as he led her to his horse.

"Can't I ride Brownie?"

"No. You might get dizzy and fall off. It's best you ride with me."

She made a sound. It could have been a weak laugh or a smothered sob. "'Twill be like the night ye made off with me, won't it?"

"Mmm." He ground his teeth, not wanting to recall that night. If he hadn't stolen her from her bed, she'd be safe with her family instead of snakebit. But then his mother might be dead by now. Yet, she might still die, and what if Rose also died? No! He wouldn't let that happen. She must live.

Settling her in front of him on his gelding, he gathered up Brownie's reins and fastened them to his saddle. Then, holding Rose securely against him, he sent his horse into a gallop across the prairie, skirting the mountains. There wasn't time to pick their way through rocks and brushy gullies now. As it was, they'd do good to reach his mother's village by midnight.

Somewhere along the way, he'd need to switch horses. It wouldn't do Rose any good if he rode the gelding into the ground. But would her temperamental stallion allow him on his back with

Dearest Irish

her? He would, Jack vowed, even if he had to knock sense into the horse's head.

* * *

Even with her coat on and Jack's warmth surrounding her, Rose continued to tremble with cold. Her foggy brain told her it must be a result of the snakebite. But why had Jack's hands also shook while he was tending her? Was he afraid for her? The possibility brought a pleased smile to her lips, until a sudden wave of dizziness swept over her. Closing her eyes, she let her head fall back against Jack's shoulder. That helped a bit but it didn't stop the throbbing in her arm, which grew worse with the jouncing of the horse.

"'Twas a rattlesnake that bit me, aye? And they're very poisonous," she managed to say.

"They can be," Jack replied after a silence, his deep voice resonating through her.

"I might die."

"No! You're not gonna die. I won't let you."

From somewhere, she called up a broken laugh. "Och, are ye God then, to be deciding such a thing?"

"Far as you're concerned, I am. I'll get you to my mother and she'll fix you up."

Rose was too weak and in too much pain to debate the matter with him. She lost track of time as her thoughts became more and more disjointed. At some point they stopped and Jack dismounted. It was growing dark by then. When he lifted her down, she grew frightened. Was he going to cut her arm again?

"What are ye doing?" she mumbled, pushing ineffectually at his shoulder.

"Easy. We're just switching horses." The next thing she knew, she was perched atop Brownie, swaying dizzily. "Hold on," Jack ordered, wrapping her good hand around the saddle horn. "I'll be right back."

"Aye, aye, sir," she said, slurring her words. She tried to grin but her lips seemed frozen. Still, she was amused by his frown. Why, she couldn't say. She wasn't sure of anything at this point. Watching Jack step in front of Brownie and grasp his halter, she blinked in confusion, groggily wondering what he was about.

"Horse, you're gonna let me ride you," he said, sounding half angry. "Because if you don't, she'll die. You don't want that, do you?"

Ah, ha! So she *was* going to die. But only if Brownie refused to let Jack ride him. It crossed her befuddled mind that it would serve him right – Jack, not Brownie – if she did die. That would teach him not to go kidnapping women. But she didn't want to die! Holding onto that thought when Jack climbed up behind her, she bent forward, lying along the stallion's neck.

"Ye must allow him to ride ye, my dear," she forced out. Brownie tossed his head as if to argue, but he didn't buck. She patted his neck. "There's my darlin' boy."

"Sit back." Jack commanded, gently drawing her upright against him once more. His voice sounded choked. Or was she imagining it?

Then Brownie was racing through the night, lulling her into a pained stupor. Soon, she knew nothing at all.

* * *

When Rose went limp in his arms, Jack knew a moment of panic. Tipping her head back, he held his hand under her nose. At the soft touch of her breath, he expelled a ragged sigh. She was unconscious but alive. Cradling her close, he urged the stallion to an even faster pace. He'd left his gelding behind. They still had miles to go and the exhausted horse would've slowed them down.

Hearing Rose mumble something, he felt a surge of hope, thinking she'd come to, but he quickly realized she was talking in her sleep. No, not sleep. She was out of her head, trapped in a nightmare by the sound of it.

"Nay! Don't!" she cried, twisting as if trying to escape. "Don't hurt me, please!"

"It's all right, you're safe," Jack said in her ear. "No one's gonna hurt you. Not while I'm alive." She must have somehow heard him, because she quieted, relaxing against him once more. He knew now that he'd guessed right, that she'd been terrorized and beaten by a man in her past, and from what she'd told him, he assumed that man was her father. If he ever got his hands on the

Dearest Irish

bastard, Jack swore he'd kill him.

Cupping Rose's face with his hand, he experienced a new wave of fear. She burned with fever. It was his fault. He should have taken better care of her. She was a greenhorn. He shouldn't have left her alone even for a minute. He'd known she was upset because he hadn't thanked her, hadn't so much as nodded at her offer of sympathy when he told her about his friend who died in the stampede. Instead, he'd pulled away from her touch, hurting her feelings and making her mad. Mad enough to ignore his warning not to risk stepping in a prairie dog hole. Yeah, he'd warned her about that but not about the danger of running into a snake.

What was the matter with him? He knew rattlers liked to crawl down burrows after prey. Why hadn't he told Rose that? Hell! The reason was plain enough for even a fool like him to see. He'd been too busy fighting his desire for the woman, and anxious to get away from her, to think of anything else. Now she was paying the price for his stupidity.

He had no business letting this yellow-haired white girl drive out his common sense. She wasn't for him. He'd told himself that time and again. Yet, he desired her more than any woman he'd ever known. Taking her to his bed a time or two – if she'd ever have him – would not satisfy that desire, he feared. He wanted more, more than he dared admit.

They reached his mother's village about an hour before midnight, sooner than he'd expected thanks to the fleet-footed stallion. The camp fires were out, the lodges silent as they charged past. He brought Brownie to a skidding halt outside his mother's lodge. The horse's sides heaved with exertion as Jack carefully dismounted, easing Rose down with him. She sagged in his arms, head lolling like a wilted flower. Praying he hadn't gotten her here too late, he took a step toward the tipi entrance but halted when someone ducked out. In the dark, he wasn't sure it was his mother until she spoke.

"Jack? Is that you?" she asked.

"Khaw, Rose is snakebit," he blurted. "It was a rattler!"

He heard Ghost Woman catch her breath. "Bring her inside," she ordered sharply.

Bending low, Jack carried Rose into the lodge and laid her on the bed of furs opposite his mother's. His arms felt suddenly empty without her; she seemed to belong there by now.

"Let me look at her," his mother said, nudging him aside and kneeling beside her unconscious patient. She felt the pulse in Rose's neck, lifted her eyelids to look at her eyes, and clicked her tongue over the injured arm. It had turned reddish-purple and was even more swollen than before their breakneck ride, Jack saw to his dismay.

"Will she live?" he asked, dreading the answer.

"How long since the snake bit her?"

"It was seven, maybe eight hours ago."

"That is bad," his mother said, jolting him with the unvarnished truth. "But there is still a chance for her," she added, pushing to her feet with difficulty. "I will make a poultice. Bring more wood for the fire, my son. Now, where are my medicine pouches?" she muttered, digging through her piled belongings.

"Oh, and take off her shirt," she absently directed.

About to duck out after firewood, Jack straightened abruptly and stared at her bent back. Did she realize how he felt about Rose? Did she know what she was asking of him? Glancing over her shoulder, she frowned at him.

"Why do you stand there? Get the wood."

He nodded and went about his errand, carrying an image of Rose bared to the waist in his mind's eye, tempting him unmercifully. A short while later, with the fire blazing and Khaw busy concocting a poultice, Jack knelt beside his innocent looking temptress. Flushed with fever, she rolled her head from side to side, mumbling broken words, evidently caught in another nightmare.

"Don't be afraid. You're safe with me," Jack whispered. He continued to speak softly as he worked the tails of her shirt free from her riding skirt. She slowly quieted, making no attempt to stop his hands when he began unbuttoning her shirt. It came as a relief to find she wore an undergarment beneath the shirt. A camisole he thought it was called. Trimmed with lace and pink ribbon, it was pretty, but not half as pretty as what it encased. The thin, soft fabric molded to Rose's slender torso, displaying the curves of her high, full breasts and allowing Jack to see the shadowy outline of her nipples.

His mouth went dry. His hands itched to cup those perfect breasts, but the woman was unconscious. How could he think of touching her when she lay helpless, in danger of dying? Ripping his gaze from her feminine charms, he gently lifted her shoulders and eased the shirt off. As he laid her back, his mother stepped to his side.

"The poultice is ready," she said. "While it cools, I will clean her up. Take that dirty rag away."

Wondering what she would think of his crude doctoring, Jack removed his bandana from Rose's arm, peeling away most of the lumpy poultice along with it. His mother snatched the rag from his hand, fingered the mixture and sniffed it. Flicking her long, thinning gray hair over her shoulder, she eyed him curiously.

"This is buffalo currant bark. Did you cook it?"

"No. There wasn't time. I chewed it."

"Mmm. You did well. Now you must leave."

"Leave? No, I want to stay. What if she needs me?" he protested, drawing a sharp, narrow-eyed glare from Khaw.

"Is she your woman?"

Jack hesitated for a split second before shaking his head. "No, but I –"

"Then you must not look upon her. You have already seen too much. I should not have told you to take off her shirt. It put bad thoughts in your head."

Jack could have denied that, but it would be a lie, and his mother was right. He had no right to see Rose unclothed, much as he might want to. Much as he *did* want to. "All right. I'll wait outside. Tell me when it's safe to come back in. I . . . I want to be here if she wakes."

"She will not wake this night. Maybe tomorrow or the day after. Maybe never."

Jack's stomach plummeted. Incapable of speech, he stooped and went out. Brownie stood right where he'd left him, head drooping in exhaustion. Feeling a new kinship with the horse, Jack unsaddled him, took off his shirt and used it to rub down the lathered stallion. "I'm glad she saved your life, boy," he said gruffly. "You paid her back tonight. Leastways I hope you did."

The horse nickered as if in agreement.

CHAPTER TEN

Rose awoke stiff and sore from lying in one place too long. Groaning, she pushed up onto her elbows and looked around. She recognized Ghost Woman's lodge and saw light seeping in around the tipi flap. The old lady herself was nowhere in sight. Neither was Jack.

The memory of being bitten by a snake surfaced, sending shivers down her spine and causing her to glance down at her right forearm. A cotton bandage was wrapped around it, but the swelling she recalled had gone down, and although the arm ached a bit, that was nothing compared to the pain she'd experienced during the dark, agonizing ride in Jack's arms. She must have lost consciousness along the way because she had no memory of their arrival here. How long ago was that?

"Hello. Is anyone there?" she called out, surprised by the hoarseness of her voice. She was terribly thirsty, she suddenly realized. Hoping for Jack to appear and give her a drink of water, she was disappointed when his mother entered the lodge.

"Ah, you are awake," Ghost Woman said. Crossing to Rose's bed, she knelt and laid a bony hand on her brow. "The fever is gone. That is good."

"Water, please," Rose croaked.

The old woman reached for an animal skin water bag and poured water from it into a cup carved from a buffalo horn. Holding the cup to Rose's lips, she allowed her to drink her fill then said, "Lie back. You are weak."

With her arms about to give out, Rose obeyed. "Thank ye, ma'am." Receiving a nod in reply, she asked, "How long have I been here?"

"This is the third sun since my son brought you to me."

"So long!"

"Mmm. You were very sick. I was not sure you would live."

Rose gulped. "Thank ye for saving my life."

Ghost Woman shook her head. "It is Jack who saved you. He did what was needed . . ." She pointed at Rose's arm. ". . . and he rode hard to bring you here."

"I'd like to thank him. Where is he? Might ye send him to me?"

The woman's gaunt copper features took on a closed expression. Rising, she stared down at Rose for a moment before saying in a rather clipped tone, "He is with the men. I will tell him you ask for him."

Rose watched her leave, getting a strong impression that the woman didn't like her asking for Jack. Why? She only wanted to thank him. Had his mother decided she didn't want her around him anymore, perhaps because she was white? No, surely not. Ghost Woman's own husband had been half white. Not that Rose held any ideas about wedding Jack. That was unthinkable. She'd vowed never to marry. She couldn't, not only because of her fear but because she wasn't fit to be any man's wife.

Her brooding thoughts were cut off when Jack thrust aside the tipi flap and ducked in. Rose caught her breath as he straightened. He'd cast off his cowboy attire. Bare-chested, with only a breechclout and leggings covering his lower half and his ebony hair flowing loose over his broad shoulders, he reminded her of the day she'd watched him at work in the smithy back on the Double C. Only now, he seemed even more primitive, like some beautiful untamed creature whose dangerous allure threatened her peace of mind.

He halted to gaze at her for a tense moment. Then he padded silently over to her in his moccasins. Heart pounding, she found it hard to breathe when he squatted beside her.

"It's good to see you awake, P'ayn-nah. Welcome back," he said in a husky voice. His dark gaze traveled over her, seeming to caress her everywhere.

"Glad I am to be back," she replied, sounding equally husky to her own ears.

"How do you feel?"

"Much better." Struggling to keep herself from staring at his glistening copper chest, she tugged her blanket higher, almost to her throat. "I owe ye my life. Thank ye for saving me."

He scowled. "Don't thank me. I almost got you killed."

"Why d'ye say that?" she asked in confusion. "'Tisn't your fault I was bitten by the snake. Ye warned me not to walk out into the prairie dog town. I should have listened to ye."

"Yeah, you should have, but I'm still to blame. I didn't warn you about rattlers hiding in the burrows, and I never should have left you there alone. You're still a greenhorn to these parts." His lips quirked. "And after all, you're only a woman."

"Only a woman, is it?" Rose huffed, instantly annoyed. "Sir, I'll have ye know there's little a woman can't do if she puts her mind to it."

Jack grinned. "There's that Irish temper again."

Realizing he'd been teasing her, she blushed hotly. "Och, you're a wicked devil, Jack Lafarge," she chided, swatting at his muscular arm.

He caught her hand and raised it to his lips. His warm, damp kiss set off explosive tingles all over her body. Struggling to control her reaction, she called up a wobbly smile. He met her uncertain gaze, gave her hand a gentle shake and released it. Shifting on his haunches, he cleared his throat and turned serious.

"Look, I won't be around for a few days."

Rose's stomach clenched. "Wh-where are ye going?"

"The Army has kindly agreed to allow the men of this village and others to go on a hunt," he said. "Since you're doing all right now, I'm going with 'em. Maybe we'll find a buffalo or two."

"Oh. And if ye do, you'll kill them?"

"It's a hunt. That means killing."

"But ye said there are so few buffalo left. Why d'ye wish to destroy them?"

His raven brows formed a slash above his arrow-straight nose. He leaned toward her and gritted, "Because the government allotments are never enough. Because half the time the meat is spoiled and the flour's full of weevils. If the people don't hunt, they starve."

Shocked, Rose stared into his angry eyes. "I . . . I didn't know."

His scowl faded. He drew back and bent his head, hair falling forward to shadow his expression. "I know you didn't. I'm sorry for growling at you."

She reached out to touch the hand clenched on his thigh. "I'm sorry, too, for your mother and her people. 'Tisn't right they're treated so poorly."

Jack opened his hand and caught hold of hers. Nodding, he said gruffly, "Anyway, you'll have time to get your strength back while I'm gone. When I return, I'll take you back to Fort Sill. There's a stage that runs through there. It'll get you over to the railroad, and you can take the train down to Texas. I'll telegraph your brother to meet you in Denison."

"But your mother," Rose blurted, caught off guard by his matter-of-fact announcement. "I haven't healed her." She unknowingly clutched at his hand, a lump forming in her throat at the thought of parting with him.

"And you don't believe you can. Do you?" Prying her fingers loose, he pressed her hand to the blanket beside her, demanding honesty with his steady gaze.

"I . . . I don't know. But I could try again."

He sighed. "We'll see when I get back." Rising, he looked down at her. "Take care of yourself, P'ayn-nah." With that, he turned and left.

Rose fought the tightness in her chest and the sting of tears behind her eyes, telling herself Jack was right. The chances of her being able to truly heal his mother were slim at best. She should accept that and go back to her family. There was nothing here for her, certainly not Jack. She knew that. Why then did the thought of bidding him farewell cause her so much pain?

* * *

Tye Devlin tossed back a shot of whiskey and nearly choked. It burned like liquid fire and made his eyes water. "Phah!" he gasped. "That stuff will rot a body's insides."

Seated across the battered table from him, Jeb Crawford chuckled. "It probably came from some still hereabouts. Best take it slow or you'll wish you had."

"Aye, I don't doubt it." Slouched in his chair in their dim

corner, Tye glanced idly around the crudely built log structure that passed for a hotel and saloon in this out-of-the-way stop in the road. He and Jeb had come across it after another long, fruitless day of searching for Rose and that no-good *bithiúnach* who'd made off with her. They'd stopped at every small hamlet and solitary cabin along the hilly, winding trail through woods and farmland. None of the Choctaws they'd questioned knew anything about Choctaw Jack or a young white woman riding with him. Or so they said. The few whites they'd run into were of no help, either.

Dispirited by their failure to find his sister over the past weeks, and longing to be with his wife, Tye eyed the few customers scattered at tables around the room. He'd already asked if any were acquainted with Rose's abductor. All had denied ever hearing of him. So had the barkeep, an aged Indian with no teeth and a map of years creasing his face, who now stood gossiping with a stout patron at the far end of the bar.

"Place ain't much for atmosphere, is it," Jed commented, drawing Tye's gaze.

"Nay, but it suits my mood."

Jeb nodded. "Yeah, mine too. We sure haven't had much luck."

Tye poured another shot of whiskey from a clay jug the barkeep had supplied them with and took a smaller swallow, making a face at the taste. Needing something to take his mind off their futile search, he said, "I know ye lived in these parts years ago, but I'm wondering what brought ye here. If ye don't mind telling me."

Jeb studied him for a moment then shrugged. "I don't like talking about it, but seeing you're one of the family now, I reckon you oughta know." Shifting in his chair, he began, "I was a young buck out for adventure when I left home over in Arkansas. Del stayed behind to help Pa work the farm. Ma had passed on a few years earlier, and our other brother and sisters all died young, so Pa was alone except for us two boys. Del felt it his duty to stay, him being the oldest.

"Anyhow, I started west, figuring to see what the Indian Territory was like, then maybe ride north and hook up with a wagon train heading for Oregon. That was a few years before the big gold rush to California, or I woulda been on the trail there, I reckon. As it was, I just wanted to see the country. What I didn't take serious enough was how lawless this territory was back then. Outlaws, both Indian and white, roamed through here, still do for that matter. I sure didn't count on being shot and robbed of everything I owned by one of the sidewinders, and left for dead."

"*Beggorah!* But ye survived."

"Yeah, thanks to a Choctaw farmer who heard the shots and got curious. I was out cold when he found me, so I don't remember him hauling me back to his cabin. When I woke up the next day I was laying in bed buck naked with a pretty little Indian gal giving me a bath." Jeb grinned at the memory and Tye laughed.

"That must have been a wee bit shocking. For the both of ye."

"Sure was for me. She pretended she wasn't bothered any, but I saw her cheeks flush, so I knew better. Her name was Poloma, meaning dove. Her daddy, the man who found me, spent most days working his fields or hunting meat for supper, so Poloma and me were alone a lot. She didn't speak much English, but we managed to talk some while she took care of me. As I got stronger, it wasn't long before we did more than talk." A nostalgic smile flitted across Jeb's face.

"I kinda reckon her pa wanted her to find a husband, or he wouldn't have turned a blind eye to what was going on between us. Pretty soon he had himself a son-in-law, and a grandbaby on the way."

"Ye had a wife and a child? But you've never spoken of them." Even as he said it, Tye felt the other man's buried pain and knew what was coming.

"Paloma died birthing our son," Jeb confided in a choked whisper, staring into his glass of pale whiskey. "The baby had trouble breathing. He died two days later. I named him Jacob Otapi after my pa and Paloma's pa, and I buried him next to her. I've never loved another woman since."

"I'm sorry, man," Tye forced out past the waves of grief swamping the place in his head that allowed him to experience exactly what Jeb was feeling. "I know ye grieve for them still, as I would for Lil and our child were I to lose them. God forbid!"

"Don't even think that," Jeb barked. "That gal's like a daughter to me. If she was to . . . well, it's ain't gonna happen. It can't."

"I pray you're right. But tell me, what did ye do after losing Paloma and wee Jacob?"

Jeb went on to explain how he'd stayed on with his wife's father for close to a year, having no heart to resume his westward journey. Then his brother had tracked him down to deliver news of their father's death the previous winter. With nothing to hold him on the home place, Del had set out to follow Jeb west, along with the brothers' close friend, Judd Howard – a man Tye was acquainted with due to circumstances he'd rather forget.

"When they found me and learned what had happened, Del and Judd tried to talk me into moving on with them. I hadn't made up my mind about it when Rebecca showed up at Otapi's place in the middle of a spring gully washer, begging for shelter. She and her youngun, Toby, were near drowned, shivering with cold and half starved. They'd been on their way back to Rebecca's Cherokee kin, after that bastard who stole her and murdered her ma got himself killed. She never made it there."

Jeb snorted in amusement, his mood lightening. Grateful for that, Tye sighed in relief as the sympathetic pain in his head receded. "I take it Del changed her plans."

"He sure enough did. He took one look at her and Toby and fell tail over head in love with both of them. It took him a while to convince Rebecca he wasn't like the snake who fathered Toby, but he eventually won her over. They got hitched and pretty soon Del came up with the idea of heading down to Texas. It was a lot closer than Oregon or California, and it seemed safer for Rebecca, seeing as she was already carrying Lil. I had nowhere else to go, so I said goodbye to Otapi and went with them. So did Judd, but you already know that."

"Aye. Ye settled in Bosque County, while Howard chose to build his ranch west of Fort Worth."

Jeb shrugged. "Wasn't quite that simple. We moved around some first, learned how to push cattle and picked cotton for a spell near Waco. That was the most miserable work I've ever done." Frowning, Jeb paused, evidently reliving the unpleasant task. Then he continued, "It wasn't long before Judd had enough and headed off on his own. A short time after that, Del and me heard land was opening up to the northwest, along the Bosque River and the creeks that feed into it. We picked up stakes again, meaning to grab a piece of prairie before it was all taken, and we did."

"And was Lil born on the Double C or –?" Distracted by the sound of the saloon door opening, Tye didn't finish his question. He glanced toward the entrance just as a long-haired Indian walked in. He reminded Tye vaguely of Choctaw Jack, although he was shorter than Rose's kidnapper.

The newcomer looked around the room, studying the customers. When his gaze landed on Tye and Jeb, he hesitated a moment, then walked toward them.

"Company comin'" Jeb muttered. "Could have a gun or a knife under that duster."

Thinking the same, Tye straightened, wondering if the stranger's set expression boded good or ill.

"You the ones asking after Jack Lafarge?" he asked, halting near their table. Plainly sensing their wariness, he held aside the flaps of his coat, revealing a slender frame and no visible weapons.

Tye exchanged a mystified glance with Jeb and replied, "The man we're searching for goes by the name of Choctaw Jack. He's about six feet tall with long hair, and, unless I'm mistaken, you're related to him. Am I right?"

"You are. Mind if I sit?"

"Nay, not a'tall." Holding his growing excitement in check, Tye shoved out a chair between him and Jeb with his booted foot. "Would ye care for a drink?"

Shaking his head, the man dropped into the chair. "No thanks. I never touch the stuff."

"As ye wish. Might I ask your name, sir, and what relation ye are to Choctaw . . . I mean Jack Lafarge?"

The Indian smiled crookedly. "You couldn't pronounce my Choctaw name, but my American name is Ben Harris, and Jack is my cousin. His pa's mother was sister to my grandfather," he explained, tipping his hat back.

"Indeed? And have ye seen him of late?"

"Naw. He doesn't show his face much in these parts since the war."

Tye's stomach sank along with his burst of hope. "D'ye have any idea where he might be found?"

"Last I heard he was blacksmithing over west at Fort Sill. That was a couple winters ago, but I expect you might find him there or on the Kiowa reservation."

"Why would he be with the Kiowas?" Tye asked, frowning in confusion.

"Because his ma's there. She's Kiowa."

"What!" Jeb erupted, slamming the glass he'd been holding down on the table. "I thought she was Choctaw. That's what he told us."

"He probably figured you'd put a bullet in him if you knew he's half Kiowa, and Cousin Jack is good at saving his own skin," Harris sneered. "How do you fellas know him? And who's the white gal I heard you're after?" He cocked an eyebrow at Tye. "She your wife?"

Tye pinned him with a hard glare. "She's my sister. Your cousin convinced her to trust him. Then he kidnapped her. I mean to get her back and make him pay."

"Oh. Sorry, mister. I hope you catch him and hang him high."

"Those are harsh words coming from his own kin. Would ye mind saying why ye wish him dead and why you're telling us all this? Others we've spoken to have denied even knowing the man."

Harris smiled wryly. "That doesn't surprise me. My people don't trust strange white men who ask questions about other Choctaws, even polecats like Jack." Drumming his fingers on the table, he added, "As for why I'd like to see him laid six feet under, it's because he deserted our outfit during the war. He's a yellow coward."

Tye stared at the man in astonishment. He might hate Jack for stealing Rose, but he'd never considered him a coward.

"The devil you say!" Jeb declared. "Jack deserted? I don't believe it. He fought alongside my nephew and came to us after the war to let us know how Toby died. That strikes me as honorable, not cowardly."

Harris's brow creased. "You mean Toby Crawford?"

"The same. You knew him?"

"Course I did. He was in the same outfit as Jack and me. He was a good fighter. We were all sorry to lose him, Jack most of all, I reckon. He was just a kid back then, and when his pa got killed, Toby's the one who pulled him through. After Toby died, though, Jack lost his backbone. He was like a whipped dog, wouldn't pick up a gun to save his life. He likely would have been sent home or shot for refusing orders, but then his ma turned up, why I dunno. The next thing we knew, both of them took off in the middle of the night. That's the last we saw of Jack."

After a long silence, Jeb muttered, "Sounds like that boy went through hell."

"We all did," Harris snapped. "But most of us didn't turn tail and run."

Tye had heard enough about Jack's past. "Right now I only care about finding my sister and bringing her home. I'm grateful to ye, Harris, for advising us where to look." Leaning forward, he offered his hand to the Choctaw.

Harris shook, then pushed back his chair and rose. "I've said my piece, and I've got a long ride home. Good luck to you." Touching his hat, he turned and walked out.

"Well sir, I 'spose we'll be heading for Fort Sill," Jeb commented, "but not until sunrise. I'm done in. My creaky old bones need a rest." So saying, he climbed stiffly to his feet.

Scowling, Tye rose and followed him to the room they'd rented for the night. What he wanted to do was saddle up and ride west through the night.

CHAPTER ELEVEN

By the day after Jack's departure, Rose was strong enough to sit up for short periods, enabling her to feed herself and tend to her personal needs. High on that list was to bathe and wash her hair, but first she had to work the knots from her tangled tresses. Juana, who'd been helping Ghost Woman care for her, lent her a brush made from a porcupine's tail ingeniously mounted on a stick.

Left to her painful task, Rose wondered where Jack was at this moment, how the hunt was going, and if she crossed his mind now and then as he chased after buffalo. She pushed aside the annoying thought when Juana returned with water, rags and a small wooden bowl containing foamy, cream colored liquid.

"This is yucca root soap. It is good for washing your hair and the rest of you. And to clean clothes." She indicated Rose's freshly washed garments, including her carefully mended shirt, which she'd returned earlier.

Rose smiled in gratitude. "Thank ye for helping me in so many ways."

"I am happy to do this. Jack and my husband are blood brothers, and you are Jack's . . . friend. It is right for you and I to be friends also, *si?*"

"Aye, of course." Telling herself Juana's slight hesitation over the word *friend* meant nothing, Rose picked up the bowl of soap and bent to sniff it. "Mmm, this smells wonderful."

"I added a little ground sage leaves. Tsoia likes the scent in my hair. Perhaps Jack will like it in yours."

Jerking upright, Rose nearly overturned the bowl of liquid soap. There was no mistaking the woman's intent this time. "Sure'n I don't care if he likes it or not. 'Tisn't as if I wish to attract him."

Juana cocked her head and smiled. "I think you do, but you are afraid to try. Why, I do not know. Jack is a good man. He would make a fine husband for you."

"Nay! I'm not looking for a husband, and I'm quite certain Jack has no desire to be wedding me."

"No? But why did he not leave your side when you were so ill, except when his mother and I tended you?"

"H-he did that?"

"*Si*, he was so worried for you, he would not sleep, and Ghost Woman had to make him eat."

Stunned, Rose stammered, "I . . . I had no idea."

"Then I have given you much to think on while he is gone. Bend over now and I will wet your hair."

Rose could think of little else *but* Jack while Juana helped her wash her hair and towel it dry with a faded piece of gingham. He lingered in her mind while the other woman gently scrubbed her back, and afterward while left alone to complete her bath. Again she wondered if he thought of her, if he missed her even the tiniest bit, as she missed him.

Over the next several days as she grew stronger and resumed helping Juana and the other women with their chores, Jack continued to dominate Rose's waking thoughts. He even appeared in her dreams, smiling, teasing her, invading her mouth with slow, deep kisses until she awoke with an unfamiliar yearning that hardened her nipples and drew moist heat between her thighs.

Shocked and frightened by her body's treacherous reaction, she fought to suppress it but failed utterly. What was happening to her? After all the vows she'd made to herself, after being so certain she would never want a man in *that* way, how could Jack affect her so? How, how, how?

* * *

Jack squinted into the distance but saw no sign of buffalo, the same story as the past three days. So far, the hunt was a failure. They'd shot enough small game to feed themselves, but nothing they could take back to their women, children and elders like his mother.

"Do you see anything, Ah-p'ah-be?" Tsoia asked. Mounted on his paint next to Jack, he too scanned the horizon, shading his eyes against the lowering sun.

"No, nothing. And you?"

"No. The buffalo have all left us. They graze now with Father Sun."

Fearing his friend was right, Jack recalled his last conversation with Rose, and her innocent question as to why he wanted to kill the last remaining buffalo. Despite his angry reply about his mother and the Kiowas facing starvation if they didn't hunt, he could not escape the guilt Rose had awakened within him. Anymore than he could escape his smoldering desire for her, desire that stirred in his loins every time he pictured her lying on her bed of buffalo furs, blanket up to her chin, but with her bare shoulders glowing like ivory satin in the firelight, tempting him unmercifully.

Get out of my head, woman! he silently commanded. *"You're not for me. I would only bring you pain.*

"Time to make camp," announced the sergeant leading their bluecoat escorts, causing Jack to jump in his saddle.

"Brother, are you well?" Tsoia asked, eyeing him uncertainly.

"I'm fine. Just tired of taking orders." It was half true.

Lying on his blanket later, with his head propped on his hands, Jack stared at the stars overhead. Did they look down on the Kiowa people and weep? Or did they laugh at their pitiful attempt to hold onto the old ways?

"The spirits curse us," said one of the other men. "We should have protected our friends the buffalo from the white hunters. We failed them. Now we cannot find even one small calf to feed our people."

Jack recognized the speaker's voice. It belonged to a young brave from a village upstream from his mother's. He was called Wolf-who-limps because of his wild, unruly nature and because of a broken leg that hadn't set right, leaving him with a limp.

"We tried to protect them," another voice said. It belonged to Tsoia's cousin Blue Elk. "We fought hard against the hunters and the bluecoats, but they were too many."

Wolf-who-limps gave a contemptuous snort but said no more. Just as well, since he didn't know what he was talking about. Blue Elk was right. No matter how many buffalo hunters the Kiowa and their allies killed, more had always taken their place. Pushing

Dearest Irish

away melancholy thoughts of the past, Jack rolled onto his side, tugged his blanket around him, and stared into the campfire's low flames, seeing Rose's blue agate eyes in his mind. Even when sleep overtook him, her shy smile and innocent glances haunted him.

When day dawned he wanted to linger in dreams with his beautiful P'ayn-nah, but the purpose for the hunt came back to him, forcing him awake. As he, Tsoia and the others prepared for another day of searching, he prayed it would not end in more disappointment.

Perhaps the Great Buffalo spirit heard him. Either that or by sheer luck, they came upon a narrow ravine when the sun was high in the sky, and there they found a dozen or so buffalo, nearly all cows, grazing on tufts of spring grass among boulders and scrub trees. At sight of them, cries of joy went up among the hunters, startling their prey. The cows milled and grunted in fear while the herd bull, an old boy with craggy horns, pawed the ground and bellowed, the sound echoing off the enclosure's rocky walls. Then he lowered his huge head and charged. In a heartbeat the whole herd was stampeding toward the hunting party.

"Look out!" yelled the bluecoat sergeant, signaling a scramble by soldiers and Kiowa to escape the narrow ravine before the enraged bull and his harem slammed into them. Jack made it out without any problem, but it was a near thing for the last man, a young soldier on a slow horse. He cleared the neck of the ravine and cut his mount sharply left seconds before the herd thundered past.

Once the buffalo were on open ground, Jack and the Kiowa braves gave chase, racing to see who could bring down the first shaggy beast. Tsoia had that honor. His arrow caught one of the larger cows behind the shoulder. It struck her heart and she tumbled over, plowing up clods of grass and red earth. Hurtling ahead, Jack came even with the huge bull and one fleet-footed cow up front. He took aim at the bull with his rifle but held his fire. Rose's question and his own conscience stopped him. Instead, he fired into the air. The rifle's loud report lent new speed to the fleeing pair.

"Run, brother and sister! Run for your lives!" Jack shouted.

"What are you doing?" cried an angry rider behind him. "You let them get away!"

Jack slowed his mount and swung the horse around, deliberately blocking the other man's path, forcing him to draw back hard on his pony to keep from colliding with Jack. He was Wolf-who-limps, the brave who'd railed against his people last night for not protecting the buffalo.

"Move aside, coward!" he demanded. "I will catch them and do what you were afraid to do."

"No, you will not. They must live."

Baring his teeth in fury, the young Kiowa tried to ride past him, but Jack grabbed his pony's rawhide halter and jerked him to a halt. Snarling, the brave whipped out his knife and slashed at him. Jack yanked his arm back in time to avoid the blade but couldn't prevent it from slicing into his thigh. Growling in pain, he prodded his horse aside, putting space between himself and the hotheaded youth. His leg was bleeding heavily. He pressed his hand to the wound and glanced over his shoulder, seeing the pair of buffalo kick up dust in the distance. They were the only survivors of the hunt.

"Would you kill the last two on earth?" he shouted. "You, who blame our people for not saving them from white hunters?"

The brave glowered at him then shot an uncertain look at the disappearing animals. Lowering his knife, he muttered, "I . . . I did not think."

"No, you did not." Drawing his own knife, Jack cut off a length of rawhide from his long Indian style rein to use as a temporary tourniquet.

At that moment, Tsoia rode up. "Ah-p'ah-be, I saw what happened. Are you bad hurt?"

Jack shook his head. "My leg bleeds, but the cut's not deep." He tied the rawhide strip around his thigh above the wound, holding back a grimace as he tightened it.

Tsoia glowered at Wolf-who-limps, who wore a look of unease. "This man is my friend, my brother. Why did you attack him?"

"He let the bull and his mate escape. I thought him a coward. He angered me and I –"

"Fool! He is no coward. He proved himself a great warrior when you still rode with your mother. I raided with him and I saw –"

"Tsoia, no," Jack barked. "That time is gone. Do not speak of it."

"But, Ah-p'ah-be, he must learn –"

"He will learn in his own way. Come, you must claim your

kill, and I need to bandage this cut." Not waiting for further argument, Jack kneed his horse toward the scene of death. There was much butchering to do before they could haul the meat back to their hungry people. Before he could return to Rose.

* * *

Rose used a spoon carved from buffalo horn to scoop up a mouthful of watery corn soup. Chewing a small bite of stringy meat, she glanced furtively at Ghost Woman across the fire pit. They'd brought their sparse meal into her lodge to escape the fierce wind that howled outside, kicking up swirling dust. The old woman ate in silence, ignoring her. Rose wondered if this was a good time to ask the question that had been plaguing her.

Uncertain, she forced down a few more spoonfuls of soup then set the bowl aside. Trying for a casual tone, she asked, "Does Jack have a wife among your people?" He was obviously not attached to Star-girl, but there were other villages and other women.

Ghost Woman looked up sharply. "No, but when he is ready, he will take a Kiowa wife. He must not choose a white woman like you."

Rose stiffened. "I never thought he would. And I've no desire to wed him." Receiving a skeptical glance in reply, she frowned. "Would ye mind telling me why you're opposed to Jack marrying a white woman? Your husband was half white, was he not?"

The old woman stared at her for a moment. Then she bent her head, gaunt features shadowed by lank gray hair, and slowly stirred the remainder of her soup. "He was, and we were cast out by his people," she said bitterly. "The whites called Étienne, my husband, squaw man like his father. That is why we left Louisiana and went to Texas."

"And his Choctaw kin? Did they also cast you out?" This drew a contemptuous snort from across the fire.

"They feared the Kiowa and did not want me near. Later, though, some of the men worked for us."

"Aye, Jack mentioned that. But what of your people? Would they not accept your hus . . . I mean Étienne?"

"We did not go to them. I feared they would kill him and our children. In that time Kiowa warriors were very fierce. They scorned the Choctaw and others who walked the white man's road."

"If there were such bad feelings between the Kiowa and the Choctaw, however did ye meet Étienne?"

Ghost woman laughed dryly. "We met because I was foolish, and my cousin did a stupid thing. He took me on a raid after my father forbid it and –"

"Ye went raiding? A woman?" Rose stared at her wide-eyed, meeting a disdainful glare.

"Kiowa women often raided with their men in the old times. But I was only twelve summers when I asked to go. My father said no, I must wait until I wed. Then I could go with my husband if he allowed it. But I would not listen. I begged my cousin until he agreed to take me with him.

"We rode east with others and attacked a Choctaw village. All went well until one of the enemy shot me from my horse."

Rose gasped and gripped her cross. "Were ye hurt bad?"

"Not so bad. The bullet hit me here." Ghost Woman lifted her hair aside, revealing a thin white scar across her right temple that disappeared into her hair. "The wound was not deep, but it made me fall into darkness."

"Ye were unconscious?"

She nodded. "My cousin did not see me fall. The fool! He promised to watch over me. Instead, he left me there. Later, after I returned to my people, I learned he told everyone I was dead, killed in the raid."

"But what happened to ye after the raid?"

"An old Choctaw woman healed me against her people's wishes, and I became her slave. Her name was Mantema. She worked me hard but was not cruel, and later she called me daughter. We lived apart from the village because they feared me. They thought I would kill them in their sleep." Ghost Woman laughed at the memory.

"Mantema taught me much about healing. I lived with her for four summers. Then Étienne came to visit his grandmother, who lived in the village. She was sick, and one day he came asking for medicine for her. He saw me and I saw him. We wed in the month of picking plums. June, you call it."

"That's very romantic," Rose murmured.

Ghost Woman smiled. "Yes, but we knew great sadness

Dearest Irish

when his people turned us away. I do not want my son and his wife and their children to be alone as we were. Now you see why he must not take a white wife, yes?"

"Aye, I see." Rose considered saying her brother was married to a part-Cherokee woman and they seemed happy, but she resisted the urge. It might sound as if she actually wanted to wed Jack, which she didn't. It was out of the question. Not that he was interested in marrying her, she assured herself.

* * *

The wind blew itself out and morning dawned sunny and pleasant. After a breakfast of leftover soup and a small piece of frybread, Rose joined a circle of village women. Each had some type of work to keep her hands busy. Two were sewing calico shirts, another began shaping a pair of child-size moccasins. Star-girl's mother, Walks Softly, carefully cut long, thin fringe along the sleeve edges of a hide dress. Pale fawn in color and decorated with a myriad of colored beads and small shells, it was a work of art.

Juana, who sat next to Rose, was stretching hide over a wooden frame that would be a small saddle for Tsahle-ee, her son. Rose held the frame upright for her.

"Turn it a little," Juana instructed, and Rose absently obeyed, attention riveted on Walks Softly's delicate task. She was caught by surprise when Juana leaned close and whispered behind her hand, "The dress is for her daughter's marriage. If any man will have the spoiled infant."

Rose choked down a laugh, then immediately felt sorry for the older woman, who obviously loved her daughter. Unfortunately it was also obvious from Juana's comment, and others, that Star-girl was strongly disliked by the other women because of her selfish ways, making Rose even more grateful to them for offering *her* their friendship. Never before, even while in the convent, had she experienced the easy acceptance shown her by these people. They all knew of her efforts to heal Ghost Woman, and they'd no doubt heard about her peculiar method, yet they never looked at her as if she were some kind of monster. She appreciated that more than they could know.

Misty-eyed, she blinked away the moisture and glanced over

to where an older gentleman with gray streaked long hair sat outside his lodge with the village children gathered around him. His Kiowa name meant Wise Hawk, she recalled. From his hand gestures and exaggerated expressions, Rose guessed he was telling the children a story.

All the other men had gone on the buffalo hunt. Would they return soon? Part of her hoped they would for the sake of the villagers, who were running critically low on food, just as Jack had said. Another part of her dreaded the men's return, for that would mean leaving here. And leaving Jack.

She stifled the gloomy prospect, allowing a more pressing matter to surface. Ghost Woman had enlisted two young women to go with her into the woods to gather plants for her medicines. One of the two was a good-natured girl named She-who-laughs. The other was Star-girl, who'd been far from eager to assist with the chore. They'd been gone for well over an hour, and Rose couldn't help worrying. She hated to think Star-girl might do anything to harm Jack's mother, but . . . .

"Ghost Woman and the others have been gone a long time," she said quietly. "D'ye think I ought to go look for them?"

Juana paused in her stitching and looked up. Arching a fine dark brow, she glanced at Star-girl's mother, considered for a moment and nodded. "I think we will both go."

They met Ghost Woman and her companions a short distance into the woods. They walked slowly toward the village with the old woman leaning heavily on She-who-laughs. Her lips were set in a thin line of pain and her wrinkled copper cheek bore a scraped patch, as if she'd struck it on a rough surface. Star-girl strolled along a few steps away, swinging a basket filled with greens on her arm and humming an odd tune, without a trace of concern for the injured elder.

"Ghost Woman, you're hurt!" Rose cried, running up to her and slipping an arm around her frail back.

"I was clumsy and fell."

She-who-laughs caught Rose's eye and darted a sidelong glance at Star-girl.

Rose inhaled sharply and glared at the beautiful Kiowa maiden, who blithely ignored her. "Ye caused her to fall, didn't ye," she accused.

Star-girl favored her with a haughty glance. "You not blame me, Yellow Hair. Old one clumsy like she say." She smirked and resumed humming.

Juana, who'd walked silently beside Rose until now, stepped in front of Star-girl, forcing her to halt. *"Bruja!* Witch! You say you did not hurt the medicine woman, but I see the truth. You are evil."

Star-girl's face contorted in rage and she shrieked a string of Kiowa words. Juana cut off her tirade with a sharp slap. The startled girl gasped, stumbled back a step and pressed a hand to her cheek. Narrowing her eyes, she spat at Juana, dropped the basket of medicinal plants and took off running toward the village. Rose and the other women stared after her as Juana wiped spittle from her blouse and squatted to clean her hand on the grass. Ghost Woman sighed heavily.

"The girl spoke against you." She tilted her head toward Rose. "I said you are my son's guest and she must show you respect."

Rose stared at her in surprise. "Ye took up for me against her?"

"Jack would wish it so."

"Did she strike you?" Juana asked as she retrieved the basket and the plants that had fallen out of it. "If she did, I will slap her again."

"No, you must not. I do not wish to hurt her mother." The old woman shrugged. "And it was my own foolishness. I should not have let her anger me, but she shouted in my face. I pushed her away, my legs shook and I fell."

"I'm sorry it happened because of me," Rose said.

"You did not cause it. Star-girl did. She loves only herself. She does not think of others as you do." The casual words of praise were hardly out of Ghost Woman's mouth when she suddenly gasped and bent over. She would have crumpled to the ground had Rose and She-who-laughs not held her up.

"What is it? What pains you so?" Rose asked in fresh alarm.

The old woman slowly straightened. Her face was almost gray. "You said the thing inside me . . . was not dead. You spoke true," she rasped, laboring for breath. "It eats at me again."

Rose swallowed hard. "I feared as much. I'll try again to kill it if you'll let me."

Ghost Woman smiled at her with resignation in her dark eyes. "No, no more. If it is my time to die, I am ready."

"But I might be able to –" A chorus of shouting from the nearby village cut off Rose's attempt to argue.

"The men have returned!" Juana exclaimed, her face lighting up. "And it sounds like they had a good hunt. Let us go and greet them." Not waiting for a reply, she hurried ahead.

"Come! I wish to be there," Ghost Woman cried, urging Rose and She-who-laughs to a faster pace. All but carrying her, they hurried after Juana.

CHAPTER TWELVE

They reached the village seconds before the men rode in escorted by a small troop of soldiers. The Kiowa braves rode horses pulling travois laden with mounds of what must be meat. Each mound was covered by a dusty fur pelt, the hide of a dead buffalo, Rose realized.

The village women and children swarmed around the returning heroes, chattering and laughing excitedly. Juana rushed ahead to greet her husband. When Rose hung back, Ghost Woman broke away from her and impatiently urged She-who-laughs onward to join the welcoming throng.

Rose followed more slowly. She'd instantly spotted Jack riding with Tsoia at the head of the hunting party but was uncertain how to greet him, and how he would react to seeing her. From her position at the back of the crowd, she admired the ripple and bunch of muscles across his chest and down his arms. Then, as he dismounted, she noticed a gash in his left legging and a dark stain trailing downward from it. Blood! It was dried blood.

Alarmed, Rose pushed through the onlookers, intent on getting to Jack. He was speaking to one of the other men, but as if sensing her presence, he glanced over his shoulder and snared her gaze. She stopped, held motionless by his glittering ebony eyes. His nostrils flared and a tantalizing smile curved his lips. She returned his smile, the sound of joyous villagers fading into the background. Then he shifted to face her and she saw him flinch.

Released from his compelling gaze, she took a step toward him but halted when Ghost Woman hobbled up to him. "You are hurt, my son," she said.

"It's only a scratch," he replied. Frowning, he touched her

scraped cheek. "But what of you, Khaw?"

She waved aside his concern. "I'm fine. Come with me. I will look at your wound." She wrapped both hands around his arm and tugged him toward her lodge.

Jack tossed a swift glance at Rose over his shoulder then let himself be led away. Rose wanted to hurry after him and offer to heal his wound but resisted the urge. He was not hers and never could be. She must remember that. Let his mother tend his leg. Turning her attention to the scene around her, she encountered Star-girl's malevolent stare. Lifting her chin, Rose refused to look away. She would not be intimidated by the bad-tempered vixen.

"Toppah, we must take care of the meat and prepare a feast for tonight," Juana said, walking over to her. "Do you wish to help?"

"Aye, I'll be happy to." Breaking eye contact with Star-girl, Rose spared her no more thought as she was put to work slicing buffalo meat into thin strips. These were hung over wooden racks to dry. Later, Juana explained, the dried strips would be pounded into fine pieces and mixed with hot buffalo fat and berries to make pemmican. Better portions of meat were cut up to be roasted over the campfires for tonight's celebration.

Several women set to work staking out the buffalo hides and concocting a jelly out of buffalo brain and liver mixed with water. Used to tan the hides, Juana explained, the mixture was heated, cooled a bit and worked into the hides by the women. Rose didn't envy them the arduous, nasty smelling chore.

Kneeling at her own task a while later, she felt a presence behind her and twisted to look. Jack stood there watching her.

"Hello, P'ayn-nah."

"H-hello, Jack." Laying aside the knife she'd been wielding, she hastily wiped her bloody hands on the grass and rose to face him.

"I'm glad to see you recovered from the snakebite."

"Aye, I'm well over it, but what of you? I saw your leg was injured. How is it?"

"It's fine. *Khaw* patched it up for me."

"Ah, well, I'm glad." Nervously licking her lips, she asked, "How were ye hurt? Was it a buffalo that did it?"

He shook his head, causing his long raven hair to caress his bare shoulders, as Rose's fingers itched to do. "No, I got in the way of a knife. My own fault."

"Oh." Realizing she was staring at his bare chest, she dropped her gaze to his moccasins and unconsciously gripped her cross. She gave a start when he wrapped his hand around hers and gently tugged it free of the small, comforting symbol.

"You are afraid of me again. Why? I told you I will not hurt you."

"Afraid? Nonsense! I'm not afraid of ye," she said, avoiding his eyes.

"No? Then why are you so skittish?"

Rose searched for words. She couldn't tell him his primitive masculinity called out to her in a way she had never experienced before. Finally, she said in a rush, "'Tis embarrassing to see ye like this, is all." She gestured at his chest with her free hand.

He glanced down and pressed the hand he held against his warm flesh, making her catch her breath and lashing her with tongues of fire. "You've seen me without a shirt before. More than once as I recall."

"I-I know," she choked out, not knowing where to look. Out of desperation, she squeezed her eyes shut.

After a moment's silence, he said, "So you want me to put a shirt on, is that it?"

"Yes! No!" she blurted, eyes popping open. Thoroughly flustered, she amended, "I mean I don't care. Do as ye please."

Jack narrowed his eyes. "What's wrong, P'ayn-nah? Tell me the truth."

She jerked her hand away and backed up a step. "There's nothing to tell. Please, I need to get back to work. There's much to be done."

He scowled, seeming ready to argue. Then he sighed. "Very well, I won't keep you from it. I'll see you later at the feast." Pivoting, he strode away, leaving Rose to stare at his retreating form, helplessly fascinated by his masculine grace and the flex of powerful muscles along his flanks.

"Señor Jack is much man. You like to look at him, sí?" Juana said from the nearby drying rack where she was working.

"What? Nay, he distracted me and . . . I was merely thinking about something." Flustered all over again, Rose knelt, picked up her knife and sliced another strip of buffalo meat, trying to ignore the other woman's knowing laughter.

* * *

Jack grinned at Tsoia's exaggerated description of how the big bull buffalo had charged them in the narrow ravine. His friend had a knack for storytelling, embellished by contorted expressions and hand movements that held his listeners captive. Gathered around a roaring campfire, with their bellies full for a change, the people were enjoying themselves. Even the bluecoats, who'd decided to stay the night, laughed at Tsoia's lively performance.

Amused as he was, Jack would have preferred a few quiet moments, maybe hours, alone with the woman who ruled his waking thoughts and tormented him in dreams that left him half loco with wanting her. Turning his eyes her way across the circle of firelight from where he sat, he watched her as he often had over the course of the evening. Seated with the other women, between his mother and Juana, who must have lent her the blue skirt and embroidered Mexican blouse she wore, she smiled and laughed and looked duly impressed as Juana translated her husband's tall tale. All the while acting as if *he* wasn't even there, Jack noted in annoyance.

Earlier, he'd caught her gazing at him once, making his blood run hot. He'd wanted to stride over there, grab her hand and pull her away from the others, into the darkness where he could hold her and kiss her and touch her in all the ways he longed to do. She'd swiftly looked away, though, and he'd let the moment pass. She hadn't glanced at him since, at least not that he'd noticed, and it irritated him to know she could so easily ignore him.

The fact that she hadn't come to him when his mother was tending his wound also irked him. And afterward, when *he'd* gone to *her,* she'd acted terrified, the same as when they first met. Oh sure, she'd said she wasn't afraid of him, that it was only his lack of a shirt that bothered her, but he didn't believe that. He knew fear when he saw it.

But what had he done to make her fear him again? Was it because of the snake bite, because he hadn't protected her the way he should have? Or was it the man from her past – her father, Jack firmly believed – who haunted her, standing like a wall between her and every man she met?

Wrapped up in thoughts of Rose, Jack didn't realize Tsoia had stopped speaking until an elbow in his ribs got his attention. His

Dearest Irish

blood brother grinned and pointed his chin toward Rose.

"Toppah is lonely. You should go to her," he said.

"She's not alone. She has plenty of company."

"Ah, but she wants to be with you. I see this in her eyes when you are not watching and she dares to look at you. Do not be a fool. Go and claim her."

Jack studied Rose's face again. Had she been secretly watching him as Tsoia said? Had he imagined the longing in her eyes a while ago or was it real? She'd turned away so swiftly that he couldn't know for certain.

As he watched, his mother leaned close and said something to Rose that made her frown and shake her head. They exchanged more words. Then Rose shot to her feet and darted off into the night toward the creek.

Jack met his mother's gaze and sent her a questioning frown as he sprang from the ground. The crackle of wood in the campfire filled the sudden silence as everyone waited to see what he would do. Leaving them to gossip about him and the yellow-haired white girl, he raced after her.

* * *

Rose wept bitter tears as she stumbled through the underbrush, between gnarled trees that seemed to reach out for her in the darkness. Only this morning Ghost Woman had seemed to praise her, if merely in passing, saying she cared for others while Star-girl did not. Yet, moments ago the old woman had barked at her to stop watching Jack and wishing for what could never be, and telling her to go home to her own people where she belonged.

But I have no people! I don't belong here or with Tye and Lil, or anywhere! I'm a pariah, cut off from everyone because of –

"Rose!" Jack's voice called from the darkness behind her, causing her to cry out and whirl around.

"Ye frightened me," she choked out, a hand pressed to her galloping heart.

"Sorry, but you shouldn't be out here in the dark."

"I'm all right. Stop following me." Dabbing at her wet cheeks with a sleeve of her borrowed blouse, she pleaded, "Just let me be."

"Uh-uh, can't do that." He was close enough now for her to see him shake his head in the starlight filtering through the sparse trees. "I want to know what Khaw said to make you run off like that."

Rose longed to turn and run again but knew he'd only follow her if she did. "She . . . she reminded me of something I should have remembered and . . . she said I should go home. But I don't have a home. I don't b-belong anywhere!" With that, she broke down weeping again.

Jack muttered something in Kiowa. She heard a stick snap underfoot as he stepped close. His arms enfolded her, pressing her to him, pillowing her head against his shoulder. Her tears dampened his shirt, the shirt he'd put on for her sake, she knew. "Don't cry, P'ayn-nah," he whispered, stroking her back. "You belong right here, with me."

"Nay, I don't," she said, struggling to stop her flood of self-pity. "Your mother's right. I should leave."

"No! She's wrong. You must stay."

Rose lifted her head, seeing the stern silhouette of his jaw. "But ye said you'd be sending me back to Tye as soon as ye returned from the hunt."

"I was a fool. I don't want you to go. Now tell me why you avoided me today. Are you angry because I didn't keep you safe from the snake?"

"What? Of course not! That was my own doing, as I've said before."

"Then why are you afraid of me again? And don't lie and say you're not."

"But I'm not, I tell ye. 'Tis simply that I . . . I don't wish to upset your mother."

"My mother again?" He cussed in English this time. "Just what did she say to you while I was away?"

Rose stepped out of his embrace, needing space between them. She started to reach for her cross but, recalling how Jack had tugged her hand away from it earlier today, clasped her hands instead. Sniffling to clear her clogged nose, she replied, "She told me how she met your father and how his people shunned them. She doesn't wish ye to suffer as they did, so ye . . . ye must wed a Kiowa woman, not a . . . ." Her tongue froze, unable to say the rest.

Dearest Irish

"Not a white woman," Jack finished for her. "A white woman like you, P'ayn-nah?" he said, moving closer and setting his hands on her shoulders.

"Aye, 'tis what she said. Not that I had any such notion," she declared hoarsely.

"Mmm, of course you didn't," he murmured with a smile in his tone, while his hands glided slowly across her shoulders and up the column of her neck. Tunneling under her hair, his fingers gently massaged her scalp while his thumbs stroked her cheeks, causing her to close her eyes and sigh in delight. His male scent enveloped her as he once more brought her against him. He was a magician, casting a spell over her senses.

It seemed natural and right when his mouth settled on hers, caressing her lips, coaxing them apart. His warm breath mingled with hers as his tongue delved within, dancing over the sensitive flesh of her mouth and teasing a shy response from her own tongue. She slipped her arms around him and splayed her hands across his back, feeling the swell of his hard muscles and making her wish he hadn't donned a shirt. At the same time, his arms enclosed her, pressing her breasts to his chest.

A groan escaped him. His mouth slanted across hers and his tongue plunged in and out with growing ardor. Through the fabric of her skirt, she felt something else rise and grow against her belly. She knew what it was. Panic gripped her. Tearing her mouth from Jack's, she turned her head aside and pushed at his encroaching chest.

"Let me go!" she cried.

"What the . . . ?" Jack loosened his hold but refused to release her. "What happened? Did I hurt you?"

"N-nay. I'm sorry, but ye must let me go. Please!" she begged, voice trembling.

"Not until you tell me what makes you so terrified of loving."

"Nay! I can't." She shook her head wildly and began to struggle again. When he suddenly let go, she stumbled backward, nearly falling before she managed to steady herself. She didn't take time to think. Dashing past him, she fled back to the village, to safety. Ghost Woman glowered at her when she slipped into a spot between two other women. She dreaded what the old woman would say when they retired to her lodge.

Jack didn't return, leaving Rose to wonder where he'd gone

and what would happen the next time she had to face him. Would he be furious with her for rejecting him again and refusing to tell him why? It tormented her to think he might hate her after tonight. Along with that dreadful thought, came the realization that she loved him. Aye, she loved him with all her heart, but she was incapable of giving herself to him. The mere thought of him doing *that* to her sent a cold tide of terror rushing through her, making her shiver despite the campfire's heat and the warm bodies next to her.

More than the pain involved in the act itself, she feared being trapped like some helpless animal. Did that make her a coward? And was this the way she must live her life, governed by a horrific memory, afraid to love and be loved? Or could she muster the courage to find out if it might be different with Jack? If he ever spoke to her again, that is.

* * *

Jack started after Rose but halted, knowing it would do no good to chase her down. He wanted to shake loose her secrets, to confirm what he suspected her father had done to her. At the same time he wanted to somehow prove to her that he would never hurt her the way that bastard had done.

Neither was possible tonight. She was too frightened and he . . . he was too angry to trust himself near her. If he lost his temper trying to drag the truth out of her, she'd only fear him more. Snarling a string of oaths, in English because the Kiowa language had no such words, he stomped over to the nearest tree and slammed his fist into it, bruising his knuckles. He did the same with his other fist. The pain was a welcome distraction from the anger and frustration boiling through him.

What the hell was he to do now? He couldn't go back to the village and look at Rose across the campfire, pretending nothing was wrong. Scraping his aching hands through his hair, he made up his mind. He had to get away from here.

He stalked from the trees, heading for the corral and the small herd of horses the Indians were allowed to keep. He wished for his swift bay gelding, but the horse hadn't found his way back since the night Jack had abandoned him. He regretted losing the bay, but he'd do the same again to save Rose's life. Settling for the sturdy

Dearest Irish

roan mare he'd used for the buffalo hunt, he threw himself on her back and sent her into a gallop toward Rainy Mountain. He needed a quiet place to sort out his jumbled thoughts.

A short while later he drew to a halt at the base of the mountain. Really just a rounded hill poking up from the prairie, his mother's people venerated it as a guardian of their homeland. Right now it offered solitude.

Hobbling the mare to make sure she didn't stray too far, Jack started up a winding trail to the peak. The climb wasn't steep until near the top, but he took his time, being careful not to slip on loose rocks in the dark and fall. He didn't care to land on one of the prickly pear cactuses scattered over the mountain and come away with spines in his hands and knees, or maybe his backside.

When he reached the mountaintop he paused to catch his breath and gaze at the stars in the blue-black sky, feeling as if he could reach out and touch them. The moon had also risen, allowing him to see the shadowed land below. Finding a level spot to sit cross-legged, he stared at the dim horizon and sifted through everything he knew about Rose, seeking a way to convince her to confide in him.

She was hard to understand, a confusing mix of fear and bravery. When they first met, he'd thought her as timid as a frightened rabbit, a comparison she didn't like, he recalled with a chuckle. Then she'd turned his opinion of her on its head, riding a horse most men wouldn't dare mount. True, she'd held an edge, having formed a bond with the stallion that Jack still couldn't fathom, but nevertheless it had taken courage to trust her life to that fragile bond.

She'd also shown courage during their hard ride from Texas, and in dealing with his mother. Thinking of Khaw, he ground his teeth, determined to put a stop to her troublemaking. He would take a wife of his own choosing, not one she chose. That thought immediately brought Rose back to mind. He'd denied wanting her for his wife to Tsoia, to his mother, to himself, but was it a lie? Did he want Rose for his own? And if he did, was it fair to ask her to be his wife? Was she strong enough to endure the slights she would face from whites with him at her side?

He recalled the surprising way she'd stood up for him during their meeting with Colonel Mackenzie and against that popinjay

Lieutenant Proctor and his bluecoats. Jack scowled, also recalling Nahotabi, the renegade Choctaw, and his sneered remarks. He'd grudgingly explained to Rose why the whiskey runner called him yellow, but he hadn't told her everything. What would she think of him if she knew the rest?

Ha! She'd run from you as she did tonight, and she'd never let you near her again.

Jack stiffened. Was he wrong? Might Rose surprise him again? If he revealed his worst, most painful memories to her, would she open up and trust him with hers? Lying back, he gazed at the stars again, considering the idea. It was worth sleeping on, he decided.

CHAPTER THIRTEEN

Rose awoke early and slipped out to greet the day, leaving Ghost Woman still asleep. She'd waited to retire last night until well after the elderly woman had gone off to bed, avoiding the dreaded unpleasantness. Evidently of the same mind, Ghost Woman did not approach her when she emerged from her lodge a bit later that morning. Even so, the tension between them hung in the air.

Seeking to occupy her hands and mind, Rose volunteered to help wash tanning jelly from the buffalo hides. She and Juana had just carried two clean, dripping hides back from the creek when Jack rode in. Wearing a stern expression, he didn't glance their way but rode straight to Ghost Woman, who sat in the sun with another older woman, doing some mending. Tensing, Rose dropped her wet hide onto a pile of others and took a step after him, fearing what he might say to his mother.

"No, you must not," Juana said sharply, gripping her arm to stop her.

"But Ghost Woman is unwell again and Jack looks angry."

"As he should be after what she said to you last night."

"Ye heard that?"

Juana nodded. "So did others. And they all saw you run away, with Jack after you. Now they wait to see what he will do."

Groaning in dismay, Rose glanced around and saw several pairs of curious eyes staring at Jack. Like them, she watched him slide from his horse as Ghost Woman rose to face him. He motioned for her to follow and strode toward her lodge. His mother hobbled after him leaning on a sturdy walking stick she'd taken to using after her fall the previous day.

Jack waited until she joined him, away from listening ears,

then spoke to her. Even from where she stood, Rose could read his scowl and the sharpness of his words. His mother made a denying gesture, but Jack held up his hand, cutting off whatever she'd started to say. He said something more, causing the old woman to nod and bend her head in acceptance. Then he marched back toward the camp, leaving her standing there, staring after him.

Rose stepped forward as Jack approached. "What did ye say to your mother? Ye shouldn't have –"

"I told her to stop meddling. She will not choose my wife. I will."

"Oh! B-but she only thinks to save ye from hurt."

"I know," he snapped. Sighing, he flicked a hank of raven hair back over his shoulder and glanced around at their curious audience. "We need to talk, but not here."

Catching her hand, he started to lead her around behind the nearest tipi, probably guessing she wouldn't wish to go near the trees with him after last night. But he halted when Tsoia called his name and ran up. The bare-chested Indian spoke excitedly in Kiowa and gestured at a small group of young braves gathered near the flimsy corral, which was no more than rope strung between trees and bushes. Rose had seen two of the men ride in earlier from another village, evidently to continue celebrating the hunt.

"Haun-nay," Jack said firmly, meaning *no,* one Kiowa word Rose understood.

"Is there trouble?" she asked, touching his arm.

He smiled and patted her hand. "No, no trouble. There's going to be a horse race. Tsoia wants me to ride in it." Focusing on his friend, he repeated, *"Haun-nay,"* and shook his head.

Juana came to stand beside Rose while her husband argued, clearly trying to change Jack's mind. The group of braves also sauntered over, led by a young man who limped slightly on his right leg. He made a laughing comment that caused Juana to clasp Rose's hand.

"Wolf-who-limps asks if the old man is afraid to race him," she translated quietly.

Rose caught her breath, fearing Jack's reaction. To her surprise, he chuckled and spoke calmly.

Leaning close, Juana whispered, "Jack says he would be happy to race one so young if he had not lost his best horse."

Wolf-who-limps quickly retorted, jabbing his thumb toward the small horse herd enclosed by the corral. Before Juana could translate, Jack turned to Rose. "He asks why I don't race the big brown stallion."

"Brownie? Nay, ye can't. He won't let ye."

Jack frowned in thought. "He let me ride him to get you back here, but I think you're right. He probably won't let me on his back without you." Facing his challenger again, he shrugged and gave a brief reply.

Rose didn't need anyone to translate what Jack had said – or the mocking laugh and finger pointed at her by Wolf-who-limps. She stiffened in outrage and glared at Jack when he, too, laughed. Ready to castigate him, she held her tongue when he spoke to the fractious youth and gestured toward the horses.

Wolf-who-limps stared at him for a moment then puffed out his chest. Nodding, he swung on his heel and limped swiftly toward the corral, followed by his friends.

"What did ye say to him?" Rose blurted.

"I told him to see for himself that the stallion can't be ridden by anyone but you."

"He's going to try riding Brownie?"

"Yup." Jack winked and took hold of her elbow. "Come on. This should be interesting."

"But ye had no right! Brownie's mine," she protested. "That boy could be hurt, or he might do something to harm Brownie."

Jack cast her a sidelong glance. "Quit worrying, P'ayn-nah. The stallion can take care of himself and it won't hurt the kid much to be dumped on his backside."

By the time they reached the corral, Wolf-who-limps and one of the other young men had gotten a braided leather halter on Brownie. The horse stamped and blew but didn't seem truly angry as he was led from the enclosure. That changed the moment Wolf-who-limps vaulted onto his back. Brownie danced sideways, neighed shrilly and reared. To his credit, the Kiowa brave stuck to the stallion as if glued there.

Undeterred, Brownie tucked his head, stiffened his legs and bucked for all he was worth. Wolf-who-limps managed to hold on for several seconds but lost his seat when the horse twisted in mid-air, throwing the unwelcome weight from his back. The brave landed hard and lay where he'd fallen for a moment. Then he caught sight of the wrathful beast charging at him with teeth bared. Crying out, Brownie's would-be rider scrambled to his feet and ran, limping, for cover behind the other youths, who looked equally terrified.

Afraid for them and for Brownie if he injured one of them, Rose dashed forward. Jack yelled at her to stop but she ignored him. Waving her hands frantically, she cried, "Nay, Brownie, ye mustn't hurt them!"

He pounded to a halt inches away from her, blowing hard, the whites of his eyes showing how enraged he was. Crooning softly to him, Rose stepped close and stroked his neck.

"Be calm, my dear. I'll not let him near ye again."

The stallion tossed his head as if to shake off his anger. Then he nickered and nuzzled her shoulder, drawing awed whispers from the men, all except Wolf-who-limps. Hearing his disgruntled voice, Rose turned to face him. He'd pushed to the front of his cohorts and stood eyeing her and Brownie balefully.

"He says the horse is loco," Jack explained, coming to stand beside her. "And just because he lets you touch him does not prove you can ride him."

"Is that so?" Rose narrowed her eyes at the young Kiowa. "Boost me up, will ye?" she asked of Jack. Stepping to Brownie's side, she wrapped her hand in his mane.

"Wait. He's not saddled. You've never ridden him bareback."

"No matter. I'll only ride him around the village a bit." She cocked an eyebrow when Jack scowled at her without moving.

"All right," he said grudgingly, "but don't try anything faster than a trot."

"Aye, aye, sir!" She grinned and gave him a pert salute.

Muttering under his breath, he bent, cupped his hands for her foot and lifted her smoothly onto Brownie's broad back. It felt strange without a saddle, but remembering what Jack had taught her, she gripped the stallion's sides with her legs and signaled him to walk. He obeyed eagerly, carrying her past lodges, cook fires and gaping villagers. They circled the campground three times; then she brought him to a halt before the crowd of men and women who'd congregated to watch. Jack caught her by the waist as she slipped to the ground, steadying her. Her hands rested instinctively on his shoulders.

"That was wonderful! I didn't realize how much I've missed riding."

"Mmm, you looked wonderful too."

Surprised by his compliment, she stared into his caressing dark eyes, unmindful of anyone else until Wolf-who-limps distracted her. His guttural words dissolved the mesmerizing hold of Jack's gaze. He released Rose and pivoted to confront the brave.

"Haun-nay!" he barked, making a sharp scissor motion with his hands. He added more, sounding angry.

"What did he say?" Rose asked, fearing real trouble.

"It matters not," Jack snapped, eyes locked with the other man's black glare.

"Yes, it does. Tell me what he said," she insisted.

"He dares you to race him and the others," he ground out.

"Oh!" Fixing wide eyes on Wolf-who-limps, she met his taunting grin. It infuriated her.

"I told him no, you won't do it."

"What! Tis my decision, not yours, and I say I will race him."

"No, you won't. You've never raced in your life. It's too dangerous."

"I raced *you* once, don't ye remember?" she shot back. "And I beat ye."

"Shi . . . oot! That was only play, woman. These boys aren't playing. They've been racing horses since they were knee-high, and they'll do anything to win. You could be killed out there." He flung his arm wide, indicating the wild country beyond the village.

Rose gulped down a spurt of fear. Should she heed his warning? Glancing at Wolf-who-limps, she couldn't stomach letting the smirking brave think she was afraid to accept his challenge. She turned pleading eyes to Jack.

"Yesterday, I denied being afraid of ye, but that was a lie. I've been a coward, afraid not only of you, but of myself. For years, I feared my God-given gift, hiding it behind the convent walls, and since leaving there I've done nothing but run away. Until now I wouldn't have dreamed of riding in a horse race, but this mad adventure ye forced upon me has changed me. *You've* changed me, Jack. I'm tired of being afraid. I want, I need to do this. Ye mustn't try to stop me."

With that, she brushed past him to face Wolf-who-limps. "I'll race ye," she declared with a curt nod.

He grinned, taking her meaning.

* * *

Jack ground his teeth, wanting to drag Rose away and make her listen to reason. He hadn't exaggerated. She could get herself killed riding against a bunch of high-spirited Kiowa braves. Yet, he realized she was right. She needed to do this to prove to herself that she was no coward. Hoping it would free her from the ghosts of her past, he sighed in resignation. So be it, but he was going to set some ground rules or there'd be no race.

With a little convincing, Wolf-who-limps agreed to Jack's stipulations. The race would be between him and Rose alone, no others, and it would be run on a straight, fairly level course about a quarter mile out to a lone hackberry tree and back again. Once that was settled, Jack approached the bluecoats who were just now getting ready to leave, evidently having enjoyed themselves well into the night, with a flask or two of whiskey judging by their bloodshot eyes and hangdog looks.

Fortunately, their sergeant had been awake long enough to see Rose ride Brownie, and he was willing, even eager to officiate the race. He also agreed to post his men at intervals along the course to make sure Wolf-who-limps didn't pull any nasty tricks that might endanger Rose. Having done all he could to make the event safe for her, Jack saddled Brownie, checking to make sure the tack was in good shape. By then Rose had changed from her borrowed skirt and blouse into her riding duds.

"Are you sure about this?" Jack asked before helping her mount up. "It's not too late to change your mind."

"I'm sure. I'll be fine." She smiled and patted the stallion's neck. "Brownie will take care of me."

Skeptical about that, he pulled off his bandana and handed it to her. "Tie this around your head. It'll keep any hair from blowing in your eyes if it comes loose. You need to see where you're going."

"Thank you." Knotting the folded rag at the back of her head, over her braided hair, she smiled once more, blue eyes glittering with excitement. "Give me a boost now, please, and stop worrying."

"I'll stop worrying when the damn race is over," he growled, giving her a hand up.

"Such language! For shame, sir!" she scolded, laughing as if she didn't have a care in the world.

* * *

Rose was far less confident than she led Jack to believe. As she lined up Brownie next to Wolf-who-limps and his buckskin pony, her mouth went dry and her palms began to sweat. Furtively wiping them on her riding skirt, she cast a quick glance at her opponent and saw him jerk back on his rein, trying to contain his nervous mount. He'd shed his hide leggings and disposed of any saddle blanket he might ordinarily use, leaving nothing but his breechclout between him and the skittish horse. Like her, he'd wrapped a bandana across his forehead, but unlike her, he also carried a braided leather quirt. Rose frowned at the thought of him using it on his horse.

Turning her attention to the soldier who was to give the starting signal, she waited for him to fire his pistol. He held off until the Kiowa youth had his horse under control. Then he nodded, raised his arm and fired. The shot cracked, Wolf-who-limps gave a blood curdling yell, and his buckskin broke into an all out run. Rose was a second or two slower away from the starting line, but when she tapped Brownie's flanks with her heels, he lunged forward as if shot by a giant spring. She bent low over his neck and hung on for dear life as he pounded after the Indian pony, swiftly cutting the distance between them.

Within seconds she was riding abreast of her cocky challenger. She glanced across the small space separating them. Wolf-who-limps met her eyes, gave a taunting grin and lashed his horse with the quirt, causing the animal to spring into the lead again, if only for a short distance. Pitying his mount, Rose fixed her gaze ahead, senses focused on Brownie's powerful body moving fluidly beneath her, on the wind whipping his mane across her face, and on the ground flying by in a stream of green, gold and dusty red-brown. Now and then she spotted one of the uniformed sentinels stationed along the way but paid them little mind.

Through skill and the liberal use of his quirt, Wolf-who-limps stayed even with Rose all the way to the tree where they were to turn for home. But once they rounded the tree, Brownie stretched out his long legs, seeming to sail over the ground while the Kiowa's buckskin gradually began to drop back. Hearing Wolf-who-limps fire off a volley of furious words she thankfully didn't understand, Rose glanced behind her and saw him lash his poor horse unmercifully. She cringed at the sight. Couldn't he see such cruelty was pointless? Brownie was simply too fast. He flew across the finish line several yards ahead of the slower animal.

A roar went up from the crowd of watchers. Rose laughed exultantly as she drew rein. An instant later, Wolf-who-limps slammed his horse into Brownie, nearly unseating her. She cried out and grabbed her saddle horn as the stallion reared. He came down hard, front hooves striking the other horse and its rider. Both screamed in pain.

Fighting to stay in the saddle, Rose saw the Kiowa brave topple to the ground. He let out another scream when he landed, while the buckskin limped away, obviously injured. To Rose's great relief, Jack pushed through the crowd and caught hold of Brownie's halter, helping her bring the horse to a standstill. Shaking in reaction, she slipped from her saddle, straight into his arms. He crushed her against his chest and she clung to him, grateful for the feel of his arms around her and his big, hard frame next to hers.

"Are you all right?" he rasped.

"I'm fine. Only hold me a moment, aye?" Her voice trembled like the rest of her.

"I'm not letting you go, P'ayn-nah. Ever."

Breath catching in her throat, Rose raised her head and gazed into his warm, dark eyes. Slowly, he started to dip his head toward her. She parted her lips, waiting for his kiss. Then a loud voice called out urgently.

Jack straightened and stared past Rose's shoulder. "Tsoia?" he said impatiently, adding a few Kiowa words. Receiving a brief, insistent reply, he looked down at Rose and loosened his embrace.

"Wolf-who-limps is hurt. It's his bad leg. Tsoia thinks it broke. He asks if you will help the boy." Pausing, Jack shook his head. "You don't have to. After what he just did to you, no one will blame you for refusing to heal his leg."

Dearest Irish

Rose eased out of his arms, pivoted and trained her eyes on the young Kiowa writhing on the ground not far away. No one had gone near him, not his friends, not even Ghost Woman. The old medicine woman should have been the one to care for the injured brave, but she stood silently with the others, making no move to help him.

"Why doesn't someone go to him?" she asked, half turning to Jack.

He frowned. "The people will do nothing for him. You won the race fairly. He has brought shame upon himself by attacking you."

As much as she detested the hot-headed brave's vengeful assault on her and Brownie, and his brutal treatment of his own horse, when Rose beheld his agonized expression and the way he clutched at his twisted leg, she couldn't turn her back on him. "I'll see what I can do for him. Will ye look after his horse? I think the poor creature is hurt."

Nodding in assent, Jack went to see about the horse, while she crossed to Wolf-who-limps and knelt beside him. Wild-eyed with pain, he growled something through gritted teeth. If she was to help him, Rose needed his cooperation. She searched the circle of watching villagers and spotting Juana, motioned her over.

"I need ye to translate for me," she said as the other woman squatted next to her.

"You would help this shameful child who calls himself a man? After he tried to hurt you?"

Rose smiled at her friend's apt description of Wolf-who-limps. "Aye, I must. 'Tis my duty as a healer."

Juana frowned but nodded. "As you wish, I will translate."

Thanking her, Rose turned her attention to the injured brave. "Your leg is broken. If you'll let me, I may be able to mend it for ye." She waited while Juana repeated her statement in Kiowa, drawing a pained, distrustful glare from Wolf-who-limps. Juana added something more. At Rose's questioning glance, she explained.

"I told him you are a great medicine woman and he should allow you to repair his leg."

Rose didn't see herself as a *great* anything, but the Kiowa youth was plainly impressed. He eyed her with newfound respect and nodded his permission. With Juana translating again, Rose enlisted Tsoia, Blue Elk and one other man to hold her patient still while she straightened his leg so that she might attempt to heal the broken bones. Aligning them required her to twist and tug on his leg at the same time, no easy task. It was made more difficult by the fact that the leg had been broken before and hadn't set properly. Wolf-who-limps snarled in agony through the ordeal and screamed when the bones finally popped into place.

Letting him rest, Rose sat on her haunches, head down and breathing hard. After several moments, she felt strong enough to continue. With an encouraging smile for the sweating, unnaturally pale youth, she positioned herself carefully, chafed her hands together and laid them on his leg directly over the break. He grunted at her heated touch but didn't try to pull away. Blocking out the hushed crowd, she whispered the healer's prayer, calling forth her power. It flowed outward through her hands, finding and surrounding the injured bones. She exerted pressure, forcing them tightly together, encouraging them to knit.

Exactly how her gift worked, Rose couldn't say, but she always knew when it succeeded. That magical sensation burst upon her now. Hearing Wolf-who-limps cry out, she gasped and swayed on her knees, drained of energy. Juana caught her, slipping a supportive arm around her.

"Toppah, you are weak. You must rest."

"But the boy, he needs me," she mumbled in a daze.

"Others will care for him now that they know you forgive him. Come." Helping Rose to her feet, Juana started to lead her away, but Jack stepped into their path.

"I will take her to my mother's lodge," he said, clasping her arm.

"No, there are bad feelings between Toppah and Ghost Woman," Juana protested, refusing to let go of her. "She will now stay with Tsoia and me."

"I spoke to my mother. There will be no more bad feelings. And I will see that Toppah rests."

"No, I say! She will come with me. You are not her husband. You have no say in this."

Jack looked positively flummoxed, Rose thought, still feeling dazed.

"Many men will wish to claim her after today," Juana added.

"Some might try to steal her. She must be guarded well. Tsoia and I will do this."

"By damn, no man will claim her but me!" Jack roared loud enough for the entire camp to hear. "She's mine!"

Rose's jaw dropped. Abruptly alert, she stared at him. Had she heard him right, or were her ears playing tricks on her?

"You have already laid with her?" Juana demanded fiercely. At the same time she squeezed Rose's arm as if warning her to keep quiet.

"No! That's not what I meant." Scrubbing a hand down his face, Jack appeared as perplexed as Rose was feeling.

"Then you mean to take Toppah for your wife?" Juana prodded.

Jack's face went blank for a moment. Then his eyes turned to Rose, capturing her gaze. "Yeah, that's what I mean to do. If she'll have me," he said quietly.

Rose forgot to breathe. She'd vowed never to marry, certain she could never find love with any man, but she'd been wrong about that. Like a seed buried in frozen earth, love had begun to sprout in her heart the first day Jack had stepped into her life. That love was now a spring bud ready to open – or be crushed beneath the weight of her fears. Which would it be?

Choosing to risk everything for a chance to experience love in full flower, she took a deep breath and answered, "Aye, she'll have ye, Jack Lafarge."

Juana released her, and giving a glad cry, Rose flew into Jack's arms. He smothered her face with kisses, landing at last on her eager lips. His tongue plundered her open mouth, and she gloried in it, not the least bit afraid. They might have gone on like that if laughter and tittered remarks from their audience hadn't intruded.

Breaking off their kiss, Rose glanced around and felt a fiery blush sweep up her throat into her cheeks. Jack chuckled and gave her a squeeze. She looked up and watched him grin. It made him look younger and more handsome than ever. She would give him reason to smile often, she vowed.

A moment later, as the gathering broke up, Rose caught sight of Star-girl standing alone near her mother's tipi. Encountering her murderous glare, Rose allowed herself a small, victorious smile.

CHAPTER FOURTEEN

Rose let Juana lead her away, glancing back once to smile at Jack. Joyous as she was at the prospect of becoming his wife, she was still exhausted from healing Wolf-who-limps. She needed to rest before their marriage ceremony, set to take place later that very day, and Juana insisted she do so in her and Tsoia's lodge. Jack was not to see her again until the appointed hour.

"After you sleep, we will make you ready," Juana said while Rose settled on the fur bed she'd slept in on her first night in the village. "You must be clean and sweet-smelling for your husband tonight." Not seeing Rose blush at her reference to the night ahead, her friend knelt to rummage through a pile of belongings on the far side of the lodge. A moment later, she rose holding a white dress made of soft hide and elaborately beaded across the yoke and top of the sleeves.

"What a lovely dress," Rose said, reminded of the garment she'd watched Star-girl's mother laboring over.

"Yes. I wore it when I wed Tsoia. It was a gift from his mother. She is gone now, taken by a sickness two winters ago. I wish you to wear this for your wedding."

"Begorrah!" Rose blurted, pushing up on one elbow. "'Tis a very generous offer, Juana, but . . . are ye sure?"

"I am sure. Remember Jack and my husband are blood brothers. When you become Jack's wife, we will be sisters. As your sister, it pleases me to do this for you."

Rose swallowed hard. She could hardly refuse such a kindness. "Thank ye, Juana. I shall be honored to wear your beautiful dress and call you sister," she said thickly.

Her new sister smiled brightly and laid the dress aside for

later. "Sleep now. I will wake you later." With that, she ducked out, leaving Rose alone.

Amazingly, she was able to sleep despite being as nervous as a caged sparrow. When Juana woke her she felt more refreshed but was still a basket of nerves.

"It is time to make you ready. I brought water. Take off your clothes while I mix the yucca soap and . . . ." Juana gasped as she stepped to the bed she shared with Tsoia, where she'd laid out her wedding dress. She shrieked a torrent of angry Spanish.

"What's wrong?" Rose rushed to her in alarm. "Saints preserve us!" she cried in horror when she saw the dress. Someone had splashed red paint over the front of it.

"Did you hear someone enter while you rested?" Juana gritted, fists balled at her sides.

"Nay, but I swear I didn't do this."

"Of course you did not. There is only one who hates us both enough to do such evil."

Rose instantly knew who she meant. "Star-girl? B-but how did she get in here without ye seeing her? And how could she know about the dress?"

"I went to help the women prepare a feast for your wedding. She must have heard me tell them you were to wear my dress, and she came to destroy it. You are lucky she did not kill you in your sleep. She will pay for this!" Snatching up the ruined dress, Juana dashed out.

Rose ran after her, calling her name. The people they passed stopped what they were doing and stared after them. Juana ran straight to Star-girl's and her mother's tipi. The vengeful young woman stood just outside, arms crossed, wearing a gloating expression. It changed to fright, however, as Juana charged, flinging the dress in her face. She had time enough to screech; then she hit the ground with the enraged Mexican woman on top of her.

"When I'm done with you, *puta,* no man will want you!" Juana snarled, raking her nails down Star-girl's cheek, drawing a scream from her.

"Someone stop them!" Rose cried as the two women rolled in the dirt, kicking, biting, and trying to fend off one another's clawing hands.

Star-girl's mother, Walks Softly, ran up shrieking in Kiowa.

Thank God, Jack and Tsoia pushed through the crowd – gathering for the second time that day to watch. Tsoia grabbed his spitting, snarling wife and yanked her to her feet, while Jack did the same with the hysterically weeping Star-girl. Both women were covered with rusty red dirt.

"What the hell started this?" Jack demanded to know.

"Sh-she attack me! See my face!" Star-girl wailed, fingering the bloody tracks marking her cheek.

"Bruja! I should kill you for what you did," Juana shouted, fighting her husband's grip. Switching to Kiowa, she pointed at the red streaked dress lying crumpled on the ground, obviously reporting what Star-girl had done. This resulted in angry rumbles from the villagers.

Walks Softly uttered a strangled cry and stared at her daughter, an appalled expression on her weathered face. She shook her head and said something that made Star-girl look away. Turning her back, the older woman approached Juana and spoke in a hushed tone, apologizing for her offspring's despicable deed, Rose gathered. Juana nodded stiffly. Then Walks Softly turned to Rose, eyes downcast, and said something that drew a furious shriek from Star-girl. Without so much as glancing her way, her mother turned and entered their tipi.

"What did she say?" Rose asked, looking to Jack.

He released Star-girl's arms and wiped his dirt coated hands on his leggings. "Walks Softly said because her shameful child ruined the dress you were to wear for our wedding, you will instead wear the dress she made for that one." He jerked his thumb toward Star-girl, who had moved off a few steps and now stood glaring daggers first at him, then at Rose.

"Oh! But . . . but I don't wish to –"

"She has been shamed before the people. She does this to save face. You must not turn her down," Jack warned.

Before Rose had a chance to reply, Walks Softly emerged from her tipi carrying the pale fawn dress. She walked to Rose and extended the garment, speaking in a subdued voice.

"She says the beading isn't quite finished, but she hopes you will accept her poor gift to replace that which was destroyed."

Rose smiled tentatively and nodded. "Thank you," she murmured as Walks Softly laid the garment in her arms. Knowing it had been created out of a mother's love for the daughter who now caused her shame, she wanted to weep for the poor woman.

Star-girl chose that moment to erupt in broken English. "Take dress! Star-girl hate it! Hate all you!" She pointed at her mother, Juana and Jack, and spat in Rose's direction, missing by a good bit. Then she ran toward the corral. Moments later she could be heard galloping away.

With the troublemaker gone, everyone seemed to breathe a sigh of relief, except for Walks Softly, who retired to her lodge. Rose felt sorry for her, but her emotions were in such turmoil over her approaching marriage that she could think of nothing else as Juana helped her bathe and dress. She tried to express her regret over the loss of her friend's treasured dress, but Juana would have none of it.

"Do not think of it. This is a happy day for you. You must smile and laugh, not be sad."

Taking her advice, Rose pasted a smile on her lips a short while later as Juana and Tsoia, acting as her family, walked her to the communal circle where Jack waited. In honor of the occasion, he'd donned a fresh blue shirt and the denim britches he'd worn during their journey from Texas. With his copper skin and long raven hair, he was a blend of his white and native ancestors. To Rose, he was the most handsome man she had ever laid eyes on.

His gaze swept over her, making her heart race. Did she please him this way, in the lovely Indian dress, with her hair loose around her shoulders? She hoped so. When she reached his side, he caught her hand, giving it a reassuring squeeze.

The wedding ceremony took only a few moments. Wise Hawk, the elderly storyteller who, it turned out, was also a minor chief, presided. Juana stood nearby, quietly translating his words for Rose. He asked Jack if he would provide food for their lodge and protect her and any children to come. Jack vowed that he would. Then the old man asked Rose if she would make their lodge a happy one. She promised she would do her best. That was that. They were now married in Kiowa eyes.

In white society, in her family's eyes and the eyes of the church she'd been raised in and had nearly given her life to, she and Jack would be living in sin. So be it. She didn't care.

Ghost Woman had kept her distance since Jack had

reproached her that morning. Now she stepped from the circle of observers, leaning on her walking stick, and faced Jack. "You have chosen your mate, my son. I am happy for you," she said with great dignity.

"Thank you, Khaw," he replied in like manner.

Nodding, the old woman addressed Rose. "Welcome, Daughter." With a smile, she extended her arm invitingly.

Tears welled in Rose's eyes. Unable to speak, she stepped into her mother-in-law's one-armed embrace, careful not to bump her walking stick and unbalance her. Feeling how thin and frail Ghost Woman was, and knowing the demon still gnawed at her vitals, Rose feared for her. Unless she could yet drive out the monster with her healer's touch, Jack's mother had little time left. They held each other tight for several seconds. When they parted, Ghost Woman cleared her throat.

"I moved my robes to Walks Softly's lodge. She needs me now, and you will wish to be alone tonight," she said to them both.

Rose glanced at Jack in surprise. She had not expected Ghost Woman to relinquish her lodge for them, and while the act of consummating their marriage hung heavy on her mind, she also had not considered the problem of privacy. Apparently Jack had, judging by his relieved expression.

"You are kind to do this, Khaw. We thank you," he said more warmly than before.

His mother nodded and went to help with final preparations for the feast. Several other villagers approached to offer their good wishes. Rose was delighted when Wolf-who-limps strode toward them no longer limping.

Elated over this miraculous recovery, he babbled a spate of excited Kiowa words.

"He wishes us good fortune and many strong sons," Jack said, "and he thanks you for making his leg straight, Medicine Woman."

Rose lifted her eyebrows. "Tell him I'm glad my medicine worked. I thank him for his good wishes and I hope to have strong sons *and* daughters who will ride like the wind."

Jack chuckled and passed on her words, causing Wolf-who-limps to frown, but he quickly appreciated her sly reference to their race. Grinning, he nodded, delivered a parting shot and trotted off to join his friends.

"He say's he is now Wolf-who-runs-swiftly," Jack told Rose with a rakish wink.

* * *

Night had fallen. The celebration continued, but Jack led Rose away, wanting only to be alone with his bride. She was quiet as he escorted her to his mother's lodge, now their lodge. He held the flap aside and she entered ahead of him. Once inside, he knew a moment of uncertainty, watching her stand there hugging herself with her back toward him.

Stepping close, he laid his hands lightly on her shoulders. "P'ayn-nah, don't be afraid. I promised I would never hurt you. If you're not ready, we don't have to –"

She swung around and pressed her hand to his lips. "Please, don't say anymore. I don't want to hear it." She drew a ragged breath. "I want ye to make love to me, Jack. I need to know what it's like with you."

He stared at her, guessing what she didn't say, that she needed him to show her it would be different between them than with the bastard who'd raped her. Because he was dead certain someone had, probably her father.

"Are you sure?"

"Aye, I'm very sure." Lowering her eyes, she grasped her cross. "But perhaps ye think me too forward for saying so."

"Uh-uh. I think you're sweet as honey, P'ayn-nah. I think you're kinder than anyone I've ever met, and more beautiful than a summer sunset. I want you so much it nearly kills me to be near you and not touch you."

She gave him a trembling smile and blinked fast to hold back the tears pooling in her eyes. One escaped to trail down her cheek. Closing the small distance between them, Jack kissed away the lone tear.

"Don't cry, little love," he murmured, nuzzling her ear. "You are mine and I am yours. Nothing else matters." Kissing his way to her mouth, he slipped his arms around her, pressing her close. She parted her lips, inviting him in while her hands climbed upward to his shoulders.

"Ah, P'ayn-nah, I love the feel of you."

"And I you, *a muirnín.*"

Jack drew back slightly. "What did you say?"

"I called ye my sweetheart."

"Did you now?" he drawled. "Say it again."

"A *muirnín.*" Her breath fluttered at his throat. She kissed him there, setting off charges that rippled outward from the spot she touched.

He ran his hands over her slender back and repeated her strange words next to her ear.

She giggled. "Ye just called me a scallop."

"A what?"

"A scallop. 'Tis a small shellfish."

He shook his head, mouth twitching. "Guess I'll stick to calling you P'ayn-nah, sugar."

"Aye, that'll do. I've come to like it."

"I've come to like *you.* A whole lot." He sealed her lips with his, kissing her long and deep. When she began to moan softly, he broke off and whispered, "I want to see you and touch you all over. Will you take off that pretty dress for me?"

Rose caught her breath and threw her head back to stare at him. This was it, her final chance to say no before matters went too far. But she'd made her choice and taken Jack as her husband before the whole village. She couldn't back out now. She didn't want to.

Managing a wobbly smile, she eased out of his arms and slowly began to loosen the leather laces that held the dress in place, first at one shoulder then at the other. She wore nothing beneath it, as Juana had instructed. Taking a shaky breath, she let the garment fall away. Jack blinked once and swallowed, Adam's apple bobbing, while his obsidian gaze travelled over her like invisible fingers. Her heart galloped in her chest. She shivered, feeling defenseless and terrified. Unable to watch the fire burning in his eyes, she stared into the shadows behind him.

"Don't be afraid," Jack said quietly, closing the space that separated them. "Look at me, Rose," he directed, surprising her with his use of her white name, and reluctantly she obeyed.

"You are my wife. I gave my word to protect you . . . even from myself. I will never raise a hand to you in anger or force myself upon you. I wish only to bring you pleasure." His hands lightly stroked her arms, making her shiver again. "Do you believe me?"

She nodded hesitantly. "I believe ye, Jack," she said, "but

there's fear in my heart, and I can't drive it out."

His brows knitted for a moment but then a determined expression replaced the frown. "We will drive it out together, P'ayn-nah." Bringing her against him, he kissed her gently while his arms encircled her. His shirt grazed her sensitive nipples, causing them to stiffen. His hands, meanwhile, glided up and down her back. It felt surprisingly pleasant. Distracted by these new sensations, she kissed him back and twined her arms about him, but when one large hand moved lower to explore her bottom, she jumped.

"Easy, it's okay for me to touch you there, and everywhere. I'm not hurting you, am I?'

"N-nay. It only . . . surprised me."

He laughed softly and kissed the tip of her nose. "You're in for a lot of surprises this night, little love. Nice ones, I hope."

His kisses delved deeper, driving out thought and urging her response. One roving hand found its way to her breasts, shooting lightning through her veins. Cupping and molding the soft flesh, teasing the points until she could hardly stand anymore, he awakened a hunger deep inside that drove her to boldness.

"Take off your shirt. I want to feel ye against me," she breathlessly pleaded.

"Yes ma'am!" Releasing her, he tore his shirt off and undid the top button of his britches. Hearing the panicky sound she couldn't contain, he stopped. "Too soon for that, I guess," he said in a thick voice. "That's okay. We'll take things slow. Come here."

She gasped as he pressed her to his naked, muscular chest. Her aroused nipples burrowed into his skin, drawing a groan from him as he reclaimed her mouth. His hands roamed at will, always gentle, never hurried, teaching her that a man's touch could bring delight instead of pain. When he scooped her up and carried her to the bed they would share, she offered no protest. Lowering her upon a buffalo robe that both tickled and soothed, he stood over her, eyes hooded and unreadable as he gazed at her.

"I must step out of these, P'ayn-nah," he warned, tapping his britches. "If you want to close your eyes, it's all right."

"Nay, I wish to see ye just as you're seeing me." She only prayed her courage would hold up. She didn't want to see the approval in Jack's eyes turn to disappointment and anger.

He removed his moccasins and, without rushing, finished

opening the closure of his britches. When he pushed them down and stepped out of them, Rose drew a sharp breath. His hips were lean, his legs long and powerfully muscled, but it was the male member standing proud amid a thatch of springy dark hair that riveted her gaze. It was big, bigger than she expected. How could he possibly fit inside her? Licking suddenly dry lips, she turned her face away.

"P'ayn-nah, I know you are still afraid, but I will make this good for you, I promise." He knelt beside her and ran his hand lightly over her, reminding her how much she liked his touch.

Rose brought her gaze back to him. "I want to believe ye, I do. 'Tis just that you're . . . a bit large. I-I fear you'll tear me apart," she choked out.

His mouth crooked up and his dark eyes sparkled in the firelight. "I guess maybe I could take that as a compliment, but you don't need to worry. We'll fit together just fine, you'll see."

With that, he bent to kiss her. His hands resumed their roaming and before long she was sighing with pleasure. When he gently nudged her legs apart she tensed, expecting him to mount her then and there, but he didn't. Instead, he petted and played, exploring her intimately in a way she'd been completely unprepared for. The sensations he evoked shot through her, causing her to writhe uncontrollably. She slapped a hand against her mouth and bit down on her knuckle to keep from screaming, not in pain but in excruciating delight.

Jack was lying beside her now, with one arm holding her close while the other worked his devilish magic. His mouth slid down her throat, kissing, tasting, moving lower until he reached the summit of her breast. Taking it between his lips, he drew upon it just hard enough to send an electric jolt to her woman's parts. That coupled with what his hand was doing made her insides convulse. She cried out, bursting with pleasure she'd never dreamed existed and floated away on a river of pure bliss.

She was barely aware of Jack shifting to lie between her legs. His lips returned to hers, his tongue diving between her teeth. She didn't think she was capable of responding to him, so meltingly weak was she, but she soon learned otherwise. At her husband's coaxing, her arms rose to hold him. Feeling hard muscles ripple along his back as he leaned above her on his elbows, she gloried in his masculine strength.

His hungry mouth, questing hands, and the pressure of his shaft against her moist, sensitive opening played havoc with her senses. In a short time she was moaning and twisting beneath him, eager to experience the bliss he'd given her before. It didn't even enter her head to resist when he adjusted his position and began to push into her.

"Does it hurt?" he asked, pausing.

"Nay, not a'tall." He'd told her there would be no pain and it was true. All she felt was fullness and an arousing friction when he delved deeper, burying his formidable length within her. Fear was a thing of the past as he began to move slowly in and out, setting off fiery charges that echoed throughout her body.

Jack locked his teeth, struggling to go slow, to be as gentle as possible. It was torture. He longed to pump into her hard and fast, but forced himself to hold back. He hadn't overcome her fear just to ruin it now by treating her roughly – like the animal who'd stolen her virginity.

Blocking out angry thoughts, he concentrated on bringing them both to the peak of pleasure their bodies craved. When it finally came, Rose screamed into his mouth and, with a growl of victory, he erupted inside her. Once the fiery flood receded, he collapsed upon her, drawing air like a bellows and heart pounding. He buried his face against her throat, drinking in her moist woman's scent. She held him, uncomplaining beneath his weight, though he knew he was too heavy for her slight frame.

As soon as he could force himself to move, he withdrew from her and rolled onto his back, tucking Rose against his side. She laid her head on his shoulder and gave a hum of contentment that made him smile. He was half asleep moments later when she spoke.

"I never knew it could be so wondrous. And ye were right, there was no pain."

"That's good," he said drowsily.

"But d'ye not hate me now?"

That brought him wide awake. "Why should I hate you?"

"Because now ye know I was no virgin. I should have told ye before, when ye asked me to be your wife, but I couldn't. I'm a coward."

Heart going out to her, Jack kissed her forehead. "A coward would not dare to race a Kiowa brave the way you did. And I already knew you had lain with a man – against your will."

She rose up on one elbow and stared down at him with wide blue agate eyes. "How could ye know that? I never told ye."

"Your fear of loving told me long ago, P'ayn-nah." Finding her maiden's barrier gone had only confirmed the fact. He laced his fingers through the strands of her hair, glowing red-gold in the firelight. "The fault is not yours. It belongs to the one who forced you."

"But doesn't it disgust ye to know I'm . . . *used goods?*"

"No! You are not," he said sternly, making her jump. He'd heard white men apply the ugly term to women they regarded as soiled. Where Rose had heard it, he didn't know and didn't care. "I do not think of you that way, and you are not to think such things either."

"Aye, husband," she whispered, bowing her head.

He drew her down into his arms again. "I'm sorry for barking at you. The one I wish to kill is he who hurt you."

"'Vengeance is mine; I will repay, sayith the Lord,'" Rose quoted. "And He's already taken vengeance for me." Her voice held a fierce note Jack had never heard from her before.

"What do you mean?"

"I mean the filthy fiend is dead."

"But I thought –" He stopped, unwilling to admit he'd believed the *fiend* to be her own father, who was still alive, he recalled her saying. "P'ayn-nah, tell me how it happened. Please."

She stayed silent for a long moment, making him wonder if she would refuse his request. Finally, she began to speak. "'Twas raining that day, the day after I departed the convent. The place was located a fair distance outside Chicago, so I'd stopped for the night with a farmer and his wife who were kind enough to take me in. Gray clouds filled the sky in the morning, and the woman tried to convince me to stay with them until it cleared. I should have stayed, but I didn't wish to impose on them any longer.

"Well, as ye might guess, I'd only walked a mile or two when it began to rain, not too hard at first but steady. Before long, I was soaked to the skin and shivering, for this was in September and a cold spell had blown in. My shoes were soon caked with mud, my hair dripping in my face. Knowing I couldn't go on like that, I was about to trudge back and beg the farmer and his wife to take me in again . . . when a horse and buggy happened along.

"The driver pulled up and called out, asking if I wanted a ride into the city. I said no, fearing to trust a strange man, but he claimed he just hated to see a woman walking the road in such weather. He seemed a descent sort, smiling and swearing he intended me no harm." Drawing a wavering breath, Rose continued, "Right then the clouds burst open. Feeling like I was about to drown, I gave in and climbed into the buggy."

"And then he forced you to . . .?"

"Nay, he was kindness itself at first, covering me with a warm lap robe and shielding us from the rain with his slicker. We talked a bit as he drove the poor horse onward through the downpour. He told me he was returning from a visit with country kin, and he asked where I was bound. I told him and he said he'd be glad to deliver me to my father's house. All seemed fine until we reached the city. By then the storm had passed by, the sky was clear and I felt grateful to Emil – that was his name – for bringing me home, almost. When he said he needed to stop and let his wife know he was back before driving me to Da's, I couldn't very well object.

"He lived in the gatehouse of a large estate on Chicago's north side. The whole place had been rebuilt after burning to the ground in the Great Fire. D'ye know about the fire?"

"Mmm. Your brother's mentioned it a time or two."

"Ah. Well, anyway, Emil was the head gardener for the estate. 'Tis why he had that little house to himself . . . and his missus, so he said. When we arrived there, he invited me in to meet her, and idjit that I am, I followed him like a lamb to the slaughter. The moment he got me inside, he hit me over the head with something. There was a blinding pain; then everything went black.

"When I came to, I found myself without a stitch of clothes and tied to his bed with a gag in my mouth. Don't ask me what he did to me. I can't speak of it, ever."

Jack squeezed his eyes shut and hugged her tight, wishing he could turn back time and prevent all of it from happening. Barring that, he sincerely wished he could stake the bastard out naked in the desert and let the animals take care of him.

"Later, I pleaded with him to untie me so I might relieve myself, saying it was either that or wet the bed. He cussed a bit but finally cut me loose. Why he didn't simply let me use a chamber pot,

I don't know. Perhaps he thought it untidy. For whatever reason, he ordered me to dress, no doubt fearing some other worker on the estate might see him with a naked woman, and he led me out to the privy. I took my time in there, wondering what to do, praying for a chance to escape. It came when I stepped out. He was angry with me for dallying and started to drag me back into his house, where he was going to *punish* me, he said."

Rose laughed bitterly. "As it turned out, he was the one punished. Ye see, as we rounded the corner of the building a man called out to him. We'd been spotted, and I suspect the man was his employer, for he was well dressed. When the fellow started toward us, Emil panicked. He snarled at me to get in the house. I refused. He lost his head and slapped me. The other man shouted for him to stop. Distracted, he let his hold on me slip and I took off running just as fast as my feet would carry me."

Pausing for a moment, she seemed caught in the memory. Jack nudged her gently. "Then what happened?"

"He ran after me. I'll never know why. He could have just let me go."

"Maybe he was afraid you'd go to the law and he'd be arrested."

"Aye, perhaps, but I wouldn't have. I was too ashamed. Whatever drove him to it, he chased me down the street. I kept ahead of him, but he was catching up. When I reached the cross street, I was so terrified, I didn't even slow down, though 'twas a busy thoroughfare. I made it safely across, but Emil wasn't so lucky. He ran into the path of a dray hauling a load of lumber. I heard him scream and turned to look. 'Twasn't a pretty sight, watching the draft horses stomp him to the ground, but I confess I felt no pity for him."

Rose bent her head back to meet Jack's gaze. "Does that make me an evil person?"

"No. He was no good. He died too quick. I would have made him suffer for days." He cupped the back of her head and resettled her against him. Stroking her velvety back, he asked, "What did you do then?"

She shrugged one shoulder. "I found my way home to Da. He was shocked to see me, especially looking dirty and bedraggled. I blamed that on the rain storm and a long walk from the convent. He allowed me to stay, though old wounds lay between us. I feared I might carry a child as a result of what happened, but thank the saints, that didn't come to pass."

Rubbing her cheek on his chest, she murmured, "Now ye know the whole sordid tale. If ye no longer want me, I'll understand."

"Don't talk foolishness. Nothing will make me stop wanting you. You are my woman. No other man will ever touch you again." Sealing his vow with a hungry kiss, he set to work showing her he meant what he said.

After they lay spent and drowsy once more, it crossed Jack's mind that this was the time to reveal everything about his past to Rose, as she had done for him. It was his last thought before falling asleep.

CHAPTER FIFTEEN

Star-girl rode through the night with vengeance in her heart. She would make that Mexican whore, Juana, pay for humiliating her in front of the whole village. But first she intended to get rid of the white woman who had stolen Jack. Once she was out of the way, Star-girl would console him. After he begged her forgiveness, that is.

In order to carry out her plans she needed help, and she knew exactly who to enlist as her partner. She'd overheard Jack tell Tsoia about the Choctaw whiskey runner who'd been captured by the bluecoats. He'd said there was bad blood between them from long ago, when they fought together in the white man's war. Star-girl would find a way to free the Choctaw. Naturally he would be grateful. Convincing him to help her shouldn't be difficult.

She arrived at Fort Sill sometime after midnight. The moon was a quarter full, providing only weak light, perfect for her purposes. Tying her horse to a small mesquite tree, she made her way onto the grounds of the fort. She knew where the guard house stood, having seen it many times on allotment days, when the government agent handed out meager rations to reservation Indians. Keeping to the deep shadows, she slipped from one building to another, cautiously watching for any soldier who might not be in his bed where he should be at this time of night.

At one point she tripped over a rock and nearly fell. It gave her an idea. Stooping, she picked up the fist-sized rock, thinking it would make a good weapon, and a quiet one.

Nearing the guard house, she spotted a lone sentry on the wide porch that ran along the main floor of the prison, several feet above ground. He walked casually back and forth, rifle cradled in the bend of his elbow, silhouetted by pale yellow light from narrow

Dearest Irish

windows on either side of the closed door. Crouching behind a horse trough, Star-girl observed the man for several minutes, waiting for an opportunity to sneak up on him. She considered sticking her knife in his back, but he might scream. Better to knock him out with the rock.

She watched impatiently, wondering if the stupid bluecoat would ever turn away long enough for her to carry out her plan. Finally, he halted at one end of the porch. Standing his gun against the wall, he fiddled with the front of his pants, making ready to piss, Star-girl realized. This was her chance!

Dashing from her hiding place, she crept soundlessly up the steps to the porch and approached the unknowing soldier from behind. He was doing up his buttons when she struck his head with her rock as hard as she could. He folded like the corn husk dolls her mother had made for her when she was a child, collapsing with a thud at her feet.

She tossed her weapon aside, stooped and searched the man's uniform for keys to the prison cells. He didn't have them. Muttering to herself, she hurried to the door, opened it a crack and peeked in. The room was empty and silent. Stepping inside, she spied a ring of keys hanging from a nail on the wall. Fearing the soldier might regain consciousness before she had time to free the whiskey runner and escape, she grabbed the keys and padded down dark, narrow stairs to where the jail cells were located.

"Choctaw, where you are?" she called in English, not knowing the Choctaw language. A moment passed; then she heard a shuffling of feet from a cell to her right.

"Nahotabi is here," a deep voice answered. "Who asks for me?"

"I am Star-girl. I come to free you." Moving carefully in the dark, she crossed to his cell door and tried several keys before one fit the lock. She turned it with some difficulty, opened the door and the foul smelling Indian stepped out, nearly knocking her over in his haste.

"Ayyee! Be careful, you stinking fool!" she flared in her own tongue. He didn't understand her words, a good thing, she supposed. She didn't want to anger him. She needed him, for now.

"Sorry."

"Come. We must hurry." She led the way up the stairs.

"Why you do this? Why free Nahotabi?"

"I tell after we get away from fort."

He didn't argue. Once outside, he saw the bluecoat lying on the porch and strode over to him, crouching beside the still body.

"What you doing?" Star-girl impatiently demanded.

"I take guns." Within seconds, he rejoined her with the soldier's pistol tucked under his belt and carrying his rifle. "Also need horse," he said as they descended the stairs. Not consulting her, he veered toward the stone corral, keeping to the shadows as she had done earlier. "You have horse?"

"Yes. Outside fort." Disgusted because she hadn't thought to bring a horse for him, she trotted along at his heels. Once at the corral, he quietly cut out an animal, leading it as they made their way past the soldiers' parade ground, toward the outer edge of the compound. They'd almost made it when a voice called out.

"Who goes there?" the soldier shouted.

"We must ride!" Nahotabi cried, flinging himself on the horse's back. "Up!" he ordered, extending his arm to Star-girl. She grasped it and he hoisted her up behind him, kicking the horse into a run as she threw her arms around him.

"Hey, stop!" A shot rang out, but the bluecoat's bullet went wide.

"My horse over there," Star-girl told the Choctaw, pointing off to the left. They located her mare and she slipped from Nahotabi's horse, glad to put space between them. He smelled like a skunk!

"Hurry!" he barked. "We cannot stay here."

"I know," she snapped. Grabbing a handful of mane, she jumped and swung her leg over the mare's back. "Let's go. We have long ride."

The Choctaw followed her lead without complaint for a while, but once they'd ridden a safe distance from the fort, he caught her horse's long single rein and pulled her to a halt. She protested, but he paid no attention. "Now you tell why you free Nahotabi. I not know you. Never see you before. What you want with me?" he questioned suspiciously.

"I want you to steal woman," she said bluntly, yanking her rein from his hand.

He gave a startled laugh. "You want woman? You no like

men?"

"No!" she shouted, highly insulted. "I want you steal Jack Lafarge's woman."

"Lafarge's woman? The yellow hair I see with him?"

"Yes, that one."

"Why you ask me do this?" He sounded suspicious again.

"What you care? You no like Jack, this I know. If you steal woman, you hurt him."

He said nothing, but she caught the movement of his hand as he scratched his chin, considering her words.

"You not want to try his woman? She is pretty, for white woman," she added, hoping to tempt him, although she couldn't help sneering the last few words.

"Ha! Now I know why you ask me do this thing." The Choctaw laughed again. "You want Yellow Jack. You want pretty white woman gone."

"Yes!" Star-girl shot back. "She steals him from me."

Nahotabi grunted. "And what I do with yellow hair after?"

She kneed her mare closer. "You kill her," she hissed, poking his arm between each word for emphasis.

He caught her hand and laughed again. "Maybe I steal you instead, little Kiowa."

Whipping out her knife with her free hand, she leaned in and held it to his throat. "You try, Choctaw, and I cut you bad, leave you for vultures."

He instantly released her. Kicking his horse away from hers, he raised his hands in surrender. "No worry. You too mean and skinny. I no want you."

"You too dirty!" she shot back. "Now tell, you steal woman or no steal?"

"Maybe. First you say how I do this. I no want get caught. Bluecoats hang Nahotabi for stealing white woman."

"You no get caught. I tell Kiowa I see wild horses. Men go chase them, Jack go too. While they gone, you come take yellow hair. Ride fast away." It was a simple plan. Star-girl saw no way it could go wrong.

The Choctaw grunted again. "This good plan. You skinny but pretty smart. I do it."

She sighed in relief. "Good. Now we go. Still long ride to

Kiowa camp." Leading out once more, Star-girl eagerly anticipated seeing the last of her yellow-haired enemy.

* * *

Morning dawned on a new world for Rose. The sky seemed bluer, the rising sun brighter, the air sweeter. She gazed over the broad, sweeping prairie and thought it the most beautiful sight she'd ever seen. When she turned to her husband as he stepped from their lodge, she also thought him the most handsome man and herself the luckiest woman on the face of the earth.

"Morning, P'ayn-nah," he said, teeth flashing as he walked up to her. "You're up early."

"I couldn't sleep any longer."

"You should have waked me. I would've made you sleepy again." Slipping an arm around her, he bent and nibbled a spot below her ear. It tickled, causing her to giggle and lift her shoulder, trying to block his access to that sensitive area.

"I wanted to greet the day, and a glorious one it is. Everything looks so fresh and new."

Jack lifted his head and followed her gaze, looking over the vast landscape. "Spring is here. For the land and for us." He turned her and kissed her tenderly, melting her insides. When at last he lifted his lips from hers, she clung to him, wanting more of the same.

"You've given me the greatest gift a man could want," he murmured, framing her face between his hands. "I hope I can make you as happy as I am right now."

She had to speak past a sudden lump in her throat. "I am happy, Jack. You freed me from the past last night and showed me how to be a woman. I lo –"

Before she could declare her love for him, little Tsahle-ee raced up. He gushed something in Kiowa to Jack and grinned precociously at her.

Jack burst out laughing. "Tsahle-ee asks if we made a friend for him to play with last night."

"What!" Rose drew away from him, feeling her cheeks burn. She'd never known a child, an adult for that matter, to ask such a frank question. Flustered, she pressed a hand to her midriff, suddenly realizing she might already carry Jack's baby.

He replied to the boy in a jocular tone, bent over and tickled his bare stomach. Tsahle-ee gave a high-pitched squeal, turned and ran off.

"What did ye say to him?" Rose asked.

"I told him I hope we did make a baby. But just to be sure, we'll keep working at it 'til we do."

Her mouth fell open in shock. "Jack, he's a child! You've no business saying such a thing to him. He shouldn't even know how babies are made at his age."

Cocking a raven brow, he pulled her into a loose embrace. "P'ayn-nah, as you have seen, Kiowa children sleep near their folks. By Tsahle-ee's age they all know how babies are made."

Her face grew hot all over again. "Oh. I . . . I wasn't thinking." She dipped her head, too embarrassed to meet his gaze. "Ye must think me a perfect fool."

His finger lifted her chin, gently prodding her to look at him. "Perfect, yes. A fool, never." He kissed her, lightly this time, and said, "I'm starving. Come on, let's get something to eat." Catching her hand, he tugged her toward the main camp where cook fires blazed.

Their breakfast was accompanied by amused looks and teasing comments that gradually overcame Rose's embarrassment, allowing her to smile and laugh along with the good-natured tormentors. Even Ghost Woman seemed genuinely happy for Jack and her, having truly accepted their marriage. However, Rose didn't miss the occasional grim set of the old woman's lips and the fact that she wasn't eating much. The pain of her illness was obviously worsening, a realization that marred the beautiful morning.

Star-girl was nowhere to be seen, for which Rose was grateful, but her mother was also absent. Concerned about her, Rose knelt beside Jack's mother and asked how Walks Softly was doing.

"She stays in her lodge," Ghost Woman said. "She is ashamed to face the people after her daughter's disgrace."

"Poor woman! Ought I to take her a bit of food?"

"I took her some before, but she ate little. She worries because Star-girl has not come back. I told her the foolish child will return when she is ready, but Walks Softly still fears for her daughter."

For her mother's sake, Rose hoped Star-girl would return,

although she'd personally be glad never to see the little witch again.

Jack had been talking with Tsoia and another man over near the corral, taking some joshing, Rose gathered from their laughter and playful nudges. Now he came and squatted next to Rose. "I'm going to ride to the fort and telegraph your brother," he said. "He and your sister need to know you're safe."

"Will ye tell them we're wed?"

His dark eyes probed hers. "Do you want me to?"

"Aye, of course I do." She bit her lip. "Only I . . . I fear what Tye will do."

He squeezed her hand. "He cares for you. He would never hurt you, of this I am sure."

"'Tisn't myself I'm worried about. 'Tis you."

Jack kissed her brow. "I will make peace with him, I promise. When I return we'll talk more and make plans. Until then, do not worry, little love." With that he rose and strode back to the corral. Sending her a reassuring smile moments later, he rode off on his errand.

Rose watched him until he disappeared from view, wondering what kind of plans he had in mind. Would they remain here with his mother's people? Or would he wish to move on? He'd wandered between two worlds, white and Indian, for years. Did he have it in him to settle in one place with her and the children she hoped they'd create?

Her thoughts were interrupted by the pounding of a horse's hooves. Glancing toward the sound, opposite the direction Jack had taken, she saw Star-girl gallop into the village. Stiffening at the sight of her, Rose wondered what new deviltry she might attempt.

* * *

Star-girl threw herself off her winded pony, knowing all eyes were upon her, exactly as she intended. She caught Juana's angry glare and Toppah's cold blue gaze, but ignored them both. Picking out the braves scattered among the watchers, she directed her words to them.

"I have seen wild horses!" she cried in her native tongue.

The men drew closer, excitement written on their faces. "Where?" one asked.

"To the north, beyond Rainy Mountain. They are fat and sleek."

An eager buzz went up among the gathering. It had been many moons since the people had chased a wild horse band, and they were in need of new, young stock. Several of the ponies the bluecoats had allowed them to keep out of their once mighty herd were aged and slow. The braves reacted quickly, making ready to go after the non-existent wild herd, just as Star-girl had expected. However, White Eagle – Jack – was not among them.

Alarmed, she approached She-who-laughs. "Where is White Eagle?" she questioned, knowing the timid maiden would not dare refuse to answer.

"He rode away, toward the soldier fort."

"No!" Star-girl blurted. If White Eagle went to the fort, he would hear of Nahotabi's escape and of the girl who helped him. *He might guess it was me!* The thought sent a wave of fear rushing through her. He would kill her if he learned she'd put the renegade Choctaw up to stealing Toppah and killing her.

"Is that a bad thing?" She-who-laughs innocently asked.

Star-girl opened her mouth to berate the stupid girl, but just then her mother appeared, touching her arm and smiling.

"Ghost Woman told me you had returned. I was afraid for you, my daughter," she said in a tearful voice. "You should not have stayed away all night."

"I had to get away," Star-girl replied curtly, vexed with having to explain herself now, when she needed to think, to decide what to do.

"Where have you been all this time?" her mother persisted.

"Riding. Do not nag at me," she snapped.

Walks Softly flinched. "I'm sorry. I did not mean to nag, but I was worried about you."

"Well, I'm back so stop worrying." Refusing to listen to any more of her mother's whining, Star-girl walked away. She watched the men mount their horses and ride out, cursing fate because White Eagle was not with them as he was supposed to be. Nervously rubbing her arms, she studied the horizon to the north, from where Nahotabi would come.

She'd left him hidden in a thick patch of mesquite near Rainy Mountain, with orders not to approach her village until mid-morning

– after the men were long gone on their wild horse chase. The plan had seemed flawless. Now she wished for a way to call it off, but she couldn't think how. If she raced away from here again so soon, to intercept the Choctaw, she'd raise everyone's suspicions.

Glancing around, she saw that most of the women watched her even now, waiting to see what she would do. Toppah ignored her, or pretended to. Hating her, Star-girl decided she wouldn't stop Nahotabi even if she could. Seeing the white-faced *puta* suffer was worth the risk of White Eagle discovering her part in the plot.

* * *

Tye Devlin found himself under attack by a sea of rage as he and Jeb Crawford rode into Fort Sill. The mental walls he'd erected over his lifetime to block out emotions from everyone around him threatened to crumble away. He hadn't come under such pressure from all sides since the night of the Chicago Fire, more than four years ago. Flinching at the bursts of pain exploding in his head, he squeezed his eyes shut and fought to reinforce his protective barriers.

"Looks like a beehive on the warpath around here," Jeb remarked.

Tye opened his eyes as the pain began to recede. With his internal shield back in place, he glanced around. Everywhere he looked soldiers were rushing about, saddling horses, checking weapons and mounting up, obviously preparing to depart on an urgent mission. "Aye, it does," he agreed.

"I wonder what's got 'em so riled up."

"Perhaps we'll find out over there." He pointed to a building with a flag flying out front and three officers gathered on the porch talking. Guessing it was the post commander's office, Tye angled his horse in that direction along with Jeb. They halted in front of the building, drawing the attention of the three officers. One, who looked to be the man in charge, pinned Tye and Jeb with an impatient stare.

"If you men are here on business, it'll have to wait," he said bluntly. "I have a serious situation on my hands. I've got no time for anything else."

"Sir, we only need a few moments," Tye said, refusing to be put off. They'd suffered too many delays already from Jeb's attacks of rheumatism and his own horse going lame. "'Tis also a serious matter. My sister's life is at stake."

The man scowled, but after a moment's consideration, he dismissed the other two officers. "All right, climb down and come with me," he ordered Tye and Jeb.

Once inside the building, he led them into an inner office and sat down behind a scarred oak desk. On it sat a nameplate with *Col. Ranald S. Mackenzie* lettered on it. So this was the ferocious Indian fighter so many Texans lauded. He didn't look particularly ferocious – until you looked into his eyes. Those pale eyes drilled into Tye.

Crossing his arms, Mackenzie said, "I have a wounded soldier and an escaped prisoner to track down. This had better be as serious as you said."

"It is. My sister was abducted several weeks ago and we've searched for her ever since. The man who took her is half Kiowa. We've reason to think he may have brought her here to his mother's people."

Mackenzie's eyebrows lifted sharply then dropped into a frown. Unfolding his arms, he leaned forward, hands planted on the desk. One hand was missing two fingers. "Are you talking about Jack Lafarge and the white woman riding with him?"

"Aye! That's him. You've seen them?"

"I have. They stopped in here a while back. The girl, your sister, didn't act like a captive. In fact, she spoke up for Lafarge and said she'd come to help his ailing mother."

Tye exchanged a surprised glance with Jeb. Was it possible Jack had duped Rose into running off with him, claiming his mother needed her healer's touch? How he'd learned of that, Tye had no idea, but innocent as Rosie was, had she fallen for his lies and gone with him willingly? Without telling her family? No, she'd never do that.

"She also said she trusted Lafarge," Mackenzie added.

"The devil she did! 'Tis more likely she feared what the villain would do to her if she spoke the truth." Tye refused to believe otherwise.

"Could be, but I doubt it," the colonel said. "She seemed quite sincere. I might add that Lafarge has never given us any trouble so far as I'm aware of."

"Seems like the only way we'll know one way or t'other is to find the two of 'em and ask Miss Rose herself," Jeb pointed out.

"True enough. You'll find Lafarge's mother in one of the Kiowa villages. Let's go talk to my adjutant. He can give you directions."

Shortly thereafter, Tye headed northwest with Jeb, intent on rescuing Rose and making Jack regret he'd stolen her.

CHAPTER SIXTEEN

Jack had ridden less than halfway to Fort Sill when he encountered an army patrol headed toward the Kiowa villages. The captain leading the bluecoats was older and wiser than Proctor, the greenhorn lieutenant he and Rose had locked horns with. This man's name was Fuller. Jack had found him courteous in the past, but not today.

"What are you doing out here, Lafarge?" he demanded in a clipped tone.

Casually adjusting his hat, Jack said, "I'm headed to the fort. Need to pick up supplies." He *was* planning to buy a long overdue hat for Rose, and he didn't figure Fuller needed to know about the telegram he intended to send.

The tired looking, unshaven officer scowled. "Not a good idea. The post is no place for an Indian today."

"Why's that?"

"A prisoner escaped last night. He had help from a young Indian woman. She knocked the guardhouse sentry over the head, damn near killed him. Colonel Mackenzie is hopping mad. He has half the troops out searching for the whiskey runner and his gal."

A bad feeling gripped Jack. "Was the whiskey runner a Choctaw?"

Fuller narrowed his eyes. "Yeah, Nahotabi by name. You know him?"

"From years back. He's no good."

"And you knew he'd been captured?"

"I crossed paths with the patrol that brought him in."

"What about the woman? Got any idea who she might be?"

Hoping his vague suspicions were wrong, Jack shrugged.

"Can't rightly say. You said she's young. Did somebody get a look at her?"

"Not up close. One of the other sentries spotted the pair as they were making their escape. He took a shot at them but missed. He did say the woman wore buckskin, not calico, with long fringe, either Comanche or Kiowa style. I'm on my way to search the Kiowa villages on Rainy Mountain Creek. You came from there, didn't you?"

Jack nodded absently. His bad feeling was now a knife in his gut. Images flashed across his mind: Star-girl's destruction of Juana's dress, the dress Rose was supposed to wear for their wedding; the spiteful girl's humiliation at Juana's hands; the hate-filled glares he'd seen her give Rose over the past weeks; and finally, the furious way she'd ridden off yesterday. To Fort Sill, Jack guessed, to break Nahotabi out. She meant to use the Choctaw to take vengeance. On Rose!

He spun his horse around, shouting, "I must ride back and warn my wife!"

"What? Why?"

"Nahotabi is my enemy," Jack said impatiently. "I fear he will go after her to get back at me." Done explaining, he kneed his mount into a gallop.

"We'll follow!" Fuller called out.

Jack didn't bother to respond. Stretching out low over his horse's neck, he pounded across the prairie, praying he'd get to Rose before Nahotabi did. Rage ripped through him at the thought of the bastard hurting her. If he did, he would pay!

* * *

Rose watched Star-girl accept the bowl of stew her mother carried over to her, not even bothering to thank the woman who loved her despite everything. Walks Softly dejectedly returned to where she and Ghost Woman were cutting out a buckskin dress for Juana to replace the ruined one. Feeling sorry for her, Rose wondered how the kind, gentle woman had come to have such a selfish, cruel daughter.

Standing apart from the other women, ignoring their baleful glares, the obnoxious girl wolfed down her food. When finished, she

Dearest Irish

carelessly discarded the bowl and strolled over to her mother's lodge, where she seated herself in the tipi's shade and idly toyed with her hair.

"*Bruja!*" Juana hissed, aiming a killing look at Star-girl as she handed Rose two empty water skins, keeping two more for herself. "Come, help me fill these. It is more pleasant by the creek, away from that one." She thrust her chin toward the object of her hatred.

Rose had to agree. It was peaceful and quiet by the rippling water. Screened by the trees, the two of them talked and laughed while filling the skins, avoiding any mention of Star-girl. When they returned a short while later, Rose deposited her heavy load near the cook fires to be used later. Then she stopped to stare at Star-girl, who'd taken to pacing back and forth, arms locked across her chest, glancing at the northern horizon every so often.

The girl's agitated behavior made Rose uneasy. Apparently, it also bothered Ghost Woman. Rising with difficulty, she said something to Walks Softly; then, leaning on her walking stick, she tottered over to Star-girl, stopping in her path, and spoke sharply in Kiowa.

"Ghost Woman asks who she watches for," Juana translated, stationing herself at Rose's side. She listened to Star-girl's reply and said, "The wicked one says she is anxious for the men to return with the horses."

"'Tis far too soon for that, isn't it?" Rose asked.

"*Sí*, that is what Ghost Woman says to her. And she asks what wickedness the girl is planning now."

Face twisting in anger, Star-girl snarled a reply.

Juana gasped. "The *bruja* says she does not answer to an old crone who belongs in the ghost world."

"*Begorrah!* How dare she?"

"She is without honor. The Kiowa do not speak so to their elders."

Angry mutters sounded from the other women, who had forgotten their chores to observe the confrontation. Still crouched over the hide she was cutting, Walks Softly looked on in distress as Ghost Woman replied in a reproving tone.

"She says Star-girl brings shame on her mother and the memory of her father. No man will want such a disrespectful one for his wife." Juana laughed low in her throat. "Ghost Woman speaks true."

Emitting a feral growl, Star-girl shouldered the old woman aside, nearly knocking her down. The insufferable witch started to stride away but halted abruptly to stare off to the north. Tossing a quick glance in that direction, Rose saw a horse and rider swiftly approaching, but she ignored both as she rushed to Ghost Woman's side and placed a steadying arm around her. Only then did she take time to study the rider who neared the village, shading her eyes to see him more clearly.

Her breath caught when she recognized the Choctaw, Nahotabi, who'd called Jack yellow. But he was a prisoner, or had been. What was he doing here?

Star-girl threw her a malicious glance. Rose knew in that instant that the outlaw Indian had come for *her,* and she couldn't smother a frightened cry.

"What have you done?" Ghost Woman spat in furious English at Star-girl.

The she-devil shrugged. "I do nothing. I not know this man," she claimed with wide-eyed innocence that fooled no one, least of all Rose.

Nahotabi halted a few yards away and dismounted. He paused a moment to take in the scene, giving a nod to Star-girl, confirming they'd plotted this together. Then he stalked toward Rose, an evil grin revealing missing front teeth.

"Run!" Ghost Woman hissed, pushing Rose away.

She stumbled back a step and whirled to run, but rough hands caught her, hauling her back against a foul smelling body. Shrieking in terror, she fought to break free. The outlaw wrapped an arm around her and squeezed hard, forcing a whoosh of air from her lungs.

"You not escape me, Yellow Hair," he taunted, sour breath fanning her face.

"Let her go!" Ghost Woman shouted.

Rose heard a dull thunk and felt Nahotabi jerk. She guessed her mother-in-law must have clouted his back with her walking stick. The Choctaw snarled and swung around, keeping hold of Rose with one arm. He drove his other fist into Ghost Woman's stomach. She gave a strangled scream and crumpled to the ground, curling on her side, clutching her belly.

"Monster!" Rose shrilled, pounding at his imprisoning arm. "Are ye proud of yourself striking a sick, helpless old woman?"

"Be silent!" he growled. Spinning her to face him, he slapped her, driving her to cry out. Her head swam from the force of the blow, the side of her face burned like fire and she tasted blood from where her teeth had cut the inside of her cheek. She was dimly aware of women's raised, angry voices. Her vision cleared enough to see Walks Softly crouch beside Ghost Woman's writhing form. Juana and the others stood a few feet away, some carrying sticks, others knives, looking ready to attack her captor.

The outlaw's hand came up holding a pistol. Cocking it, he waved it back and forth at the group of women. "Stay back or I shoot!"

Rose caught Star-girl's vengeful smile. Then Nahotabi clamped his hand around her arm and started to drag her toward his horse. She dug in her heels and gritted her teeth when his grip tightened, cutting into her flesh. It was useless; he was much too strong for her. With a painful yank, he forced her to stumble after him.

"Nay! I'll not go!" she shrilled when they reached his horse. She tried to claw his face, but he deflected her attempt and, seizing both her hands, wrenched her arms behind her back, making her scream in pain.

"You do what Nahotabi say, white gal, and maybe I no kill you right away," he said. Giving a dirty laugh, he lifted her off her feet, preparing to throw her onto his horse, but he froze at the sound of a horse's thundering approach.

"Turn loose of my wife, you bastard!" the rider bellowed.

Rose spotted Jack and gave a glad cry. Nahotabi roared furiously, threw her aside and fired his gun as she fell on her backside. She couldn't see if his bullet found its mark or missed. Either way, it didn't stop her enraged husband. Leaping from his galloping steed, he hurled himself at the outlaw. They crashed to earth with Jack on top.

Nahotabi's gun went flying, landing within Rose's reach. Instinctively, she grabbed it. The thing was heavier than she expected, but she hung onto it and scooted backward as the two men grappled with each other, snarling and cursing. With an effort, she climbed to her feet and backed away.

* * *

Nahotabi's bullet had grazed Jack high on his left side, but in his fury he barely noticed the pain. He'd left his own .44 behind this morning, depending on his Winchester for his ride to the fort, and he hadn't dared fire it with Rose in the Choctaw's grasp. Fiercely glad to punish the lowdown coyote with his fists, he blocked a wild punch and landed one of his own, splitting open his enemy's bottom lip, making him yelp. He drew back his arm, ready to deliver another blow, but Nahotabi tossed a handful of dirt in his face, blinding him.

Blinking and swiping at his eyes, Jack couldn't stop the fist that slammed into his chin, throwing him sideways off his adversary. He shook his ringing head and rolled unsteadily to his feet, still blinking fast to clear his eyes. Although blurred, his vision was good enough to see Nahotabi also get to his feet – with a knife in his hand.

"You think you beat me, Yellow Jack?" the bastard mocked. "Nahotabi good fighter, not easy to beat." He wiped blood from his lip with the back of his hand. "I kill you and take your woman."

"Like hell you will!" Drawing his own knife, Jack prepared to meet an attack as the Choctaw circled him, sunlight glinting off his blade. Staring into his hate-filled eyes, Jack saw them flicker and sidestepped just in time, escaping the sudden strike that would have torn open his belly. At the same time, he swung his knife up and ripped it across the whiskey runner's arm.

Nahotabi shrieked and stumbled back, blood dripping from the gash. Unfortunately, it wasn't his knife arm, or he might have dropped his weapon. As it was, the wound only infuriated him further. Emitting a feral growl, he lunged again, this time fending off Jack's blade by grabbing hold of his wrist.

Jack reacted swiftly, catching Nahotabi's knife arm in a steely grip. Locked in a test of strength, he returned his opponent's glare, muscles straining and teeth bared. Neither gave an inch as they twisted and turned, trying to break one another's hold. Gradually, though, Jack felt Nahotabi weaken. Confident it was only a matter of time, he meant to put an end to the outlaw's miserable existence.

Suddenly, Nahotabi snared Jack's leg with his booted foot and threw him off balance. They tumbled to the ground, this time with the Choctaw on top. Jack's hold on his knife arm broke. He had no chance to regain it. Lifting the knife high, the bastard was about to drive it into Jack's chest when a gun barked.

Nahotabi's body jerked and he gave a strangled scream. He hung suspended over Jack for a second or two. Then the knife dropped from his hand. When he started to collapse, Jack shoved him aside. He flopped onto his back and lay motionless on the ground.

Pushing onto his elbows, Jack took in the look of disbelief frozen on the outlaw's face. Then he glanced around, wondering who had shot him. His heart skipped a beat when he saw Rose standing a short distance way, holding Nahotabi's smoking gun. Slowly lowering the pistol, she stared wide-eyed at the dead man, red-gold hair swirling like a halo around her head.

Picking himself up, Jack went to her. He gently lifted the gun from her hand and stuffed it behind his back under his belt. Rose looked up at him, pale with shock and trembling.

"I killed him," she whispered vacantly.

Jack drew her close. "You saved my life, P'ayn-nah."

She drew a ragged breath and came back to herself. With a choked cry, she locked her arms around him, sobbing in reaction, and Jack held her tight, ignoring the now stinging bullet graze under his left arm. Her storm of tears passed quickly. Sniffling and wiping at her eyes, she stepped back and abruptly caught her breath. "You're wounded!"

He looked down and saw a bloody patch running down the side of his shirt. "It's nothing, just a scratch."

"Perhaps, but it needs –" Rose was cut off by the sound of Juana's angry voice.

"This is your doing, *bruja!*"

Jack turned with Rose and spotted Juana near the center of the village. Fists clenched, she advanced on the treacherous Kiowa maiden who had set Nahotabi loose and obviously plotted with him to harm Rose.

"No! I did nothing," Star-girl cried, backing away. Her look of fear gave Jack grim satisfaction.

"You lied! There are no wild horses, are there?" Juana accused. "You wanted the men gone so your *amigo* could ride in and steal Toppah."

Jack didn't know about any wild horses, but he realized the only man in sight was old Wise Hawk, standing outside his tipi with the village children clustered near him, observing the situation. A short distance beyond them, several women crouched around someone lying on the ground. Standing apart from them, Star-girl's mother held a hand pressed to her lips as tears streamed down her face.

"Do not touch me!" her daughter screeched. She whirled and tried to run, but Tsoia's furious wife grabbed her by the hair and jerked her to a halt, extracting a scream from her.

"You won't escape me, evil one," Juana vowed. Yanking off Star-girl's beaded rawhide belt, she twisted her arms behind her back and swiftly bound them with the belt. Then she dragged her shrieking captive over to Wise Hawk's tipi and forced her to the ground, scattering the flock of children. "She is not to move from here," she said, getting a nod from the old man.

Jack returned his gaze to the group of women. "Who is that lying on the ground? Did Nahotabi injure someone?"

"Your mother! The vile animal struck her. I must go to her." Drawing away from him, she ran toward the group of women and the prone figure they surrounded.

Jack shot a ferocious glare at Nahotabi, wishing the varmint wasn't dead so he could tear him apart with his bare hands. Then he rushed after Rose with fresh fear riding him. She was kneeling beside his mother, holding her hand, when Jack caught up. The other women parted, allowing him close.

"Khaw," he said thickly, going down on one knee opposite Rose. Shocked by his mother's contorted, pain-filled features, he caught her other hand in his.

She opened her eyes and cried, "Kill me! End this torture!"

He reared back, appalled by her request, and heard Rose gasp in shock. "No! Do not ask this of me," he said, shaking his head.

"I must. It is a snake . . . eating at me. I cannot stand . . . any more," she forced out between labored breaths. "You must help me."

Rose bent low and gently stroked his mother's brow. "It needn't come to that. Let me try again to kill the snake. Please!"

Khaw groaned in agony and shook her head. "No. You will only . . . drive it back. It will return . . . to tear at me."

"'Twill be different this time. Jack will lend me his strength,"

Rose said, sounding desperate. She raised her eyes to him, meeting his surprised gaze. "Won't you?"

He nodded. "Sure. Anything you need." He wondered exactly what she had in mind. Not that it mattered. Whatever she asked of him, he would do.

"What if it still . . . does not work?" Khaw gasped, staring at him. "Will you end this pain for me?" Her eyes pleaded with him.

He wanted to say no, absolutely not. She was his mother. How could he kill her? But was it fair to let her go on suffering like this? Wouldn't it be kinder to let her find peace with her ancestors? He looked at his wife, seeking an answer. She returned his stare, obviously distressed, and gave a small shake of her head. Was she saying no, don't do it? Or was she telling him he must find his own answer?

Making the hardest decision of his life, he swallowed hard and met Khaw's tortured gaze. "If Rose cannot heal you, I will do as you ask."

Rose gave a choked cry but said nothing.

"Thank you," Khaw whispered. Fighting the pain, she squeezed her eyes shut for a moment. When she opened them again, she looked at Rose. "Daughter, let us see if . . . your medicine is strong enough this time."

* * *

Rose followed Jack as he carried his mother to her bed in Walks Softly's lodge. As he settled her on her buffalo robes, she noticed his bloodstained shirt and insisted Rose tend to him before doing anything else.

"There's no need," Jack argued. "The bleeding has already stopped."

"Even so, your wife . . . must clean and bandage it," Ghost Woman stubbornly declared, despite her own pain.

"It won't take me long," Rose said, signaling Jack not to delay matters with further arguing. "Take your shirt off while I gather what I need."

He frowned but did as she said, unbuttoning the bloody garment and pulling it off. Armed with a bowl of water, a rag for cleaning the wound, and a roll of calico strips Ghost Woman used for bandages, Rose set to work. Jack flinched once as she wiped blood away from the cut, which was as shallow as he'd said, thank the saints. Otherwise, he sat stoically without moving, except to lift his arm out of the way now and then.

Rose had just tied off the ends of the bandage when dogs began to bark and frightened women's voices sounded outside.

"What the devil?" Jack muttered. Rising, he crossed to the tipi entrance, pushed the flap aside and stuck his head out to see what had caused the commotion. He drew back, swearing under his breath.

"I forgot I met an army patrol on my way to the fort. That's how I found out Nahotabi had escaped. The bluecoats followed me. They're here now," he hastily explained. Coming to squat beside Rose, who'd moved to Ghost Woman's side, he touched his mother's arm. "I'd best go speak to them. I'll return soon."

"Go. Do not let them . . . make trouble. I will wait."

He exchanged a grim look with Rose, stood and went out to meet the soldiers. Once he was gone, Ghost Woman groaned and writhed in agony. For her sake, Rose prayed Jack would be quick. She knew she didn't possess enough strength to destroy the demon inside his mother without his help. Would the crazy idea she'd come up with work? It must! If it didn't, Jack would feel duty-bound to fulfill his promise to end his mother's pain.

The thought of him killing his own mother horrified Rose. How would he live with himself afterward? Moreover, she feared for both his soul and Ghost Woman's. She had no idea how the Kiowas regarded such an act, but as a Catholic, she believed murder and suicide were mortal sins. If Jack were to kill his mother with her permission, he would be guilty of murder, even if he saw it as merciful. And his mother would be committing suicide by her son's hand.

"Let's get ye ready," she said, telling herself she would succeed. She must save Ghost Woman no matter what it cost her.

Jack returned minutes later. "The bluecoats are gone," he announced, kneeling beside Rose. "They're on their way back to Fort Sill with Nahotabi's body. I told them I shot him when he tried to kill me. Didn't figure they needed to know different. They'd want to ask you questions, and that would take too much time."

"Aye, it would."

"What about Star-girl?" Ghost Woman asked, managing to contain her pain for a brief moment.

"She's with her mother and Juana. Walks Softly begged me not to turn her over to the soldiers. Her punishment can wait until later, after you are feeling better." He turned to Rose. "What do you want me to do?"

"I need you to kneel behind me," she replied, starting to turn back the blanket covering Ghost Woman's mid-section. She had already pulled her long dress up out of the way.

The old woman clutched the top edge of her blanket. "My son should not . . . see me this way," she said, again gasping for breath.

"He won't see ye when he's behind me." Rose sent Jack a pointed glance and he moved, positioning himself at her back.

"My wife speaks true. I can't see you now." It likely wasn't entirely true, Rose suspected, but it satisfied his mother.

"Good. Let us be done with this – one way or the other."

Doing her best to ignore those ominous words, Rose spoke over her shoulder to Jack. "Place your hands at my waist and lean against me." He did as she asked. "When the power begins to flow through me, you may feel a burning, but do not pull away. I hope, nay, I *believe* your strength will increase the power and give me more time to destroy the snake."

"I won't pull away. I'll be right here for as long as you need me."

Reassured by his promise and by the warmth and solidity of his body, she smiled at her patient. "Snake is a good word for it. Before I attack it, I must speak the prayer of healing. As I told ye before, it comes from my long-ago ancestors in Ireland. They prayed to their ancient gods of nature."

"Your elder ones were wise. The Kiowa people . . . also pray to such spirits." Gritting her teeth, the venerable medicine woman said, "Speak then!"

CHAPTER SEVENTEEN

Rose bent her head, closed her eyes and murmured words that traced back to a pagan religion lost in time. They conflicted with her Catholic faith but were part of the healing ritual and she dared not omit them. In English, they roughly meant:

Guardians of earth, sky and the sacred waters,
Consecrate this body and make it an instrument of healing,
Enter this mind and draw forth the power of fire,
Guide these hands that they may find the source of affliction.
And restore the sufferer to good health and peace.

As always, the prayer calmed her. Breathing deep, she chafed her hands briskly while the inner fire leapt to life, spreading to all parts of her body and concentrating in her fingertips. She heard Jack catch his breath and felt his hands tighten on her waist. The fire stung him as she'd thought it might. True to his word, though, he didn't pull away. When she leaned forward to lay hands on his mother, he moved with her, keeping his body pressed firmly to her back.

Ghost Woman flinched at her touch. "I had forgotten the heat," she said.

"I'm sorry for the burning. 'Tis necessary if I'm to heal ye."

"It is nothing. Do as you must."

Lightly probing her patient's swollen belly, Rose closed her eyes and traced the ragged edges of the invasive growth, seeing it in her mind. "'Tis more uneven in shape than before," she said absently.

"Is that bad?" Jack asked.

"Not bad exactly, but I think I must destroy it in parts, not all at once." Opening her eyes, Rose met Ghost Woman's pain-racked gaze. "'Twill take longer, but it should work. If you're ready, I'll begin."

"Yes, do it!" the old woman gasped.

Closing her eyes again and gathering her power, Rose surrounded one protruding section of the demon with all ten fingers and attacked. Fire shot from her mind, down the pathways to her fingertips and into the voracious killer. It writhed and tried to shrink from her touch, but she persisted until the part she was bombarding broke off from the large central mass. Ghost Woman cried out, but Rose barely heard, so focused on her task was she. A few seconds more of the cauterizing fire, and the small dismembered part of the demon died. She quickly smashed it into scorched, miniscule bits that would pass harmlessly from their host's body.

She allowed herself and her patient a brief respite before calling up her power for another attack. Taking aim at a slightly larger extension of the invader, she concentrated on severing it. The cut was clean and quick. She felt the monster shudder beneath her fingertips and somewhere in her brain she registered Ghost Woman's choked cry. Knowing the best way to end her pain was to finish this, Rose dealt with the second severed piece of the *snake* the same way as the first.

Again, she rested to restore her power, a bit longer than before.

"You all right?" Jack asked, massaging her shoulders. It felt wonderful.

"Aye, I only needed a bit of a rest. I'm fine now." She sighed in regret when his hands dropped back to her waist. Collecting her power, she took aim again, sliced away a third ragged extension of the invader and destroyed it. She repeated this process several more times, taking a little longer to recover after each attack. Without Jack's support, she couldn't have progressed as fast as she did.

However, the worst was yet to come. She had whittled away at the demon until it was reduced to the size of a large orange, but that was still much bigger than any of the segments she'd already destroyed. Killing the thing would require more strength than she had left. For that she would have to tap into Jack's store of energy.

Needing a longer rest before the final assault, and knowing

Ghost Woman did too, Rose sagged against her husband, letting her head loll backward onto his shoulder. He brushed hair from her damp brow and hugged her tight.

"You're done in," he murmured. "Why don't you rest up over night and finish the job tomorrow?"

"No." She rolled her head back and forth. "That would give the thing a chance to recover. I must kill it now, and ye must help me."

"How?"

"When I call up my power this time, I'll reach out to ye with my mind and attempt to draw upon your strength." She turned enough to gaze into his ebony eyes. "I'm not a'tall sure that's possible, ye understand, but if it works, you'll likely feel something, a weakening of your body, I fear. And ye mustn't resist, Jack. If ye do . . . ." She shook her head.

"I won't. Take whatever you need and don't worry about me. Just make sure you're all right because . . ." He paused to swallow. ". . . because I need you. I love you."

Rose caught her breath. Tears of joy welled in her eyes. She reached up with trembling fingers to caress his beloved copper features. "I love ye too," she whispered.

"You chose well for your wife, my son," Ghost Woman said in a dry, cracked voice, reminding them of her presence. "Much better than I would have chosen for you." She caught Rose's hand, giving it a squeeze.

Brushing tears from her eyes, Rose smiled tremulously. "Thank ye, Khaw. May I call ye that? It has been a very long time since I lost my own mother."

"You honor me. Of course you may call me Khaw or mother as you like. I am proud to have a daughter such as you."

Rose stifled a sob and, lifting her mother-in-law's frail hand, kissed it with genuine love for the woman.

Jack cleared his throat. "Now that you've got that settled, maybe we'd best get on with the healing." He sounded embarrassed by their show of emotion, and his own, Rose suspected.

"Aye, that we should," she agreed. Settling to her work again, she focused her inner sight on the remaining growth, carefully positioning her fingertips around the outer edge of the uneven sphere. "I'm reaching out to ye now, Jack. Don't resist."

"I won't," he again promised. He gasped and stiffened briefly as she breached his natural defenses, seeking the core of his being. She felt him open to her, allowing her in. A sense of wholeness, of unity with him, swept over her, almost like the bliss she'd found last night, when he'd brought her to the height of passion. This was different, though. Rather than an explosion of pleasure that left her satiated but drained of strength, this melding of their energy suffused her with glowing warmth and a feeling of limitless power.

She drew upon that power to blast the demon invader with an invisible beam of fire that should have killed it on the spot. However, while the thing was badly singed, it refused to die, tenaciously clinging to its victim. Rose gave it no respite, blasting it again and again. The third time brought results. The mass broke partially loose, wrenching a scream from Ghost Woman.

"'Tisn't dead yet," Rose said. Determined to destroy it once and for all, she gathered another burst of energy and launched it, ruthlessly searing the monster until it released its last hold on her mother-in-law. The old woman made a strangled sound, more surprise than pain. Rose's attention stayed riveted on the object of her wrath. With one final all-out assault, she burned and smashed the vile demon to harmless bits.

"'Tis done. The thing is dead," she said with a tired sigh. She had little chance to rejoice in her victory. The moment she relaxed, her union with Jack dissolved and a tide of weakness flooded her body and mind. Limp with exhaustion, she heard Jack cry out her name and felt his arms encircle her. Then she sank into darkness.

* * *

Jack cradled Rose in his arms and pushed to his feet, grunting with the effort. His legs wobbled for a second, but he forced them under control and carried his wife from the lodge, leaving his mother asleep. He'd called in Walks Softly to watch over her. The woman looked in need of something to keep her busy and her mind off her daughter's treachery.

He worriedly studied Rose's face as he strode toward their isolated tipi. Her auburn lashes lay fanned against her cheeks, accentuating her paleness. When she'd collapsed after the healing, he'd been too drained of strength by their strange bonding to do more than hold her for several moments. He'd recovered for the most part now, but she remained unconscious, and fear for her tore at him like knives.

She still hadn't come to by the time he got her settled on their bed of buffalo robes. Finding a clean cloth, he wet it and dribbled a few drops of water between her parted lips. She swallowed, encouraging him to give her more. When he figured she had enough, he used the cool, damp rag to pat her face. She didn't move or make a sound. Tossing the rag aside, he absently donned a fresh shirt and sat down next to her, watching, waiting for her to come back to him.

At last, after what seemed like hours, she stirred. Clasping her hand to his chest, Jack stroked her brow and murmured her name. Relief flooded him when she opened her eyes and smiled at him.

"Jack? What happened?" she asked softly.

"You finished healing Khaw and swooned, P'ayn-nah. Scared the daylights out of me." Bending close, he brushed her lips with his then studied her closely. Her cheeks were pink now instead of bone white, he was glad to see. "How do you feel?"

"Just a wee bit tired."

"Mmm. What you did, it took too much out of you." He frowned. "I saw how much it cost you last time. I shouldn't have let you try it again."

"Don't be daft," Rose scolded. "We couldn't allow that vicious thing to kill your mother. I'm glad I was finally able to destroy it, and I couldn't have done it without your help." She reached up to thread her fingers through his hair, where it had fallen forward. "Are ye feeling all right? I didn't hurt ye?"

"No. I'm fine." He didn't see any point in telling her how weak he'd been for a while. That was over and done with. "Now listen, you're not to move from here. You need to rest. I'll see about –"

"Jack, may I enter?" a woman's voice called from outside the lodge, cutting off his words. It sounded like Juana.

"Come on in," he replied, exchanging a glance with Rose and turning toward the low entrance.

Juana ducked inside. Straightening, she darted a worried look at Rose and spoke to him. "Two men have come. They do not seem friendly. The younger one wants to know if you are here and if a white woman is with you." She shifted her gaze to Rose. "He says he is the woman's brother."

Rose gasped. "Tye's here?" She pushed up on her elbows, eyes wide with fright. "Jack, he doesn't know about your mother. He's sure to be furious over me disappearing the way I did, and he –"

"It's all right. I'll handle this. You stay here and rest," he ordered, gently pushing her back. "You're too weak to stand."

"But I can't just lie here while –"

"Do like I said. Stay here," he repeated. Rising, he told Juana, "See that she doesn't move." Getting a mute nod from her, he stooped and went to face Tye Devlin's wrath.

* * *

Tye eyed the Kiowa women clustered around Jeb and him. They didn't look any too friendly. In fact, he half expected them to attack at any moment. Where were their men, he wondered, and where had that Mexican woman run off to? She appeared to be the only one who spoke English, but as soon as he'd stated his business, she'd melted away into the crowd. Had she gone to warn Jack Lafarge? Was that no good woman stealer about to make another run for it with Rose?

Gritting his teeth, Tye took a step forward, ready to force his way through the crowd of women, determined not to let his quarry escape. Jeb caught his sleeve, stopping him.

"I wouldn't make a move. These gals all carry knives. They'll cut you to ribbons if they think you're out to make trouble."

Tye shook off his hand. "What am I to do then, stand here and let Lafarge sneak off with my sister again? To someplace where I might never find them?"

"I'm not sneaking off anywhere," a man's voice called out.

Recognizing it, Tye shot a furious glare toward the source and watched the women part, allowing Choctaw Jack to walk toward him. He halted a few feet away.

"Howdy, Jeb," he said. "Good to see you."

"Jack, it's been a while," Jeb replied mildly, drawing an irritated glance from Tye.

"Devlin, I wondered when you'd turn up."

"Where's Rose?" Tye demanded. "I've come to take her home. After I kill ye for what you've done to her, ye bastard!" He started for the filthy defiler of young women, meaning to pound him to a bloody pulp. Rose's sudden appearance beside her abductor brought him up short.

"Tye Devlin, don't ye dare lay a hand on my husband!" she shouted, blue eyes blazing.

"Husband!" he blurted. "Ye wed the *bligeard?*"

"Aye, and I'll thank ye not to be calling him nasty names." Shifting her gaze to Jeb Crawford, she softened her tone. "Hello, Jeb."

"Howdy, Miz Rose. I'm mighty glad to see you. Jack, you led us on quite a chase. You've got some explaining to do, I reckon."

Lafarge gave a curt nod and snapped at Rose, "I told you not to get up."

She smiled sweetly at him. "And I told ye I couldn't just lie there."

The Mexican woman Tye had spoken to stepped out of the crowd. "Toppah insisted she must come to you," she told Lafarge. "I could not stop her."

"Rosie, are ye hurt?" Tye questioned, alarmed when she suddenly swayed, causing Lafarge to put his arm around her for support.

"Nay, nay, I'm fine, only a wee bit tired from healing Jack's mother."

"His mother?" Baffled, Tye shook his head and scrubbed a hand down his face. "Rose, kindly stop speaking in riddles. What's this about healing his mother? And for pity's sake, tell me why ye wed the man who stole ye from your bed in the middle of the night."

"Because I love him. Can't ye tell?" The tender glance she gave Choctaw Jack left little doubt that she spoke the truth. If that wasn't enough, the emotion flooding Tye's brain confirmed it. As with his other sister, Jessie, he'd never been able to completely block out Rose's emotions, as he could with most others. Even though he didn't see how she could love her kidnapper, he had no choice but to believe she did.

"As for how I came to heal Jack's mother, Ghost Woman, 'tis a rather long story, and as I said, I'm a bit tired. So, if ye don't mind, I'd like to sit before we begin." She gestured toward a low burning campfire in front of the nearest tipi.

Tye would rather have beaten the daylights out of her *husband* than sit down with him, but he couldn't refuse her request. Once they were seated around the fire, the young Mexican woman, who Rose addressed as Juana, produced a battered coffee pot and a small pouch of coffee. While she prepared the brew, Rose clasped Choctaw Jack's hand and began to explain.

"First, ye need to understand why Jack spirited me away from the Double C. His mother was close to dying, ye see, and he was desperate to save her. He knew of my healing gift, having seen me heal Brownie's leg, and he resolved to bring me here to help his mother."

"Indeed?" Lifting a skeptical brow, Tye glared at Jack. "If that's the case, why didn't ye come to me and explain the situation instead of kidnapping my sister?"

"You ordered me to keep away from her, remember? You sure as hell wouldn't have let her ride all the way up here with me."

"*Begorrah!* You've got that right, ye no good deserter!"

Rose gasped and a look of surprise flashed across Jack's face. "You talked to some of my Choctaw relatives," he said.

"Aye, and we heard how ye turned yellow and deserted during the war. Not only are ye a kidnapper, you're a coward!"

Fury glittered in the black eyes glaring at him across the fire. Tye tensed, ready to meet an attack. But Rose clutched Jack's arm when he started to rise, holding him back.

"Nay! I'll not watch the two of ye beat each other bloody. Tye, ye don't know the whole story. Jack had good reason for walking away from the war."

"Oh, aye? And just what might that be?" he challenged, crossing his arms.

Rose scowled and shook her head. "'Tis a long story, one best left for later. Right now, I only want ye to believe Jack and Tsoia – Juana's husband – had no choice but to steal me away and bring me up here. I admit I wasn't best pleased at first." She darted a teasing grin at Choctaw Jack that made Tye clench his jaw. "But I changed my mind along the way."

"And it's taken ye all this time to heal his mother? Surely ye could have done the job weeks ago and he could have brought ye home." He pointed at Jack. "But that wasn't your plan, was it? Nay, ye meant to keep her here all along, didn't ye? And use her for your own –"

"Enough!" Rose flared, jumping up. "Either stop your ugly accusations, brother, or leave." Stamping her foot, she clenched and unclenched her hands, looking as if she'd like to tear strips from his hide like the panther he'd once fought.

Nonplused, he stared at her hardly believing this was his meek little sister.

"Sit down, P'ayn-nah," Jack said. "I can fight my own battles."

Rose frowned at him. "But he –"

"It's all right. Sit," he repeated, catching her hand and giving it a tug. This time she obeyed, scowling at him.

Despite his simmering anger, Tye almost grinned. He bet Rose's husband, if they truly were wed, was in for a tongue-lashing later.

Jeb cleared his throat. "Maybe we oughta listen to what Jack and Miz Rose have to say, Tye. Could be there's a good reason they haven't headed back to the ranch."

"Thank ye, Jeb," Rose said in a calmer tone.

"Fine. Go ahead, spin your tale," Tye barked. He might be faintly amused, but it would take a lot of convincing to make him welcome Jack Lafarge into the family.

Learning about the failure of Rose's first efforts to heal Jack's mother forced Tye to concede his sister's need to remain here longer. Her enthusiastic description of her stay in the Kiowa village eased his mind some, but her claim that she'd ridden in a horse race against an Indian brave and won, was more than Tye could swallow. He laughingly scoffed at the absurd claim, drawing her furious glare.

"Quit your laughing, ye *idjit!* And don't be calling me a liar!"

Juana, who was just then refilling his tin cup with steaming coffee, looked up. "It is true, *Señor*. Toppah and the brown stallion flew like the wind. They were *magnifico.*"

Tye stopped laughing. "Toppah is her name in Kiowa?" he asked distractedly, staring at Rose in amazement.

"*Sí,* it means yellow-hair, but she has other names also. After the race, the young man she defeated grew angry and did a stupid thing. Toppah's horse struck him to protect her, and the foolish boy's leg was broken. Your sister used her magic to heal his leg. We

Dearest Irish

all saw her do this. Many now call her Heals-with-her-hands."

"I didn't know that," Rose said, clearly astonished.

Juana smiled at her. "It is so. Others just call you Wise Woman."

"She's also a good shot," Jack said, tilting his head to look at Rose. "She saved my skin today." He continued to watch her as color flooded her cheeks.

"What are ye talking about?" Tye asked. As Jack recounted Rose's near abduction by the escaped prisoner from Fort Sill and how she'd killed the man in order to save her husband's life, Tye was left speechless. Never again would he think of her as his sheltered baby sister.

As if he didn't have enough startling facts to think about, Jack cleared his throat and said, "There's one more thing I want you to know. Rose mentioned I took her into the mountains a while back, but she didn't tell you how that ride ended."

"Jack, no!" Rose blurted, clutching his arm. "There's no need."

He patted her hand. "Yeah, P'ayn-nah, there is. He's your brother. He's got a right to know." To Tye, he said, "We were ready to head back to the village. I went to refill our canteens first, leaving Rose alone. While I was gone, she got bitten by a rattlesnake and almost died before I got her back here."

Tye's bemusement turned into fury. "Ye bastard! Ye nearly got her killed!" he roared. Springing to his feet, he was about to lunge across the space separating them when Rose shrieked at him to stop.

"He just admitted leaving ye alone," he fired back as she stood to face him. "'Twas his fault ye were bitten."

"Nay, as I've told Jack time and again, 'twas my own fault for not waiting for him where he told me to. I was put out with him over some silly thing and thought to teach him a lesson. As it turned out, I'm the one who learned a painful lesson. And 'twas Jack who saved my life, with his mother's help."

A long moment passed as Tye digested her confession. Finally, he broke the tense silence. "Rosie, Jessie's temper has gotten her into trouble time and again. Now it seems you're taking after her. I'm not happy to see it."

Turning to Jack, who had risen to stand beside Rose, he said sourly, "Which doesn't excuse ye for leaving her alone."

"No, it doesn't, and if you still want to beat the tar out of me, I won't stop you."

Tye had noticed the fresh bruise on Jack's jaw, no doubt a result of his fight with the escaped prisoner Rose had killed. Now he considered adding a matching bruise to the opposite side of that square copper jaw, but the idea of punching a man who wouldn't defend himself left a bad taste in his mouth.

"When ye decide to put up a fight, I'll gladly trade blows with ye."

"Fair enough," Jack said, holding his gaze. He started to say something else, but an ear-splitting scream cut him off.

Pivoting toward the sound, Tye saw flames curling along the bottom of one of the tipis.

Dearest Irish

CHAPTER EIGHTEEN

Jack's stomach clenched when he saw flames threatening to consume Tsoia and Juana's lodge. Another scream sounded, reminding him Star-girl was tied up in there. Much as he detested her for conspiring with Nahotabi to harm Rose, he didn't wish her to burn to death.

At that instant, Juana returned from the creek, where she'd gone to refill the coffee pot. Seeing her lodge on fire, she screamed and dropped the pot, splashing water around her feet.

"Tsahle-ee!" she shrieked. "I sent him to get more coffee." She ran toward her burning lodge with Jack after her. She would have thrown herself at the hide flap covering the low entrance – already catching fire – if he hadn't stepped in front of her.

"Wait!" he barked. "Setting yourself on fire won't help him."

She gave a wordless cry but stood frozen as he tore off his shirt and used it to beat out the flames barring the opening.

"Mi bebe!" Juana cried, trying to dive past him the moment the way was clear.

"No! Stay here," he ordered, pushing her back. "I will get him." Crouching, he lunged through the opening. The scorched hide cover slapped him, stinging his bare skin. He coughed and squinted through a swirl of smoke, searching for Tsahle-ee.

"Help me!" gasped Star-girl. She was lying on her side near the fire pit, ankles bound and hands tied behind her back.

"Where's the boy?" Jack demanded above the crackle of flames climbing up the hide walls surrounding them.

"H-he is there." She tilted her head toward Tsoia and Juana's sleeping place. "But you will cut me loose, yes?"

"First the boy." Ignoring her strangled pleas, he kept low

where the smoke was less and duck-walked over to the bed of furs. "Tsahle-ee? It's Jack." He turned back the top buffalo robe and found the terrified child curled up crying.

"It's all right. I've got you," Jack said in Kiowa, scooping him up. He knew a rush of protectiveness as the little boy wrapped his arms and legs around him, whimpering against his throat.

"Don't leave me!" Star-girl croaked, barely audible above the fire's growing roar, as he made for the exit with his precious burden.

"I'll come back for you."

"No need," Tye Devlin said, tearing away the singed hide flap and ducking inside. "I'll bring her out."

Jack nodded gratefully and snaked out of the burning tipi. Juana was instantly there, lifting her son into her arms.

"*Mijo!* Thank the Blessed Virgin!" She hugged him close, both of them weeping.

Rose knelt beside Jack as he coughed smoke from his lungs. She helped him climb unsteadily to his feet. Brushing back the long hair plastered to his face by sweat, she looked him over and checked the bandage wrapped around his upper torso. "Are ye all right?"

"Yeah, I'm okay," he rasped between coughs. "But your brother, he . . . ." He glanced back at the tipi, now fully engulfed by fire.

"I know. He hasn't come out yet," she whispered, voice trembling. She'd barely spoken when Tye's head popped out of the fiery trap.

Jack rushed to help him drag Star-girl's limp body out. She groaned weakly as they moved her clear of the inferno, seconds before it collapsed in a heap of charred hides and burning lodge poles. Hearing a woman's choked cry, Jack turned to see Walks Softly drop to her knees beside her daughter. She shook Star-girl's shoulder and called her name, getting only a gurgling moan in response.

"Release her!" the woman demanded hysterically. "She cannot breathe this way."

"No!" Juana shouted. "She caused the fire and almost killed my son."

Tsahle-ee lifted his head from her shoulder. "No, *Madrecita*, Tsahle-ee do it."

"What?" Juana stared at him doubtfully. "What do you

mean?"

"Tsahle-ee burn lodge. I fall and hit stones. They hot." He held up his arm, showing her a red burn mark on his small forearm. "It hurt. Then stick jump from fire, hit wall." Tears dripped down his cheeks and he wailed, "I sorry!"

"Madre de Dios!" Juana squeezed him tight. "It's all right, *Mijo*. You did not mean to start the fire."

"What did he say?" Rose whispered to Jack, and he quickly translated the boy's confession. "So it was an accident, not Star-girl's doing," she said.

"Now will you release my daughter? Please!" Walks Softly begged.

Getting a stiff nod from Juana, Jack knelt and cut the thong binding Star-girl's wrists, then did the same to the one at her ankles. Breathing in shallow gasps, she lay unmoving. Her mother rolled her onto her back, pleading with her to wake up, to come back to her.

"Will she die?" Juana asked quietly.

Frowning, Jack stood and shrugged. "She doesn't sound good."

Rose pushed past him, crouched beside Walks Softly and touched the tearful woman's shoulder. "May I help?" she asked, pointing first at herself then at Star-girl's inert form. She got her meaning across.

Walks Softly hesitated only a second. Then she nodded and moved to give Rose room. Jack watched his wife rub her hands together lightly and move them over the nearly unconscious girl as lightly as butterflies seeking a place to land. They paused over Star-girl's chest then homed in on her throat.

"She's burned inside," she said, more to herself than to those gathered to watch. Again rubbing her hands together, briskly this time, she bent her head and murmured the strange but now familiar prayer she always spoke before a healing. Had it only been an hour or two since she'd recited it over his mother? To Jack, it seemed far longer.

Repositioning herself, Rose carefully placed both hands on her patient's throat and closed her eyes. Not a sound could be heard from the watchers as she knelt there, concentrating. Suddenly Star-girl coughed and sucked in a rasping breath. Rose moved her hands lower over the damaged lungs and resumed her healing magic. The girl's breathing gradually quieted and grew more even. At last, her eyes fluttered open and Rose drew back.

Giving a glad cry, Walks Softly moved close and helped her daughter sit up. At the same time, Jack drew Rose to her feet. Pale and exhausted, she swayed against him until he bent and lifted her into his arms.

"I'm taking you back to our bed and you'll stay there this time," he said sternly.

"Yes, Jack," she said tiredly, resting her head on his shoulder.

Tye Devlin stepped into his path. "D'ye have any tea? A cup of it with sugar will help restore her. 'Tis what our mother gave her and Jessie after one of their . . . spells."

"My mother probably has some kind of tea." Jack hesitated then added, "Thanks for getting Star-girl out."

"Glad to help." Stepping aside, his brother-in-law allowed them to pass.

Settling Rose on their bed moments later, Jack kissed her lightly. "Rest. I'll look in on Khaw and see if she has tea."

She slipped a hand around his neck. "Ye won't fight with Tye?"

"Not if he doesn't start trouble, and I don't think he will now."

"Nay, I don't think so either." Releasing him, she covered her mouth to hide a yawn.

"Rest," he repeated.

"Aye." Her eyes were already closing. "Wake me when . . . time to eat," she mumbled.

He stood and ducked out quietly, thinking he wasn't going to wake her for anything, even tea if he found some.

* * *

Rose awoke in darkness. It took her a moment to remember where she was and to realize night must have fallen. Jack hadn't lit a fire, leading her to wonder where he was and why he hadn't waked her as she'd asked him to do.

Folding back the blanket he'd placed over her, she rose unsteadily and waited for her legs to stop wobbling. Her stomach rumbled, reminding her that she needed food. Making her way outside, she drank in the cool spring night air, shivered and looked around. Stars were peeking out overhead. In the near distance she saw men gathered around a blazing fire. The Kiowa braves must have returned.

She finger-combed her snarled hair and walked toward the fire's inviting warmth. As she drew near, she heard a heated exchange between Jack and Tsoia. Although she didn't understand their Kiowa words, she guessed their discussion had to do with the day's events and the one who'd set them in motion. No doubt Tsoia had been shocked to return and find his family's lodge destroyed. He and the others also had a right to be angry over the wild goose chase – wild *horse* chase, she corrected – that Star-girl had sent them on.

After living with the Kiowa for several weeks, Rose knew women were expected to stay out of the men's discussions, but since she'd been Star-girl's intended victim, she thought she had a right to know what they meant to do with the culprit. Clearing her throat, she stepped into the circle of firelight. All the men's eyes turned her way. Seeing Tye and Jeb among them, she nodded to them.

"P'ayn-nah, is something wrong?" Jack asked, immediately on his feet. He came to her side, a worried look in his eyes.

"Nay, I'm fine, only hungry. Ye didn't wake me as I asked ye to do."

"No, I figured you needed sleep more than food." Smiling, he took hold of her elbow. "Come on, I'll get you a bowl of stew at the women's fire."

"Wait." She dug in her heels. "I want to know what you're planning to do with Star-girl."

His lips thinned and his brows bumped together in a frown. "We haven't decided yet, but you don't need to worry. She won't make anymore trouble, I promise."

"What does he want to do to her?" She inclined her head toward Tsoia, noting the hard set of his mouth.

The muscles along Jack's jaw bunched as he followed her gaze. "He blames her for the fire, even though Tsahle-ee started it. He wants to punish her and turn her over to the Army."

"Punish her? How?"

"You don't want to know."

"Aye, I do want to know," she said stubbornly.

Planting both hands on his hips, he said through his teeth, "He wants to cut off her nose."

Rose gasped and shot a disbelieving glance at Tsoia. "Ye can't be serious."

"I'm dead serious. It's a Kiowa way to punish dishonored women."

She stared at him aghast. "That's horrible! Surely ye won't let him do such a thing."

"I've argued for exiling her from the village, but the other men have a say in this too. If they see things Tsoia's way, I can't stop them."

Aghast at the thought of any woman, even Star-girl, being mutilated, Rose turned slowly around, examining the faces of the men staring back at her. She knew most of them by name, though she'd had little to do with them, having spent most of her time here with the women or with Jack. One or two grumbled to a neighbor, evidently annoyed by her interruption, others appeared merely curious.

"I'd like to speak to them," she said. "Will ye translate for me?"

"Rose, women don't speak when the men are in council. You shouldn't even be here."

"I know that, but if anyone should have a say in what happens to Star-girl, 'tis I. I'm the one she tried to have kidnapped and no doubt killed. I also healed her, if ye recall." Crossing her arms, she said, "Either ye translate for me or I'll get Juana to do it."

"Dammit, woman, I –"

A burst of laughter from Tye cut Jack off. "Brother, you've turned my baby sister into a tiger. Ye may as well let her have her say."

Jack aimed a piercing glare his way then studied Rose. "Fine, but don't say I didn't warn you. They aren't going to like this."

"They don't need to like it, they only need to listen."

Scowling, he snapped off a few words to the group in their native tongue, drawing several loud protests until the old chief, Wise Hawk, held up his hand for silence. Once he had the men's attention, he spoke briefly in a calm voice. The others looked none to happy, but they didn't argue with him.

"Wise Hawk says he will hear Heals-with-her-hands's

words," Jack translated.

"He's calling me that too?"

"That's your new name, I guess."

Liking it better than Toppah – Yellow Hair – Rose smiled at Wise Hawk. His lips crooked slightly and he motioned for her to begin. She opened her mouth, ready to denounce the Kiowas' cruel methods of punishment, but she held back, realizing a calm approach might yield better results. Clearing her throat, she looked from one man's face to the next. Some turned their eyes away while others stared at her impassively. Tsoia frowned at her, making no secret of his angry impatience.

Holding his gaze, she said, "Star-girl has caused much trouble. Like you, I wish to punish her." While Jack translated, she chose her words carefully. "But after the fire, when she almost died, I healed her. Now we are . . . connected." She laced her fingers together to demonstrate her meaning. "I feel responsible for her."

Pausing again, she rubbed her forehead, searching for a way to make them understand. Finally, she said, "It would cause me pain to see her tortured. I ask you to be kinder than she has been. Punish her, but be merciful. Thank you for hearing me. That's all I have to say."

Silence reigned after Jack finished translating her words. The men exchanged looks, seeming uncertain what to think. Afraid she had failed to convince them, Rose turned to Jack.

"D'ye think they'll do as I asked? Should I say something more?"

He shook his head. "You said enough. There's nothing more –"

Wise Hawk's interrupted him, speaking in his customary calm tone.

"What's he saying?" Rose whispered.

"He says Heals-with-her-hands speaks well. She – you – have given them much to think on." Listening to the elder for a moment more, Jack added, "They will discuss the matter further and give their decision in the morning."

"Oh, but surely –"

"You had your say. If you argue, you'll only make them angry." Firmly gripping her arm, he turned her away and led her from the circle, not even allowing her a moment to speak to her brother and Jeb.

"Where are we going?" she asked, wishing he would slow down.

"To get that bowl of stew I promised you. Then I'm taking you to bed, again. And this time you'll stay there."

"Will ye stay there with me?" she asked hopefully, longing to taste more of the delights he'd introduced her to on their wedding night. Had it really been only last night?

"Yes," he said curtly, causing her to wonder if he was angry with her for daring to voice her plea before the men. He seemed to confirm this while she ate. Sitting beside her, staring into the low-burning cook fire, he said nothing except for distracted replies to her attempts at conversation.

The stew sat like a lump in her stomach as they trod the path to their lodge. Once there, Jack told her to get in bed while he squatted to build a fire. He kept his back to her as she disrobed, not glancing at her once. His disinterest brought her close to tears. Lying down on their fur bed, she drew the blanket over herself and waited.

Despite his taciturn behavior, Rose couldn't help but enjoy watching her husband strip out of his shirt and pants. His copper flesh glowed in the firelight. Muscles bunched and rippled with his every move, and when he turned toward her, the sight of his aroused state awakened an answering need in her lower belly.

She scooted over, making room for him under the blanket, then rolled on her side and pressed against him, reveling in his masculine strength. His arms enfolded her and he kissed her temple, but he didn't fuse his mouth with hers or run his hands over her as she recalled from last night. He just laid there. Hurt and bewildered, Rose pushed away from him. Sitting up, she hugged the blanket to her chest and gazed down at him through pools of tears.

"What's wrong?" she choked out. "I thought ye wanted me, but now ye don't."

Really looking at her for the first time since he'd practically dragged her from the men's council circle, Jack's gaze softened. He reached up to thread his fingers through her hair and cup the back of her neck. Smiling sadly, he said, "I want you more than I can say, P'ayn-nah."

She brushed the dampness from her eyes. "Then why d'ye seem so . . . so cold toward me tonight?"

"I'm not cold, far from it. But I'm afraid."

"Afraid?" Rose frowned in confusion. "Of what?"

He sighed and let his hand fall away from her. "Of you hating me."

A startled laugh burst from her throat. "Are ye joking? I love ye. I could never hate ye."

"No, I'm not joking. And after you hear what I've got to say, you might not want to be near me ever again."

Mystified and somewhat alarmed, she shook her head. "I doubt that, but for saints' sake, stop trying to frighten me. What is this dreadful thing you're so sure will drive me away?"

Jack sat up and turned to face her. "I told you I deserted the Confederate Army after Khaw told me how my brother and sister were killed. Remember?"

"Aye, I do." She remembered the terrible story all too clearly.

Looking down, he traced the blanket's dull brown plaid with his finger. "Mmm, but I didn't tell you how I stole horses and rode west with Khaw to join her people."

"Is that all? I don't blame ye for stealing a pair of horses. Ye had to."

He glanced at her from beneath lowered brows then went back to tracing the plaid pattern. "No, that's not all. It took us a while to track down Khaw's band, and once we did, it took even longer for the Kiowas to accept me. They didn't trust me because of my white blood. The only one to speak up for me was Tsoia." Jack grinned. "He was young and wild back then, and curious enough about my life with the *bcdalpago* – the hairy mouth ones – that he was willing to give me a chance."

"The hairy mouth ones? What does that mean?"

He chuckled. "Many white men grow a mustache and beard. Indians don't."

"Oh, yes, I've noticed that ye don't shave."

"None of the braves do. If a stray hair sprouts, we pull it." His humor quickly fled. "Getting back to the point, with Tsoia's help I convinced the others to let me ride with them on a raid into Texas."

Rose caught her breath. Too shocked to speak, she clutched her cross. She couldn't hide her reaction when he raised his head to meet her horrified stare.

"You've heard about some of the raids, I see. I'm sure your brother will welcome you if you run to him for protection from me." His resigned tone and the grim twist of his lips made clear he expected her to jump up and run.

"Damn ye, Jack Lafarge!" she flared, forgetting her momentary shock. "Even though we took no such vow, I wed ye for better or worse, sir, and I'll not be walking away."

He blinked and his mouth worked, but no words came out. Glad to see she'd set him back on his heels, she discarded modesty, allowing the blanket to fall into her lap. She crossed her arms, deliberately drawing his gaze to her breasts. Let him look! Maybe he'd think twice before again suggesting that she leave.

"Now, tell me about this raid ye went on. Did ye kill women and children?"

His eyes lifted, anger burning in their black depths. "No! I never touched any woman or child. I couldn't, not after what happened to my brother and sister."

"Hmm. But ye did scalp and mutilate their men?"

He turned his face away, unwilling to confirm her guess. He wasn't going to get off that easily, she determined.

"Answer me! Tell me the truth, all of it."

His head whipped around. "You want the truth? Fine," he gritted. "I took my share of scalps, sure, and I listened to men scream while they were being tortured. I'm not going into the details because they'd make you sick." He screwed his eyes shut and bent his head, long black hair shadowing his tormented expression. "Lord knows it sickens me to remember some of the things I saw and did."

Rose swallowed hard. Seeing his genuine remorse, she couldn't stay angry. Still, like drawing poison from a snake bite, she sought to draw out as much of his festering secrets as possible. "Did ye go on other raids?" she asked.

He nodded, took a shaky breath and looked up. "I rode with Tsoia and the others three times. When we returned from the last raid, we learned the white man's war was over."

"How did the news reach ye way out here?"

"It came from Comancheros, New Mexicans who traded with the Kiowa, Comanche and other tribes." He shrugged and rubbed his bandaged chest. "After that, Khaw started nagging me to go back to the white man's world. She sensed what was coming for her people and didn't want me caught up in the battles. Finally, I gave in to her, put on the torn duds I'd worn while fighting with the Rebs, and rode into Fort Sill. That was ten years ago."

Taking a deep breath, Jack concluded, "Later I headed down to the Double C to let Toby Crawford's folks know I was with him when he died. I've wandered back and forth between there and the fort and here ever since."

Rose reached out to stroke the sculpted line of his jaw. "And you've been lonely, haven't ye," she whispered. It wasn't a question. She knew she was right because she'd suffered the same awful loneliness during her years in the convent.

Jack caught her hand and pressed it over his heart. "Yeah, until I met you, P'ayn-nah. I'm never lonely with you. That's why I couldn't bring myself to tell you about the raids. I was so afraid you'd leave me. Still am, but seeing how horrified you are by what Tsoia wants to do to Star-girl, I knew I had to confess. You need to know what kind of man you hooked up with. I had to give you the chance to walk away, even if means losing you."

"You'll never lose me, my love. We both have terrible memories, but together we'll banish them."

His adam's apple bobbed and she detected the glisten of moisture in his eyes. Without a word, he rose to his knees, placed his hands at her waist and pulled her up against him. She caught her breath, feeling her breasts pillow against his chest. He buried his face in her hair while one hand slid around her to caress her back. His other hand began a slow journey down her side, touching off tiny bolts of lightning. He nuzzled her throat, his tongue flicking out to taste her, and traveled lower. When he reached the crest of her breast, he made her cry out with his talented mouth. His hands roamed over all the sensitive places he'd found last night, reclaiming them for himself.

She clasped his head between her hands. "Kiss me!"

"My pleasure, darlin'," he said thickly, bringing his mouth to hers. While their tongues performed a delicious dance, he parted her thighs with his knee and moved his hand to where she most wanted it. Opening her, he delved into her passage with one then two fingers, lighting a bonfire within her. She twisted in his arms, desperate for him to satisfy the need he'd created.

Tearing her mouth from his, she begged, "Jack, please! I

want ye inside me!"

"All right!" he gasped. Gripping her parted thighs, he positioned her over his jutting staff. She groaned as he pushed into her, loving the sensation of being filled. He lifted her almost off then sheathed himself again. She wrapped her legs around his hips and threw her head back, crying out each time he drove upward, caressing her internal flesh. He went slow, bringing her close to completion but never quite allowing her to reach it. When she couldn't stand one more moment, she pounded at his shoulders.

"Finish it!" she cried.

He growled deep in his throat and, laying her on her back, he pounded into her fast and hard. Within seconds, she cried out, this time in ecstasy. Almost immediately, he gave a matching cry and convulsed within her.

How she came to be lying on her side moments later, with Jack's arms around her and his body fused to her backside, Rose didn't know. Had she passed out from exhaustion after that explosive burst of pleasure? She couldn't remember but decided it didn't matter. It was enough to know he was there with her, that he wanted her as much as she wanted him, and that he had trusted her with his last dark secret. The past was over and done with. From now on they would walk into the future together.

Feeling the slow rhythm of her husband's breathing, she sighed contentedly and joined him in slumber.

CHAPTER NINETEEN

The next morning, Rose knelt beside the creek, washing the pretty skirt and blouse Juana had lent her a few days ago. Finished rinsing yucca soap from the garments, she wrung them out, stood and draped them over a low tree limb. As soon as both were dry, she would return them to Juana, who'd lost her few extra clothes in the fire, along with all her family's belongings.

Tsoia's cousin, Blue Elk, had welcomed him, Juana and Tsahle-ee into his lodge last night, and Rose supposed they would be spending several more nights there until a new tipi could be erected for them. That would require many yards of canvas, since there were no buffalo hides available, and new lodge poles. Most of the men, including Jack, Tye and Jeb, had set out earlier in search of tall, straight pine trees to serve as the poles.

Meanwhile, the village women had collected as much canvas as they could spare from their meager stores and were now busy cutting out sections that would be sewn together to form a large semi-circle for wrapping around the pole framework. Walking back to camp, Rose spotted Juana down on her knees cutting canvas. She went to kneel beside her.

"Can I help?"

"You should be with Ghost Woman, caring for her," Juana said, glancing at her without pausing at her task.

"I'll look in on her in a while. She ate well this morning and she was asleep when I left her. It will take time for her to regain her strength, but I think she'll recover fully."

"That is good. She has suffered much."

"So have you, my friend," Rose said softly as she drew the knife Jack had given her and set to work cutting another side of the tough material. "I'm terribly sorry for bringing so much trouble to you and your family."

Frowning, Juana shook her head. "I told you before it's not your doing. Star-girl is to blame for all of it. And she will pay."

"Have the men decided what to do with her?" A knot formed in Rose's middle at the thought of the brutal punishment they might mete out.

"No. They will hold another council after they return with poles for our new lodge. Then they will decide. I hope they choose to beat her." Juana's voice rang with vengeful anger. "I wish to strike the blows."

Rose swallowed a protest, recalling Jack's warning not to make the men angry last night. Juana was too furious to listen, she surmised, and it would do no good to argue with her. All she could do was wait and hope the Kiowa braves came to a merciful decision.

* * *

Wiping sweat from his forehead with his hand, Jack was glad he wore only his breechclout and leggings. Going shirtless made the warm day easier to tolerate, but cutting down trees and chopping off branches was still hot work. With that task completed and the slender tree trunks lashed to horses, ready to be dragged to the village, he and the other men mounted up for the trek back.

Tye Devlin and Jeb Crawford rode up, flanking him on either side. This surprised him since they'd barely spoken to him all morning.

"Jeb and I have a proposition for ye," Tye said.

"That right?" Jack eyed him warily.

"Aye, we'd like to hire ye on as assistant foreman for the Double C."

"And blacksmith," Jeb added.

Astonished, Jack glanced back and forth between the two. "Did Rose put you up to this?" he asked suspiciously.

Tye scowled and said testily, "Nay, she knows nothing about it. 'Twas Jeb's idea."

Jack turned his head, meeting Jeb's friendly smile.

"You're mighty handy with a hammer and tongs, and you know your way around cattle better than most," the older man said.

"And Tye here could use some help running things. 'Sides, I figure Miz Rose might like to be near her kin. Don't you think?"

"She might." Jack had been thinking exactly the same thing. "But you've never had an assistant foreman before. Why do you need one now? You and Del aren't ready for rockers yet, are you?"

Jeb chuckled and shifted in his saddle. "Not by a long shot, young fella, but Del has him a touch of reumatiz and spending all day in the saddle makes it worse. As for me, I could be away from the ranch for a spell. I've got in mind doing some visiting."

"Aye, with a certain widow woman and her boys, I'm guessing," Tye said with a grin.

"Could be you're right," Jeb allowed with a glint in his eyes. Then he aimed a probing stare at Jack. "So, what do you think? You interested in the job or not?"

Wondering what widow woman Tye referred to, Jack shrugged. "I might be. I'll think about it. Thanks for the offer."

"You'll talk it over with Rose, I hope," Tye said. "She deserves a say in the matter."

Jack glared at him in irritation. "I know that. She'll have her say." Kneeing his horse, he rode ahead to catch up with Tsoia.

As the afternoon passed, the job offer weighed on his mind. If he hired on fulltime at the Double C, he wouldn't be near his mother over winter to make sure she had enough food and warm blankets. Tsoia and Juana would watch out for her, he knew, and he could send money up here for supplies, but that wasn't the same as being nearby in case she needed him. Still, he had a wife now. He must think of her and the children he hoped they'd soon have. Rose did deserve a say in this. Tye Devlin hadn't needed to tell him that. He fully intended to talk the matter over with her. No doubt she'd prefer to live near her kin, and he wanted her to be happy. But his mother . . . .

He sighed. This was not going to be an easy decision.

The sun was going down in a blaze of red and purple when they arrived at the village. Flickering campfires and the cheerful voices of women and children welcomed them back. Tsahle-ee came running as fast as his short legs could carry him. Shrieking happily, he flew into his father's arms as soon as Tsoia alighted from his paint. Juana followed close behind him, anxious to greet her husband and inspect the poles for their new lodge.

Jack spotted Rose as she hurried to meet him. Her sweet smile banished his ponderous thoughts. Arms encircling her slim curves, he kissed her soundly, not caring who watched, including her brother.

"I missed you," he murmured.

"I missed ye too." She turned in his embrace to look over the poles now being unlashed from the tired pack horses. "'Twould seem ye had good luck finding the proper trees."

"Yeah, we should have plenty to put up a new tipi," he agreed, moving to stand at her side, keeping one arm around her.

Tye and Jeb walked over to join them. Slapping his hat against his leg to knock off the accumulated dust, Tye said, "Sis, you're a bit flushed. You're not feverish, are ye?"

Rose tipped her head back to meet Jack's caressing gaze, a warm pink painting her cheeks. "Nay, I'm simply glad to see my husband."

He grinned, hungrily staring at her lips.

"Och, newlyweds! I should have known." Sounding disgusted, Tye crossed his arms and shook his head. "Ye can't wait to get him alone, I suppose."

Feeling Rose tense and seeing her duck her head in embarrassment, Jack scowled at her brother. He opened his mouth to warn the Irishman not to say anymore unless he wanted a fist in his teeth, but Jeb's snort of laughter saved him the trouble.

The older man cocked his head, eyeing Tye. "How long have you and Lil been married now?" he asked, scratching his whiskered chin.

Tye frowned at him. "'Twill be a year come July. Why?"

"Oh, I was just recalling a while back when you and David Taylor went off hunting for a couple or three days. The evening you got home, you barely wolfed down your supper before you hustled Lil upstairs. Guess you're still newlyweds, hmm?"

Tye flushed dark red. "I'm thinking I'll wolf down some food right now, away from you, ye auld scoundrel." Clamping his hat back on, he stomped off.

Jeb chuckled. "Sorry, Miz Rose. He didn't mean no harm. He's been mighty worried about you and set on putting a bullet in Jack for making off with you the way he did."

"But he knows there's no need for that now."

"He does, and he's not about to do anything that'd hurt you. It's just that he's still getting used to the idea of you being Jack's wife." Touching his hat to both of them, he sauntered toward the cook fires.

"You want me to hustle you off to our lodge?" Jack whispered playfully in Rose's ear.

She tipped her head back, gave him a sultry smile and ran her fingertip down his bare chest. "Not just yet. First we'd best get ye something to eat. You'll need your strength, aye?"

Jack grinned, enjoying this new, flirtatious side of his wife.

* * *

As it turned out he didn't make it to their lodge as soon as he'd hoped. After the men had all eaten, Wise Hawk called them together to decide Star-girl's fate. Tye and Jeb were not invited to join them this time, but the old chief did send for the accused one and her mother. Star-girl looked terrified when she was thrust into the circle of men, as well she should, Jack thought. Tsoia still wanted to cut off her nose. Others favored beating her.

Jack himself had come to regret letting Walks Softly convince him not to turn her daughter over to the Army patrol the other day. But it was not too late. He would offer to escort her to the fort tomorrow and turn her in, he decided.

Wise Hawk spoke first. "I have invited Walks Softly to speak to us in the matter of her daughter's punishment. She told me her thoughts while most of you were gone today. I found wisdom in her words. Now you must hear her." He extended his gnarled hand, inviting the gray-haired woman to speak.

Walks Softly stepped forward, head shyly bent. Her hands clutched the sides of her long calico shirt. Worn over a doeskin skirt, the garment hung loose on the woman's thin frame. Nervously clearing her throat, she spoke so quietly that Wise Hawk had to ask her to speak up. Nodding, she took a deep breath and began again.

"I am shamed by the evil things my daughter has done." She kept her eyes lowered, refusing to look at any of the men – or Star-girl, who scowled but held her tongue. "She must be punished. I know this, but I ask you not to cruelly beat her or make her ugly by cutting off her nose. Show mercy, I beg you. Give her a chance to live as a proper woman."

She paused to draw breath and dart a wary glance at her listeners. "There is a man who will take her for his wife even knowing her evil deeds, I believe. He has offered for her more than once, but I refused because she does not care for him."

"Haun-nay!" Star-girl cried. "He is old and he already has two wives!"

Tsoia shot to his feet and charged over to her, bringing Jack halfway to his feet, ready to intervene if necessary. "Be still!" his blood brother snarled at the terrified girl. "If you speak again I will cut out your tongue." He waved his knife in front of her eyes convincingly.

Cringing before him, she slapped a hand across her mouth and said not a word. Tsoia stood over her for a long moment, looking like he wished she'd say a word, any word, and give him an excuse to carry out his threat. Finally, he slipped his knife back into the sheath at his waist and resumed his place in the circle.

Jack relaxed, but only slightly. Tsoia's furious gaze never left Star-girl.

"The man is Comanche," Walks Softly doggedly continued. "He lives far from here. If you give my miserable child to him, she will cause no more trouble for this village." She glanced coldly at Star-girl. "And her husband's wives will beat her until she learns her proper place."

Her last words drew laughter from the men. Several nodded in agreement. Tsoia scowled but shrugged in grudging acceptance. Star-girl hung her head and wept.

* * *

Rose lay awake, waiting for Jack, anxious to know what the men decreed. When he finally entered the lodge, she sat up, clasping the blanket to her breasts. "What's the decision?" she blurted.

He padded over to her, laughing softly. "Can't wait to find out, hmm? Couldn't you greet your husband properly first?" he chided, kneeling on one knee beside their bed.

"I'm sorry," she said, feeling the gentle bite of his words. Leaning toward him, she kissed him in eager welcome, letting the blanket slip as he pressed her to him.

"Much better, wife," he breathed into her mouth while his hand went exploring, causing her to gasp when he found her breast and lightly pinched her nipple. He continued his playful roaming for long moments, rousing her need for him to a fever pitch. Then he set her away and stood, gazing down at her, desire burning in his dark eyes.

"You are so beautiful," he said, voice low and husky. "Your breasts are flushed with passion and your lips glisten from my kisses. Do you know what the sight of you does to me?"

Quivering with desire and breathing fast, she whispered, "I know what the sight of you does to me." As she spoke, she reached up and wrapped her hand around his full member, jutting forward beneath his breechclout. She smiled when he gave a choked cry, pleased that she could draw such a reaction from him, and stroked her hand slowly up and down the length of him.

"Stop!" he growled, tugging her hand away. "Anymore and I'll lose control, and we'll both regret it."

Disappointed yet glorying in her power over him, Rose watched avidly as, with shaking hands, he stripped off his leggings and the dark piece of cloth that kept him from her. She caught her breath when he sprang free. Kicking away the blanket covering her lower half, she lay back and held her arms up to him. In a heartbeat, he was between her legs, pushing into her.

"You feel so good!" he groaned, leaning on his arms, staring into her eyes.

"You . . . do . . . too!" she panted between his powerful thrusts. Within seconds they both cried out, reaching the peak of passion at the same instant. As the waves of pleasure receded, Rose went limp, barely finding the strength to hold him when he slowly collapsed upon her. He was heavy, forcing her to take shallow breaths, but she didn't mind. She loved the feel of him in her arms.

She clutched him tight a moment later when he rolled over, taking her with him, reversing their positions so that she lay on top of him, with his shaft still a part of her. Rubbing her cheek on his muscular chest, she purred in contentment. He made a deep, answering sound that reverberated beneath her ear. They rested quietly for several minutes. Rose was almost asleep when Jack spoke.

"Do you still want to know what we decided to do with Star-girl?"

"Och! I forgot all about her." Levering up with her hands on his shoulders, she saw him grin and frowned down at him. "Ye devil! Ye deliberately distracted me, didn't ye?"

He chuckled. "Couldn't let you get away with nagging me about her the minute I walked in. So I gave you something else to think about."

"I didn't nag!" she huffed. "I merely asked a question. Which ye never answered." She tried to disengage herself from him, but he splayed a big hand across her bottom, preventing her from moving away.

"Don't be angry, P'ayn-nah. I just wanted you so much, I couldn't wait."

"Oh!" she stopped trying to wriggle free.

"Come here and I'll tell you everything you want to know." Smiling, he gently drew her back down, nestling her against him. Kissing the top of her head, he brushed his fingers lightly up and down her spine, making her tingle. He continued to stroke her as he related Walks Softly's suggestion and the men's decision to honor her request.

"Tsoia volunteered to deliver her to her husband-to-be tomorrow."

Alarmed, Rose raised her head. "But he hates her. He might cut off her nose."

"Don't worry. Wise Hawk accepted Tsoia's offer, but he's sending Walks Softly along to formally give her daughter to the Comanche suitor. And to make sure Star-girl gets there with her nose still attached, I figure."

Rose relaxed once more. "I'm glad. Wise Hawk truly is wise."

"He is. Now, can we forget about Star-girl? I've got other things on my mind," Jack drawled, his tone as slow and thick as warm molasses. Feeling another part of him thicken within her, Rose lost interest in everything but her husband.

Hours later, she roused to the touch of Jack's lips raining butterfly kisses over her face. She smiled but couldn't force her eyes open until he nibbled her ear, making her squirm. Finally managing to open her eyes partway, she found him raised up on one hand, leaning over her.

"Is it morning already?" she mumbled.

"Not quite, but soon, and there's something I need to talk to you about."

"What is it?" She yawned and stretched, trying to wake up.

"Yesterday your brother and Jeb offered me a job as assistant foreman on the Double C."

That brought Rose fully alert. "Begorrah! After Tye being so angry with ye? I can hardly believe it."

He nodded, frowning. "I was surprised at first, but then I realized he wants you close by."

Thinking he was right, she sat up and brushed tangled hair away from her face. "What did ye tell them?"

"That I'd think about it and talk to you. You'd like to be near your kin, I reckon."

"Aye, but what of your mother? Surely we can't go off and leave her."

"I thought about that too, but Juana and Tsoia will look after her if I ask them to. They've been doing it right along anyway." He caressed her cheek, ran his hand down her throat and across the top swell of her breasts. "And I want you to be happy."

Touched by his desire to please her, she ran her fingers through his long raven hair, enjoying the touch of it against her sensitive skin, and gazed into his eyes. "'Tis your decision to make, my love. I shall be happy anywhere as long as we're together."

His adams apple bobbed and she heard him swallow. "For most of my life I told myself I would never take a white wife. I didn't want to love you, but my heart said different. Now I thank the Great Spirit for sending you to me."

She caught her breath and glad tears blurred her vision as he wrapped her in his embrace. Kissing her tenderly, he murmured, "You are everything to me, P'ayn-nah. I love you."

* * *

By the time they emerged from the lodge, the sun was well up. Tsoia had already departed on his mission with Star-girl and her mother, and Rose wasn't terribly surprised when Tye strode up to her and announced that he and Jeb would also be leaving.

Handing a tin cup filled with steaming black coffee to Jack, she sipped from her own cup and smiled at her anxious looking brother. "Of course, ye must be getting home to Lil."

"Aye, she's had the baby by now. I only pray to God she and the child are well." He gave a wry laugh and rubbed the back of his neck. "David warned me once that I'd one day learn how it feels to wait and worry while my wife struggles to bring our babe into the world. Little did I know how right he was."

"You've had it worse than most," Rose said guiltily. "I'm sorry Jack and I caused ye to be apart from Lil when she needed ye with her."

He smiled crookedly. "Aye, well, she practically ordered me to go after ye. She'll be glad to know I found ye safe and . . . happy." He turned to Jack. "Ye haven't said yea or nay to our offer." He tilted his head toward Jeb, who had sauntered over.

"I haven't made up my mind yet," Jack replied

Tye frowned. "I'd like your word that you'll at least bring Rose back for a visit soon. 'Twould set Jessie's mind at ease. She had a vision of the two of ye that frightened her half to death."

"Wh-what was the vision?" Rose asked fearfully. Her sister's visions had a way of coming true, often with dreadful results.

Tye glanced at her and frowned. "He had hold of ye." He directed a hard stare at Jack "Ye were forcing yourself on Rosie, and she was trying to fight ye off."

Rose exchanged a mystified glance with Jack. Then his eyes suddenly widened and he burst out laughing. She scowled, wondering what was so funny until, all of a sudden she, too, remembered the scene Jessie had obviously foreseen.

"'Twas the first time ye kissed me!" she exclaimed.

"Must be. That's the only time I can think of."

"What are ye talking about?" Tye demanded to know.

Jack shrugged. "It was our second or third day on the trail riding up here," he explained. "We stopped to eat and rest the horses. Rose gave me this look like she wanted me to kiss her."

"I did no such thing," she protested.

"It sure looked like it to me." He winked roguishly, and she couldn't resist smiling.

"Anyhow, I kissed her. She got scared and pounded on me with her fists, as I recall." Jack shrugged. "That must be what your sister saw in that vision of hers."

Struck by Jack's comment, Rose said, "You're not a bit surprised to hear about Jessie's ability to see the future, are ye? Ye must have known about her, but how? I'm sure I never mentioned her gift to ye."

He shrugged. "I learned about your *gift* the day I met you, remember? And I figured there was something . . . *special* about all three of you." He met Tye's wary gaze. "Most everybody on the Double C and the Taylor place knows you located the little girl that time when she went missing, but no one knows *how* you did it. And I've heard tell how your sister, Miz Jessie, predicts things, and most times her predictions come true."

"Damn!" Tye shook his head. "I had no idea there's been so much talk about us. Rumors can be dangerous for our kind. Ones such as us were called witches back in Ireland. D'ye remember our mam's stories, Rosie?"

"Aye, she said some were even burned at the stake in times past."

"Nothing like that's gonna happen here, or down home," Jeb said. "Tye, you're a hero to most folks for saving the young'un. As for Miz Jessie, you don't need to worry. David Taylor would kill anybody who threatened her, and he's got a small army of hands to back him up."

Jeb turned to Rose, a twinkle in his gray eyes. "And this young lady has Kiowa relatives now who, from the stories I've been hearing, think she's big medicine. I feel sorry for any fool who lays a hand on her." He eyed Jack, mouth quirking. "Except her husband, of course."

Jack laughed and Rose was glad to see Tye's mood lighten. When Jack promised to bring her for a visit soon, her brother actually smiled and shook his hand.

"Give me hug, then, colleen," he said, drawing Rose into his embrace. "We won't say goodbye, for I'll be seeing ye soon."

"Aye, that ye will, big brother," she whispered, slightly choked up. She kissed his cheek and stepped back, returned Jeb's genial "So long," and watched the two of them mount their horses.

With farewell waves, they rode out, leaving Rose feeling rather forlorn until Jack came to her side. He gathered her close, offering comfort.

"How'd you like to ride over to Rainy Mountain and climb to

the top? The path up isn't too steep and you might like the view."
 Excitement washed away her sadness. "I'm sure I'll love it."

CHAPTER TWENTY

When Rose went to check on Ghost Woman early the next morning, she found her sitting up on her bed of furs. Dressed for the day, she was brushing her silver hair. Surprised, Rose shot a questioning glance at She-who-laughs. The girl had kindly stayed with the old woman during the night, since Walks Softly and Tsoia had not yet returned from conveying Star-girl to her intended husband. Rose appreciated being able to spend the night with Jack, but she wondered if they'd been wise to trust his mother's care to one so young.

She-who-laughs shrugged her shoulders, pointed at Ghost Woman and shook her head, conveying her inability to stop the elder from getting up.

"Do not be angry with her," Ghost Woman said. "She tried to make me stay down, but I cannot lie here another day. I wish to feel the wind on my face again."

"Aye? Well, I hope ye don't feel the red earth on your face when your legs give out," Rose said sternly. "Ye could barely sit up to swallow your broth yesterday. What makes ye think you're strong enough to stand and walk now?" As she spoke, She-who laughs slipped out, plainly eager to escape.

"I am not strong enough without your help, Daughter." Ghost Woman smiled, dark eyes twinkling. "Come, help this foolish old woman to her feet."

Sighing, Rose threw up her hands. "Very well, but don't say I didn't warn ye." As gently as possible, she did as asked and handed Ghost Woman her walking stick to lean on. She wrapped a blanket around her mother-in-law's thin shoulders and collected bowls and spoons for their breakfast.

"Are ye sure ye want to do this, Khaw?" she asked worriedly.

"I am sure." Ghost Woman patted her supporting hand. "Help me out to the fire."

It was useless to argue. Assisting the old woman from the lodge and keeping an arm firmly around her, Rose walked her over to the cook fire and lowered her carefully to the ground. Juana stood bent over the cook pot dishing up breadroot porridge – made from prairie turnips, Rose had learned – for herself and a yawning Tsahle-ee. Glancing up, she smiled.

"It's good to see you up, Medicine Woman," she said.

"I am glad to be up."

Rose filled a bowl with porridge and handed it to Ghost Woman along with a horn spoon.

"Thank you, Daughter. Where is your husband? I do not see him."

"He went hunting with Blue Elk."

"Perhaps they will bring back some fat rabbits," Juana remarked, seating herself nearby and pointing her son to a spot beside her.

"That would be good," Ghost Woman said between mouthfuls. "We must begin making pemmican from the dried buffalo meat."

"It is already being done."

"Ah. I have missed much while lying on my back."

"It couldn't be helped. Ye were ill," Rose said, scooping up porridge for herself.

"Mmm, but your magic cured me." Swallowing another spoonful, Ghost Woman said casually, "Now you will return to your people and Jack will go with you."

Rose cut her a startled glance as she knelt next to her. "Did he say we're leaving?" she asked, folding her legs under her.

The old woman slurped more porridge before answering. "No, but you must go." She set her bowl down and gazed directly at Rose. "I told my son long ago that he must walk the white man's road. After my people gave up fighting, I thought different. I hoped Jack would make his home near me on the reservation, but that was selfish. I see now that he belongs with you and your people. It will not be easy for the two of you or your children, but it is the wisest path. There is nothing for you here."

Dearest Irish

"Medicine Woman is right, Toppah," Juana said, smiling sadly. "I love my husband and his people, but our life is hard. Tsoia told me your brother has offered Jack a fine position on his ranch in Texas. He should accept."

Stirring her lumpy porridge, Rose shrugged. "He hasn't decided yet, but he's promised we will visit my family soon."

Ghost woman nodded. "That is good. He will see with clear eyes where you belong and he will decide wisely."

Where I belong? I belong with Jack, no matter where that is, Rose thought.

* * *

They departed on a bright morning two days later. By then Tsoia, Juana and Tsahle-ee were settled in their new lodge, the canvas sections of which Rose had helped stitch together. Walks Softly was back and, although pained by an unhappy parting with her daughter, she also seemed relieved. Rose was grateful for her presence. It made leaving Ghost Woman somewhat easier.

She stood by as Jack bid his mother a quiet farewell. When she stepped forward to take her turn at saying goodbye, her mother-in-law caught her in a tight embrace.

"Take care of my son," she whispered.

"I will," Rose promised, choked up. Stepping back, she smiled and, with tears blurring her vision, let Jack boost her onto Brownie's back.

They'd already exchanged parting words with Tsoia and Juana, receiving earnest promises to watch over Ghost Woman. Now, with waves and wishes for a good journey from the other villagers, they rode out. Gripped by sadness at leaving behind people she'd come to care for, who accepted her healing ability as a natural thing, Rose found little to say. Jack, too, appeared caught up in his thoughts. It was an hour or two later when he broke the silence.

"I'd like you to see my family's plantation, what's left of it, anyhow. It's kind of out of our way, but if you agree, we can stop by there before heading for the Double C."

"Och, I'd love to see where ye grew up," she said, spirits lifting.

"Yeah, well, there isn't mush to see these days."

"Still, I'd like to stop there."

"All right. Just don't expect too much."

With that decision made, they headed southeast, taking their time, and eventually crossed the Red River at Colbert's Ferry. Once in Texas, they continued east. It was late afternoon of the following day when Jack called a halt.

"We're on my family's land," he said as they dismounted.

"Oh, aye?" Squinting into the declining sun, Rose tugged the hat Jack had bought her at a trader's store lower and glanced around. She saw no sign of human habitation. Dotted with grass, brambles and a few wind-twisted trees, the landscape appeared empty and uninviting.

"Yeah, welcome to Belle Rouge. Used to be cotton fields everywhere you look," Jack said, leaning an arm across his saddle. "This part has gone wild. When we get closer to the home place tomorrow, you'll see plowed land where I rented it out."

"Ah, and your tenants, will I meet them?"

He chuckled. "I reckon you will. They'll be surprised to see I've finally taken a wife." He rounded his horse and drew her close. "And a white woman at that."

She frowned uncertainly. "D'ye think they'll disapprove?"

"No, but like I said, they'll be surprised." He dropped a quick kiss on her lips. "Come on, help me gather wood for a fire. It's getting dark and I'm starving." He kissed her again, more thoroughly this time. "For food and for you," he rasped.

Rose caught her breath, regretting when he released her. Excitement made her heart pump faster as they scrounged for dry wood. Once Jack laid a fire, they heated bacon and beans and wolfed down their dinner, often meeting each other's hungry gazes. When they'd eaten their fill, Jack undressed her and made love to her beside the low-burning fire. Afterward, Rose fell asleep with a smile on her lips, not caring about anything but the man who held her close.

She awoke before dawn to the cold splat of raindrops on her faces. Jack pulled her from their damp nest and, snatching up boots, clothes and blankets, they ran naked and laughing for a bent tree standing about a hundred yards away. They ducked under its gnarled bows, shivering in the chilly pre-dawn air. When Rose started to don her shirt, Jack stopped her.

"Don't. Not yet. I'll warm you, P'ayn-nah." True to his word, he soon had her blood running fast and hot.

Curled together, they slept late beneath their leafy guardian and the blanket Jack had spread over them at some point. When they woke again, the rain had passed and the sun shown brightly. Speaking little but smiling often, they dressed and ate a hasty breakfast of pemmican and water, then saddled up and rode on.

* * *

Jack's stomach knotted as it always did at the sight of his family's burned out home. Clenching his jaw, he ached to get his hands on the bastards who'd done this, but he knew that would never happen. He'd tried to track them down years back, after giving in to his mother's pleas and riding back to the white man's world, but it had been useless. The raiders were either dead or long since gone from these parts, and he wasn't going to spend his life searching for a lost trail. His folks wouldn't want him to, and it wouldn't bring back his sister and brother.

Turning his head, he read the shock on Rose's face. He'd told her about the raid, but nothing could have prepared her for seeing the charred stone chimney and overgrown mound, all that remained of his boyhood home.

"Like I said, there's not much to see."

Her blue agate eyes met his, filled with grief. "'Tis a sad thing to know you and your family once called this home." She gestured at the weed and vine covered ruin. "And to think those devils could heartlessly destroy it and murder the poor children. Surely God has a special place in hell for such as them."

Jack agreed with her but held his tongue, remembering some of the Kiowa raids he'd taken part in. Although he'd never lifted his hand against a woman or child, he'd done his share of killing and burning, and he'd watched far worse things being done. Was he any better than the animals who'd destroyed his home and family? Rose had shown him understanding and love. All he could do was love her in return and hope to erase the blackness from his soul.

They sat their horses in silence, staring at the scene of devastation for several minutes. Then Rose cleared her throat. "Might ye take me to the graves? I'd like to . . . tell them hello."

Something in his chest tightened. Only his dearest wife would put it that way. "Of course," he said, voice husky. He led her to the tall bur oak that stood sentinel over the two small graves. A wooden cross marked the head of each.

"My brother, François, lies there," he said, pointing to the grave on the left. "Angelique, my sister, lies next to him."

"What beautiful names! They're French, nay?"

"Yeah, Pa named them after his own brother and sister."

"Ah. But why didn't he give you a French name?"

Jack grin crookedly. "He did. My proper name is Jacque Antoine Bertrand Lafarge."

Rose slapped a hand over her mouth, attempting to smother her giggles. "Oh my, that's quite a mouthful," she said breathlessly.

"Right, and it fits me about as good as a poke bonnet fits a mule."

She giggled out loud this time. "'Tis a fine comparison, sir, and I'm afraid I must agree." Gazing down at the graves, she grew serious. "They've been kept up. Who does it, I wonder?"

"Oscar Leggett, one of my tenants, takes care of them when I'm not here. That's most of the time," he admitted with a twinge of guilt. Changing the subject, he said, "Come on, I'll introduce you to Oscar and his wife Mattie." Laying his hand at the small of her back, he urged her away from the small graves, back to their horses.

* * *

Riding slowly along a meandering path, Rose soon gazed upon neatly plowed fields with tender green shoots springing up from the reddish brown earth. "Are these Oscar's fields?"

"That to your left is his. He's got another one farther on past his and Mattie's cabin. This field to our right is rented to another family. We'll stop by their place after we pay Oscar and Mattie a visit. Oscar was my first tenant and he collects the rents for me. Guess you could say he's my manager."

"Ah. How did he come to be here?"

Jack laughed dryly. "He walked all the way from Georgia."

Wrinkling her brow, Rose asked, "'Tis a very long way, is it not?"

"Sure is. Took him almost two years to get here, the way he

tells it."

"Goodness! What made him undertake such a long journey on foot?"

"He didn't own a horse. Walking was his only choice. See, he was a slave until President Lincoln proclaimed all slaves free. By the time Oscar heard about that, his master's plantation had been overrun by General Sherman's Yankee troops. There was nothing left, no food, no shelter, no reason to stay. He'd heard rumors of how blacks might have an easier time in Texas, so he headed west. He hid out from Confederate patrols, found work where he could, stole food where he couldn't. Along the way he met Mattie. She'd run off from some place over in Louisiana. They took to each other and she walked the rest of the way with him."

"But how did they end up here on your land?" Rose persisted.

"Purely by chance. I found them squatting here after the war, when I came to look the place over. By then they had two babies, a broken down mule and a lean-to built out of tree branches and brush. Oscar had managed to plow a small section of land and plant him some cotton. Where he got the seeds, I didn't ask, but he knew what he was doing. Guess he'd have to after being a field hand on a cotton plantation.

"Anyway, I made a deal with him. He agreed to pay me a share of his earnings from the cotton. He kept the rest and got to go on working his field. That's what gave me the idea to rent out the land. I passed word around that I was looking for sharecroppers and it didn't take long to find some takers. Tenants have come and gone since then. These days, five families live on the place. Three are former slaves, one's a white man – a widower with two half grown sons – and one's a Choctaw with a wife and three little tykes. Oscar and Mattie have three sons and a pretty little daughter named Callie."

Seeing Jack smile, Rose guessed he held a special fondness for the girl. Would he be a caring father to his own children? Or would he rule them with a harsh voice and a leather strap the way her own sire had done? No, surely not that!

Directing her thoughts elsewhere, she said, "I'm curious. How do Oscar and the others sell their cotton?"

"They send it down the Red River by boat to Shreveport,

where the cotton is ginned and marketed."

"Ah, I see. And do they have food and other goods shipped up the river?"

Jack shook his head. "Not likely. They're not that well off. Once in a while, they might trade for sugar or tobacco, maybe some calico and such at the trader's place up river. For food, they all tend vegetable patches and I see to it they start out with a milk cow and chickens. Some manage to keep a few hogs, and when I can, I drive a steer or two this way. They don't have much."

"But ye make sure they have a home and enough to eat, at least. 'Tis a good man ye are, Jack Lafarge."

He frowned and shifted in his saddle, obviously uncomfortable with her praise. "Can't let young ones go hungry. I've seen enough of that on the reservation." After a long pause, he muttered so low that she could hardly hear, "And I've done too many wrongs."

Rose leaned over to touch his arm, drawing his dark gaze back to her. "Ye can't undo the past, my love, anymore than I can. But surely the good ye do here helps balance the scales."

One corner of his mouth twitched up. "I hope you're right, P'ayn-nah."

The words were barely out of his mouth when a sturdy looking cabin came into view. "That's Oscar's place, and that's Mattie out front." Sounding relieved, he spurred his mount up a narrow path to the dwelling with Rose following close behind him.

Busy hanging wet laundry on a line strung between the cabin and a post standing at an angle to the log building, a plump, light-skinned black woman with a scarf around her head straightened at the sound of their approach. Shading her eyes with one hand, she studied them for a brief moment. Then she let out a piercing cry and shouted, "Mr. Jack! Oscar, Mr. Jack's come ta call! And he's got a white lady with him. Get on out here!"

Jack laughed as she picked up her skirts and ran to meet them. Sliding to the ground before his horse came to a complete halt, he caught the woman in a bear hug and lifted her off her feet. Then he set her lightly down. Holding her at arm's length, he said, "Mattie, you get more beautiful every time I see you."

Mattie, who was indeed lovely, snorted at his compliment and swatted the air. "Mr. Jack, you's a born charmer, but you best be

Dearest Irish

savin' those sweet words for this here pretty white lady." Smiling brightly, she turned inquisitive amber eyes toward Rose as she dismounted.

Pivoting, Jack held out his hand, and Rose stepped to his side. He slipped his arm around her as she returned the other woman's genial smile. "Mattie, this is Rose, my wife."

"You don't say! Well, ain't that just fine."

"Did I hear right?" a deep bass voice called out. It belonged to a tall, strapping black man striding toward them from the far side of the cabin. "You done took yo'self a wife?" Grinning hugely, he stuck out a hand that looked half again the size of Jack's. The two men shook hands and pounded each other on the back.

"Howdy, Oscar. Yeah, you heard right."

"I'll be, yuh finally jumped the stick!" The ebony-skinned giant laughed heartily.

Jack grinned and caught Rose's hand, drawing her forward. "P'ayn-nah, this is Oscar Leggett. Oscar, I'd like you to meet Rose, my wife."

"Mighty pleased to meet yuh, ma'am," the big man rumbled with a wide smile.

"I'm pleased to ye too, Mr. Leggett."

His wiry brows shot upward in surprise. Then he shook his head. "Just call me Oscar, Miz Rose. It's what I's used to."

She smiled. "Very well, Oscar, but in that case ye must call me just plain Rose. Please."

He sent Jack a doubtful glance as if asking his permission. Getting an amused grin in response, he said, "All right, if'n that's the way yuh wants it . . . Rose." Clearing his corded throat, he added, "I reckon yuh already said how-do to my Mattie." He laid a big paw gently on his wife's shoulder and they exchanged an affectionate glance.

"I'm sorry, I didn't have the chance, but I'm most happy to make your acquaintance, Mattie."

"Same goes for me, Rose. Come and set a spell in the shade." Pointing to the cabin's porch, their genial hostess led the way, chattering, "Land o' Goshen, it shore is warm for a spring day! I brewed us some sassafras tea a while ago. It's mighty refreshin'. And Oscar has him a jug stashed away, if you wants a taste, Mr. Jack."

"The tea will do fine, Mattie."

With a nod, she looked up at her husband, who was a good foot taller than her, and commanded, "Oscar, go fetch some ice from the ice house."

"Yessum. Be back right quick, folks," he told Rose and Jack, and he loped off to do Mattie's bidding.

Mounting the shallow porch steps, she pointed to a pair of rough-hewn chairs padded with calico covered cushions. "Set you down and be comfortable. Where'd y'all ride in from?"

"From the Territory," Jack replied, refusing a chair in favor of leaning against one of the porch roof supports framing the steps.

"Visited yore mama, I reckon."

"Yeah, I wanted her to meet Rose," he said, not mentioning his mother's illness.

"Uh-huh." Planting her hands on her ample hips, Mattie eyed them shrewdly. "How'd she take it seein' the two o' you together?"

Rose caught her meaning and stiffened while Jack merely crossed his arms and crooked his lips in a half smile. "She wasn't in favor of us marrying at first, but she came around."

Mattie opened her mouth as if to question him further, but she evidently thought better of it. "Glad to hear that. I'd best collect the tea and some cups." With that, she turned and entered the cabin, leaving the door ajar.

Rose searched Jack's face, looking for his reaction to the woman's question. Meeting her worried gaze, he moved to crouch beside her and patted her knee. "It's all right. She wasn't judging us. She's afraid for us, the same as Khaw."

Taking his word, Rose's trepidation eased. Before she could speak, Oscar returned. Jack rose and stepped back as his tenant – and clearly his friend – took the steps in one giant stride. He carried a bucket filled with chunks of ice, no doubt chipped from a larger block.

"This oughtta do us. We'll have that tea nice n' cold. Just yuh wait n' see." Grinning, he marched into the cabin to help Mattie prepare the drinks.

Moments later, as promised, Rose enjoyed her first swallow of the iced drink from a cold tin cup. "Oh, that's delicious! Ye must give me your recipe, Mattie."

"Glad yuh like it, M . . . er, Rose. Ain't nothin' to makin' it.

Just boil some chopped up sassafras root, strain it good and add honey, or sugar if you got it."

"Think I could have some more?" Jack asked.

"Lawsy me, course yuh can." Taking his cup, Mattie dashed inside to refill it.

Oscar, who sat sprawled on the top step with his back against the post opposite Jack's, cleared his throat. "What y'all doin' over this way, Mr. Jack? It ain't rent time yet, if'n yuh don't mind me sayin' so," he said guardedly.

"No need to worry, Oscar, I'm not here to collect any rents. I only wanted Rose to see the place before we head south to her brother's."

"Oh, well, that's good then," the big man said, tone brightening.

"Where are Callie and the boys?" Jack asked once Mattie returned with his refilled cup.

"I sent the boys out to hoe the far field," Oscar replied. "Callie's over to Red Gardener's place. He asked for her to give him a hand with mendin' his boys' duds."

Mattie sighed as she sat down in the vacant chair next to Rose. "Those pore boys' britches is so patched up, it's a wonder they don't fall apart," she said grimly.

Jack scowled. "Gardener's still drinking up his profits, I take it."

Oscar nodded. "He shore is, and it's pure disgustin' the way he treats those two young'uns."

"He's taking a strap to them again?"

"Yessir. Their raggedy shirts don't hide their marked up backs. I'd do the same to their no-good pa if'n I dared," Oscar growled. "But he'd have his hooded friends down on us sure as shootin'. I cain't risk Mattie and my own young'uns."

Rose watched Jack stiffen. Seeing the fury in his eyes, she feared what he had in mind when he handed her his empty cup.

"Stay here. I'll be back in a while."

Letting the cup drop along with hers, she jumped to her feet. "Nay! Whatever you're thinking, don't do it. That man might be dangerous!"

He caught hold of her arms. "P'ayn-nah, I can't walk away and let him beat hell out of his sons. You know that."

She swallowed hard, wanting to argue, but as he said, she knew he couldn't turn his back on endangered children. And she knew why. They reminded him of his brother and sister. Giving a reluctant nod, she whispered, "Be careful. Please."

"I will. Stay here with Mattie and Oscar. I won't be long."

He spoke true. He wasn't gone more than a quarter hour, but it seemed like forever to Rose. Refusing Mattie's suggestion that she wait inside the cabin, she huddled in her chair on the porch, watching for Jack. Seated quietly beside her, Mattie took her hand, and Rose clung to it tightly. She didn't draw an easy breath until she saw Jack riding up the path toward them. On his lap, he held a young girl, perhaps eight or ten years of age – Callie, Rose surmised.

Shooting from her chair, she rushed down the steps to meet him. She waited impatiently while he dismounted and stood the little girl on her feet. Callie eyed her for a moment then called out to her mother and went running for the safety of her arms. By then Rose was wrapped in Jack's arms and kissing him boldly, screened by his long black hair. So absorbed was she in the feel of him that she didn't hear Oscar's bass chuckle or Mattie's delighted giggles until Jack broke off their hungry kiss.

Blushing, she stepped back when he released her. Only then did she notice his swollen cheek and the blood trickling from a cut near his left eye. "Och! You're hurt!" she cried, lightly fingering his injury.

He caught her hand and kissed her fingers. "It's nothing. Gardener looks a lot worse." He grinned, clearly pleased with himself.

Rose turned her hand, catching hold of his. "Your knuckles are bloody too. Come on, I'll clean them for ye. And you'll tell me everything that happened."

Jack favored her with a crooked grin. "You're getting downright bossy, P'ayn-nah."

They ended up spending the night with Mattie, Oscar and their family. Jack told the story of his encounter with Gardener to Rose and their hosts, reporting how he'd pounded it into the drunken lout that he was to buy decent clothes for his sons and was not to beat them again. If he didn't obey those orders, and if he dared cause trouble for Oscar and Mattie or any of the other tenants, he could expect far worse when Jack learned of it.

Much to his chagrin and Rose's amusement, he was begged to repeat the whole tale when the three Leggett boys, smaller versions of Oscar, returned home from working their father's field. It also came out that Oscar was engaged in building on to the back of the cabin, where he and Mattie would finally have a room of their own, away from their offspring. After a night spent trying to sleep among the noisy brood, Rose well understood that necessity.

She and Jack said goodbye early the next morning and, forgoing their plans to visit the other tenants, headed southeast toward Bosque County and her family. As they rode, Rose thought more and more about the offer Jeb Crawford and her brother had made to Jack. She knew he disliked the idea of living so far from his mother in the winter months when life was hardest on the reservation. As did she, but Ghost Woman's sage advice remained ever on her mind. For the sake of the children she and Jack hoped to conceive, accepting the position of assistant foreman on the Double C seemed the wisest course.

At the same time, Rose wished there was some way they could live on the Lafarge plantation. Not only would they be closer to Ghost Woman, but they'd have the companionship of Oscar and Mattie. It was this thought that planted an idea in her brain. She didn't know if it would work and hesitated to bring it up, but during their second day on the trail she decided to mention it. The sun was high in the sky, the day pleasantly warm when they stopped to eat and rest the horses.

Setting aside her half empty plate, Rose took a deep breath and said, "Jack, I've been thinking about the job Tye and Jeb offered ye."

He glanced up with a forkful of beans partway to his mouth. "Yeah?"

"Aye, and I've an idea. If ye were to accept their offer and work for them for, say three or four years, perhaps we could save up enough to begin rebuilding your family's home and plant a cotton crop of our own. What d'ye think?"

Wrinkling his brow, he asked, "Would you really want to scratch out a bare living? It'd take years to build up the plantation enough to make a profit." He looked down, idly stirring the remains of his meal. "Besides, I've got no stomach for throwing out Oscar, Mattie and the others who've worked and sweated to feed their families."

Anger surged through Rose. "I wouldn't dream of doing that," she snapped, glaring at him. "How can ye think I'd ever wish to do such a thing?"

His copper coloring turned dark red. "Sorry. I didn't mean to insult you. But how do you think we'd rebuild the plantation when over half of it's parceled out to tenants?"

She blinked, having no idea what to say. Finally, she muttered, "I don't know."

Jack was kind enough not to scoff at her ill-conceived idea, though she felt like a fool for suggesting it. Still, as they resumed their trek, it continued to buzz around in her head like an angry bee that refused to leave her alone. Sometime later, inspiration struck.

"What if we all joined together in a . . . a cooperative?" she burst out.

"Huh?" Startled from his thoughts, Jack stared at her.

"Suppose each family owned an equal share in the plantation," she said excitedly, "and we all worked together, plowing, planting, harvesting as a group. Surely we'd be able to raise more cotton and bring in more profits for everyone. Wouldn't we?"

Jack continued to stare at her as if thunderstruck, causing her to fidget in her saddle, which in turn caused Brownie to dance sideways. She settled him down, all but holding her breath as her husband gazed into the distance, thinking. Pulling off his hat, he raked his fingers through his hair, slapped the hat back on and finally looked at her again.

"It just might work." He nodded and grinned. "I married me one smart white lady."

Overjoyed, Rose basked in his praise.

CHAPTER TWENTY-ONE

The closer they got to the ranch, the quieter Rose became, Jack noticed. He figured he knew why but didn't say anything until their last night on the trail. Camped under a cloudless sky, with a fire holding the dark shadows at bay, they'd eaten their supper and were finishing the last of the coffee.

Relaxed with his back propped against his saddle and his legs outstretched, he studied his wife. She sat hunched over next to him, elbows on her knees, coffee cup idly turning in her hands. A frown marred her smooth features as she stared into the flames.

"You look like a condemned prisoner waiting to be hanged at dawn," he said.

She sat bolt upright and turned startled eyes his way. "I-I'm sorry. I don't mean to –"

"It's all right. I know you're wondering what kind of reception we'll get at the ranch when you ride in with me."

"Nay! I . . . ." She went silent, shoulders slumping. Looking away, she said, "Aye, I admit I'm a bit worried. Even though Tye and Jeb must have explained the circumstances, I fear some may still accuse ye of kidnapping me for evil purposes. And, as your mother warned, they may not accept us."

"I don't think you need to worry about the Crawfords. Like you said, Tye and Jeb have set them straight by now, and don't forget Miz Rebecca and Lil are part Cherokee. They won't see anything wrong in us marrying."

"Aye, but what of Jessie? After her frightening dream and how she misunderstood it, I'm not so sure she'll believe Tye or me."

He swirled the coffee grounds in his cup. "I don't know your sister, but if she loves you the way I think she does, I hope she'll want to see you happy. And I mean to make you happy, P'ayn-nah."

She smiled sweetly. "Ye already have. I only hope Jessie sees that."

Watching her closely, Jack asked, "What if she doesn't? Will you still be my wife?"

Her eyes widened and she shook her head. "How can ye ask me that? I love my sister, but you're my husband. You're forever a part of me. Would I cut out my own heart?" She tapped a fist over her heart and shook her head vehemently. "Never!"

Tossing aside his cup, he opened his arms for her. "Come here," he said thickly, and with a soft cry, she flung herself against him. He pulled her onto his lap and kissed her with desperate urgency, needing to reassure himself and her that they'd always be together. Caressing the soft inner flesh of her mouth with his tongue, he delved deep, the way his body burned to do in her woman's passage. She answered him eagerly, her tongue weaving a spell that drove him loco.

He tore his mouth from hers and frantically tugged her shirt free of her riding skirt, needing to look at her and touch her. Getting onto her knees between his legs, she helped him with the buttons and fought free of the shirt. Her camisole met the same fate, baring her to the waist, a feast for his hungry gaze. She clutched his shoulders and arched her back, offering him her beautiful pink-tipped breasts. Eagerly, he encircled them with his hands and gently kneaded their fullness, tweaking the stiff points with his thumbs.

A trembling sigh broke from her lips. He looked into her half-closed eyes, recognizing a desire equal to his own. She gripped his head, twined her fingers through his hair and urged him downward. Knowing what she wanted, he ran his tongue around an eager nipple then took it in his mouth and drew strongly upon it. She cried out and dug her fingers into his shoulders. Glorying in her response, he turned his attention to her other breast. At the same time, he undid the fastenings of her skirt and loosened the tie of her drawers. Sliding his hands under both garments, he pushed them down to her knees. He caressed her hips and flat belly, her flesh quivering at his touch.

"Oh, Jack! I need ye so!" she gasped.

Abandoning her breasts for the moment, he reclaimed her mouth while nudging her knees apart as far as her bunched clothes allowed. Then he went searching in the damp nest of curls surrounding her tender parts. Finding what he sought, he stroked her slowly, lovingly, feeling her jerk in reaction and swallowing her wild cries. Unable to stand much more, he gripped her waist and drew back a fraction.

"Can you wait for me?" he rasped, heart galloping and breath coming in loud gusts.

"Aye, but hurry!" Scooting backward onto her already spread blanket, she kicked off her boots, skirt and drawers while he hustled out of his own clothes. She watched avidly as he skinned off his pants, causing his erection to pulse and grow harder still.

"Get on your hands and knees," he said, wanting to teach her a new way of loving.

She frowned at him. "Why? What d'ye think to do?"

He chuckled. "It's all right, P'ayn-nah. There are many ways I can pleasure you. This is one of them. You want to learn, don't you?"

After a brief hesitation, she nodded and got into position on her blanket as he'd directed. She looked over her shoulder when he knelt behind her, nudging her legs father apart. Grinning at the picture she presented, he caressed the white globes of her bottom and heard her catch an unsteady breath.

"It's all right," he repeated softly. "I'm just going to touch you." For long moments he did nothing but stroke her back and thighs, occasionally slipping his hand around to fondle her breasts and belly. He waited until she began to moan and writhe beneath his caresses. Then he slid one hand lower, parted her folds and, knitting two fingers, entered her. She gasped and tossed her head as he moved his fingers in and out. Within seconds she was ready for him. Taking hold of his staff, he wet the tip in her juices and began pushing into her. She tensed briefly then shifted, trying to accommodate him.

"Bend your elbows and lean down," he directed, voice thick with passion. She did as he said and he drove farther into her. Watching her for any sign of pain but seeing none, he buried himself to the root, clenching his jaw, fighting for control. Hearing her gasp, he managed to ask, "Are you all right?"

"Aye. 'Tis just . . . it feels . . . as if you're . . . under my heart," she panted.

"Does it hurt?" Alarmed, he was about to pull back.

"Nay, only I . . . need ye to move. Please!"

"Yes ma'am!" Drawing back, he pushed into her again and again, increasing his speed until she was bumping against him frantically and they were both breathing like race horses. Feeling Rose's inner muscles convulse around him and hearing her shriek of victory, he pumped into her one last time and cried out with the force of his own climax.

When she slowly collapsed under him, he went down with her, not wanting to lose their connection. Drained of energy, he lay over her, unable to move for a long moment.

"Jack, you're crushing me," she gasped.

He immediately rolled off her. "Sorry, love, I didn't mean to. You stole my strength."

She turned on her side and snuggled close, laying her head on his shoulder. He spread his hand across her bottom and sighed in tired contentment.

"I hated to have ye leave me," she whispered, "but ye were squashing these." She touched her breast, where it molded against him.

Chuckling, he petted the abused orb. "Can't have that. They're two of my favorite parts of you."

She giggled. "I suspected as much. And what other parts of me d'ye favor?"

"Many parts." Tipping her head back, he murmured, "Here and here and here," as he gently kissed her brow, her eyelids, her cheeks. "And here." Coaxing her lips apart, he kissed her thoroughly, tasting her reawakened passion and feeling himself ready for her again. Slipping his hand between them, he touched his very favorite part of her. "And here," he growled.

Moaning softly, she opened herself to his explorations and soon they were teetering on the edge of ecstasy once more. This time they soared over the precipice in unison and fell into exhausted slumber under the stars, with coyotes yipping in the velvety night.

* * *

Around mid-afternoon of the following day, Rose sighted the Double C buildings. A short while later, she drew Brownie to a halt near the corral where she'd first met Jack. He drew rein beside her as a man stepped out of the barn, evidently curious to see who'd ridden up. Rose recognized Micah Johnson, the ranch hand with only one good arm.

"Well I'll be, if it ain't Choctaw Jack," he said sarcastically. "Didn't figure on seein' yuh again, not after yuh stole Miz Rose." He eyed her as if he wasn't quite sure how to greet her. Opting for politeness, he touched his hat to her. "Howdy, ma'am."

"Hello, Mr. Johnson," she replied coolly, swinging off of Brownie. "Is my brother anywhere about?"

"I reckon he's in the house with Miz Lil and their young'un. He's stuck close since he got back a few days ago."

Jack had also dismounted. Taking Brownie's reins from Rose, he led both horses over to Johnson. "You don't mind taking care of our horses, do you, Micah? My wife and I need to head up to the house."

The other man's mouth fell open. "Your wife!" he blurted, darting a glance at Rose. "Now ain't that somethin'."

Jack didn't reply. Thrusting the reins into Johnson's hand, he strode back to Rose. "Come on. Let's get this over with." Taking hold of her elbow, he marched her to the house and up the front steps.

"Wait!" she cried, grabbing his wrist when he reached to open the door. "Perhaps we ought to knock."

He scowled at her. "Why? Your brother lives here. Don't you think he –"

The door was yanked open from inside, cutting him off. Jessie stood there, eyes wide. "Rosie!" she burst out. "I thought I heard your voice. Thank the saints you're home safe!"

"Jessie, I –"

Not giving Rose time to finish, her sister charged out onto the stoop and dragged her into a vise-like embrace, forcing a gasp from her throat. When she finally managed to free herself and turn to Jack, she saw he'd backed down a step to give them space on the stoop. He stood watching them, hat held at his side and raven hair waving in the wind.

Smiling at him, she said, "Jessie, this is my husband, Jack Lafarge."

"We've met before, only I knew ye as Choctaw Jack then,"

her sister said dryly.

"Yes ma'am, that's what most white folks call me."

"Mmm. I also recall ye helped save my daughter's life. 'Tis a debt I owe ye, sir, and the only reason I don't scratch your eyes out for stealing my baby sister away."

"Jessie, ye don't understand," Rose said hastily. "Jack had good reason to –"

"Och, I heard about it from Tye, but your darlin' husband near frightened the life out of me when he appeared with ye in my dream."

"I'm sorry for that, Miz Taylor. If I'd had any other choice, I wouldn't have made off with her the way I did." He gazed at Rose and grinned roguishly. "Can't say I'm sorry for how things turned out though."

Instantly reminded of their lovemaking last night, she felt her face heat up and lowered her eyes. But she couldn't suppress a grin.

Her sister cleared her throat. "Call me Jessie, Jack. We're kin now. And come in, both of ye. Everyone will wish to greet ye."

Hugely relieved by Jessie's welcome, Rose followed her inside, tightly clasping Jack's hand. The next thing she knew, Tye, Lil and Rebecca Crawford were gathered around them, hugging her, shaking hands with Jack in her brother's case, and talking all at once. She basked in their warmth, thankful and relieved, especially for Jack's sake.

"Ye had your babe, I see," Rose remarked to Lil, noting her flattened stomach. "Is all well with ye and the wee one?"

"Sure did. We have a son," Lil replied, beaming at Tye, who stepped close and wrapped his arm around her. "He took his sweet time about it, but he's almost two weeks old now. He oughta be awake from his nap. I'll go fetch him." Drawing away from Tye, she turned and dashed upstairs.

"Come and sit," Rebecca invited, gesturing toward the right side of the long room that served as both kitchen and parlor. She pointed Rose and Jack to the sofa, while she and Jessie took straight chairs framing the hearth and Tye dragged one over from the kitchen table, leaving the one easy chair for Lil.

"What brings ye to the Double C, Jess?" Rose asked. "I'm glad to see ye, mind, but I didn't expect to find ye here today."

Jessie exchanged an odd sort of glance with their brother and knitted her hands tightly in her lap. "I, ah, wanted to see the baby again. Maria Medina and I stayed here during Lil's lying in, but we returned to the River T soon after. David and Luis, Maria's husband, were gone with the trail drive by then, ye see, and the woman I asked to look after both Maria's brood and my own, was anxious to go home. So I haven't seen the little fellow since just after he was born."

Darting another, desperate looking glance at Tye, Jessie fell silent. He shifted uncomfortably on his chair and avoided Rose's bemused gaze. She was about to ask the cause of their odd behavior when Lil returned carrying her blanketed son.

Her sister-in-law walked up to her and said, "Rose, I'd like you to meet your nephew, Patrick Delancy Devlin. Uh, Delancy is Pa's proper name. You want to hold him?"

"Aye, but I've never held such a wee one before. D'ye trust me with him?"

Lil snorted at her question. "Of course I trust you. Just hold him steady and be sure to support his head." She bent and carefully laid the baby in Rose's arms. "That's it. See, it's not so hard."

Gazing into the little boy's innocent dark eyes, Rose gently stroked his silky cap of dark curls and whispered, "Hello, wee Patrick. Aren't ye the handsome boy. I'm your Auntie Rose." Aware of Jack's arm across her shoulders and his watchful gaze, she smiled lovingly at him. "And this is your Uncle Jack."

Her big, brave husband warily brushed the baby's hand. When Patrick wrapped his tiny fist around his finger, Jack grinned. "Hey there, boy, you mean to take my finger off?"

His comment brought laughter from all the adults. In the midst of it, Rose heard heavy footsteps descending the stairs from the upper floor. She raised her head, thinking it must be Del Crawford. She cried out in shock when she saw her father.

"Da! What are ye doing here?"

"I meant to tell ye, Rosie," Jessie began, "but I didn't know –"

"Shush, daughter, I can speak for meself," their father said, halfway down the stairs.

Rose didn't realize she was clutching baby Patrick tight until he let out a loud squall. She immediately loosened her hold. "Oh, little one, I'm sorry. I didn't mean to crush ye."

Lil hurriedly reclaimed her son. Placing him against her shoulder, she gently patted his back and crooned to him. He quieted within seconds.

"I'm so sorry," Rose repeated remorsefully. "Did I harm him?" Feeling Jack squeeze her shoulders, she was grateful for his presence.

"No, he's all right. He just got a might scared," Lil assured her. Walking over to Tye, who'd risen in alarm, Lil said, "I'll take him upstairs and feed him."

He nodded and kissed her brow. "I'll be up in a bit."

By then, Seamus had reached the bottom of the staircase. Pausing there, he patted Patrick's small head. "That's a good lad," he said gruffly. Then he smiled at Lil and moved aside, allowing her to climb the stairs. Facing Rose, he said, "Ye needn't act so shocked at the sight of yer auld da, Rose Marie. Since all me children choose ta live in this great huge state, I decided I may as well join ye." He gripped the suspenders holding up his baggy trousers and studied the floor. "A man wants to end his days with his family around him. Don't ye see?"

Rose's throat constricted. With a glance at Jack, she stood and crossed to her father. "Of course I see, Da, and I'm glad you're here." She kissed his stubbled cheek, noting that his beard was turning white just like his hair, which had once been dark auburn like Jessie's.

He caught her to him and bussed her cheek in return. "We've had our differences, colleen. Me own doin', I admit. But I'm done with that now and I hope ye'll believe me when I say I've always loved ye."

Her eyes grew misty. "I believe ye, Da. And I hope you'll forgive me for being a trial to ye. 'Twas never my intention."

"Och, I know that." He cleared his throat and looked past her. "Now, will ye kindly introduce yon long-haired fellow who's starin' at ye like he owns ye?"

Rose tensed, fearing she might yet face his outrage. Stepping back, she pivoted and saw Jack on his feet, waiting quietly. And he was indeed watching her with a possessive set to his chiseled copper features. She squared her shoulders and nodded to him, prepared to defend their union. She wouldn't allow anyone, even her father, to disparage the man she loved.

Jack came to her side and placed his hand at the small of her back, clearly asserting his claim upon her.

"Da, I'd like ye to meet my husband, Jack Lafarge. Jack, this my father, Seamus Devlin." She held her breath, praying Da wouldn't unleash his hot temper.

He studied Jack, brows knitted above his hawkish nose. "So ye're the *bligeard* who made off with me daughter in the middle of the night, are ye?"

Rose opened her mouth to protest, but Jack forestalled her.

"Not sure what you just called me, sir, but I did kidnap Rose and take her up to Indian Territory. And like I told Miz Jessie, I can't say I'm real sorry. Rose saved my mother's life and gave me hope for the future. She healed my spirit."

Touched by his words, she choked on a sob.

He turned his head and gazed into her tear-wet eyes. "I love her with all my heart."

Lips trembling, Rose couldn't hold back the happy tears that slipped down her cheeks.

Her father coughed and cleared his throat. "Well, that's fine," he said gruffly, "but I must ask if the nuptials were performed in a church, in the proper way?"

Rose hesitated, afraid to answer.

"We married in my mother's village, in the Kiowa way," Jack replied evenly.

"Aye, but was the marriage blessed by the church?"

"If you mean by a Catholic padre, the answer's no."

Da pursed his lips and shook his head. "That won't do," he said sternly. Then he turned to Jessie. "Where might we find the nearest priest? I want Rosie wed in the eyes o' God to himself here before she bears a child."

Tye chuckled while Rose grew hot with embarrassment, but Jessie swiftly assured Da there was indeed a Catholic church not too far distant. Arrangements for a wedding would be made as soon as possible.

Del Crawford walked in the front door a moment later. He'd been out riding over the ranch, checking the water level in the creek and keeping an eye out for late calves, it turned out. His arrival set off a wave of explanations followed by a brief discussion between the men about the assistant foreman's job Jack had been offered. Del knew all about it from Tye and expressed his approval. Rose watched Jack shake hands with him and her brother, sealing his acceptance – with the understanding that he would work on the Double C for a few years only, just long enough to save up funds to begin rebuilding his family home.

With that settled, Tye bounded up the stairs, anxious to be with Lil and their son. He'd be leaving in a day or two to catch up with the northbound trail drive and would be gone for two months or more, he'd said with obvious regret. Rose felt bad for him and Lil. They'd been apart when Patrick was born – thanks to Jack and her – and now they were to be separated again. She silently vowed to help Lil with the baby and ease her loneliness in Tye's absence as much as she could.

Needing a few moments' privacy with her own husband, Rose drew him outside. They strolled down to the corral, where Brownie and Jack's Indian pony stood in sleepy relaxation. Raising his head, the big brown stallion nickered and trotted over to them. Rose scratched around his ears the way he loved and laughed softly when he snuffed against the palm of her hand, looking for a treat.

"I'll bring an apple for ye later, ye big beggar."

Jack reached over and patted the stallion's neck. "He's earned an apple now and then."

"Aye, without him, we might never have met. Ye wouldn't have discovered my secret and kidnapped me to heal Khaw."

Turning her into his arms, Jack kissed her tenderly. "And I never would have found the one woman in the world for me."

Rose gazed into his eyes. "Jack, will it offend ye to marry me in the white man's way as Da wishes?" she asked solemnly.

"No." He framed her face with his hands and murmured, "For my P'an-nah I will do anything." Bending close, he kissed her again, chasing away thoughts of everything but him.

EPILOGUE

Belle Rouge Plantation; July 1880

Rose was thankful for a dry wind blowing down from the Indian Territory. It dissipated the summer heat somewhat, though not a lot. Seated with her mother-in-law on a blanket Jack had laid out for them beneath a spreading live oak, she patted her damp forehead with a handkerchief and glanced around the yard of her Red River home. She was glad to see so many friends and family had accepted the invitation to today's picnic barbecue. Most had also found patches of shade.

"You have given my son two daughters. Each is beautiful in her own way," Ghost Woman said, drawing Rose's attention.

"Thank ye for saying so, Khaw," she replied, watching the old woman slowly wield her fan, made of feathers bound to a wooden handle, to cool her sixteen-month-old granddaughter, Chloé, who'd fallen asleep in her lap.

Gazing at her youngest child, Rose had to agree. Each of her daughters was beautiful, but in very different ways. Her older girl, Angelique – named for Jack's departed sister – had her father's black hair but Rose's light skin, a dramatic contrast. Chloé, on the other hand, had inherited Rose's hair color but her skin was neither pale nor copper. Instead, it was gold tinted. With her red-gold hair curling about her round face, she brought to mind a cherubic angel. At the moment, Rose feared she was also causing her grandmother discomfort.

"She must be making ye hotter than ever," Rose said. "D'ye want me to take her?"

"No, she is fine. I do not hold her often. The next time I see her, she will not want to be held like this."

"It needn't be so. This was your home once. Ye know you're welcome to stay here with us, Khaw. We'd love to have ye."

Ghost Woman nodded. "I know, Daughter, but my place is with my people. I will not leave them again."

Rose sighed in resignation. She and Jack had asked his mother to live with them several times, but her answer was always the same. Turning her thoughts elsewhere, she once more gazed around at the people she loved. They were all here: her father, Jessie and David with their three children, Tye and Lil with their two boys and Lil's parents. Even Jeb Crawford and his wife of three years, Abigail, and her two sons had ridden in from their ranch.

They'd come to celebrate the restoration of the Lafarge house. The place was far from fancy and the rebuilding wasn't finished, but it had progressed far enough for Jack and her and their daughters to move in a month ago. Any furniture they hadn't been given by family, her husband had constructed with the help of their friend, Oscar Leggett.

Oscar, Mattie, their daughter and sons were also here today, as were the other former sharecroppers who now belonged to the Belle Rouge Cotton Cooperative. With one exception – Red Gardener. The vicious drunk had beaten his sons again despite Jack's warning. Not long after that he'd disappeared. No one knew what had happened to him. Rose had her suspicions but kept them to herself, not wishing to question Oscar's truthfulness, or anyone else's.

Left alone, Gardener's sons had been more or less adopted by Mattie and her gentle giant husband. From then on, the other tenants – now owners – had pitched in to work Gardner's field. And when Jack approached them with his proposal for a cooperative, they'd unanimously insisted the Gardner boys, now almost grown, should have their pa's portion.

A child's angry shriek jolted Rose from her reverie. Recognizing the high-pitched voice of her three-year-old, Angelique, she climbed to her feet, pressing a hand to her mounded belly. Seven months into her third pregnancy, she felt the baby give a strong kick and smiled to herself. This time she was having a boy, she just knew.

"I'd best see what's wrong," she said, eyeing the gaggle of children, some white, some black, some Indian, who stood watching her seven-year-old niece, Nora Taylor, and the wailing toddler she was struggling to restrain in her small arms.

"Go. I will watch over the little one."

With a distracted nod, Rose hurried past several women who'd also risen in concern. Ignoring them and the other children, she lifted her red-faced, crying daughter from Nora.

"Hush, sweetheart, don't carry on so." Brushing back Angelique's sweat-dampened black hair, she glanced at Nora. "What happened?"

Nora bit her lip and looked to Vittorio, the eldest son of Maria and Luis Medina. He, his parents and siblings had accompanied Jessie and David up here from Bosque County. Vittorio was four years older than Nora, but the two were inseparable.

"We were going to choose teams for Red Rover," the dark-haired adolescent explained. *"La nina* wishes to play but she is too young. She grew angry when we told her no."

"I see." Quite certain Nora was the one who'd said no, Rose gave her a stern look. Her niece flushed and lowered her eyes. "Perhaps you could have two games, one for the older children and one for the younger ones."

"But we won't have enough players for our teams," Nora hotly protested. Like her mother, Jessie, she was quick to lose her temper.

Rose cocked an eyebrow at her. "Oh, I think ye can manage, young lady."

"Your aunt is right, *mija,"* Vittorio said swiftly, diffusing Nora's temperamental outburst. "It will be fun to try it with smaller teams. Come, Angelique, you can play with the younger ones," he declared, holding out his arms and smiling shyly at Rose.

She returned his smile and handed over her now excited daughter. "Thank ye, Vittorio."

"De Nada, Señora," he said with a nod. As she watched, he set about dividing the children into age groups, coaxing a still petulant Nora to cooperate.

Admiring his leadership skills, Rose didn't hear Jack approach. She jumped when he came up behind her and laid his hands on her shoulders.

"You all right, P'ayn-nah?"

"Aye, I'm fine," she replied, turning to face him. "When will the meat be ready, d'ye think? We've some hungry guests."

"It won't be much longer."

"Good. I'd best go help Jessie and Lil set out the other dishes. They're doing all the work while I sit around."

"I heard them tell you to take it easy. Good advice. I don't want you overdoing." He glanced at her expanding midsection and grinned. "Go keep Khaw company. That's an order."

Exasperated, she stuck her tongue out at him. He chuckled, turned her toward the big live oak and gave her a gentle push.

The rest of the day passed in a warm haze of abundant food, friendship and laughter. By sunset the neighbors had all left, needing to put their tired offspring to bed. Tye, Jessie, Rose and their spouses and various in-laws stood on the front porch of the house, watching the oldest of their children chase fireflies in the dim twilight. Leaning back against Jack's muscular chest, Rose sighed when he wrapped his arms around her to gently stroke her stomach. She was tired and her back ached, but never had she felt so contented.

The Children's laughing chatter was suddenly cut off by Nora's urgent command to hush. A silence also fell over the adults as the girl stared into the shadows near the huge bur oak tree guarding the graves of Jack's sister and brother.

"Hello, I'm Nora. What's your name?" she asked the empty darkness.

"What the devil?" David muttered, making a move toward the steps.

"No! Wait," Jessie whispered, clutching his shirt sleeve.

"Angelique? That's my cousin's name too," Nora said artlessly.

Jack stiffened and clamped his hands around Rose's arms. His mother cried out in Kiowa.

"This is my brother Reece," Nora added, pointing to the boy who stood nearby. "No, I can't see your brother. Where is he?"

"Oh. Maybe he'll come with you next time." She waved at the being only she could see. "Goodbye."

The children resumed their play as if nothing had happened. No one on the porch moved or spoke for a long, tense moment. Then Ghost Woman broke the silence.

"She spoke to my daughter, Angelique, who is with the spirits of our people. This child has great power."

"I've heard her speak to someone who wasn't there before, in the nursery next to our room," Jessie murmured, clinging to David's arm. "She told me she was talking to a little boy. I thought it was her imagination, but it wasn't, was it?"

Her husband caught her to him. "My mother lost a baby, a boy, when she was six months along. I remember Pa laying the little fellow, my brother, in the cradle in the nursery." David's voice grew thick. "Do you think . . . ?"

Jessie looked up. "Did your parents name him?"

"Pa did. When he buried him, he cut *Jeremy* into the cross marking the grave.

"Jeremy was the name of the boy Nora spoke of."

Turning in David's arms, Jessie looked at Tye and Rose. "It's happening again."

"Aye, I've already seen signs in Patrick," Tye admitted, catching Lil's hand in his. "He's had dreams. Like yours, Jess. Hasn't he *mavourneen?*"

Lil nodded. "He told me he'd have a brother to play with three months before Nicholas was born," Lil confirmed. "He dreamed it."

Rose laid her hand over the child moving within her, wondering. "I've seen no sign from either of our girls, but they're so young. Perhaps in a few more years."

Seamus Devlin gave a deep, rolling laugh and looked skyward. "Nora, me love, ye can tell the *auld ones* their race is in no danger of dyin' out just yet."

The End

About the Author

Lyn Horner resides in north Texas with her husband and beloved cats. Trained in the visual arts, Lyn worked as a fashion illustrator and art instructor. After quitting work to raise her children, she took up writing as a creative outlet. This hobby grew into a love of historical research and the crafting of passionate love stories based on that research.

The author says, "Writing a book is much like putting together a really big jigsaw puzzle. It requires endless patience and stubborn determination to see your ideas come to life, and once hooked on the process, you're forever addicted."